An alien visits the International Space Station to provide a potential solution to climate change, for a price!
—"The Trade" by C. Winspear

A house is how you live on, how you keep giving to those you love after you are gone. It's not an easy thing to escape.
—"Foundations" by Michael Gardner

How does one interpret the most profound human concept so an alien can understand?
—"A Word That Means Everything" by Andy Dibble

For a single day of glory and the settlement of a dispute among immortals, is a life a satisfactory price?
—"Borrowed Glory" by L. Ron Hubbard

Will yours be a good death or a bad one? You'll have to catch it to find out.
—"Catching My Death" by J. L. George

Just what wonders or misery can a cereal box prize offer?
—"A Prize in Every Box" by F. J. Bergmann

How often would you reset time to save the love of your life?
—"Yellow and Pink" by Leah Ning

The Phoenix has always been the guardian of Dembia. Now there's trouble in the land, and mysteriously, the Phoenix has left two golden eggs.
—"The Phoenix's Peace" by Jody Lynn Nye

Know there is nothing here to harm you. Only your choices. Only yourself. The educational tapes will prepare you for your choice, "I accept" or "I decline." There are no other options.
—"Educational Tapes" by Katie Livingston

What would you do if the air was taken from you but you couldn't die?

—"Trading Ghosts" by David A. Elsensohn

Alien performers capture the imaginations of human audiences, but what is the cost to the performers and their people?

—"Stolen Sky" by Storm Humbert

A young woman seeks her destiny in the African winds of Harmattan.

—"The Winds of Harmattan" by Nnedi Okorafor

A landmine decommission expert struggles to connect with his nonhuman partner in the midst of an endless war.

—"As Able the Air" by Zack Be

The human race may not understand the alien race of *skyylls*, but we can feel their pain.

—"Molting Season" by Tim Boiteau

A troupe of androids risks everything by breaking the three laws of robotics to win the praise of a roving theater critic.

—"Automated Everyman Migrant Theater" by Sonny Zae

The magic is strong in the Green Tower, and two young girls struggle to discover its secrets.

—"The Green Tower" by Katherine Kurtz

L. RON HUBBARD

Presents

Writers of the Future

Anthologies

"Speculative fiction fans will welcome this showcase of new talent....Winners of the simultaneous Illustrators of the Future Contest are featured with work as varied and as exciting as the authors."   —*Library Journal* starred review

"Writers of the Future is always one of the best original anthologies of the year."   —*Tangent*

"The Writers of the Future Award has also earned its place alongside the Hugo and Nebula awards in the triad of speculative fiction's most prestigious acknowledgments of literary excellence."
—*SFFAudio*

"Where can an aspiring sci-fi artist go to get discovered?... Fortunately, there's one opportunity—the Illustrators of the Future Contest—that offers up-and-coming artists an honest-to-goodness shot at science fiction stardom."

—*Sci-Fi* magazine

"The series continues to be a powerful statement of faith as well as direction in American science fiction."

—*Publishers Weekly*

"The book you are holding in your hands is our first sight of the next generation of science fiction and fantasy writers."

—Orson Scott Card
Writers of the Future Contest judge

L. Ron Hubbard PRESENTS

Writers of the Future

VOLUME 36

L. Ron Hubbard PRESENTS

Writers of the Future

VOLUME 36

The year's twelve best tales from the
Writers of the Future international writers' program

Illustrated by winners in the Illustrators of the Future
international illustrators' program

Four short stories from authors L. Ron Hubbard /
Katherine Kurtz / Jody Lynn Nye / Nnedi Okorafor

With essays on writing and illustration by
L. Ron Hubbard / Mike Perkins / Sean Williams

Edited by David Farland
Illustrations Art Directed by Echo Chernik

GALAXY PRESS, INC.

For information, contact Galaxy Press, Inc. at 7051 Hollywood Boulevard, Los Angeles, California, 90028.

"The Trade": © 2020 C. Winspear
"Foundations": © 2020 Michael Gardner
"A Word That Means Everything": © 2020 Andy Dibble
"Steps in the Right Direction": © 2010 L. Ron Hubbard
"Borrowed Glory": © 2008 L. Ron Hubbard
"Catching My Death": © 2020 J. L. George
"A Prize in Every Box": © 2020 F. J. Bergmann
"Yellow and Pink": © 2020 Leah Ning
"The Phoenix's Peace": © 2020 Jody Lynn Nye
"Educational Tapes": © 2020 Katie Livingston
"Trading Ghosts": © 2020 David A. Elsensohn
"Stolen Sky": © 2020 Storm Humbert
"The Winds of Harmattan": © 2013 Nnedi Okorafor
"As Able the Air": © 2020 Zack Be
"Molting Season": © 2020 Tim Boiteau
"Automated Everyman Migrant Theater": © 2020 Sonny Zae
"The Green Tower": © 2002 Katherine Kurtz
 Illustration on pages 8 and 31: © 2020 Arthur Bowling
 Illustration on pages 9 and 62: © 2020 Aidin Andrews
 Illustration on pages 10 and 80: © 2020 Heather A. Laurence
 Illustration on pages 11 and 122: © 2020 Cassandre Bolan
 Illustration on pages 12 and 141: © 2020 Kaitlyn Goldberg
 Illustration on pages 13 and 163: © 2020 Ben Hill
 Illustration on pages 14 and 199: © 2020 Irmak Çavun
 Illustration on pages 15 and 259: © 2020 John Dale Javier
 Illustration on pages 16 and 294: © 2020 Mason Matak
 Illustration on pages 17 and 319: © 2020 Anh Le
 Illustration on pages 18 and 339: © 2020 Brittany Jackson
 Illustration on pages 19 and 353: © 2020 Brock Aguirre
 Illustration on pages 20 and 389: © 2020 Daniel Bitton
 Illustration on pages 21 and 413: © 2020 Phoebe Rothfeld
 Illustration on pages 22 and 428: © 2020 John Dale Javier

Cover Artwork and pages 7 and 233: *Uncertain Egg* © 2020 Echo Chernik
Interior Design by Jerry Kelly

ISBN 978-1-61986-659-1

Printed in the United States of America.

WRITERS OF THE FUTURE (word and medallion) and ILLUSTRATORS OF THE FUTURE and its logo are trademarks owned by the L. Ron Hubbard Library and are used with permission.

CONTENTS

INTRODUCTION   1
by *David Farland*

THE ILLUSTRATORS OF THE FUTURE CONTEST
     AND THE ART OF THIS ANTHOLOGY   4
by *Echo Chernik*

ART GALLERY   7

THE TRADE   23
by *C. Winspear*
     Illustrated by Arthur Bowling

FOUNDATIONS   47
by *Michael Gardner*
     Illustrated by Aidin Andrews

A WORD THAT MEANS EVERYTHING   75
by *Andy Dibble*
     Illustrated by Heather A. Laurence

STEPS IN THE RIGHT DIRECTION   107
by *L. Ron Hubbard*

BORROWED GLORY   113
by *L. Ron Hubbard*
     Illustrated by Cassandre Bolan

CATCHING MY DEATH   135
by *J. L. George*
     Illustrated by Kaitlyn Goldberg

A PRIZE IN EVERY BOX   157
by *F. J. Bergmann*
     Illustrated by Ben Hill

YELLOW AND PINK   181
by *Leah Ning*
     Illustrated by Irmak Çavun

MAKING COLLABORATION WORK FOR YOU
     OR CO-WRITING WITH LARRY AND SEAN   201
by *Sean Williams*

THE PHOENIX'S PEACE   211
by *Jody Lynn Nye*
   Inspired by Echo Chernik's *Uncertain Egg*

EDUCATIONAL TAPES   241
by *Katie Livingston*
   Illustrated by John Dale Javier

TRADING GHOSTS   289
by *David A. Elsensohn*
   Illustrated by Mason Matak

STOLEN SKY   307
by *Storm Humbert*
   Illustrated by Anh Le

BREAKING IN   323
by *Mike Perkins*

THE WINDS OF HARMATTAN   329
by *Nnedi Okorafor*
   Illustrated by Brittany Jackson

AS ABLE THE AIR   349
by *Zack Be*
   Illustrated by Brock Aguirre

MOLTING SEASON   375
by *Tim Boiteau*
   Illustrated by Daniel Bitton

AUTOMATED EVERYMAN MIGRANT THEATER   393
by *Sonny Zae*
   Illustrated by Phoebe Rothfeld

THE GREEN TOWER   421
by *Katherine Kurtz*
   Illustrated by John Dale Javier

THE YEAR IN THE CONTESTS   443

Introduction

BY DAVID FARLAND

David Farland is a New York Times *bestselling author with more than fifty novels and anthologies to his credit. He has won numerous awards, including the L. Ron Hubbard Gold Award in 1987, and has served as Coordinating Judge of the Writers of the Future for more than a dozen years.*

He has helped mentor hundreds of new writers, including such #1 bestselling authors as Brandon Sanderson (The Way of Kings*), Stephenie Meyer (* Twilight*), Brandon Mull (* Fablehaven*), James Dashner (* The Maze Runner*), and others. While writing Star Wars novels in 1998, he was asked to help choose a book to push big for Scholastic, and selected* Harry Potter, *then helped develop a bestseller strategy.*

In addition to his novels and short stories, Dave has also assisted with video game design and worked as a greenlighting analyst for movies in Hollywood. Dave continues to help mentor writers through the Writers of the Future program, where he acts as Coordinating Judge, editor of the anthology, and teaches workshops to our winning authors. He also teaches online classes and live workshops.

Introduction

Welcome to *L. Ron Hubbard Presents Writers of the Future Volume 36*.

The Contest judges and I, with the help of our first reader Kary English, take pride in discovering the world's best new authors in the field of speculative fiction every year.

I only have one goal for this anthology: to make each volume better than the last.

That's a tough job. Finding publishable stories isn't hard, but last year's anthology was so wonderful, how can we beat it? It became a bestseller and won an award, as did the one before that. So we hope that today's new authors will really wow us.

I think that we've succeeded. The writing and artistic talent in Volume 36 is exceptional!

Of course, the stories are still judged blind. We don't get to know who sent the story, what race or gender the author is, or what country the story came from. We only judge each submission based upon the quality of the story.

I ask myself questions like, "How original is this idea?" "On the level of plot, does it hold me enthralled?" "How great of a stylist is this author?" and "How does this one stack up against the many other submissions in this quarter?" "Does it affect me emotionally?" and "Is it memorable?"

Maybe those are the reasons why the anthology is so good.

Both Contests grew larger and the number of submissions were at their highest ever. The competing writers and artists are aware just how hard it is to win, so they give it their best.

In this volume, we have a dozen new authors to introduce from the United Kingdom, Australia, and the United States.

The writer winners featured in the anthology are paid for publication. In addition, they're paid prize money just for winning, and will fly to our awards ceremony in Hollywood, California, where they will be treated to a workshop taught by some of the biggest writers in the field of science fiction and fantasy—folks like Kevin J. Anderson, Orson Scott Card, Nina Kiriki Hoffman, Nancy Kress, Katherine Kurtz, Larry Niven, Nnedi Okorafor, Tim Powers, Brandon Sanderson, and more. Of course, the workshop itself was created by the Contests' founder, L. Ron Hubbard, and he is represented in the workshop by his own written materials.

Then, one of the first-place winners of the Writers' Contest will be awarded the grand prize of $5,000. When you consider the value of the prizes and payment for publication, this becomes the top market in the world for new writers.

In the same way, aspiring illustrators send in art each quarter, hoping to win a prize. These fantastic images are judged first by the Coordinating Judge for the Illustrators' Contest, Echo Chernik, then go to a blue-ribbon panel of judges, including such legendary figures as Ciruelo, Diane Dillon, Bob Eggleton, Craig Elliott, Larry Elmore, Val Lakey Lindahn, Mike Perkins, Rob Prior, Dan dos Santos, and Shaun Tan. The quarterly winners are then commissioned to illustrate one of the winning stories from the Writers' Contest—included in this volume—and with them they compete for the Illustrators' Contest $5,000 grand prize.

We've also got great stories from Jody Lynn Nye, inspired by our cover, and from our new judge Katherine Kurtz, who brought us a tale from her Deryni universe, and an African-based fantasy story from Nnedi Okorafor, along with a classic tale from the founder of the Contests, L. Ron Hubbard.

The anthology also boasts articles with sound advice from Contest judges Sean Williams, Mike Perkins, Echo Chernik, and timeless guidance from L. Ron Hubbard.

So without further ado, sit back and enjoy!

The Illustrators of the Future Contest and the Art of This Anthology

BY ECHO CHERNIK

Echo Chernik is a successful advertising and publishing illustrator with twenty-five years of professional experience and several prestigious publishing awards.

Her clients include mainstream companies such as: Miller, Camel, Coors, Celestial Seasonings, Publix Super Markets, Inc., Kmart, Sears, Nascar, the Sheikh of Dubai, the city of New Orleans, Bellagio resort, the state of Indiana, USPS, Dave Matthews Band, Arlo Guthrie, McDonald's, Procter & Gamble, Trek Bicycle Corporation, Disney, BBC, Mattel, Hasbro, and more. She specializes in several styles including decorative, vector, and art nouveau.

She is the Coordinating Judge of the Illustrators of the Future Contest. Echo strives to share the important but all-too-often neglected subject of the business aspect of illustration with the winners, as well as preparing them for the reality of a successful career in illustration.

The Illustrators of the Future Contest and the Art of This Anthology

The Writers and Illustrators of the Future Contests were created by L. Ron Hubbard with the purpose of discovering precious talent and providing the means to give it wings to fly.

It is every artist's dream to create something perfect, something special and beautiful, to share their creation and have the world appreciate it. Yet so many wonderful gems remain undiscovered. It is challenging and difficult to bring these creations to the world, which is why the Writers and Illustrators of the Future Contests are so important. These Contests give authors and illustrators a way to share their talent, to be recognized by their idols, and to receive support and help lift them to even higher levels of success.

We, the judges and past winners of the competitions, want to see you succeed in your dreams and fly high! The judges are all successful, seasoned writers and artists who know how difficult the path to success can be, which is why we give our time and expertise so freely to those who are just beginning their journey.

I am honored to be the Coordinating Judge for the Illustrators of the Future Contest, and to have the very special opportunity—in the words of L. Ron Hubbard—to "give tomorrow a new form" by helping young illustrators achieve a strong start.

Participating is easy and free. The judging is all done blind, so the judges don't know anything about the entrants other than the quality of their work. This Contest is legitimately one of the best opportunities a young artist can have.

We see entries from all over the world, and entrants don't

even need to speak English to enter or win. This year we have winners from Iran, Turkey, Vietnam, and across the United States. Each quarter three contest winners are chosen, so at the end of the year there are a total of twelve winners for the year.

The winning illustrators enter a second competition for the grand prize Golden Brush Award and $5,000. Each artist is commissioned to create an illustration to accompany a Writers of the Future Contest winning story. These amazing pieces are all included in this anthology.

All winners are flown to Hollywood for a huge black-tie celebration and book signing. They also spend an entire week learning the ins and outs of being a successful commercial artist in today's world. There are seminars and lectures by famous illustrator judges and guest speakers. It's an invaluable experience centered on providing benefit and a head start to the Contest winners, with the goal of leaving the young professional artists full of the knowledge and confidence needed to succeed.

In addition to all of that, this year I was invited to conceive and design the cover for *L. Ron Hubbard Presents Writers of the Future Volume 36*. It was important to me to reflect the spirit of the Contest.

The *Uncertain Egg* is a piece about undiscovered potential. It's about hope, dreams, and the unknown. The illustration is also about being supported and encouraged—and given the wings to fly. L. Ron Hubbard dreamed of helping undiscovered talent soar and succeed, and we strive to continue that legacy by providing support, encouragement, publicity, and education to the burgeoning talent that is upcoming.

It doesn't matter how old you are, or how long your treasures have been hidden—success as a writer or artist can be found at any age or point in your life. I encourage you to submit your work to these Contests, and to keep submitting every quarter. Believe in your dream, and never get discouraged. With perseverance and hard work, you can bring your dream to life, and the Writers and Illustrators of the Future are here to help launch you to fly as high as you can dream!

ECHO CHERNIK
Uncertain Egg

7

ARTHUR BOWLING
The Trade

AIDIN ANDREWS
Foundations

HEATHER A. LAURENCE
A Word That Means Everything

CASSANDRE BOLAN
Borrowed Glory

11

KAITLYN GOLDBERG
Catching My Death

BEN HILL
A Prize in Every Box

13

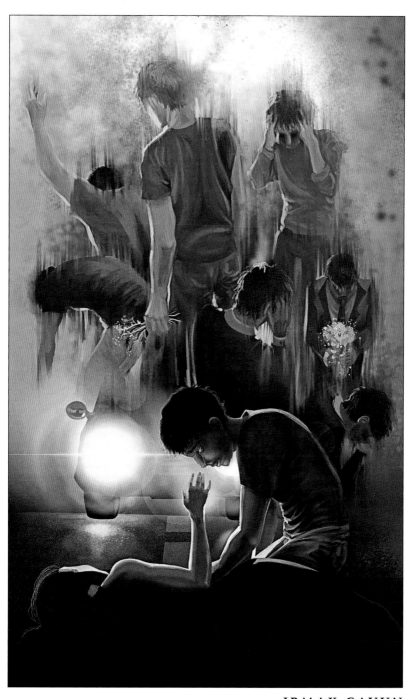

IRMAK ÇAVUN
Yellow and Pink

JOHN DALE JAVIER
Educational Tapes

15

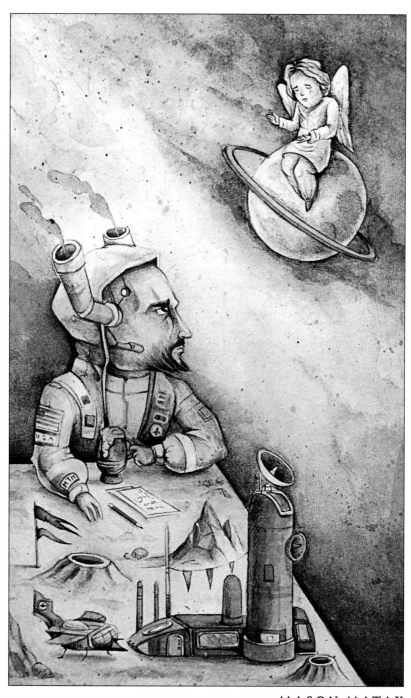

MASON MATAK
Trading Ghosts

ANH LE
Stolen Sky

BRITTANY JACKSON
The Winds of Harmattan

BROCK AGUIRRE
As Able the Air

19

DANIEL BITTON

Molting Season

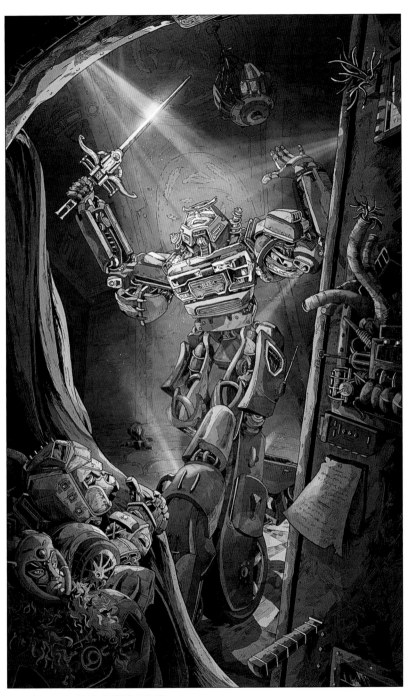

PHOEBE ROTHFELD
Automated Everyman Migrant Theater   21

JOHN DALE JAVIER
The Green Tower

The Trade

written by
C. Winspear

illustrated by
ARTHUR BOWLING

ABOUT THE AUTHOR

Chris Winspear is an Australian author and poet with a master's in creative writing from the University of Technology Sydney. He ran his own 3D printing business before working for the Transport Department. He dreams about how much more efficiently transport will run once the AIs take over.

He was a state-level fencer, but we assure you that there are no laser swords in this story.

Chris is obsessed with travelling, having volunteered in Peru, studied in Korea, and worked in upstate New York. He hopes to visit Mars one day—but will settle for the Moon.

He is currently seeking an agent to represent his standalone novels All for Birth *and* 1001 Nights under the Sun.

ABOUT THE ILLUSTRATOR

Arthur McKinley Bowling III was born in 1990 in the small town of Devil's Lake, North Dakota. He's known as Kenny by friends and family.

Arthur has always had an interest in drawing, using whatever tools he could to depict his favorite characters from video games, TV shows, and anime.

He began to see art as a career option thanks to encouragement from his family. While Arthur was still in high school, his parents nurtured his artistic pursuits by signing him up for classes with Art Instruction Schools to learn the fundamentals of art and design. He later graduated from Minnesota State University, Moorhead's art program with a bachelor of fine arts in illustration and bachelor of arts in painting.

After college Arthur continued to push his work to the next level, studying under acclaimed artists such as Jon Foster and Donato Giancola through independent mentorships. He is currently living in Columbia, Maryland, where he continues to develop his artistic skills through mentorships, workshops, and the online arts community. He hopes to bring his work to games, books, and magazines soon.

The Trade

It was the best view humanity had to offer, but I still felt unfulfilled.

I held my camera a few millimetres from the zenith window of the International Space Station's cupola and gazed down at what had become the common sight of Earth hanging beneath me. From up here, you couldn't tell that the planet was heating up, or that the nations had nuclear ICBMs pointed at each other. I zoomed into clouds and continents and snapped shot after shot, hunting for something in that arcing landscape of blues and whites, maybe angels. Whatever it was, I didn't find it.

I stood on top of the world, but today the view made me feel uneasy. Odd. Maybe I'd feel better if I was over the moon.

I swung the camera around and snapped my daily selfie. "Husband tax," Oleg called it. Sometimes I felt bad for not missing him as much as he missed me. I checked the photo and grimaced at my unruly zero-g hair and the wrinkles under my eyes. At least my smile looked bright and cheerful, convincing enough even for Oleg, who should have known better.

My unease remained, a silent siren of discomfort in the back of my mind. What was the problem? It couldn't be vertigo or fluid shift. I'd adjusted to all that. I glanced out the port window at the Space Station Remote Manipulator System, the station's huge Canadian robotic arm. Wasn't the SSRMS supposed to have moved along by now in its survey? Ground must have found something. Maybe I was anxiously anticipating their call.

Or maybe I felt uneasy because the magic of space had already become dull and routine, as if the majestic sight of Earth from orbit was no more special than the view out of my old kitchen window. I'd made it up here onto the ISS, and yet after two months this amazing life in microgravity no longer produced any sense of thrill or achievement.

What was wrong with me?

My name, Lena Sokolov, would be engraved in the lists of early astronauts, glorified for as long as humanity survived. But that wasn't enough. I wanted to go to Mars. I wanted to go to Alpha Centauri. I wanted to be immortal and to lead the disheartened human race into a more optimistic future. Even then, the unknown thing I hunted with my camera might still remain out of reach.

I glanced again at the photo and my unease heightened alarmingly. In the background of the image, the stars looked wrong. Too bright. I turned to the bow window and noticed what my subconscious had picked up half an hour ago.

But I couldn't believe it. The stars weren't skewed or faint. There had to be something wrong with my eyes. My consciousness, unlike my instincts, possessed incredible powers of denial. Only after a few minutes of blinking and experimenting with the camera did I accept what I saw.

A transparent wall hung past the bow of the station, stretching and skewing the stars beyond. A wall or a hull? The effect reminded me of those incredible deep-sea fish that could change their skin to match the ocean floor beneath them.

Something gigantic had camouflaged itself and crept up on us, coming to rest outside our main docking adapter.

I glanced back to the SSRMS, which remained stationary. Had the transparent thing also cut off our communication with Ground?

"Lena, Node Two, now!" Yuma's scream reverberated through the station.

I pulled myself down, gripping blue handle after blue handle, turning at Node One and throwing myself down the US module

Destiny. Yuma floated ahead of me at Node Two, looking out the hatch window.

The walls shuddered.

My unease turned to panic, then to excitement. At last something interesting, something we hadn't trained for!

"A vessel's trying to dock," Yuma said. "Radio's jammed. Are we being invaded? Where's Nat?"

I looked through the little circular window of the hatch. I couldn't see anything outside. At first this disappointed me, but then I remembered I should've seen stars. Something was out there, blocking the view.

"Natalie! Node Two!" Yuma shouted. Then he whispered to me, "Who could it be? The Chinese?"

The wall of camouflage I'd seen from the cupola covered a gigantic volume, enough to contain all the satellites and shuttles ever launched from Earth.

"Not human," I answered.

"What?"

The hatch clacked.

Yuma grabbed its steel latch and held it in its locked position. I almost criticised him for this desperate action—as if spacefaring aliens couldn't get through a simple lock—and what if we offended them? But I couldn't send poor Yuma into an even worse panic. That would be bad "expeditionary behaviour."

The steel latch jumped out of Yuma's grip. The hatch opened with a pop and a hiss. Compressed air from the other side spilled into Node Two, tasting more earthy and natural than our own. The gust pushed us away.

By the time Yuma and I grabbed a handle and oriented ourselves, a man had emerged from the open hatch. He was dressed in a navy-blue jumpsuit identical to our own uniforms, although stripped of its badges, flag, and nametag. The module behind him didn't appear alien at all, more like a mirror image of our Node Two.

"Hello, humans!" The man waved his palms wide.

Yuma yelped.

I made sure I had a good grip on the surfaces around me.

"Am I first?" the man asked. "Tell me I'm first."

We stared.

"Yep. I can see from your faces that I'm first. Hell, yeah!"

He fist-pumped the air, kicking and catching handles to do a 180° sideways flip. He continued talking to us upside-down.

"Numero uno, baby! It's a real pleasure to welcome you to the galactic community. I'm here to— Sorry, is this distracting?"

He flipped his body back round the same way as us, his head now perfectly level with my own. Although the alien looked human, I'd never met anyone who could so confidently toss themselves around in microgravity.

"*I* am a trader. I trade things for other things, et cetera. You can call me—let's have a look—how bout Daikoku, in honour of Yuma here? Swell. Listen, my arrival is fantastic news for you. And not just because I've got over two hundred million tons of goodies that have travelled at relativistic speeds for you to browse."

We stared.

"Hmm. Your faces"—he pointed at each of us—"are not nearly in proportion to the scope of this opportunity. You gotta pick up that excitement by about 2000%. Okay?"

Yuma nodded automatically. Even I found myself smiling, erring on the side of politeness.

"Better. You've made it guys! At the next convention, I'll add you to the trade routes, and then you'll have visitors all the time. So, let's talk. If you could have anything in the universe, what would you want?"

I thought of Oleg at home, a frown across his face as he told me about the latest swarm missile test. I'd watched the news myself and seen banners with red letters, "The dead don't pollute," while on the other side of the world another country voted against the UN's carbon tax, its new leaders expressing their confidence in laser-based antimissile defences. Everyone knew those defences didn't work against swarm missiles but talking about lasers made everyone feel better anyway. They reminded people of the '80s, when things were simpler.

"I think we're going a bit fast here," I said. "Yuma, are you okay?"

"I'm fine," Yuma responded, though he was clearly hyperventilating.

"He'll be fine," the trader insisted. "Now, if you could have anything at all?"

No. We needed a second to process this. And where the hell was Natalie? I thought of something to slow this all down.

"It's rude for us to negotiate without offering something first," I said. "Would you like a drink?"

The man's eyes seemed to glow green as his grin spread wide. "Free?"

We turned around and began the short journey to the next module, Destiny. Each second gave my brain a better chance of processing that this was really happening.

An alien. A real alien. The trader must have made a deliberate choice to appear human, to match our navy-blue uniforms, and to board through a replica of Node Two. His voice had an American accent and he enunciated his words with all the punch and emotion of a TV star. Maybe he'd learned English by listening to broadcasts from orbit. Meanwhile, his pick of a Japanese name showed he knew of our nationalities and cultures. How long had he been observing us?

I whispered to Yuma. "What does Daikoku mean?"

"It's like a god of commerce."

"Let's use Daiko for short," said the trader, who evidently possessed better hearing than a natural human.

If things turned violent, we had no idea what we were up against. I glanced at the tools on the wall. Node Two's big wrench had chosen a good time to go missing from its Velcro strap. Though, realistically, none of our weapons could match those of a being powerful enough to travel between stars.

"So where have you come from, Daiko?"

"Ohh, I'm old. Where I came from doesn't exist anymore. A few laps around the galaxy will do that to you."

Laps around the galaxy? Even at relativistic speeds, that would have taken millions of years.

We floated on through the narrow rectangular hatchway into Destiny. The walls were littered with screens, papers, camera lenses, wires, and tubes, everything delicately stuck or strapped down. I felt a domestic need to apologise to our guest for inviting him into such a messy home.

"And what brings you to Earth?" Yuma asked, trying to sound nonchalant.

"Why, you guys, of course! This system sits in a part-DMZ– part-national-park between two competing civilisations. While passing through, I picked up some of your primitive radio signals and changed course. Finding new intelligent life, being first, that's a big deal in my circles. Worth the detour."

The dispenser hung overhead. Yuma stuck in his water pouch. While it filled, we decided by tacit consensus to rotate ourselves, putting our heads to port, our feet to starboard, and the water dispenser in front of us. Yuma removed his pouch and glared at Daiko as he drank, as if hoping the alien would disappear after a few gulps of water. No such luck.

I thought of what I could offer Daiko. "Green tea?"

"Why, thank you kindly."

As I filled the drink pouch, Daiko pushed himself down by the four monitors of the robotic workstation, the unused backup controls for the SSRMS.

"You guys don't realise that you've found a jinni in a lamp here. We're talking space lift...."

One of the dark monitors came alive, showing a thin, curved tower that stretched out of the atmosphere, space vessels docked in a ring at its apex. I'd heard of theoretical projects that would launch equipment into orbit without the need of heavy fuel and rockets, starting a rush of space exploration and asteroid mining.

ARTHUR BOWLING

I'd never imagined I could see that sort of development in my lifetime. Our nations were too busy dealing with failed crops, engineered viruses, and power shortages.

"Or maybe some solar farms for your little global warming issue…" said Daiko, as if he'd read my mind.

The next monitor showed a web of solar panels floating in space. They looked much cleaner and darker than our current tech. The image zoomed out to a map of Sol, showing three solar farms in very low orbit around the sun, even lower than Mercury, beaming their energy back to Earth. The monitor flicked to a diagram depicting the complex network of orbital relays and ground receivers that would distribute the near limitless energy supply around the world, forestalling our potential war over power generation and climate change.

"Still too much for you? I guess you guys haven't even really got into wave and tidal power yet. Seriously, tide comes in, tide goes out. Waves crash against the shore. Where there's movement, there's energy. Get on it."

Daiko snatched the green tea out of my hands. He slurped as a video began to play on the third monitor. Waves crashed against devices of all sorts: some concrete walls, some buoys that bobbed around, some turbines under the sea. The video then showed an expanse of water covered with a green, mossy film.

"That's algae," Daiko explained. "You can use that to take CO_2 out of the air. Also helps with your overfishing issue."

Right on cue, the film plunged under the waves, showing dozens of colourful fish. I knew I was watching a marketing presentation, but I didn't care. I was awestruck. By waving his technological wand, Daiko could make all our problems go away.

"Though your issue isn't really tech, is it? It's more those brutal economical-political systems. How 'bout some hyperintelligent AIs to run things? You'll never need to work again."

The last monitor, which had displayed the controls for the station's robotic arm, changed over to a video depicting a city of bubble-like skyscrapers. Hundreds of little quadcopter drones flew between the buildings. The video cut to a factory floor packed with thousands of robotic limbs, not a single human worker to be seen.

But how could we possibly power such industry? Every robot had a dozen unnecessary lights across its frame. Then again, Daiko didn't have to think about climate change, did he? That's how things must have been in my parent's day. People could marvel at an invention for its own merit, without lunging at its CO_2 implications like a drowning man at the floating debris of a sunken ship.

Daiko looked up at Yuma's open-mouthed expression and the monitor went blank.

"Oh, too far? I'm sorry. Maybe you'll settle for an automated antinuclear defence system because, damn, you guys are badass! Like seriously, you're lucky you're in a DMZ. You're so uncivilised the guys spinward from you would classify you as food, and under their law you'd have less rights than their favourite sweet and sour fungi. But then again they're obsessed with taste. Let's call 'em 'Longtongues.' The way humans have visual arts, novels, film, and games; these guys have salty, sweet, sour, and savoury. All their art is about taste. To be fair, their tongues are so sensitive that it's like tasting in 3D colour compared to—"

"What do you want in return for these things?" asked Yuma.

For the first time, Daiko's arms ceased waving around and came to rest by his side.

"It's always about the cost," he sighed.

I, for one, didn't care about the price. I remained engrossed in the future he'd presented, one where we could skip the woes of global warming and potential world war, where space exploration could begin in earnest with the space lift, where energy came cheap, where the air cleared up, and where AIs took care of all mundane labour so we could dedicate ourselves to our passions.

Gazing at the monitors, I wanted it all. I needed it all. Our existence seemed so primitive, so perilous, and so pathetic compared to the potential Daiko saw in us. Any price seemed reasonable. Anything—

"One billion people."

I blinked. "What?"

The trader glanced to port. "Sorry, forgot to do a pop count on your planet. You're a little behind average. Let's say, two hundred million people. Hey, one for every ton of my cargo."

"You want our people?"

"Yeah, a few people. And I need the rights and permissions to take a scan of your planet, its art, and its digital networks. To be honest, I've already taken the scan, but certain civilisations insist on getting the natives' permission."

Yuma and I stared at each other. I could see he was thinking the same thing: Did we even have a choice in this deal? The Spanish conquistadors hadn't bothered to buy the Inca's gold; they'd simply taken it.

"Hey, fellas, look at it from my view. Your main selling point is that you're so damn cute. I mean, look at this can...." The trader knocked on the wall. "Aluminium, adorable! And your art...Wow! Your wars...Prime simulation potential! I mean, I'm practically your agent here. I want the galaxy to hear you sing. But I can't do a tour off a recording. I need real personas to represent the culture. The Dwellers—my best customers—aren't interested in museum pieces, they're interested in flavours of consciousness. So I need people."

"Slaves?" I said. "You're saying you want us to sell you two hundred million slaves?"

The trader scrunched up his face. "*Slaves* is a harsh word."

I glanced at Yuma, who seemed to be hyperventilating again.

"Look," the trader continued. "I sell to lots of civilisations. I can't guarantee the legal rights of the repurposed population. But at worst they'd be treated like indentured servants, or minimum-wage workers. If they're lucky, they might even live luxurious lives as household pets."

Pets! The trader wanted to sell us as pets! How could I respond to that? Yuma's eyes offered no suggestions, only panic. Where the hell was Natalie? I needed to buy time again, slow things down.

"We'll need to talk this over with our superiors."

The trader laughed. "No."

I felt my pulse quicken. Did Daiko really expect Yuma and me to make a decision for all of humanity?

"But—"

"Listen, I've been down that path before. If you had a united planetary government, maybe. But the best you have is some piss-weak, pretty-please-if-you-could council that can't even stop climate change. Besides, if your people know I'm giving you anything, then they'll fight over it. The things you buy, I'm going to make it look like you discovered them yourselves. And I'll leave a few drones behind to make sure the tech spreads around evenly."

In addition to his hyperventilating, Yuma now seemed to be turning blue.

"Come on. Have some respect for yourselves," Daiko added. "In some cultures, early astronauts are royalty and the space station is a very tall throne."

"But surely there must be someone else on your ship you need to check things with?"

"Nope. No one but lonely old me."

Two hundred million tons of goods owned by one person? I found that unlikely. But then again, I had no idea of the trader's true physiology. Maybe he was a hive-mind, or a machine, or some sort of organic space-leviathan.

Daiko threw up his arms. "Okay. You've got a lot to take in. Let me retire for twenty-four hours. You can find your missing crew member, and we'll talk tomorrow."

He began floating back towards Node Two.

I didn't trust Daiko to show himself out, but I struggled to keep up with him as he flung himself through Destiny, nimbly grabbing handles to adjust his direction without stopping.

I would have lost him if he hadn't paused before the hatchway that led into his replica of Node Two.

"Thanks for the tea." He smiled at me and handed back the drink pouch. "Just knock if you have any questions."

As he turned back to the hatchway, I noticed a shadow pass over us. Before I could register what was happening, Natalie flew in from Columbus and smashed Daiko's head with Node Two's missing wrench. I heard the crack of bone.

"Ah, you must be Natalie." Daiko spun himself around, smiling despite the dent in his skull.

Natalie swung again, holding onto a blue handle with her other hand so she could put some force into the blow. She still struggled in microgravity to make much of an impact.

Daiko just stood there. In fact, he seemed to wave his hand in encouragement as her clobbering became gradually more effective.

He'd begun to twitch by the time it occurred to me to scream. After the sixth blow, he went limp, blood oozing over his face, occasional red orbs breaking off to drift around the module and stick to whatever they touched.

"What have you done?" Yuma shouted, behind me.

"Relax." Natalie puffed with exertion. "I heard everything. It's over now. No slaves."

"But you killed him. There might be others."

I couldn't take my eyes off Daiko's body. Dressed in the same uniform as me, it gently brushed against the emergency equipment locker.

"Get a grip, Yuma. And Lena, look at me. Lena."

I looked at Natalie's Barbie-blonde hair and blue eyes.

"It's okay now," she said. "We have his ship. We'll be able to pull all that tech out. We'll be ready for whoever comes next."

"But you can't just kill the first alien we meet," Yuma argued. "You have no idea what the consequences could be, what his ship might be programmed to do without him..."

I had trouble listening. I felt sick. There was a corpse where seconds ago there had been a person, maybe of completely different origin to me, but certainly intelligent and conscious.

Natalie and Yuma kept shouting.

Academically, I understood Natalie's argument. Everything we knew about Daiko suggested that he wanted to take our people, either to sell into servitude or to exhibit in his relativistic travelling zoo. He certainly had the tech to take whatever we refused him. Not to mention, in all of history, the colonisers had rarely treated their technologically inferior brethren with anything less than abuse.

"But that thing wasn't human," Yuma pointed out. "It only looked human."

True. We'd made the assumption that Daiko would obey human logic, would follow the behavioural arcs of human history. But we had no idea what ethics he abided by. Maybe galactic laws protected indigenous populations like us. Or maybe Daiko's spacefaring kin tended to have a kinder nature than us humans. When he'd mentioned the Longtongues, it had been with amazement and horror, implying that their culinary aggression was a rarity in the civilised galaxy. Now we would never know.

My sense of unease returned, stronger than ever.

"But it was too easy," I whispered to myself.

Natalie heard me. "What do you mean?"

A new figure appeared out of the hatchway, floating towards us with outstretched hands. Natalie screamed and pushed herself backwards. Yuma instinctively spun back and then—unable to reach the walls—continued to spin round and round in the middle of the module. Only I held my ground, glancing between the old body of the trader and the identical copy that had just stepped through the hatchway.

"Wooo-hoo," shouted Daiko's new body. "This really is the Wild West! You guys are Class-Four Barbarians, for sure. How did you make it this far? You should have blown yourselves up by now."

We stared back, children awaiting their punishment.

"Anyway." Daiko waved at Natalie. "Lovely to meet you. Since you're all here, I thought I'd leave a short list of my most popular items." He pulled a piece of paper out of his pocket and let it float towards us. "Have a think. Have a chat. When you make a decision, just shout out. Okay?"

He reached down, picked up his old body, and perfunctorily tossed it through the hatchway back towards his ship. Maybe he didn't want us analysing the corpse. Later, I'd find some of the blood that had floated onto the walls and take a sample.

"Daiko, before you go."

"Yes, Lena, my sweet?"

He looked straight into my eyes and I realised he somehow knew me better than Yuma or Natalie did, maybe even better than Oleg at home. I had the feeling he'd been listening to my thoughts earlier and somehow measured my lust for achievement, my insatiable need for ever-farther boundaries to exceed. His eyes seemed to scan me to the soul.

I said, "You mentioned that other traders would come after you. Will they be...friendly, like you?"

"I'll be frank. I am the most friendly, most sophisticated, and most-damn-elegant trader you'll meet in a whole galactic cycle. But what you're really asking me is, 'Will the next trader enslave all of mankind?'"

I nodded.

Daiko stroked his chin. "It's looked down upon. But given you're Class-Four Barbarians with at least 37% chance of eradicating yourselves this century...then certain arguments could be made to repurpose your populace for your own good. It really depends on who comes, and what shape you're in when they get here."

Daiko pointed to the list floating in the air. "If you take my tech, it won't be too long before you elevate from Barbarians to Spacefaring. Then you'll be able to defend yourselves, both legally and militarily. I don't want to say it's an easy decision, but..."

He shrugged, waved bye, and closed the hatch after him. The hatch should not have been that easy to shut, but as soon as Daiko was out of sight it seemed to seal by itself.

Through the little circular window, I saw nothing but darkness.

We fell back to the Zvezda module in the Russian segment, to the aft-most dining table, away from Daiko. Natalie wiped the blood off her hands and began heating meals for all of us, beef stroganoff, rice pilaf, and chicken teriyaki.

Natalie sucked her stroganoff straight out of the food pouch. I carefully used a spoon to pick at the pilaf. Yuma didn't eat at all. In front of us lay the list Daiko had written in inhumanly neat handwriting. I noticed he'd put an asterisk next to the inventions that could save us.

Popular Items, sorted by cost:

* Renewable energy suite. (Seriously,
     tidal power. Get on it.):
     3p
* CO_2 reducing algae:
     1,000p
  Construction nanites:
     25,000p
  Space maps, as current as my own,
     400 light-years radius:
     50,000p
  Encyclopaedia of Species, Empires, Civilisations, and Systems by M.A.2332.Xenatlesack:
     100,000p
  Hyperefficient super-crops (bye world hunger):
     500,000p
  Immortality via genetic manipulation:
     1,000,000p

* Automated antinuclear defence system:
    5,000,000p
  Full-immersion VR + immortality via digitalisation:
    10,000,000p
  Networkable mind-tech (hive-mind!):
    20,000,000p
* Solar farm, 50–65 PWh per year:
    35,000,000p
  Self-erecting space-lift/catapult,
    initial capacity 400t/h:
    50,000,000p
  Asteroid-mining fleet, 17 x 2 Gt vessels:
    70,000,000p
  The Totality of Science, a mind-print for the enlightened
    Spacefarer, edited by Mnulamnuamlani CCXVI:
    100,000,000p
* AI Master (a nice one):
    125,000,000p
  Autonomous defence fleet (3rd class), sufficient
    to defend against the nearest four aggressor
    civilisations, INEFFECTIVE AGAINST TRADERS.
    (This tech is beyond what I can ethically give
    you, so it'll have to operate independently
    from human control.):
    150,000,000p
  All of the above and more, bulk discount, only:
    200,000,000p

Note: p = Repurposed Population (not slaves).

Any purchased item will also incur the following
additional costs: signed authorisation for a complete
planet scan, right of sale for any and all cultural worth
contained within, and official acknowledgment of
first contact and market registration. Consult your
trader for full terms and conditions.

"We can't give him anyone," I said.

"The 'super crops' alone would make up for the population loss," Natalie rebuked, gently. Too gently. She knew she'd already lost.

"They're not our lives to give," Yuma said. "Besides, we don't know what the tech might do to us after Daiko leaves."

Natalie gazed down at the grey, utilitarian dinner table, with its built-in food warmer and trash bags wrapped around the handles. I saw what she saw, a spaceship made of recycled cans. The list only sold one thing: the future. And the prices were all the same: our humanity.

"He only wants three people for the renewables," Natalie said. "We could give ourselves up. It's the most good we could ever do for our countries. Remember all that talk about expeditionary behaviour. Well, this is it."

Yuma didn't have a response to that, but it didn't matter.

"The list is a trick," I said.

They both stared at me. How hadn't they seen it?

"Yuma, what was the first thing he asked when he saw us?"

"Something like, 'Am I first?'"

I banged my fist on the table. "That's what he cares about! No matter what we buy, he's going to register us as his discovery. That's why he wants people, to show off his find at some traders' convention."

"And no matter what we buy, we end up registered." Yuma's eyes went wide. "Even if we buy nothing at all, he'll still tell other traders where to find us."

"But if we upgrade our tech enough, we'll have autonomy," Natalie argued. "We'll stop global warming and we'll have extraterrestrial rights as a 'Spacefaring' race."

"We don't know how those rights work," I challenged. "And we'd never be able to resist anything at Daiko's tech level. Think about it, Natalie. He probably invented the Longtongues to scare us into making a purchase."

Daiko may not have been human, but he *was* a salesman. We couldn't know how he'd calculated our odds of surviving the next century, but between global warming and nuclear war, we had enough fears to satisfy the equation, and to believe that buying these goods might be a necessary evil. In case we weren't persuaded enough already, Daiko had added monsters in the darkness between the stars.

"Human nature doesn't change because our tech does," Yuma said. "If these traders think we're barbarians, then we're barbarians, and we'll have to evolve over time. A sudden technological shift could be the most dangerous thing of all."

Natalie raised her voice: "If we do nothing, the next time a trader comes there might not be anyone left on Earth to visit."

"People will solve the climate crisis by themselves."

"Bullshit!" Natalie spat. "People are ignorant, greedy morons and you know it. Without our help, they'll shout and scream and march themselves to their deaths."

"If that is so, then our species deserves to die." Yuma shook his head. "But I don't think that's the case. I believe we'll go through this process of change and adapt for the better. Cheating, by using tech bought with slaves, will have terrible ramifications for our culture. I'm not talking Japanese culture, I'm talking about all our culture, human culture. We may survive through selling our own, but what sort of race would that make us? And without that human spirit, how will we deal with alien invaders or whatever the next crisis might be?"

"Also, better tech means better weapons," I added. "You only need to watch the news to know that's the last thing we need."

"So what's your plan?" Natalie threw down her empty food pouch. It bounced off the table and floated off overhead. "To simply pass on all this potential?"

"There's one thing we have to buy."

They both stared at me, again.

"Our anonymity. We have to stay off the market."

"That's right," Yuma said. "If we remain a secret, no other trader can come and repurpose us."

"And you think Daiko's just gonna fly away empty-handed?

You think he'll keep his discovery quiet out of the goodness of his heart?"

I turned towards the bow. "We'll have to find out."

Back in Node Two, the hatch opened as soon as we knocked. Daiko pushed through, again hooking his feet around the blue handles so he could wave his hands.

"Full disclosure: I could hear everything you said, and you're making a terrible mistake."

"It's all we want, Daiko," I said. "You will leave us off your maps. You'll tell no one where we are. And you'll make sure no one backtracks along your trail."

Daiko groaned. "You gotta give me something. I can conceal your location, but I want to claim that I was first. The least you can do is formally acknowledge me."

"As long as you conceal our location, fine."

"But a document's not enough," Daiko protested. "These galactic trade conventions, they're full of sceptics. I'll need your permission for the planet scan, the right of sale, and at least a hundred people."

"No. You can have the other things but you're not getting any people. You were never getting anyone from us. We care for our own. We're not barbarians."

"I'll be the judge of that." Daiko scratched his head where Natalie had clubbed his last body to death with the wrench. "Listen, without any people, the other traders will say I faked it all. Creating a fake planet scan is not difficult for an AI, but creating a living being, with a whole different mindset, that's a different story."

"No."

He caught my eye, and something seemed to pass between us. He smiled at me, and again I had the feeling that he knew me too well.

He lifted a single finger.

"One person. You'll give me one person and the permissions,

and I'll make sure no one finds you till the next happy accident, likely tens of thousands of years."

I looked back at Yuma and Natalie. That was a mistake. My silence denoted acceptance.

"Whoever's coming, close the hatch behind you." Daiko threw himself backwards through the hatchway and down into his own ship. The lights on his side switched off, his version of Node Two disappearing into an unnaturally deep darkness.

Clinging to our blue handles, Yuma, Natalie, and I glared at each other, three astronauts caught in a Mexican standoff. But there was no need for discussion. Yuma had two children at home. Natalie had three. A few years ago, Oleg had asked for kids. I'd sacrificed that life to get to space faster. I would have regretted that decision, if not for the trader.

I realised what had passed between Daiko and me when he'd met my eye. He must've known my wanderlust, sensed my excitement when I'd first seen his ship, and detected that travelling around the galaxy with an alien did not seem like a great sacrifice to me.

But I also got a glimpse of him in return, not his physical form, but his mind. I saw that he too travelled with an insatiable desire for accomplishment and significance. The hunt had taken him through thousands of worlds, civilisations changing too fast for him to ever revisit. He crawled through the galaxy, imprisoned by the speed of light, always wanting to see more, own more, change more, be more. I'd seen in his eyes that, though different in so many insignificant ways, we shared the same need.

I let myself drift into the mouth of the hatchway and turned to Yuma and Natalie.

"Tell Control..." I said. "Tell Oleg..."

Yuma nodded. Natalie wiped the tears out of her eyes and helped me with the heavy hatch.

"Good luck," they both said, repeatedly.

The hatch sealed, leaving me in darkness. I tried not to think about Oleg. I didn't want the trader to see me cry.

Daiko's ship provided plenty of distraction as I heard the docking mechanism uncouple and felt myself being pulled forward, towards the bow. Actually, I was beyond the bow now. The ISS's orientation no longer applied.

Now I would travel farther than I could've ever dreamed. This ship—I felt it rumble—this is what I'd been hunting.

Something in the air made me feel drowsy. I didn't mind. I suspected that when I woke I would be the only human to have ever left the solar system.

First!

Foundations

written by
Michael Gardner

illustrated by
AIDIN ANDREWS

ABOUT THE AUTHOR

Michael Gardner lives in Canberra, Australia, where he is an economist by day and a writer of fantasy and horror by night. Strangely, he aspired to do both as a teenager, and was encouraged by an English teacher who didn't mind that his creative writing assignments were always about the supernatural and were influenced heavily by Clive Barker.

Yet he lost his way in his twenties. Not quite knowing how to take his writing forward, he focused on his new career in a new city. But those years were in no way a waste, as that was when he met his patient and supportive wife, and later they had two wonderful kids. The experience of fatherhood continues to find its way into his stories.

It was about six years ago that he fell in love with writing again. And this time he fell hard.

The key moment arose when his sister signed him up for a course run by a former Writers of the Future winner Ian McHugh. And it changed everything. Inspired, he started writing again, and soon submitted his first story to a magazine. The story was promptly rejected.

But he persisted, because what other choice did he have when writing about strange things made him so happy, proud, and satisfied?

His work has appeared in Aurealis, Andromeda Spaceways Magazine, *and* Metaphorosis. *He is also a two-time finalist for the Aurealis Awards. This is his first professional sale.*

ABOUT THE ILLUSTRATOR

Aidin Sol Andrews is an artist residing in the beautiful bayside town of Bellingham, Washington. Encouraged to pursue his interests from a young age, he has had a fondness for the arts as long as he can remember.

Some of Aidin's most pervasive personal inspirations are his mother, Annie, who owns her own jewelry business, and his high school art teacher, Katy Shanafelt. Artists such as Aaron Horkey, Shaun Tan, and Felix Colgrave are also a constant inspiration to him, and a reminder of how amazing art and illustration can be.

Foundations

Where have you been?" Dad demanded when I opened the front door. I pulled up sharply, startled. Damn, they got home early.

He was halfway down the ornate staircase, a hand clutching tightly at the carved banister. He stood tall, rigid, green eyes glaring. His grey hair was unkempt, his mouth a tight line.

"Out," I said.

"Out," he repeated. Then nothing. He waited, as if he thought I would suddenly intuit what was wrong. Which was crazy, I thought. But then I did sense something.

The house smelt different. Stale. The blood-red runner under Dad's feet seemed less vibrant. And the walls felt closer, older, and there were small cracks in them that I hadn't noticed before. The house couldn't have aged that much in the few hours I'd been away and yet, I felt it.

I swallowed, suddenly nervous.

From the first floor came my mother's voice. "Is that Poppy?" She sounded tired, and frail.

"Yes, Mum," I said.

"Can you come up here, please?"

There was silence then. A silence in which my father continued to glower, in which I heard my heart beating hard, the blood coursing across my temples.

I'd reluctantly agreed to look after Lacy for a few hours while my parents visited a friend in the hospital. But then I'd got a call from Johnnie, and I really wanted to see him, so I'd left my sister by herself with the house. I'd convinced her it would be fine, challenged her even, and she'd convinced me that she could handle the house now that she was eight. And if I'd had doubts, I'd pushed them down so that I wouldn't feel guilty.

But something must have gone wrong.

I closed the front door and began to ascend the stairs. Halfway up, I eased past my father, who fell into step behind me.

The stairs opened into our parlour. It looked different as well. The walls were darker and bowed. The gold lounges at the centre of the room looked worn. The fireplace was cold, and the ancient swords crossed above the mantle appeared dull and neglected.

Across the room I saw Mum huddled between the drinks cabinet and the large, arched window that overlooked the back creek. Her eyes were red, as if she'd been crying. A sharp pain jabbed up under my ribs. Guilt and shame, and a dash of dread.

"Go," my father said from close behind. "Go and see what you've done."

I wanted to run from his accusations and whatever was waiting for me, but I didn't. I walked slowly toward my mother and, as she stood, I saw Lacy. I took in a sharp breath, my body quivering. Oh, God, what had I done?

She was held up about four feet off the floor by wooden tendrils that had snaked up out of the parquetry and enveloped her midsection. She lay on her back, her body arched and limp, her head hanging backward. Her eyes were open—cloudy, white orbs, not seeing, not blinking.

The wall of the house was cracked, and from the fissure in the plaster a skeletal hand had broken free and clutched my sister around the wrist. Her skin was bruised under that tight grip. Uncle Carlton's tight grip.

"Lacy," I whispered, but she didn't respond. Her breathing came shallow, her chest barely moving.

"But why?" I said quietly. "Why would the house turn on her?"

"I don't know," my mother said. "But it did, and she was too young and inexperienced to resist."

"That's why we'd asked you to look after her," Dad snapped.

"Derek," my mother said, turning to glare at him. "This isn't the time."

I knew he'd blame me. He always did. I was suddenly annoyed. As if Dad needed another excuse to be disappointed in me. I wanted to shake Lacy. To pull her from the embrace of the house's floor, to slap her and say, what the hell? How had you been so stupid, or unlucky, or naive to get caught by this slow-moving, behemoth of a house? But just as quickly as the anger flared, it died, leaving me empty.

Dad sighed. "I'll call the engineer."

My mother nodded, then placed a hand on Lacy's forehead.

"What can I do?" I asked.

"I think you've done enough for the time being, don't you?" Dad said. My face grew hot and I felt that stabbing pain in my chest again.

Mum frowned at him, then turned to me with a softer expression. "Why don't you talk to Grandma Dee and find out what she knows."

I nodded, turned, and hurried away.

I opened the heavy oak door covered in glyphs and symbols. If they'd meant anything once, they didn't now, not to me. The basement beyond was hidden in darkness—a thick, black ooze. I reached inside and felt around for the light switch, flicked it, and a single bulb fizzed to life. It cast just enough sickly light to force back the gloom into the corners of the sunken room.

The stone steps leading down were smooth and worn as if two million feet had trodden this path a million times. I stepped carefully so as not to slip, ducking my head under the wooden beam that supported the ceiling. It was cool under the house, and it smelt damp and earthy.

The room was nearly empty. There were only a couple of rolled rugs in the corner next to several half-empty paint cans. And then there was Grandma Dee.

I walked across the uneven stone floor toward her. Her face protruded from the wall only a couple of bricks up from the floor, as did one lean arm and the toes of a foot. The rest of Grandma Dee's emaciated body was walled into the foundations of the house. Her eyes were closed.

I sat beside her on the cold floor, and looked over her face—leathered skin, thin lips, grey, wiry hair hanging partway over her forehead.

"Hello, Grandma Dee," I said.

She snorted, and her eyelids fluttered open, exposing rheumy eyes. I watched her irises contract, then expand, then she turned toward me. Her mouth twitched, smiled, the frail skin on her cheeks wrinkling.

"Hello, dear," she croaked. She cleared her throat. I saw her exposed toes wiggle.

Grandma Dee wasn't actually my grandmother. She was my great, great, great, great-grandmother, but it was easier to call her Grandma Dee.

"Lacy's in trouble, Grandma Dee," I said. She frowned, then closed her eyes tight. I watched the flickering movement beneath her lids as her eyes coursed back and forth. When she opened them again she appeared disappointed. I felt sick of adults being disappointed.

"Lacy's let the house in," she said. "Why?"

I shrugged noncommittally.

"How did the house get past you and your parents?"

I hesitated. "We weren't there," I eventually mumbled.

"Oh," Grandma Dee said. She didn't accuse me like Dad had, and yet there was enough in the silence that followed to make me uncomfortable. She allowed the silence to build, and build, like waves on waves, doubling in size until they were crashing down around me. I cracked.

"She said she was okay," I said. "I believed her. I mean, I was fine with the house by the time I was her age."

"You were always strong," Grandma Dee said. "Not all children are the same."

"Lacy's strong," I said, and I wanted so hard to believe it. I was still hoping she'd miraculously fight off the house.

"Yes, dear," Grandma Dee said. She sighed. "We all make mistakes. Me included. I should have been watching. It's your Uncle Carlton, isn't it?"

I nodded.

"He's been unhappy. He doesn't like the way your father is running his factory."

"What's that got to do with Lacy?"

"Your father won't listen to your Uncle Carlton, but he thinks your father may listen to Lacy."

"That's crazy. He's going to destroy a little girl for nothing."

"He doesn't see it like that, dear. He doesn't want to hurt Lacy, just swap with her. She'll live on, in the house."

I swallowed, thinking over what Grandma Dee had said. "So what do we do now?"

"We wait for the engineer."

"Wait," I repeated. I couldn't believe that was our only option. "Why can't we just expel Uncle Carlton? He's turned on his own. He doesn't deserve our protection."

Grandma Dee sighed again. "It's not that simple, dear. The factory was Carlton's business originally, and he's linked with it and our home. Like him or not, he helps hold our estate together."

I rubbed my hands together, eyes downcast. Finally, I took a breath and looked back at Grandma Dee.

"I wonder sometimes," I said, tasting the words as I said them, not sure if I should continue. But if not with Grandma Dee, then with who?

"Yes?" she said.

"I wonder if it would be so bad to be houseless."

The raw cackle that escaped her cracked lips surprised me. It rose around me, and then shattered and fell like broken glass.

She exhaled loudly. "I suppose you think it would be freeing."

"But it would. No pressure, no ancestors weighing down on you with responsibility, with expectations, with..."

I didn't know what else I meant. It just felt heavy here, claustrophobic and crowded. It didn't feel like that with Johnnie.

"Your parents became part of the house for you and Lacy."

"But I never asked for it."

"No. Not many of us did. And yet if you neglect your role in the house, fair or not, it is often not you that is hurt, but the others that look to you for support."

The ice shard that stabbed at my heart was swift and cold. I lowered my head, fighting back hot tears.

"Don't fret, dear," Grandma Dee said. "If there's one thing I know, it's that broken things can be mended."

My sleep was filled with troubled dreams, so I felt relieved when I woke. But the feeling didn't last.

The room was biting cold, and the light that spilled through the stained-glass image of my Great-great-uncle Roman was dull and grey. A thick layer of dust feathered the canopy above my four-poster bed as if it had stood for an aeon, unused. My room didn't feel welcoming anymore.

I shimmied out from under the covers and padded across icy floorboards to find a dressing gown and slippers amongst the pile of dirty clothes in the corner. Then I opened my door carefully and slipped outside before making my way downstairs to check on my sister.

In the parlour I felt surprised to find Mum crouched next to Lacy, her hand on Lacy's stomach. Mum had a blanket around her shoulders, and her head rested on her chest, asleep. Had she stayed with Lacy all night?

I moved closer, past the faded lounges and my ancestor's swords, which now had a hint of rust on the blades. Lacy was still encased in tendrils of the house, looking like a surrealist coffee table. Her eyes remained sightless orbs, and her hair hung to the floor. Outside the back window I could see willow trees swaying in the breeze, long branches caressing the creek water.

My mother roused, her head rising slowly, eyes looking without seeing until her dreams shook free from her head. When she spied me, her eyes hardened and she frowned, which hurt. Once again I felt like a moth fluttering at a window, confused and unable to get inside.

"How is she?" I asked.

Mum cleared her throat, glanced at Lacy and then back at me. "She hasn't changed."

I didn't know what else to say. Everything that bubbled to the forefront of my mind didn't seem to hold sufficient weight.

"Your father has arranged for the engineer to come this morning," Mum said. I watched her hand gently rubbing at the part of Lacy's stomach that the house had left untouched. I couldn't remember the last time she'd touched me with such affection. When had I stopped being a child to her?

"That's good," I said.

"What did Grandma Dee say?"

"She said that Uncle Carlton wanted greater control of the factory, and he thought he could use Lacy to achieve that."

I watched the worry work its way through Mum's features.

"Oh," she said. For a moment I thought she might cry, but instead she sniffed hard, then continued. "I could do with some tea." Her knees made popping sounds as she rose to her feet and stretched.

"Why don't I get it? You've had a long night."

She looked at me strangely, as if she wasn't quite seeing her oldest daughter, but then her expression warmed.

"Thank you, Poppy."

As I waited for the kettle to boil, my phone rang. I removed it from my pocket. It was Johnnie. A glance across the parlour showed me that Mum was still focussed on Lacy, not me, so I quietly closed the kitchen door and answered my phone.

"Hey, babe," he said. I could hear the grin in his voice. "You free tonight? I miss you already, and—"

"I can't," I interrupted. "I'm sorry."

"But Jonesy's having a party down by the river. It's going to be great, babe."

I sighed, looking out the kitchen window across our front lawns to the street beyond. There weren't as many houses as there had once been. The block across from ours was vacant, as were several blocks farther down the street. Each had had a house collapse in the last few years, one after the other, as if a contagion had spread.

"I can't. It's Lacy. I shouldn't have left her last night to see you. She's let the house in and, well, it's bad. She's in trouble and—"

"So it's my fault?" he asked.

I hesitated. Was it? Did I resent him for what had happened? Outside the window a white car turned into our street, driving steadily, veering around the potholes.

"No," I said finally. "That's not what I meant. I'm just upset, and worried about her. She's lying there, comatose, and…it's hard to explain. It's just bad."

I suddenly realised how difficult it was to make a houseless understand the gravity of a house's incursion. I mean, what did he have to compare that to? And yet he wasn't stupid. His family had come from a collapsed home once, so I expect he grasped the general problem.

"So, what now? Should I come visit? Pay my respects or something?"

"She's not dead," I hissed.

"Sorry, wrong words then. But—"

"No."

"But I want to see you, babe. I'm desperate." I loved to hear him beg, and he knew it. Despite Lacy, despite my guilt, I smiled.

"I know, me too. Soon, okay? I just have to make sure Lacy's better first."

"Okay, babe. I understand. But if you change your mind about tonight, come find me at the river."

The white car stopped by the footpath outside our house, beneath the large jacaranda. When the car door opened, a slim man emerged. He was neatly dressed in a grey suit, with round spectacles perched on the end of his nose. His hair was white and thinning.

I watched the stranger close the car door and take the path to our house.

"I've got to go, Johnnie. We have a visitor."

"Okay, sure. I love you."

Those words seemed to come so easily for him. He said them almost casually.

"I love you, too," I said, but he was already gone.

I met Johnnie at my father's factory, which was actually a large printing press. Dad employed the houseless to man the machines, collect the books, and load trucks. I'd finished another visit—"learning the trade," as father called it—and Johnnie had just finished a shift.

Dad had asked if I was okay to find my own way home. He could go with me, of course, he'd said, if I wanted. It's just he had so much paperwork. I'd assured him I was fine, which was both what he and I wanted.

On my way out I spied Johnnie. He was older than me, maybe twenty, and while he wore the white coveralls the other workers donned, they didn't fit him the same. On Johnnie they were tight, hugging him in the right places, revealing muscles. He was tall, with dark, wavy hair and darker eyes that seemed to stare into my soul. He was someone people noticed. Someone I noticed.

I guess I'd stared when I walked by, because he smiled at me. I faltered mid-stride, feeling strange.

"Hey, babe," he said.

That stopped me. I turned sharply, trying to glare.

"I'm not your babe," I said.

He didn't hesitate. "You could be. I'm sure you could do anything you put your mind to." Followed by the grin. That cheeky, sexy, I-know-what-you-want grin.

I tried to be mad, but my damn mouth betrayed me, and I laughed.

I had always been told the houseless were a sad bunch. Poor, lost, and desperate, roaming in hope of something better—a home like ours. Work, like at my father's factory, was a blessing.

That wasn't Johnnie. If he was representative of the houseless, they were free. Unconstrained. He was different from what I'd always known, and I guess that, as much as anything, was why falling for him was so damn easy.

"Hmm," the engineer said.

He waved a slender, electronic wand over Lacy, which made high-pitched sounds as it moved.

"Well?" Dad asked, standing close to the drinks cabinet, Mum's hand clutched in his. "You can fix this, right?" I could hear strain in his voice.

I stood back, leaning against the golden lounge in the middle of the parlour, watching the small man complete his examination.

The engineer turned to my father. "It's a complicated case."

"How?" my mother stammered, tears spilling onto her cheeks. I wanted to go comfort her, but I didn't. I couldn't.

"It's okay," Dad told Mum quietly. But I knew it wasn't all right.

The engineer frowned. "The house is not simply holding your daughter, they've become intertwined. Part of her has become the house, part of the house—more specifically, your ancestor here—has become her. He's managed to push most of your daughter out."

"But you can reverse it, surely?" Dad asked. "This has to have happened before?"

The engineer sighed, then brought the wand quickly around and slapped it into the open palm of his left hand.

"The problem is her age and experience. Her entry into the walls of the building has weakened them. You can see cracking here, and here," he said, pointing his wand toward the corner of the parlour room. "She can barely hold the house together as it is. If I remove her…"

"But, but," my father stuttered. "But can't you cast Uncle Carlton out and back into the house?"

He shook his head slowly. "In my experience, when an ancestor deserts a house, nothing will compel them to return."

"So he stays in Lacy?" I said, horrified. What had I done? How did I not know this?

The engineer turned and looked across at me with pity. "Expelling him is possible. But it will come at a cost to the structural integrity of your home, and anything else throughout your estate that has links to your uncle."

My father swallowed. "Our factory."

I watched anger and anxiety work their way into his face, and I knew he was thinking of me again.

"So," my mother said, new tears wetting her cheeks, "it's Lacy, or the house and factory?"

The engineer cleared his throat. "Most likely, yes."

Oh, God. What had I done? And yet, it was an easy choice, wasn't it?

"We'll need to think on it," my father said.

"What?" I said.

"I understand," the engineer replied. "It is a difficult decision."

"No, no it's not," I said, my voice rising. I hurried toward them. I couldn't believe they were all standing calmly talking about Lacy as if she were interchangeable with bricks and mortar, as if she were a thing that could be cast aside. But my father continued as if I hadn't spoken.

"How long do we have to make our decision?" he asked.

The engineer glanced at Lacy, then back again. "She'll be fine for another twenty-four hours or so. After that, the expulsion becomes riskier to the host."

"This is crazy. It's just a house," I said.

Dad turned on me. "Haven't you done enough?" The ferocity in his words hit like a punch to the guts. I tried to be strong, to roll with the blow, but felt hot tears welling. I blinked hard. "None of this would have happened if you had just done your duty and protected her instead of running off to meet up with whatever piece of street trash you've picked up this time. And now you dare to tell us what the right decision is? Leaving your little sister alone to her history was wrong. She's too young to do anything but let them in. Don't you get it? Even if we free her, she may never be the same. And the house, our legacy..."

He grew quiet then, as if his outburst had shocked and drained him. His face had grown pale, and his hands shook.

The engineer looked at me as if I were a naive child. And mother wouldn't even catch my eye.

With tears beginning to fall, I turned and fled the room.

"You're upset, dear," Grandma Dee said, looking up at me from beneath drooping eyelids.

I nodded.

"What's wrong?"

"The engineer says he can't just bring Lacy back, not without damaging the house, and maybe the factory. And Mum and Dad, they...How, Grandma Dee? How could they even consider putting the house before Lacy?"

Grandma Dee sighed, and shifted her withered arm until it brushed up against my hand. I took her hand in mine, her skin papery.

"The house is bigger than one person, dear. It's hard to understand when you are still so young."

I pulled my hand back, holding it to my chest. "That's rubbish. Lacy's alive. She has to come before the house."

Grandma Dee paused, and I felt for a moment I could read her thoughts—she wanted to ask me why I'd left Lacy on her own then. But she didn't.

"When you approach the end of your life, you wonder what you will leave behind. It's the nature of things. A repeated pattern.

"A house is a marker. Something to say that your time meant more than just the life you lived. A house is how you are remembered, how you live on, how you keep giving to those you love after you are gone. It's not an easy thing to let go of.

"Lacy is to be part of that, whether it is today, or in the future. Choosing to forgo the house would ruin Lacy's legacy as well as yours, and your father's, and your mother's, and mine, and everyone who lives on in the house."

I looked at Grandma Dee, her leathered face entombed within the bricks of the basement. Did she really think this was something special? Something bigger than the sum of its parts?

"I'm not sure I believe that, Grandma Dee. I've met the houseless. They seem free in a way we aren't. Is it so bad to concentrate on the here and now, living each moment without constantly scanning the horizon?"

"Perhaps," Grandma Dee said.

I watched her close her eyes, drifting back to sleep as if our talk were finished.

"I'd tear the house down tomorrow to save Lacy, and then she could stay with me," I said quietly. "I've met a boy, Grandma Dee. He'd look after us, me and Lacy. I think we'd be fine out there without the constraints of a house."

Grandma Dee's eyes snapped open, her hand sprang out and grabbed my wrist. "But is that what Lacy wants? Or this boy, for that matter? Is that what you really want?"

I tried to pull away from her bony grasp, but couldn't. And suddenly I could feel the house as if it were an electrical current that flowed through Grandma Dee and into my veins. I felt the history, the struggles and triumphs and rebellions and hurts and love of my family, the sacrifices made so that I could be safe and warm, protected. It hit me so hard I almost believed.

But then I remembered what the house had done to Lacy, and I wrenched my hand back from Grandma Dee. I watched warily as her sharp eyes searched my face.

"The houseless are not freed, they're lost. They haven't escaped, they just haven't found a spot to plant roots. Neither have you. It doesn't mean you have to wander forever. It just means you have to look, and find something worth staying for."

AIDIN ANDREWS

I lay on my bed, unable to sleep, listening to the quiet murmur of my parents talking down the hall. I couldn't distinguish specific words, but I knew they were discussing Lacy. She was on my mind too.

I felt powerless. I was to blame for Lacy's predicament, but I didn't have a say in how to resolve it. Everyone told me I was part of the house, but I felt like a tiny cog trying to spin against the churn of the machine.

The only person who made me feel different was Johnnie.

I sat up in bed and glanced at my window. Moonlight streamed through the stained glass features of Great-great-uncle Roman. It was the wrong decision, but I no longer cared.

I eased off of my bed and changed into the freshest-looking clothes I could find on the pile in the corner. Then I opened my window and slipped outside, using the ivy and trellis to shimmy down the side of the house.

I found Johnnie sitting on the bonnet of Jonesy's coupe, swigging liquor from a half-empty bottle. He was centre stage, surrounded by ten of his mates, most of whom also worked for my father. A fire burned in a rusty drum nearby, casting flickering light, and heat. At Johnnie's feet, purring around his ankles, was a girl I knew as Rachel.

I walked across the abandoned lot, gravel crunching under my feet as the damp, oily smell of the river filled the air. When he saw me he stopped orating, rose to his feet and waved, the bonnet groaning under his weight.

"You made it, babe," he said, grinning.

I smiled back. "Yeah. I needed to get away for a while."

He jumped to the ground with a thud, and the circle of revellers parted and allowed me to enter. He offered me his hand, which I took, and he pulled me close.

I saw Rachel rise lithely to her feet, pouting.

"You want a drink?" he said, proffering the bottle. I shook my head no.

"Can we go for a walk? Somewhere private?" I cast a quick look at Rachel, who watched us intently.

He frowned. "Go somewhere? But you just got here."

I gave an apologetic shrug to the group, then pulled Johnnie by the hand out of the circle, away from the fire and his friends. He followed like a stubborn child, feigning resistance, but he kept walking. I led him out of earshot of the party and only stopped when I saw his friends had resumed chatting amongst themselves in the light of the fire, all except Rachel who stood on the edge of the group watching after us.

"What's up with you?" he said finally.

I huffed. "Lacy of course."

"Oh, yeah. How is she?"

I wasn't sure he actually wanted an answer, but I gave one. "Not good. The engineer came this morning and said he may not be able to save both her and the house. To me, it's simple. We save her. But Mum and Dad...they're not so sure. They're thinking on it. How could they even hesitate, Johnnie? How?"

"Ah, damn it," he said, and this time he sounded genuine. "I'm sorry. That's rough." He took another swig of his liquor. "What you need is to take your mind off it. Come back to the party with me. We'll put on some music, you'll have a couple of drinks, we'll shoot the breeze, maybe dance."

I smiled. "Sounds good. But in a little while, okay? I just need a few minutes with you alone to collect my thoughts." I pulled him closer, but this time the resistance was real.

"What is it?" I said.

"Nothing. Look, I invited you to a party, not..."

"Not what?"

"Nothing. Just...Sure. Let's talk." But then he glanced back at Rachel who was still on her own waiting for us, or more likely him. I suddenly felt annoyed. He might stay out here in the cool with me for a few minutes, and I could talk, but he wouldn't really listen. Because Johnnie was Johnnie. He was honest to himself, he was free. He had no obligations, because he chose not to.

"Never mind," I said. I surprised myself when I walked away from him into the darkness.

"Hey," he called after me. "Where are you going? Party's this way."

"Maybe next time," I said as the cold night engulfed me.

It was quiet when I returned home.

I slipped inside, removed my shoes and padded softly upstairs. I thought about going to bed, but I decided to check on Lacy first.

I sat down next to her and began to run my fingers through her hair. It felt brittle. Her unseeing eyes still stared sightlessly.

"Lacy, come back, please. I want you to come back," I said. I felt hot and anxious sitting there, hoping desperately that something would change, but she didn't respond.

I placed my hand on her forehead, surprised at how cool she felt. I could feel the house beneath her skin worming around like a parasite. I could feel her struggling to hold the south wall together, bearing Uncle Carlton's responsibility. The anger came on abruptly—anger at myself and at this damn house. Fury filled me like a drowning man finally giving in and inhaling cold water.

I pulled my hand back and turned away, disgusted, and as I did my eyes settled on the swords crossed over the mantle. There was no question in my mind as to what I would do next.

The sword came free of the wall more easily than I'd expected. It was heavy in my hands, but the weight felt reassuring. I tested the balance of the weapon, swinging it to and fro, getting a feel for it before I returned to Lacy and Uncle Carlton.

I felt liberated as I raised the heft of that sword above my head, and brought its full weight down onto Carlton's arm, which cracked but didn't break. The force of the blow vibrated up my arms, and into my shoulders. I pulled the sword back and swung hard again, and this time the blade sheered through his arm and smashed into the floor, the house screaming as it did.

I worked the sword back and forth, until I could wrench it free from the parquetry. And then I went to work on the wooden tendrils clinging at Lacy.

With each jarring blow, more and more wood snapped, splintered, and split. When the protrusion began to groan, and slowly tilt, I stopped, breathing heavily, and I stepped back to watch it slowly bend, then crack loudly and topple, Lacy spilling free and sliding across the floor, only a few wooden strands still clinging to her.

Then I turned on the wall hiding Uncle Carlton. Selfish Uncle Carlton. Chips of plaster flew, then wood, then bone. The screams of the house began anew, growing insistent, and louder, rising in pitch until my ears rang, but I kept hacking away until my arms burned with lactic acid, until they barely responded to my will to move, but still I would have kept swinging if someone hadn't grabbed me from behind and wrested the sword from my exhausted grip.

"What are you doing?" Dad hissed in my ears. Before I could answer he pulled me hard backward, and my feet slid from under me, but Dad took my weight. We moved away from the wall, my feet dragging along the floor, and I noticed with confusion that the southern wall continued to crack and split even though my father had interrupted my manic work. And then, I realised with shock, the wall was giving way.

"Lacy," I said, looking around frantically. "Where is she?"

"Your mother has her," Dad said. I tried to fight, but I was too exhausted and he was too strong. We backpedalled together until we slammed into the couches in the middle of the parlour. Mum was there, cradling Lacy, who was now awake, the whiteness receding from her eyes as she looked around, muddled. The rising din of destruction drew my attention once more.

I watched in horrid fascination as cracks became fissures, and plaster fell in chunks, exposing beams of wood that were also breaking, along with the bricks behind them. And then with a roar the whole wall fell away, the window shattering violently, and I raised my arm to shield my eyes against the cloud of dust that rose from the debris and expanded, enveloping us. It kept coming thick, and I was soon coughing, tears stinging my eyes.

I closed them tight and buried my head in my hands, listening to the sounds of wreckage shifting.

When I opened my eyes again, through the dust I could see a gaping hole, and the sag of the unsupported roof. Closer than I ever imagined was the cold night, already encroaching.

I'd done this. Me. I shivered, suddenly very frightened for us all.

"And where is your father now, dear?" Grandma Dee asked.

The basement smelt damper than before. I could hear running water somewhere behind Grandma Dee's wall.

"The factory, checking the damage."

"I see."

I watched her close her eyes, the pupils fluttering beneath as she searched the connections in our house, and throughout our wider estate. Then she was back, the hint of a grin caressing her lips.

"The factory will be okay. Your father underestimated his links to the building. He does that, your father. He puts too much stock in others, not enough in himself. Uncle Carlton may have made the initial investment, but your father made the factory work."

I exhaled. "The house is a wreck, though. The entire back wall is nearly gone."

Grandma Dee looked me over, letting the words hang in the air. "What did your father say about that?" she said eventually.

I turned my mind back to last night. To freeing Lacy, to my father rescuing me before the south wall collapsed. After, he'd held me as the piles of bricks continued to shift, and the dust settled, both of us listening to the sounds of the night floating in—an owl, cars revving far away.

"He was quiet," I said, recalling his distant gaze. He'd looked defeated, and yet in his eyes there was also something new. "Very quiet for him. It was worse than yelling."

"And Lacy?" Grandma Dee asked.

"She's okay, a little disoriented, but okay. Afterward, we bathed and fed her, then put her to bed. When she was asleep, Dad mumbled something about checking on the factory, and he left."

"I see."

But I didn't. I didn't know what was going on. I'd defied him and ruined our house and I'd expected an explosion, but it had never come.

"What now, Grandma Dee? Can a house this damaged be repaired?"

"Yes, dear. But it requires sacrifice. Someone needs to replace Uncle Carlton. Someone who can buttress this family."

"And if there is no one?"

Grandma Dee stared at me, a hard stare. "We can hold on for a while, but not forever. The house will fall, and if it doesn't, the houseless will come and make sure it does. And then the factory will follow. I expect you'll be sad for a while, but you'll be free of us. And after you've buried me, and your great aunts, your Great-great-uncle Roman, after that you'll join the houseless and work for someone else if you're lucky, and survive as best you can on your own."

I couldn't reply. I couldn't even breathe.

I'd fantasised about the houseless, but I didn't really know what being houseless meant. I'd thought Johnnie was special, but that was wrong. I'd begun to realise that the attributes I'd admired in him—his honesty, his freedom—may have simply been narcissism thinly disguised.

And my family? What had once seemed like a weight pulling me down suddenly seemed warm, and comforting. Had it really taken nearly losing Lacy for me to realise? And now our home was at risk, we were all at risk.

"I need to fix this," I whispered.

I sat with Lacy on her bed, patting her thin leg beneath the covers as she ate her breakfast. Mum had delivered the eggs moments before, but then she was gone again, saying something about tea. Since Lacy had come back to us the night before last, Mum had moved into overdrive, buzzing back and forth like a bee pollinating flowers, doting on her. Dad still wasn't home, and that worried me.

When my phone rang in my pocket, Lacy gave me an inquiring glance. I hoped it was Dad, but when I checked I saw it was Johnnie.

"I'll just be a moment," I said.

"That's okay," Lacy mumbled around a mouthful of food. She sounded happy, innocent. I couldn't believe the change in her—it was as if she'd somehow wound back time to before her ordeal, as if it had never happened. She was our glimmer of joy.

I went outside her room and answered my phone, heading toward the study at the end of the hall.

"Hey, babe," he said.

"What do you want?"

"What's with the attitude, babe? I just wanted to check on you, make sure you were okay. You seemed distracted the other night."

"I'm fine," I said, stepping into the study and toward the large bay windows. I wasn't in the mood for his charm.

"Good. So...want to catch up tonight? I'll make it up to you," he said.

I glanced out across our lawns. It looked cold outside, as if the sun was still waking. I thought about asking him what had happened between him and Rachel after I'd left, but then I wondered if I really cared. He continued before I made up my mind.

"It'll be great. We're heading to Razzie's for a few drinks—"

"Then going to the river," I interrupted. Just like last week, and the week before.

"Yeah," he said.

I laughed, I couldn't help it. How had I imagined he had the answers? He was stuck in a cycle, going to the same places, doing the same things each week, with the same people, trying to feel a little control in his life. But it was a sham.

"What's so funny?" he asked. The cheer was gone from his voice.

"Take Rachel," I said.

"Aw, come on. There's nothing between us. It's you I want, babe."

But I'd had enough. I hung up on him.

When Dad returned later that night, I was waiting for him on the stairs. Mum and Lacy were asleep in Lacy's bed.

He looked wrecked, his eyes bleary and red. When those tired eyes found me sitting at the base of the stairs he stopped in the doorway, hand still clutching the door handle, eyes widening a little.

"Hi, Daddy," I said.

He smiled at me briefly, then frowned, his default setting.

"How's the factory?"

He closed the door behind him, swaying gently on weary legs. "I was worried. Uncle Carlton started that factory, put his soul into it, but apparently he wasn't the only thing holding it together."

"Grandma Dee told me there was more of you in the business than you realised."

He nodded, then collapsed onto the steps beside me and rested his head in his hands. "Still, it's taken damage," he mumbled, "but nothing that can't be repaired. It's in a much better state than..."

The house, I thought, but I didn't finish his sentence, and neither did he. He and I both knew that the factory might be okay for now, but it would only stand so long as the house stood, and without intervention that might not be long.

"It's my fault. All of it," I said.

I watched him closely, but he didn't respond. He was very still, head in his hands, hunched.

"Grandma Dee said it's not too late for the house." I cleared my throat. "I'll take Carlton's place." And when I said it out loud, I knew I meant it.

My father's head rose, his eyes narrowed. "No," he said firmly.
"But, Daddy, I—"

"No. That's not what I want for you. That's not what we did all of this for."

I didn't understand. Was his faith in me so shallow? A puddle when it might have been a pool?

But as I watched his expression soften, I realised that wasn't it. There was a foreign expression on my father's face. Concern, pride, and shame mixed together. Then he averted his gaze again, staring down at his feet. I followed his eyes. His usually neat shoes were scuffed and dirty.

"I've been hard on you. Perhaps unfairly so," he said.

"And I've disappointed you."

"No, you haven't." He sighed, turned to look at me. "Fathers like to think they're needed. We get protective, and sometimes begin to believe that our role is to protect our children from making the same mistakes we did. But that never works, because we all become who we become through trial and error.

"You're your own woman, Poppy. I may not have always liked that you were so strong-willed, and that you were unwilling to take my guidance, but I'm proud that you've grown up to make your own decisions and to own them when they are right, and wrong."

I swallowed, my eyes feeling hot. Like Grandma Dee sharing the pulse of the house with me, I felt my father's contribution to our legacy coursing in the stairs beneath me, plucking at my skin. I felt close to Dad in that moment. And I think I understood him a little. He'd always tried to make Lacy and me understand family responsibility as he did, not as an obligation, but as something that paid back on itself. And I think I did now. Love was a reward, for love.

"Then why won't you let me save the house?"

"You bringing Lacy back reminded me how much more life you girls have to live, and how much more you both have to give to the family, to each other, and to yourselves."

"But she wouldn't have needed bringing back if I—"

71

"That's in the past now, honey."

He smiled, and then did something confounding. He reached out and placed an arm around me and pulled me close. I surprised myself by letting him.

I rested my head on his shoulder and inhaled the scent of him—aftershave and ink from the printing presses.

"There's a reason I took you to the factory with me so often over the years. You were always the one I wanted to take over. And you can run it, Poppy. I know you can."

After we cleared away the rubble, the true extent of the destruction became clearer. Barely three feet of the southern wall remained consistently intact, although in each corner where it joined the east and west walls the bricks rose a little higher. About halfway along, a large window frame jutted from the bricks, but the glass was gone, shattered during the collapse.

The engineer had put in place struts to support the roof and the top floors. Tomorrow he'd begin rebuilding the wall.

Mum, Lacy, and I stood close together on the muddy lawn, a gentle breeze whipping our hair. Mum had her arm around Lacy, who rubbed her small hands together nervously. Lacy's eyes were already wet. I knew how she felt, but I was going to keep it together. Dad had asked me to. And maybe he'd asked the same of Mum because she watched on stoically, proudly even.

"It's time," Dad said. He sat on the broken wall near the eastern corner. Beside him on the lawn was a neat pile of bricks, a bucket of mortar, and a trowel.

Without warning, Lacy disentangled herself from Mum and sprang at Dad, leaping into his arms with a hug so fierce she nearly knocked him backward off the brick ledge and into the house. Dad chuckled but hugged her back hard as Lacy began to sob into his chest.

"I don't want you to go," Lacy said, sniffling.

"I'm not going anywhere, sweet one. I'll always be here."

"You promise?"

"Yes, I promise. Come talk to me often, okay?"

"I will, Daddy."

Mum began to gently pry Lacy from Dad's arms, and when she was done, she bent and took Dad in her own, hugging him tightly.

"I love you," she said. "You know that, right?"

"Of course," he whispered. "And I love you, too."

When she pulled back, he turned to me and I knew it was my turn.

I shuffled forward, hesitated, then leaned down and kissed the rough stubble of his jaw. As I did, he raised a hand to my face and cupped my cheek for just a second, but then he released me and I pulled back from him.

"Okay. Over to you," he said.

I suddenly found it hard to swallow, as if something had lodged at the top of my throat. He was letting go of an integral part of himself and passing it to me like a baton. I wasn't sure I felt ready, but I was determined to damn well try.

I bent, picked up the trowel and scooped a generous amount of mortar from the bucket. Dad lay down on his side, turning away from us so that he gazed into the house. He allowed one arm to fall inside, just like Grandma Dee.

I took a breath, which did little to calm the sporadic beating of my heart, and then I placed the mortar onto the side of his face, covering his ear. I smoothed it a little, and then stepped back to allow Mum and Lacy to affix the first red brick in place above the newest foundation of our house.

A Word That Means Everything

written by
Andy Dibble

illustrated by
HEATHER A. LAURENCE

ABOUT THE AUTHOR

Andy Dibble lives in Madison, Wisconsin, and works as a healthcare IT consultant. He has supported the electronic medical records of large healthcare systems in six countries. He has a long history of volunteering as a programming language instructor and a less fulfilling history in software development. While not writing, he spends his free time reading, running, and eating sushi.

Andy came to writing fiction by way of academia. While an undergraduate, he completed four majors—computer science, religious studies, philosophy, and Asian studies—and published a paper on two of India's great epics, the Mahābhārata *and the* Bhāgavata Purāṇa. *In pursuit of a career as a professor of South Asian religion, he completed a master of theological studies at Harvard Divinity School. Along the way, he realized writing about abstruse Sanskrit texts for a living wasn't for him. Unfortunately, giving up on academia also meant giving up on many opportunities to publish. Fortunately, writing speculative fiction brings new publishing opportunities.*

ABOUT THE ILLUSTRATOR

Heather A. Laurence was born in 1993 in Bremerton, Washington. When she was six, she decided to become an artist, and has not turned back since.

Her father inspired her by teaching her to draw and paint at a young age and telling her that anyone can be an artist. She continued to develop her skills and went to Kansas State University where she achieved a BFA in painting.

She now continues to develop her work, taking advantage of resources such as the Illustration Academy each summer and the online Art Business Bootcamp program. She works from her home studio in Michigan with her seventeen-pound gray cat watching over her. She works hard at creating book-cover compositions for her portfolio, and writing stories to make into original graphic novels and short comics.

A Word That
Means Everything

When Pius was assigned to Murk, he assumed he would be translating the Bible into the language of genius octopuses. But the first Thulhu he laid eyes on, rendered grayscale by the mist, only humped a lichen patch, distended tongue audibly slathering against rock, tentacle suckers puckering as they stuck and unstuck, vestigial wings like out-of-body lungs flagging over its backside.

Thulhus were supposed to communicate via tentacle gestures. This thrashing was it, right? But Pius's visor remained dark. No translation.

His last assignment with the Prabhakarins had been different. They knew first impressions mattered. This tentaclely brute didn't even acknowledge him.

"You're sure this thing is sentient?" he called back. His voice echoed queerly in the gloom.

"Keep it down!" Zora said in a church whisper. She was a good guide, by reputation a good ethnographer. But she treated him more like a credulous little brother than a client.

"I thought you said they can't hear."

"They can't. But the Thulhus aren't top of the food chain." Zora dangled her fingers like a jellyfish. Made them creep. The right fore-tentacle of her Thulhu-suit glided with almost feline surreptitiousness. She snatched her left hand away and her other fore-tentacle darted behind the nearest hind-tentacle of her suit.

The visor protruding from Pius's headgear flashed "Predator."

He gulped. In this fog, anything worthy of the name *predator* had to be calculating an ambush.

He was armed, but sensor mesh constricted his trigger finger. He'd chosen the noninvasive Thulhu-suit. Zora's interfaced directly with her motor cortex, so her gestures were just a symptom of the same neural impulses that animated her suit's fore-tentacles. Through obliquer mentation she could control the four hind-tentacles of her suit. If it came to flight, Pius had just one option: autopilot.

The Thulhu let up its humping long enough to radiate a spasm down its limber fore-tentacles and four stouter hind-tentacles. A shrug?

Pius's visor proffered, "Disbelief" in blocky red print. Then corrected itself, "Amused disbelief."

Pius groaned. What kind of language was this? He expected elegance, a system of symbols, like the sign language of Prabhakarin children who are deaf-mute until puberty.

"Maybe they just thrash around to mate and warn each other of danger," said Pius. "That doesn't mean they have *language*."

"Did your Church tell you that?" Zora chuckled like Socrates must have chuckled just before shredding his interlocutors' preconceptions.

"Just my guess." It could be bureaucratic blundering that consigned him to Murk, but he had to assume the One Church hadn't sent him on a fool's errand.

"Thousands of robots taking millions of pictures all over this region ran pattern recognition, *devilishly* clever algorithms. The same software derived more than a thousand languages spanning over a hundred species throughout the galaxy. Just think how few Bible translations your Church would have piddled out without it."

Church doctrine said that the Holy Spirit doesn't work through software, but brandishing dogma was a nonstarter. "Maybe a different subject would be more cooperative?"

There were other males (Zora called them men) scarfing

lichen or sloughing about as though they belonged to a patch of mist rather than a place, and fog-gray females (ahem, women) haunting the periphery of the seen world. Young clung to the floppy wings on their backs as their fore-tentacles flicked about in conversation.

"You'll have less luck with the others. We're just…" She let a fore-tentacle go slack like a burdensome limb she hadn't found the time to amputate.

The translation smote the upper left of Pius's vision. "Disobedient-other"?

In imitation, he let his shoulder drop, and the whole left side of his Thulhu-suit sagged. Pius avoided keeling over into spongy marsh only by windmilling to the other side. His suit would have formed the gesture if he had just spoken the word into his mouthpiece.

Light danced in Zora's eyes, but she suppressed her mirth.

The Thulhu let up feeding. His fore-tentacles squiggled.

"Derisive amusement," Pius's visor flared.

"Why does this one 'talk'?" said Pius. Unsure how his suit would react, he resisted the urge to make air quotes.

"Heh, he's just true to his name."

"His name?"

"Snarky."

Snarky made the disobedient-other gesture. Pius's headset flashed, "Oh, the alien is back." Snarky's fore-tentacles mimed a hug, and Pius read the translation, "And she brought a friend."

Zora nudged Pius.

"How are you?" Pius said into his mouthpiece. His suit gestured accordingly. The feed glowing on the lower-right of his visor said the accusatory gesture for "you" meant literally "other-me."

"And it has nothing interesting to say," Snarky gestured, as self-important as a four-year-old. He only stood as high as Pius's waist.

HEATHER A. LAURENCE

"You really don't think I'm a person?" said Pius.

"Of course I believe I'm a person." Snarky's fore-tentacles wrung in dizzying self-referential circles.

Did the untranslatability of "you" confuse him? "That's not what I meant."

"I know what you meant. I've been through this with her. In the end we agreed to disagree. She—sage alien that she is—believes there's a shadowy world of squishy objects behind the mist. I say it's impossible."

"Behind the mist?"

"Where else would it be?"

Pius was taken aback by Snarky's candor. "What am I then?"

"Just another alien I imagined. Proof that I'm exceptionally clever."

Or delusional.

"Maybe I'm just bored."

On second thought, Pius remembered Zora saying that the Thulhus only believe in their own minds. To them, there were no bodies, no other Thulhus; there's no lichen to eat, no mist. There are only thoughts of bodies, thoughts of other minds, mist-thoughts, lichen-thoughts.

She had lectured him on brain science. "You don't believe the hemispheres of your brain are two different people just because they communicate in order to render and interpret the world. To Thulhus, that's what talk is like."

Scant recognition on his part.

She tried again. "If you saw your brain, you'd know that the gray matter was you. But it wouldn't feel like you, right? That's how a Thulhu thinks about other Thulhus. He knows they're all *him*, even though it doesn't feel that way."

What Pius knew was that he wasn't a brain but a soul fashioned by his Creator. Zora only knew a universe in flux, constantly prototyping. Not a universe, vibrant and ushering.

A Godless materiality.

Maybe he could enlighten Snarky. "But everything persists even when you aren't looking at it. You close your eyes, open them, and—" Pius's suit broke off gesturing as Snarky leaned upsettingly close.

"Close my eyes?" His cephalopod face was so near, Pius took the hint: Thulhus don't have eyelids. Thulhus didn't have to adapt to overbearing light with the mist always about. They might as well have lived inside a cloud.

"Ah, assume you can," Pius said.

"Very well." Apparently, Thulhus have a gesture for *gross condescension*.

"When you cover your eyes," said Pius, ignoring the slight, "the whole world goes away, and when you see again, it's the same as it was. How do you explain that if all that exists is you?"

Thulhus don't have lips, and Snarky's mouth was beneath his body where Pius couldn't see it. But Pius knew Snarky would be grinning impishly were it not for his anatomy.

"How can I? I am overcome. You've shown me the error of my ways, wrestled your existence from my delusions."

Zora glanced at Pius sheepishly. But why should Snarky be polite? He believes he's just talking to himself.

Snarky flapped a fore-tentacle, an off-hand negation. "Sometimes the mist gobbles up what I see, sometimes it doesn't. This eye-blinking has nothing to do with it. Zora tells me aliens have a similar problem. Sometimes you try to remember and succeed, sometimes you fail. Mist, forgetfulness—they are the same."

Zora perceived Pius's mounting agitation. "Persistence for us isn't the same as it is for them. They only see motion, no colors, nothing that's still."

Snarky couldn't hear, but he must have inferred the purpose of their exchange because he flicked his tentacles in amused squiggles.

"Do you believe in God?" Pius ventured. The software made the fore-tentacles of his suit link together to denote belief then lifted the right in an extravagant salute, "God."

Snarky emitted a confused wavering. He imitated the extravagant salute. "Is God a person?" His fore-tentacles groped and shivered in the gesture for *person*.

As far as the software ascertained, his question was meant in all earnestness. But it posed a dilemma: "Person" means an intellect and even more than that, a will, so God is a person. But if Pius said as much, Snarky would reject God as he rejected all other persons.

"Yes, God's a person."

Snarky swayed, dithering. "Am I God?"

"No, you aren't God. We aren't God either. God is"—Pius struggled to produce a word—"outside. Beyond the mist." The software raised Pius's right fore-tentacle in a new salute, an elephantine trumpeting. Reviewing the feed, Pius realized it meant literally one-beyond-mist, which also meant one-beyond-forgetfulness.

"One-beyond-mist," Snarky gestured. Was that a question?

"Yes, that's the beginning of what God is," Pius said carefully. "What would it take for you to believe in one-beyond-mist?"

"Ah, I understand now, becoming God only requires patience." His tentacles squiggled. "Wait for the mist to clear, and I will be one-beyond-mist!"

"Did you hear what I said? *You aren't God.*"

Zora flipped her fore-tentacles disarmingly; she shot Pius a look.

"But if I can't become God, God is impossible."

"God is another person, someone *always* beyond the mist." Pius struggled to screen the tension from his voice. It came out a plea, "What would it take for you to believe in God?"

"Madness."

"Snarky likes you," said Zora.

"Likes me?"

"When I met him, he gestured incoherently just to confuse the software. You had a conversation, give and take."

"He's delusional."

"He's different. You have to bridge that difference, don't expect him to."

"And how am I supposed to do that?"

"Maybe in your translation Jesus can have tentacles. And Satan can be one of the *things* deep down in the lowlands." Her tentacles didn't squiggle like Snarky's would have, but she cracked a smile. The deep things were just rumor spawned by the same mythos that named the Thulhus.

She would've gone on, but Pius cut her short. "What you're suggesting isn't translation."

"Maybe not, but limiting your work to the bounds of this book—the Bible—isn't going to reach the Thulhus. For a Thulhu there's only one mind, one author, one work of literature. So think of the Bible as a Thulhu would, as part of a larger work, one constantly expanding and improving." She grinned. "Your translation is just the next draft."

Pius sulked for a while on the way back, but eventually Zora tried again. "Back on Earth, biologists had a saying: 'Life will find a way,' will thrive in every habitat—the driest desert, the bottom of the ocean. Once we studied other worlds, do you know how that saying changed?"

"How?" Pius begrudged.

"'Life will find *every* way.' The universe will surprise you no matter how your Bible says life should be." Her constantly prototyping universe in which Christianity is as queer and outmoded as the vestigial wings of a Thulhu.

"*Every* way? Aside from the Thulhus, I've seen sooty ferns, lichen, a few mushrooms, and whatever that's rotting so delightfully in the marsh. Not exactly biological diversity."

"Those mushrooms." Her right fore-tentacle wound in a spiral. "They *live* off radiation. Even in the lowlands where radioisotopes blanket everything."

"There are mutant mushrooms. So what?"

"There's the universe, and then there's your Bible." Her voice was low but sure, like faraway thunder. "I'll let you guess which doesn't fit within the other."

Pius was glad to be indoors. The air had an antiseptic taste, but it was unmisted, an unmurky corner of Murk. He changed out of his sweaty wetsuit, and peeled the sensor mesh from his hands and arms. The skin beneath was clammy, and it itched. There was a solar-spectrum light in his monkishly small dorm. It might ward off seasonal affective disorder (it was always the season for that on Murk), but that merry bulb didn't assuage his brooding.

He keyed a report to his superiors. "First contacted native sentient species today, *Murkaea hectopus cthulhu*, commonly named Thulhus. Findings not encouraging. The one Thulhu that condescended to communicate with us via tentacle gesticulations had no concept of God, or I suspect, any spiritual reality. His arrogance was not that of the disbeliever but of the fool convinced that his limited concepts are the only possible lens through which one may perceive the world.

"Serving God and His Word, I contend that the purported sentience of the Thulhus is an invention of the software that derived their language, if it can even properly be called a language. I humbly suggest that sentience be construed in terms of whether a species has a concept of the Divine, not the dictates of software.

"The Thulhus strike me as a hive species; every Thulhu believes itself to be queen and all the members of its cult (i.e. group) mere extensions of itself. We do not sully Scripture by translating it into the mating dance of bees. Let us not sully it with the tentacle-gesturing of the Thulhus. Recommendation is that this project be terminated."

A response could take weeks given bureaucratic shuffling. But just two standard hours later: "Your contention is unacceptable. We will send help."

Cowed by the eight-word reprimand of his superiors, Pius drifted. Should he wait for the promised, and likely degrading, help? Would the project be out of his hands once help arrived? Would he become a mere clerk at the beck and call of a new superior?

Pius prayed for answers but continued to work. Without explicit instruction to the contrary, he had to show progress in daily reports, though only God knew whether anyone would read them.

He had a place to start: the Gospel of John, the fourth and most exalted of the biographies of Jesus. After that he'd translate whatever other Greek portions of the Bible his superiors told him to, hitherto without collaboration. Synthesis happened higher in the ecclesiastical hierarchy.

He dictated the opening verses of John in the original Greek into the mouthpiece of his headgear, *"En arche en ho logos...."* The shadowy tentacles of a Thulhu homunculus rose and fell across his visor. They froze—stuttering?—then jostled to the next gesture.

He replayed with English subtitles, and right away, the problem was as plain as mist: "In the beginning was the *logos* (?)." Even the software surrendered before the translation puzzle posed by *logos*. *Logos* is not just Word, as it is commonly translated into English. Indeed, the capital *W* only gestures at the capacious semantics of *logos*, which includes just about everything having to do with language and the mind: discourse, narration, commandment, teaching, reason, intellect, proportion, expectation. In one Bible passage, *logos* means debt, in another a legal complaint. In several passages, *logos* has a derogatory connotation, as mere talk or empty rhetoric, like when Paul writes, "The kingdom of God depends not upon *logos* but on power."

Logos found a niche in most every philosophy and religion throughout the ancient Mediterranean in which John wrote his Gospel: Orphic and Dionysian mystery cults exalted their dying and vivifying gods with epithets of which *logos* was the germ. Stoic philosophers taught of a *logos spermatikos*, the rational principle undergirding everything. Aristotle rendered *logos* as rationality, the soul of humanity.

Pius decided to simply gloss *logos* as the Thulhu gesture for "word." It would altogether miss the mark, but the Thulhus obviously have no capacity to construe the expanse of John's meaning. No one could object to his treating an impossible problem with an inadequate solution.

"Translate 'word.'" An umbral tentacle rose across his field of view like a hand reaching in supplication, oddly stirring. But the subtitles that crowded beneath provoked no fellow-feeling: "Gesture, verb, word, connection, ascent, legerdemain, guile."

Pius tried again. The software repeated itself without irritation.

He groaned from a tight place in his chest. The primary meaning wasn't even "word" but "gesture," which had all kinds of implications John hadn't intended.

Pius moved on to "verb," the second meaning listed. Why should "noun" be absent? The software had to be confused, befuddled by the Thulhus and their supposed language.

The next meaning, "connection," had worth because gesturing is how the Thulhus connect. And it brought out a shade of meaning latent but not explicit in John's usage: John says the *logos* is Jesus, and Jesus is how God connects to His creation.

But the next meaning, "ascent," had nothing to do with John. "Ascent" conjured images of a Thulhu mounting a steep rise through inscrutable mists like the dread monster Cthulhu from the old Lovecraft tales, the Thulhus' namesake. Jesus could have no association with that!

"Legerdemain" and "guile" didn't help. Too underhanded. He couldn't frame Jesus in such a sinister light.

He leapt up to hammer out a report to his superiors. They'd understand that it was better to preserve John's meaning than to twist it in translation. Whatever he did would be ignored or ridiculed by the Thulhus anyway. Why even try?

But that prim reprimand stung, a crisp blow. His superiors would see this project done. At best they would ignore him. Worse, they might judge him beneath even *unacceptable*.

He sagged onto his tiny cot, defeated once by the separateness of languages and again by the aloofness of the Church to which he dedicated his life.

On the day Pius was called to Murk, he'd been watching the sunrise ritual with Prabhakarin children and their non-menstruating mothers. Beneath the banyan tree in the town square of Dhruv, men dipped teak ladles into pots of ghee, heated just to liquidity, then upended the pure oil over a preserved footprint of one of their distinguished ancestors—once, twice, three times. Murmuring a mantra in a forgotten tongue, they bowed prostrate with the fingers of all four hands intertwined like strands of an occult knot. The new sun bathed their backs.

One of the girls—pre-pubescent because her mouths were just lipless slits—caught Pius's eye with an upward grasping motion, hand-speak for sex. Thank God, it wasn't an invitation. She was just repeating what she'd seen, a reminder that Pius's abstinence was a topic of light conversation around Dhruv. He pointed upward with two pronged fingers and drew them to his eyes: *the stars are watching you.* She turned away, rasping giggles from her inchoate larynxes.

Almost half of the men rose to begin work, most in a marketplace stall, at the docks, or a warehouse. More would rise soon, but the truly pious would continue prostrations until the sun lifted fully above the horizon. No mean feat given that Prabhakara's diurnal cycle is forty times longer than a standard day. After the long night, some would keep shoving their noses into the dirt from sheer superstitious relief.

A vibration from inside his dhoti. About time the Church broke radio silence. They could page him through his headgear, but the locals deemed any adornment above the waist womanish, so he rarely wore it.

Undoubtedly, he would be reassigned, perhaps to just another Prabhakarin community, but he suspected otherwise. He'd heard through the missionary grapevine that the Church planned to cut its losses: Prabhakarins spoke too many languages, were too stuck in their ways, too fearful of an everlasting night.

God willing, his next assignment would be on Aletheia. The common tongue, spoken across the entire planet, boasted more than one million words, five thousand colors, five thousand textures, five thousand for every sense. Every mannerism, every flavor of awkwardness and triumph, every nuance of propriety, every stage in every process from nascence to ripeness to moribundity had a name. Most had several, each a near-synonym different only by a flutter of connotation. Anyone, no matter his station, could coin a new word, and if his fellows deemed it worthy, civilizations would take it up. What better language to translate the Gospel into? Pen just one translation, and he could bring billions to Christ.

He rushed into his hut to fetch his headgear. But his wife was in the way, or rather the woman the town council had designated as his wife. Her gourd-shaped head yammered from both ends, left mouth prognosticating doom: the stars would destroy him if he shirked the sunrise ritual again. Then she'd be a tainted widow unable to inherit even his impure off-world wealth. Her right mouth grumbled about stillbirths and deformities.

Murmuring polite apologies, he ducked beneath her accusing arm, knowing she wouldn't touch him, not during her period. He swiped the jute fiber sack that held his headgear, edged past her, and made for the tree line. He passed the stand of basalt idols that guarded the northern entrance to Dhruv, among them a rough-hewn statue of Jesus. It had two heads like all the other graven images. Pius ground his teeth and impotently fantasized about pulverizing the heathen thing.

The canopy, overshadowing him, had unfurled after its nightly hibernation. He covered one ear to block the cacophony of tropical birds, and donned his headgear. Loam squished beneath his tapping foot.

"You are Pius Judson, missionary of the One Church of Christ?" A machine voice, monotone, like all official Church communication.

"I am Pius Judson, missionary of the One Church of Christ," he echoed for purposes of voice recognition.

"The Church looks upon your work favorably. You are hereby reassigned to the moon of Aletheia, colloquially named Murk. Report to research station Relyeh on its southern continent at your earliest convenience."

Murk, the *moon* of Aletheia. Teasingly near Aletheia but not Aletheia. What had he done wrong? With almost no prodding from his superiors, he'd translated the entire New Testament into the Dhruvish dialect, spoken by merchants and bankers across most of the continent. He'd translated John's Gospel two more times into the dialects of outlying villages. His attempt to render John in child hand-speak had floundered, but that project was his own.

"Is someone else translating John into Aletheian?"

A pause. "It is given to you to know." An answer as cryptic as the prognostications of Prabhakarin astrologers.

"Who?"

"Father David Nestor."

Pius removed his headgear and laughed bitterly. Murk wasn't his punishment. It was his consolation prize. He'd been outclassed by the greatest Bible translator alive.

When Pius got word that the promised help was David Nestor, he wondered idly if all those sunrise rituals he abstained from provoked astrological backlash after all. But he wasn't the one tumbling from Aletheia to the shrouded moon of the hectopus cows. David must have fallen far in the eyes of the Church to be reassigned to Murk.

That thought kindled a grim green warmth in Pius. Envy didn't shame him as much as it should have. Knowing that staunched the warmth, a little.

David emerged from the decontamination chamber clothed in priestly black—slacks and a shirt, not a cassock. His cheekbones were high, his skin taut and frustratingly boyish even though he was fifteen years Pius's senior.

Pius shook David's hand stiffly and led him toward the mess hall, unsure what to say. Pius started toward a bevy of support staff, mostly Devonians, a species of black amphibious fish-people. They weren't native to Murk, but the damp suited them. Perhaps the presence of a crowd would stifle whatever probing questions David had chambered in his throat.

But David turned to the side to indicate an empty table. "How about here?"

Inquisition: unavoidable.

Pius slumped into a seat. He said nothing.

David speared a rehydrated potato on his plate with more gusto than the wrinkled tuber deserved. "The potatoes here aren't bad. See, they spice everything to oblivion over on Aletheia."

Was David rubbing it in? *Hey, Pius, have you heard of scholars' pagodas on Aletheia? In Asher—marvelous city, really—there's one just for Bible translation. It has a level for each book of the Bible! And would you believe it's built into a mountain of pink salt?*

David swallowed. "Sometimes plain rations are best."

Pius wasn't in the mood for banter. "How should we begin with the translation?"

"Let's not talk about work. Let's talk about you."

Next David would say he's no longer needed, or worse, needed but only for clerical errands. David would be the fount of all creative insight.

"I read your work on translating John into Prabhakarin languages," said David.

"Really?" Pius wasn't exactly a distinguished translator.

"I like to know about the people I work with. Your translation of *logos* intrigued me. I forget the term, but it means *action*. It struck me as a bit loose."

Loose? "I wanted to render *logos* as Word. But to the villagers I lived with language isn't about description. It's all about inciting action, so I chose *kara*, action." His mouth felt suddenly dry. "I hope you can see why it was necessary?" The last came out a plea.

"All language is about inciting action?" said David, his scholar's soul beaming.

So Pius knew something that David didn't. "They go too far, of course, but it's not so strange, if you think about it. When a mother tells her child, 'It's eight o'clock,' she's not trying to *inform* her child of anything. She wants the kid to go to bed."

"Ah, so that's why your translation was so admonishing, 'You must believe this!' and 'You must believe that!'"

Pius opened his mouth but clammed up.

"You can speak plainly to me, Pius. I'm just a priest, a pastor like yourself." That confusion in titles said much. In an earlier age, before there was One Church of Christ, they would have stood on opposite sides of an eight-hundred-year-old schism. David would be a Catholic and a Jesuit, Pius a Protestant.

"I know the tone was off, but belief is what the Gospel is about, embracing *doctrine*, I mean."

"Perhaps."

Perhaps? "How would you have translated *logos* into Prabhakarin?"

Pius thought he might've caught him off guard, but of course David Nestor would have an answer, "They have a word, *amita*, meaning boundless. It's so much richer than just some generic action."

"I know the word. *Amita* orchestrates the stars in a grand ritual, the infinite cosmic ritual that all the rituals the Prabhakarins perform on the ground supposedly emulate."

"Sounds pretty good, right? Jesus is that boundless principle, the infinite entering history as a finite being. Like in John's Gospel."

"But translating *logos* as *amita* would have made the Prabhakarins think Christianity was just a repackaged version of their religion."

"Why not exploit the cultural idiom, write an eloquent

translation, and engage Prabhakarin readers? Then we pose some real competition to the canons of the native religion."

"We can't do that at the expense of Christ." Grim warmth again, less green, redder. "You know, *Jesus*?"

"That's why there are Gospels." David didn't raise his voice. "John goes on to say who the man is that is the *logos*, what he did, who he was, his sacrifice."

"You can't *wreck* the beginning just because you think John will pick up the pieces later on." Pius gained his feet. "Let's not talk about me. Let's talk about you."

Pius meant the translation of John that had made David's reputation, his Orkish translation. The translation that should not have been. Orken One is hell, too hot for water to condense except at its poles. It has a magnetosphere, an atmosphere, wind enough to normalize temperatures through day and night. But life couldn't have a foothold; it had been molten just five-hundred million years ago. That was time enough for reels of amino acids, perhaps inklings of silicon-based life. But further complexity just shouldn't have been possible. Everyone with pull—star system governments, venerable scientific foundations, enterprising trillionaires—set their sights only on the cornucopia of Earth-like worlds with a real chance at harboring sentient life.

Orken One still attracted pioneers, wealthy tourists scudding by in a luxury cruiser. Peeping through the lenses of drones conferred bragging rights with none of them being boiled alive.

The Dantesque safari amazed them—sandstone hoodoos, geologically young but red like old blood, bearing pyroclastic slabs aloft in unbroken penance. Dunes like white-robed acolytes cowering resplendently beneath the numinous glare of Orken. The wind screaming judgment upon the ever-erring landscape, sometimes skewing it in flagellate wave patterns, other times whipping it in dust devils or driving biting sandstorms of cataclysmic size.

The footage seeped into social media. A keen-eyed researcher took notice. She found no water, nothing fossilized. But wave patterns furrowed the dunes even on windless days, even against the prevailing wind.

The second wave of drones had been equipped with translation software. They discarded any footage of patterns explicable by weather alone. But much remained, too much for chance. Biology notwithstanding, the drones' Bayes nets and Markov models found language.

It wasn't long until researchers weren't just overhearing the Orkens but conversing with them. No one ever found out what they were. Either the Orkens were holding out, or they didn't know themselves. But biological puzzles didn't faze Christian missionaries dedicated to bringing the Good News to every sentient race. None proved himself worthier of the challenge than David Nestor.

"What about me?" said David. Not a challenge, just an honest question.

"How did you translate *logos* into Orkish?"

"Sun-principle," said David. "The reason their sun burns. You know that." Every translator of the Bible alive knew that.

"Do you *want* to make Christianity sound like sun-worship?"

"It might sound like that to us," David said calmly. "But it doesn't to them. They don't worship their star Orken, they just believe their world persists through its light."

"But that's not what John meant."

"It's not? Isn't *logos* the principle that creates and upholds reality? Doesn't John call Jesus the 'light of the world'?"

"Later on, but not at the beginning," Pius protested lamely.

"Really? You know that *logos* is a philosophical term in Greek. John must've known that. And how did its use as a philosophical term begin?"

"Heraclitus," Pius conceded.

"And what did Heraclitus say the *logos* is?"

Is he going to make me say it? "A principle that animates the universe."

"And characterized by *fire*."

94

Pius sighed. "Perhaps your rendering of *logos* was acceptable." The word was out before echoes of the reprimand from on-high (unacceptable, *unacceptable*) seized him. He forged on, "But what about later when John writes, 'And the *logos* became flesh and lived among us.'"

David smiled. He knew this was coming.

"You translated flesh as *spirit*, precisely the *opposite* of what John meant!" said Pius.

"I think you know why I did that."

"I know the commentaries and the subcommentaries, but those are others' reasons. You never said why."

"That's because God's Word needs to stand by itself. If we need long footnotes and commentaries to explain it, we've already failed." David caught Pius with a level stare. "Why do you think I did it?"

There was nothing to do but answer. "The Orkens didn't have a sand-wave pattern for flesh when the explorers arrived. How could they in a world without bodies?"

"But they came up with one, didn't they? A word for us, for *humans*. They never differentiated between our flesh and flesh in general. You see the problem?"

"They would think that the *logos*-made-flesh didn't come for them, that Jesus only came for us."

"I hope you can see why it was necessary," said David, using Pius's own words against him.

Pius had to swallow before speaking. "Maybe Jesus didn't come for the Orkens. John's point is that Jesus debased himself, became flesh, to redeem us from the death of our bodies."

"Orkens die too," David said with a long stare. "Not like us, but they die. And some have died glad they knew Christ. You think if I could do it again, I would abandon the project and deny them that?"

"If God wanted everyone to live a Christian life, he wouldn't have waited billions of years before coming as Jesus. Think of the—how many? *trillions*?—dying every day throughout the universe that never knew Christ. God has a plan for them. You think we should compromise God's Word just to whittle down that number by the barest fraction?"

David regarded Pius wearily, weary as the galactic wanderer he was. "Why did you become a missionary, Pius?"

"God called me."

"What did God call you to do?"

Pius knew what David wanted him to say, so he demurred, "To safeguard His Word."

"That's all?"

"That's all I'll say."

David's lips pursed, fell in the slightest frown, said nothing.

To wipe David's disappointment away, Pius changed the subject. "You asked me why I was called, but you never said why you came."

"To help."

"That's all? I have to think our superiors have big plans for the Thulhus if they send you in such a hurry. Big plans!" David came to help? Help what?

It dawned on Pius. "You aren't here for the Thulhus. You're just the next maneuver in the political game. Our superiors don't care about the Thulhus, not really. They just want to brag about how the Church translated the New Testament into Thulhuese before the Muslims translated the Qur'an or the Buddhists translate whichever sutras are trendiest."

"Let our superiors concern themselves with politics, Pius. They do God's work too, even if they are unaware of it."

"You're David Nestor. You have to know something."

"They didn't send me. I volunteered."

Pius avoided David the following day and the next. But on the third day, Zora called them together.

David saw Zora and brightened. He offered his hand, like one dignitary meeting another, but unbeknownst to the joint delegations they were on a first-name basis. She took it. "Zora Mead, it's an honor."

Pius scanned both their faces. However Zora identified, it wasn't Christian. Why would David be honored to meet her?

"You didn't know?" said David. "Zora discovered Orkish."

"That was you?"

"Yup."

A split-second suspicion: David came for her? But that was ridiculous. Who would give up on Aletheia, come to Murk, just to shake a hand?

"Let's get down to it," said Zora. "Tomorrow there will be four minutes of mistlessness where we visited Snarky and his cult. There's a good chance they haven't migrated far. Trust me, it's a rare opportunity."

"There isn't another cult in the area?" Pius asked.

"Don't want another tentacle lashing from Snarky?" said Zora. "He learned more from you than you think. Meet him again. He'll be a different Thulhu in clear air." She glanced from Pius to David and back to Pius. "I've been tailing a different cult, but if you need me again—"

"We'll be fine," said David. "Pius can guide me, and we can radio for help if anything goes wrong."

Zora looked at Pius uncertainly, then sized David up, frowned in resignation. "All right, but go armed. There are reports of lampreys."

Scarcely thinking about how humid it'd gotten, Pius followed David to the armory, palmed the same munitions as David, and loaded them into the same model handgun.

David would confront him, he knew. Whatever David said, and however he responded, he would always be turned around. He could white-knuckle it, but for how long?

David always knew the right thing to say. He listened as though he'd crossed not only the gulf between Aletheia and Murk for Pius's sake, but the empty reaches of galactic space. How long could his convictions hold out against the enormity of David's attention?

A Devonian staff woman had already strapped David into his Thulhu-suit but had yet to help Pius.

"Junia, when you're done with the Churchmen, come back here and help me with these repairs. Dehumidifiers won't fix themselves, even on God's account," said Junia's manager, a middle-aged white engineer.

Junia strapped Pius into his Thulhu-suit harness, rushed to snap the buckles into place, and hurried to join her manager.

David called back to her, "You forgot one."

"Forgot one?" she said, her black gills flapping listlessly, huge insensate fish eyes on either side of her cleft head.

"*His* buckles," said David.

Pius shifted, scrutinized the points where his harness interfaced with his chest and legs. He lifted his right thigh free.

"Oh, sorry about that." She readily snapped the errant buckle into place.

The manager faced David penitently. "Sorry, sometimes they make mistakes."

David took to operating the Thulhu-suit easily, bounding over mist-cloaked boulders and winding around sucking marsh without hesitation. He had the brain implant, like Zora. David must have digested everything there was to know about Thulhu-suit operation just like he'd assimilated Pius's work on the Prabhakarins. But it could just be because he was David Nestor. Everything came easily to David Nestor.

Pius trailed behind David. They weren't far from the coordinates Zora had given them, where the mist would clear and night would deign to show her star-freckled face. Maybe Pius could avoid another confrontation.

But when they were ten minutes out from the station, David relaxed his pace.

"Did you hear what the manager said back at the base, when he apologized for that mix-up with your harness?" David said.

That was an odd way to brook conversation. "He didn't say it to me." *And it was my harness that was loose.*

"He said, 'Sometimes they make mistakes.'"

Recalling that the manager's subordinate was young, black, a woman, and a Devonian, the prejudice of those words slammed into Pius.

"What do you think he meant?" said David.

"By 'they'? Could've been racist? Maybe sexist? Species-ist?" Pius suggested, sharing in the joke.

"Don't forget ageist. Classist? Maybe he has something against fish?"

"He could've just meant that sometimes the people he manages make mistakes."

"But why say 'they'?" said David.

"Good question." Pius chuckled again.

"Why write *logos*?" said David.

"Good question." His humor was gone. "But I'm not sure God will tell us if we ask."

"I mean, why would John—why would *God*—write *logos* in scripture if He didn't mean something as rich as *logos*, with all its meaning, if He didn't know we would translate it and translate it again, sometimes carelessly, sometimes with all our faculty, but inevitably fail to capture His meaning?"

"He knew that we would sin in this, like we do in so many things. It's no different."

"I don't think that's it at all," said David, a touch forlorn. "Why would God entrust scripture to us if He didn't think we could carry out His will through it?"

Again David managed to turn Pius's own words around on him, make it seem that he was the one protecting scripture and bringing the true Gospel to new species, while Pius was just straying again and again. "Is there a point in this?"

"No point, just something I'm trying to gesture at." David raised his right fore-tentacle in the trumpeting salute, the software's neologism for one-beyond-mist, which might mean God. "Remember in First Corinthians Paul writes of how he spreads the Gospel? 'I am all things to all people, that I might by all means save some.' I think *logos* is like that. It began as just a word, give or take the capital *W*. Maybe John meant a certain something by it, but God knew that we wouldn't be able to get inside John's head, that throughout history and the stupendous variety of His creation, we would inevitably make it richer, even unknowingly, like the crew manager with his 'they.' I think *logos* is the Word to you and I, a solar-principle to the Orkens, and an action to the Prabhakarins. I think it's what every sentient species needs it to be, and given time, *logos* will mean everything, will be a word that means everything."

David cast his spell over Pius while speaking, but they departed again in silence. The mist occluded everything, outlasting mere words and the illusions of the man that wove them. Pius decided that David had spent too long tinkering with the stupendous variety of the Aletheian tongue. Surely, a scholarly fancy overcame him to stretch meaning further and further without regard for scripture or the Christianizing of sentient life. A word that means *everything*? Were it possible, it would mean nothing at all!

Pius plucked up his courage. Just as they were climbing the rise upon which Snarky and his cult still grazed, he beckoned, "Hold up." There was still some time before the mist would clear.

David swiveled his Thulhu-suit around.

"Why did you volunteer to come here when you already had work on Aletheia?"

"They can get on without me."

And I can't? "It has nothing to do with a word that means everything?"

"No need to think it means more than it does." David only half smiled at his own joke. "I just see the richness in *logos*, and its potential, and I see God in that potential."

Pius had to lay it on hard. "It's heresy."

"Heresy?" At last, David was the one reacting.

"Yes, however we translate *logos*, God means *something* by it. God doesn't send us in pursuit of phantoms, willing that we do violence to the text, refashioning Christianity as just every other religion it comes into contact with."

"John didn't invent this word *logos*. He found it where it was and elevated it for God's purposes. Heraclitus's fire, the Stoic *logos spermatikos*, Aristotle's soul of humanity, reason, Word—all of that was already there. You think *logos* is just a title for Christ? No, it was a title for cult deities throughout the ancient Mediterranean: Orpheus, Hermes, Dionysus." A deep anger, a lash of desert wind, stirred within David. "You think the difference between us is that you defend the truth of scripture and I corrupt it, but really I have my eye on the spirit of the Word and you defend the dead letter."

"Me? You have these blinders, this *tunnel vision*. What about the rest of scripture? Jesus wasn't Heraclitus, or a Stoic, or Aristotle, and he certainly wasn't an alien. He was *human*. He's what's decisive, and his humanity is part of that."

"If that's how you feel—"

"We don't even need to go back to your scandalous Orken translation to make my point! You know the prevailing Chinese translation of *logos*?" David jerked a nod, but Pius spoke over him, "*Dao*. Because of that Chinese speakers ever since the twentieth century have believed that the real Old Testament isn't the prophets, the Books of Moses, and the history of the Hebrews. No, they said it's the Daodejing!" Pius didn't need to remind him that the Daodejing is foundational to Daoism. And Daoism has nothing to do with any Christian creed. "*That's* what I mean by heresy."

"People misread the Bible all the time. You don't need faulty translation to find crude innovators."

"But we needn't help the innovators along! Our task is to preserve the meaning John intended. Once the alien races acclimate to us, they'll understand the Gospel as we do."

David grimaced as if his last meal refused digestion.

Let him. God didn't incarnate as a Thulhu, or any alien, but as a human.

"And how long will that take?" said David. "You think we should tell our superiors, 'Wait a few generations while we figure out how to educate a whole moon of Thulhus about the proper meaning of *logos*?'"

"If that's what it takes," Pius shot back.

"You know," David said, voice edged with disdain, "you've already styled John according to alien religion and you don't even realize it. Your translation of *logos* into Prabhakarin: *kara*, action. You had your reasons, but *logos* doesn't mean action. John's *logos* is language, reason, transcendence. Not action."

Pius recoiled, recalling his own words, *I hope you can see why it was necessary.*

David's tone lowered. "In fact, it's *Satanic.*"

"Satanic?" He couldn't mean that.

"Yes, *Satanic.* You know Faust? Sold his soul to the devil, and in Goethe's version of the legend, the one everyone reads, what did Faust translate *logos* as? *Action.*"

An ululation punctuated David's last word. A trick of the mist? Impossible.

There was a shadow. Wait. Not a shadow. A lamprey, going by the row upon row of barbs in its cyclostome maw. It writhed on six gray-green tentacles that branched from its long eel body and shivered over one another. There was no guessing how it would move. Pius's visor didn't bother trying to interpret. But when it glided—first laterally, then zigzagging nearer—he knew the hair-raising splendor of it.

Pius met its eyes last. Enormous eyes, mad with hunger, obsidian like Snarky's, but there the resemblance ended. Behind those eyes was only instinct and lithe machinery. Pius wasn't a person, not even an alien. He was a meal.

His arm shot up reflexively. His suit smacked the lamprey with a fore-tentacle. The ghastly thing stumbled. Never before had it chanced upon prey so large as a human in a Thulhu-suit.

Ululation on his other side, higher pitched. A second silhouette, slimmer than the first and mist-gray. He supposed it was female, though sexing the squirmy horrors was beyond his ken.

Distantly he worried the Thulhus wouldn't know to flee. They couldn't hear the struggle, and if they could see down from the rise (the mist was thinning), they'd only recognize him if he moved. Zora had said they could see nothing but motion. Pius swung his arm but the tentacle only curled upward like a wounded soldier.

What was he doing? He may stand as tall as two Thulhus, but a tentacle lashing from a Thulhu cult was just the price of a meal as far as these lampreys were concerned. Pius unholstered his handgun.

David was already firing at the putative male. Pius anticipated the snap of discharge, a misted vapor trail, a gory hole, perhaps ricochet.

Nothing. No explosion. Either David's gun jammed, or...

Experimentally, Pius fired. Again nothing. He cursed Murk and didn't chastise himself for cursing. David hadn't checked for dry munitions, and Pius had been too distracted to think of it.

David tested his balance on just his back hind-tentacles and bellowed at the top of his lungs. He struck with his two free hind-tentacles. But the female had already drawn back. She hadn't bargained for a plus-sized Thulhu rearing like a hellion ripe from the pit.

The male drifted into the mist after her.

"Think they'll stay gone?" said David.

"The Thulhus!" Pius scrambled up the rise, his damaged fore-tentacle dangling uselessly behind.

"Pius, you can't dive in like that!" David called after him. "We're here to interview, not interfere with the natural order."

"We already interfered! Our arguing led them here."

On the top of the rise, where the mist was thinner, the male had one of the Thulhus pinned. It slurped down a tentacle of the subdued Thulhu, its maw twisting savagely. The Thulhu's four free tentacles languished.

Three Thulhu males—men—darted forward, but the female lamprey stalked side to side, warding them back. The ghostly women Thulhus planted young on their backsides and fled through the slackening mist.

Just one option. Pius flung himself toward the male. His hind-tentacles whipped in pairs, propelling him forward. Just as he was above the male, he dropped his shoulder, making his abortive disobedient-other gesture. The side of his suit sagged; everything tilted on top of the lamprey.

Pius had the male pinned, but it maneuvered his damaged fore-tentacle into its mouth. How long until it gobbled something vital?

Whether inspired by Pius's dive or rankled over their fallen brother, the Thulhus rallied. Two lost tentacles to twisting lamprey maw, but they assailed the female relentlessly.

David reared again, and the female slunk away even without the mist to cloak its retreat.

Pius almost cried out but didn't. The male still savored his Thulhu-suit fore-tentacle. A shout might divert it.

David didn't need to be told, and he didn't hesitate. Balancing on his fore-tentacles, he flexed two hind-tentacles and strangled the male until it was dead.

The Thulhu men parted, revealing their fallen brother, Snarky. His obsidian eyes opened and closed listlessly, alive but only just. One of his fore-tentacles lifted and fell, lifted and fell again. Once Pius would have thought this wavering a spasm, but now he'd imbibed enough of Thulhu gesturing to know its cadence.

"Distance," his visor flared. "Distance and clarity"—Snarky's fore-tentacles went limp and rose again—"is a good way for the world to end."

Snarky couldn't see the night or the dead lamprey. But with the mist pulled away, Snarky saw the scrambling forms of the women and young shuffling farther up the rise. The other men gestured safety and calm. Danger was past. Knowing that, he would die, his every thought winking into oblivion, and the world would end soundlessly with him. Such is the boundless egoism of a Thulhu.

Pius could offer some gesture of apology. This wasn't chance predation; the aliens were to blame. But how could Snarky forgive—or blame—a stranger that, to him, had no more reality than a dream? He whispered evenly, feelingly into his mouthpiece. "Do you believe we exist now? Or is it still just you?" His suit gestured the message, compensating for the defunct fore-tentacle by use of the hind-tentacle nearest.

"Alien, it was never just about me." Perhaps he meant it, or maybe Snarky was snarky until the last.

The other men crowded around Snarky while the women and young snaked through the clear air to join the men. Pius and David withdrew to let the Thulhus tend to their dead.

One of the women settled beside Snarky's body. One by one, she and all the Thulhus careened their necks. Thulhu-suit flashlights cut the dark, but for the Thulhus, the darkness was total. For them, nothing moved, not Aletheia cloud-wreathed and bluely luminous overhead, neither the stars, peepholes into heaven.

In unison, the Thulhus raised their right fore-tentacles in the trumpeting salute, which meant one-beyond-mist, the translation software's coinage, its attempt at God. The woman beside Snarky felt over his body, at last raising one of his limp fore-tentacles high.

Why salute? What is the night to them in its static splendor? They had no comprehension of Aletheia waltzing around Murk too slowly for a mortal eye to recognize. They saw only motion, *action*. Pius followed the arch of their tentacles, passing over Aletheia, the jewel of the panorama according to a human way of seeing. A fat star twinkled, shifting beneath a film of atmosphere, in sullen majesty near the pole where Murk's axis processed limitlessly off into space.

Did they know that star, have a name and rank for it in their pantheon of pagan gods? They could, even though these moments of clarity and distance were rare.

105

Whatever their mythology, they had their wonder. That was enough.

Pius recalled, in the Book of Acts, the account of Paul's preaching to Greek Stoic philosophers, the most prominent philosophical tradition from which John borrowed *logos*, "Athenians, I see how extremely religious you are in every way. For as I went through the city and looked carefully at the objects of your worship, I found among them an altar with the inscription, 'To an unknown god.' What therefore you worship as unknown, this I proclaim to you."

David and Pius started back, shoulder to shoulder, enfolded everywhere by mist, which to them, was different from forgetfulness.

"Next time we grab dry rounds," said Pius.

"We could have scared both off if you hadn't keeled over on top of one."

"Heh, even so."

David agreed with silence, and after a longer silence, "I shouldn't have called your translation Satanic."

"I know you didn't mean it."

"It's not that, I mean it wasn't fair. Faust just happened to settle on the same translation as you, and he's just a man in a story."

"But he had reasons for translating *logos* as action, right?"

"Faust says that the Holy Spirit moved him, and maybe it did."

"And maybe it was Satan," Pius allowed.

"Who can say? I think you made the right choice for the Prabhakarins, though."

"And now we need to make the right choice for the Thulhus."

"Any ideas?"

Pius spoke into his mouthpiece, "In the beginning was the Gesture..."

Steps in the
Right Direction

BY L. RON HUBBARD

L. Ron Hubbard's brilliantly adventurous life and long, prolific and remarkably versatile writing career have become almost legendary in their dimensions and creative influence. Although he was always quintessentially the writer, the range of his experiences, travels and questing curiosity into the world's places and cultures was extraordinarily wide and diverse. He was both explorer and master mariner, pilot and diver, prospector and photographer, artist and educator, composer and musician.

As a youngster growing up in a still-rugged frontier Montana, he was riding horses by the time he was three, and had become a blood brother of the Blackfeet Indian tribe by the age of six. He traveled more than a quarter of a million miles by sea and land into remote corners of the Far East while still a teenager and before the advent of commercial aviation as we know it. He led three separate voyages of discovery and exploration under the flag of the prestigious Explorers Club, one while testing an experimental direction-finding system for the US government. And he barnstormed across the United States in gliders and early powered aircraft, worked as a successful screenwriter in Hollywood, was only twenty-five when he was elected president of the American Fiction Guild's New York Chapter with a membership that included Dashiell Hammett, Raymond Chandler, and Edgar Rice Burroughs, and served with distinction as a US naval officer during the Second World War.

All of this—and much more—in a life of vigorous industry and high achievement, found its way into the substance of L. Ron Hubbard's fiction, imbuing it for millions of readers with a defining hallmark authenticity.

His outpouring of fiction—often exceeding a million words a year—was prodigious, ultimately encompassing more than 260 published novels, novelettes, short stories and screenplays in virtually every major genre, from action and adventure, western and romance, to mystery and suspense, and, of course, science fiction and fantasy.

107

Although Mr. Hubbard had already achieved enormous popularity and acclaim in other genres when he burst onto the landscape of speculative literature with his first published science fiction story, "The Dangerous Dimension," in 1938, it was his trendsetting work in this field, particularly, that not only helped expand the scope and imaginative boundaries of the genre, but established him as one of the founders and creative wellsprings of what remains its most celebrated—and fabled—period of productivity and literary invention, the Golden Age of Science Fiction of the thirties and forties.

Such established L. Ron Hubbard classics of speculative fiction as Fear, Final Blackout, Typewriter in the Sky *and* Ole Doc Methuselah, *as well as his powerful, capstone novels, the precedent-setting* Battlefield Earth *and the* Mission Earth *dekalogy, continue, meanwhile, to appear on the bestseller lists and to garner critical recognition in countries around the world.*

L. Ron Hubbard's fifty-five-year career as a professional writer was distinguished, equally, by a deeply felt, lifelong commitment to helping other writers, especially beginners, become better, more productive and more successful at their craft. This culminated in 1985 with his establishment of both the Writers of the Future Contest—now indisputably the largest and most successful merit competition of its kind in the world—and the annual anthology of the winning best new, original science fiction and fantasy.

But Mr. Hubbard's earliest work with fledgling writers— undertaken even as he himself, still in his early twenties, was climbing rapidly to national prominence—found clear, cogent expression at the time in lectures at universities such as Harvard and George Washington on how to get started, and in a series of "how to" articles about writing as a craft and profession.

The article that follows—"Steps in the Right Direction"—was originally published in the January 1949 issue of Writers' Markets and Methods. *It describes the practical philosophy and energetic disciplines he applied with such telling success to his own career, voluminously turning his own life experiences, knowledge and ideas, his own probing curiosity, into memorable fiction.*

Steps in the
Right Direction

How the writer can convert his own life
and curiosity into stories
An interview with L. Ron Hubbard
By R. Walton Willems

L. Ron Hubbard grinned when I asked him for a few secrets of his writing success. "No secrets, I'm afraid." He waved a hand, as though to say that everything was open and, on the whole, not too difficult. "I believe the writer must be in debt to Life, that his plots must come from curiosity of his own making and that the most important thing in writing a story is to write the story."

The last item seemed the easiest to start with, so I asked Mr. Hubbard if the advice were really as obvious in meaning as it sounded.

"Almost," he admitted, "though I think I mean it with a harder punch than is usually the case. If you want to write a story—write it! The more time spent in planning it, thinking it over, the longer it is likely to be before the story gets written. In spite of this, many writers tell themselves that the final draft will come sooner if they put thinking time in first. Thinking time is too often stalling time. The quicker the story is down in first draft the better. Then planning, if still needed, can be done—working now with something concrete, something that can be handled and headed toward the final draft. Write while the idea's hot, while the desire to do that story is still there to help you with the story. The planning can come in then, and it will be planning without stalling."

I asked Mr. Hubbard if this would not lead to a writer doing, in the long run, more work on revisions than would be required if the story were carefully planned.

"At first, it might. Though here I think the extra work—if there were any—would be small compared to the advantage of getting the story started. Later on, though, with a lot of writing behind him, the writer will find that the story idea becomes almost self-planning as the first draft is written. The actual writing of the first draft will be done by an author who has conditioned himself to think as he writes. As time goes on he will find that the first draft is ever closer to what the final draft should be. Eventually he should be able to make that first and final draft, which is also the story-planning draft, all the same thing."

Then I remembered something I had heard about L. Ron Hubbard: How magazine editors had, at times, sent messengers to him with a cover painting of a forthcoming issue. The messenger would wait while Hubbard looked at the painting, then wrote a story to suit the illustration, and the messenger would return to the editor with painting and story ready to go to the printer. I asked Hubbard about this. He shrugged it off as not being a true part of the real business of writing.

"Though situations like that do come up, and the writer should be prepared to meet them. They present a challenge, of course, and the writer has a chance to come through with a yarn that will make the reader feel that, for once, the artist read the same story the reader did before making the illustration. However, work in that category is minor, although it always helps the writer's future to be able to help an editor out of a jam. Situations might, one day, be reversed.

"I think the writer's best story ideas and plots are ones developed in his own mind as a result of his mental prying into something that strikes his fancy.

"A method I think is good is for the writer to imagine an impossible situation, then work from there. The final story plot need have no connection with the situation you started with, and all characters and ideas in the original situation might be left out of the final story entirely. But the incident has served its purpose of getting the mind thinking in story terms, asking questions that lead to a story."

"For instance?" I asked.

Mr. Hubbard smiled, came back with a question of his own. "What kind of a story?"

"Love story," I said. "With an airplane."

"Airplane. Pilot. Something unlikely: Goldfish. A pilot who always takes a bowl of goldfish in his plane with him. Ask yourself what that has to do with the girl, what that means to him. Where does he stand with the girl, how does the future look. What has happened. What is about to happen...The story's under way—the goldfish could be made to stay in, but for the usual story they would be dropped about this time, something more plausible submitted. The unusual situation there to start with should be considered as strictly a springboard. Don't try to hold on to it after the story starts taking hold on its own."

I asked why something unusual was used.

"Merely to get the writer interested, asking himself questions, thinking along story lines. In the actual story opening the writer is going to try to get the reader curious, make him want to read the story. Same idea for the writer—he's got to hook himself into the story or there never will be a story. If the finished story idea has a place for the unusual situation that started the writer thinking, leave it in there, let it be used to hook the reader. But don't try to force it in where it no longer belongs. If, as the story grows, it wants to outgrow its creative situation, let it."

"That's two of your nonsecrets, Mr. Hubbard. How about the idea of being in debt to Life?"

"That means living and learning. It means doing all you can, studying all you can, learning all you can. It means— borrowing from the Bank of the World in ideas and knowledge and experience. Recognize this as a debt to the people around you—a debt the writer must pay back with his writing. It isn't a hard debt to pay, for the repayment will be made easy by borrowing—the greater the borrowing, the greater the ease with which payments can be made. The writer who has drawn much from the world will find that his mind is filled with material that can be used to make the payments. The more the writer throws himself into debt, the more he will have with which to repay."

I asked Mr. Hubbard to summarize the points he had touched on in our talk. He ticked them off on his fingers.

"The writer should make his own background for his writing, a background built of his own living and learning. Story ideas should grow from an appeal to his own curiosity. He should write the story while the idea is burning in his mind."

"That's all there is to it?"

Hubbard grinned warily. "Well, at least those are three steps in the right direction."

Borrowed Glory

written by
L. Ron Hubbard

illustrated by
CASSANDRE BOLAN

ABOUT THE AUTHOR

"Borrowed Glory" was originally published in October of 1941. Ron wrote the story for John W. Campbell's fantasy magazine Unknown Worlds. *The magazine was launched in 1939. But with the War and its demands on many of Campbell's stable of writers including Ron, plus war-time paper shortages, the magazine was in print for a mere thirty-nine issues. While the magazine lasted, it provided a venue for some of Ron's most memorable stories including* Fear, Typewriter in the Sky, Slaves of Sleep—*eight novel-length and six short stories in all.*

As Robert Silverberg tells it, "Hubbard would become one of Unknown's *most popular contributors and his fantasy novels for the magazine were to become classics of the field."*

Campbell had very definite ideas about what he was looking to include in Unknown. *"All human beings like wishes to come true. In fairy stories and fantasy, wishes do come true."*

And who wouldn't want to be young again, to find love and glory even for just a little while. With Ron's unmistakable touch, the lines between the real and the illusory, the here and now, begin to blur and merge in "Borrowed Glory." And for just forty-eight hours, our dreams come true—but can we truly be fulfilled by joyous memories?

ABOUT THE ILLUSTRATOR

Cassandre paints diverse, real, and strong women in the epic contexts of myths and fairytales. Her paintings are retellings of these universal stories and the women in them. She's inspired by tales of sacred femininism, Jungian psychology, women's studies, and she loves analyzing every children's TV show on Netflix with her kids!

Her clients have included Cartoon Network, Fantasy Flight Games, and Creative Assembly, as well as many inspirational indie creators, and was featured in ImagineFX magazine (2014/2019). She was a winner of L. Ron Hubbard's Illustrators of the Future Contest in 2014, featured in Volume 30.

Cassandre has lived across the world, grown up in the army, and recently spent ten years in Dubai, but mostly resides in her own little fantasy world. She is deathly allergic to schedules, normal jobs, bedtimes, and feels incredibly lucky to not only freelance but create original independent projects too. When not painting scowling middle-aged women in armor or getting rabidly philosophical about children's TV shows, Cassandre likes to mysteriously disappear into her shadowy witch's lair to work on her secret original children's book series.

Borrowed Glory

Human beings," said Tuffaron, familiarly known as the Mad Genie, "are stupid and willful. They derive intense enjoyment from suffering or else they would not bend all their efforts toward suffering."

He sat back upon the hot rock this hotter day and gazed off into the dun wilderness, stroking his fang to give himself an air of contemplation and wisdom.

Georgie bustled her wings with resentment. Her lower lip protruded and her usually angelic countenance darkened. "Know-it-all!" she taunted. "Conceited know-it-all!"

"That is no way for an angel to talk, Georgie," said Tuffaron.

"Conceited, bloated know-it-all!" she cried and then and there felt a growing desire to kick his huge column of a leg. Of course she wouldn't, for that would not be exactly an expression of love for everything. "Prove it!" she demanded.

"Why," said Tuffaron, the Mad Genie, in his most lofty tone, "human beings prove it themselves."

"You evade me. You are the stupid one!" said Georgie. "I dare you to put that matter to test. Human beings are very nice, very, very nice and I love them. So there!"

"You are under orders to love everything, even human beings," said Tuffaron. "And why should I exert myself to labor a point already too beautifully established?"

"Coward!" said Georgie.

Tuffaron looked down at her and thoughtfully considered her virginal whiteness, the graceful slope of her wings, the pink of

115

her tiny toes showing from beneath her radiant gown. "Georgie, I would not try to trifle with such proof if I were you. Besides, you have nothing to wager."

"I am not allowed to wager."

"See?" said Tuffaron. "You are afraid to prove your own point, for you know quite well you cannot."

"I'll wager my magic ring against your magic snuffbox that I can prove you wrong," said Georgie.

"Ah," said Tuffaron. "But how do you propose to prove this?"

"The outer limit of my power is to grant anything for forty-eight hours."

"Certainly, but according to the law, if you grant anything for forty-eight hours you have to have it back in forty-eight hours."

"Just so. A human being," declared Georgie, "is so starved for comfort and happiness that if he is granted all for just a short time he will be content."

"My dear, you do not know humans."

"Is it a wager?"

"A sure thing is never a wager," said Tuffaron, "but I will place my magic snuffbox against your magic ring that if you give all for forty-eight hours you will only succeed in creating misery. My precept is well known."

"The wager is stated. I shall grant all for forty-eight hours and even though I must take it back at the end of the time, I shall succeed in leaving happiness."

Solemnly he wrapped his huge black hand about her dainty little white one. She eyed him defiantly as they sealed the bargain. And then she leaped up and flew swiftly away.

Tuffaron barked a guffaw. "I have always wanted an angel ring," he told the hot day.

It was not warm in the room and one might have kept butter on the ancient radiator. A trickle of bitter wind came in under the door, gulped what warmth there was to be found in the place and then with a triumphant swoop went soaring up and out through the cracked pane at the window's top.

116

It was not warm but it was clean, this room. Patient hands had polished the floor with much scrubbing; the walls of the room bore erasure marks but no spots of smudge. The tiny kitchenette might not have a quarter in its gas meter but it had bright red paper edging its shelves and the scanty utensils were burnished into mirrors; the teatowels, though ragged, were newly washed and even the dishcloth was white—but this last was more because there had been nothing with which to soil dishes for many days. A half loaf of bread and a chunk of very cheap cheese stood in solitary bravery upon the cupboard shelf.

The little worn lady who napped upon the bed was not unlike the shawl which covered her—a lovely weave but tattered edges and thin warp and a bleach which comes with time.

Meredith Smith's little hand, outflung against the pillow, matched the whiteness of the case save where the veins showed blue. It was a hand which reminded one of a doll's.

She slept. To her, as years went on, sleep was more and more the only thing left for her to do. It was as though an exhausting life had robbed her of rest, so that now when she no longer had work to do she could at least make up lost sleep.

From the age of eighteen to the age of sixty she had been a stenographer in the Hayward Life Co. She had written billions of words in letters for them. She had kept the files of her department in neat and exact order. She would have had a pension now but Hayward Life was a defunct organization and had been so for the past six years.

Relief brought Meredith Smith enough for her rent and a small allowance of food but she was not officious and demanding enough to extract from the authorities a sufficiency.

But she did not mind poverty. She did not mind cold. There was only one sharp pain with her now and one which she felt was a pain which should be accepted, endured. It had come about three years ago when she had chanced to read a poem in which old age was paid by its memory of love and it had swept over her like a blinding flood that she, Meredith Smith, had no payment for that age. The only thing she had saved was a decent burial, two hundred and twenty dollars beneath the rug.

She had worked. There had been many women who had married out of work. But she had worked. She had been neither beautiful nor ugly. She had merely been efficient. At times she had thought to herself that on some future day she must find, at last, that thing for which her heart was starved. But it had always been a future day and now, at sixty-six, there would never be one.

She had never loved a man. She had never been loved by a child. She had had a long succession of efficient days where her typewriter had clattered busily and loudly as though to muffle her lack.

She had never had anyone. She had been a small soul in a great city, scarcely knowing who worked at the next desk. And so it had been; from eighteen to sixty. And now...

It was easier now to sleep and try not to think of it. For she would die without having once known affection, jealousy, ecstasy or true pain.

She had been useless. She had run a typewriter. She had been nothing to life. She had never known beauty; she had never known laughter; she had never known pain; and she would die without ever having lived, she would die without a single tear to fall upon her going. She had never been known, to be forgotten. Yesterdays reached back in a long gray chain like pages written with a single word and without punctuation. Tomorrow stretched out gray; gray and then black. A long, long time black. And she was forgotten before she was gone and she had nothing to forget except emptiness.

But the hand which touched her hand so warmly did not startle her and it did not seem strange for her faded blue eyes to open upon a lovely girl. The door had been locked but Meredith Smith did not think of that, for this visitor was sitting upon the edge of the bed and smiling at her so calmly and pleasantly that one could never think of her as an intruder.

"You are Meredith Smith?" said the visitor.

The old lady smiled. "What is your name?"

"I am called Georgette, Meredith. Do not be afraid."

"I am glad you came."

"Thank you. You see very few people, I think."

"No one," said Meredith, "except the relief agent each week."

"Meredith Smith, would you like to see people?"

"I don't understand you."

"Meredith Smith, would you like to see people and be young again and dance and laugh and be in love?"

The old lady's eyes became moist. She smiled, afraid to be eager.

"Would you like to do these things, Meredith Smith, if only for forty-eight hours, knowing that you would again come here and be old?"

"For forty-eight hours—to be young, to dance, to laugh, to be in love—even if only for forty-eight hours." She was still afraid and spoke very quietly.

"Then," said Georgie, "I tell you now," and she had a small stick with a glowing thing upon its end, "that for forty-eight hours, beginning this minute, you can have everything for which you ask and everything done which you want done. But you must know that at the end of the forty-eight hours, everything for which you ask will be taken back."

"Yes," said Meredith in a whisper. "Oh, yes!"

"It is now eight o'clock in the morning," said Georgie. "At eight a.m. day after tomorrow, all things I gave you will have to be returned, save only memory. But until then, Meredith Smith, all things you want are yours."

It did not particularly surprise Meredith that her visitor did not go away as a normal person should but dissolved, glowed and vanished. Meredith sat looking at the imprint on the bed where Georgette had been seated. And then Meredith rose.

YOUTH! BEAUTY!

In her mirror she watched and her fluttering heart began to grow stronger and stronger. Her hair turned from gray to soft, burnished chestnut. Her eyes grew larger and longer and brightened into a blue which was deep and lovely and warm. Her skin became fresh and pink and radiant. She smiled at herself and her beautiful mouth bowed open to reveal sparkling, even teeth. There came a taut, breath-catching curve in her throat and the unseen hand which molded her flowed over her form, rounding it, giving it grace, giving it allure and poise—

YOUTH!

A gay darling of eighteen stared with lip-parted wonder at herself.

BEAUTY!

Ah, beauty!

She was not able to longer retain the somber rags of her clothes and with a prodigal hand ripped them away and, naked, held out her arms and waltzed airily about the room, thrilled to the edge of tears but laughing instead.

"Meredith, Meredith," she said to the mirror, posed as she halted. "Meredith, Meredith," she said again, intrigued by the warm charm of the new voice which came softly and throbbingly out of herself.

Ah, yes, a young beauty. A proud young beauty who could yet be tender and yielding, whose laughter was gay and told of passion and love—

"Meredith, Meredith," she whispered and kissed herself in the mirror.

Where were those dead years? Gone and done. Where were those lightless days? Cut through now by the brilliance of this vision she beheld. Where was the heartache of never having belonged or suffered? Gone, gone. All gone now. For everything might be taken back but this memory, and the memory, that would be enough! Forty-eight hours. And already those hours were speeding.

What to wear? She did not even know enough of current styles to ask properly. And then she solved it with a giggle at her own brightness.

"I wish for a morning outfit of the most enhancing and modern style possible."

120

CLOTHES!

They rustled upon the furniture and lay still, new in expensive boxes. A saucy little hat. Sheer stockings so thrilling to the touch. A white linen dress with a piqué collar and a small bolero to match. Long white gloves smooth to the cheek. And underthings. And graceful shoes.

She dressed, lingering ecstatically over the process, enjoying the touch of the fabrics, reveling in the new clean smell of silk and leather.

She enjoyed herself in the glass, turning and turning back, posing and turning again. And then she drew on the gloves, picked up the purse and stepped out of her room.

She was not seen in the hall or on the stairs. She wrinkled a pert little nose at the sordid street.

"A car," she said. "A wonderful car, very long and smooth to ride in, and a haughty chauffeur and footman to drive it."

"Your car, mademoiselle," said the stiffly standing footman, six feet tall and his chin resting on a cloud.

For a moment she was awed by his austerity and she nearly drew back as though he could look through her and know that it was a masquerade. But she did not want him to see how daunted she was and so she stepped into the limousine. Still frightened she settled back upon the white leather upholstery.

"The...ah, the park—James."

"Very good, mademoiselle." And the footman stepped into the front seat and said to the chauffeur, "Mademoiselle requires to ride in the park."

They hummed away and up the street and through the town and soon they were spinning between the green acres of Central Park, one of a flowing line of traffic. She was aware of people who stopped and glanced toward her, for it was a lovely car and in it she knew they saw a lovely girl. She felt suddenly unhappy and conspicuous. And it worried her that the chauffeur and footman knew that this was a masquerade.

"Stop," she said into the phone.

CASSANDRE BOLAN

The car drew up beside a curbed walk and she got out.

"I shall not need you again," she said.

"Very good, mademoiselle," said the footman with a stiff bow, and the car went away.

She was relieved about it, for not once in it had she felt comfortable. And standing here she did not feel conspicuous at all, for people passed her by, now that the car was gone, with only that sidelong glance which is awarded every heart-stirring girl by the passerby.

Warm again and happy, she stepped off the walk and risked staining her tiny shoes in the grass. She felt she must walk in soft earth beneath a clear sky and feel clean wind, and so, for nearly an hour, she enjoyed herself.

Then she began to be aware of time slipping away from her. She knew she must compose herself, bring order to her activities, plan out each hour which remained to her. For only in that way could she stock a store of memories from which she could draw upon in the years which would remain to her.

Across the drive was a bench beside the lake and she knew that it would be a nice place to think and so she waited for the flow of traffic to abate so that she could cross to it.

She thought the way clear and stepped upon the street. There was a sudden scream of brakes and a thudding bump as wheels were stabbed into the gutter. She stood paralyzed with terror to see that a large car had narrowly missed her, and that only by expert driving on the part of its chauffeur.

A young man was out of the back and had her hand, dragging her from the street and into the car with him. She sat still, pale and weak, lips parted. But it was not from fright but from wonder. She had not wished for this and yet it could not have been better had she wished for it.

"You are not hurt?" he said. He was shy and nervous and when he saw that he still held her hand he quickly dropped it and moistened his lips.

She looked long at him. He was a young man, probably not

more than twenty-five, for his skin was fresh and his eyes were clear. He radiated strength and this shyness of his was only born from fright at the near accident, fright for her and awe for her beauty as well. He was six feet tall and his eyes were black as his hair. His voice was low and showed breeding.

"Is there...there any place we can take you?"

"I...wasn't going anywhere in particular," she said. "You are very good. I...I am sorry I frightened you so. I wasn't watching—"

"It is all our fault," said the young man. "Please, may I introduce myself? I am Thomas Crandall."

"I am Meredith Smith."

"It...it isn't quite proper—to be introduced this way," he faltered. And then he smiled good-humoredly at her and they both began to laugh.

The laughter put them at ease and took away the memory of the near fatality.

They drove for a little while, more and more in tune with each other, and then he turned to her and asked, "Would I seem terribly bold if I asked you to have lunch with me? I at least owe you that."

"I would be very disappointed if you did not," she answered. "That...that isn't a very ladylike speech, I know, but...but I would like to have lunch with you."

He was flattered and enthralled and smiled it upon her. Most of his lingering shyness departed and he leaned toward the glass to tell his chauffeur, "The Montmaron, please."

"You know," he said a little while later as they sat in the roof garden at a small table, "I was hoping that something like this might happen. Last night, I was hoping. Do you believe in wishes? I think wishes come true sometimes, don't they?"

She was startled that he might have read her secret, but she smiled at him and realized it wasn't so. The softness of the string music failed, after that, to wholly dispel a fear which had been implanted in her heart.

What would he think when he discovered— No, she mustn't dwell upon that. She would not dwell on the end.

He was so nice when he laughed. He was so nice.

And yet the knife of fear still probed her heart. He must not know. They would live up to the moment and then—then she—

"It's wine with bubbles in it," he was saying. "Wine with giggles in it. Drink a little but not too much."

She drank. She felt better. She almost forgot....

They went to a matinee but she had so little attention for the stage that the play, afterward, seemed quite incoherent to her. Somehow Thomas Crandall was the leading man and Thomas Crandall occasionally smiled sideways at her. When it ended he was holding her hand. He seemed very doubtful of his small advances and she had the feeling that he was afraid he might touch her and break her.

"What will your family think?" he said when they were outside. "You've been gone all afternoon and someone must have expected you somewhere. Surely anyone as beautiful as you must be missed."

She felt nervous and guilty. "Oh...oh, I...I am not from New York. I am from Boston. That's it. From Boston. And—my father and mother are both dead. I came down to see a show."

"Ah, so I've helped you attend to business." He grinned. "Then I am very much in luck. Then you can dine with me. And there are clubs and dancing and there will be a moon tonight—" Instantly he blushed. And she laughed at him.

"I am fond of the moon," she said, close against his arm. "Oh, but I must...must go to my hotel for a little while and dress."

"Tell Charles which one. No, tell me and I'll tell him. I should dress also."

"The...the Astor."

"I'll be back in an hour," he called to her from the curb. And the big car drew away.

She was filled with uneasiness to be standing there alone. She knew very little about such things and was certain she would make some mistake. But she reckoned without her beauty and the gallantry of man.

"I wish," she whispered to herself as she signed the register, "that I had a hundred dollars in my purse." And to the smiling clerk, "A suite, please. A large suite. My...my baggage will be brought in."

And the porter came through the door carrying new luggage with her name upon it.

When Thomas Crandall came back an hour later he stopped in wide-eyed reverence for the girl who came from the elevator. Her glowing chestnut hair swept down to naked shoulders and her gown, a graceful miracle in green, flowed closely to her to sweep out and to the floor. Finding it difficult to speak—for there seemed to be something in his throat—he helped her into the ermine wrap and led her through the lobby and down the steps as though he were escorting the sun itself.

"You...you are beautiful," he said. "No, that's not adequate. You are— Oh," he gave it up, "where would you like to dine?"

"Where you are going?" she said.

He laughed. They both laughed. And they went away to dine.

The world became a fantasy of bright glasses and swirling color and music, a delicate sensory world, and people laughed together and waiters were quick and kind.

"Not too much," he admonished her. "It's not the wine. It's the bubbles. They have fantasies in them. Each one contains a giggle or a castle or the moon."

They danced. And the bubbles won.

Somewhat astonished she looked about her to find the last place nearly empty. A scrubwoman was already at work upon the floor and a man was piling tables and chairs. And the orchestra, when Tommy offered more largess, was too sleepy to play. There was no more champagne. There was no more music. And the edge of the roof garden was already gray and the moon had gone.

She yawned as he took her arm. She nearly fell asleep as they got into his car. She snuggled down against him and looked up at him.

He laughed at her and then grew serious. "If I thought... if...well...I wish I could marry you."

"Why can't you?" she said.

"Why can't— Do you mean it? But, no. You've known me a very short time. You—"

"I have known you forever. We are to be married!"

"But what if...if I turn out to be a drunkard?"

"Then I will also be a drunkard."

He looked at her for a moment. "You do love me, don't you, as I love you?"

She pulled his head down and kissed him.

Somewhat dazedly afterward he said to his chauffeur: "There must be a place where people can get married quickly."

"Quickly," she murmured.

"Yes, sir," said the chauffeur.

"Take us there," said Tommy.

Suddenly she was terrified. She did not dare permit him to do this. For in—in twenty-six hours she would be— But she was more afraid that he would not.

She snuggled against him once more and sighed. Twenty-six hours left. Only twenty-six hours left but they could be full and she could be happy. And somehow, she would have to have the courage to face what came after. To face the loss of him...She drowsed.

With sixteen hours left to her she lay upon the great bed in the airy room and looked at the ceiling beams where the afternoon sunlight sent reflections dancing. He had said that he had a few phone calls to make and that there would be a party beginning at six and that the whole city—or whoever was important in the city—would be there. And she had understood suddenly that she knew about Thomas Crandall or had heard of him as a playwright, fabulously successful.

This, his home, was a palace of wonder to her, all marble and teak and ivory, filled with servants who were soft-footed and efficient—servants of whom she was secretly in awe.

She had not wished this and yet it had happened. It had been all Tommy's idea to marry her, to bring her here, to give a great party....

She did not have the courage it would take to run away now, before everyone came. For these hours were so precious that she hated to waste minutes in thinking so darkly on things. But think now she must. In sixteen hours she would be sixty-six years old, faded, delicate, starved— And Thomas Crandall—

She began to weep and, in a little while, realized that there was no solution. For what could she ask which she could retain? She could not plead that his love would not change. She knew that when he knew, he would be revolted both by her withered self and by the witchcraft which he would perceive. She could never stand to see him look at her as he would. And she could never bear to so cruelly abuse his love. For his love was not part of the wishes. If only it had been! Then he would forget—

And another knife of thought cut into her. Could she go back now, Mrs. Thomas Crandall, to a hovel on a sordid street and be happy with memory? She began to know that that could never be.

But his footstep was in the hall and he burst in followed by a train of servants who bore great boxes of clothes and flowers and little boxes full of things much more precious.

She was lost in the rapture of it. And then when she kissed him she forgot even the little boxes of velvet.

"Tommy, if this could last forever and ever—"

"It will last. Forever and ever." But he seemed to sense something strange in her and the dark eyes were thoughtful for just the space of a heartbeat. And her heart was racing.

"Tommy—don't leave me. Ever!"

"Never. In a little while the mayor and I don't know who all will be here for the wedding dinner. After your very slight wedding breakfast, I should think you would want something to eat. We'll have pheasants and...and hummingbird tongues—"

He scooped her up and carried her around the room and pretended to throw her out of the window.

And so the hours fled, as vanishes a song.

And it was four o'clock in the morning with the summer day heralded by a false dawn. Beside her Tommy slept quietly, hair tousled, one arm flung across her. A bird began to chirp himself into groggy wakefulness and somewhere in the direction of the river a boat whistled throatily. A clock was running in the room. Running loudly. She could just see its glowing face and knew that it was four. She had just four hours left. Four hours.

And she could not trust herself. She had to run away. But she could not trust herself not to afterward come back. And everything she had been given would be taken away except the memory.

The memory!

She knew now that a memory was not enough. A memory would be pain she could not bear. She would read of his plays. And hear of his continued fame. And she—she would not be able to come near him—and she would not be able to stay away. She would come back and he would not believe her. He would turn her forth and she would see a look upon his face—

She shivered.

She knew suddenly what she had to do and so she shivered.

With gentle slowness, she removed his arm and crept from the bed. He stirred and seemed about to wake and then quieted. She bent and kissed his cheek and a small bright tear glowed there in the cold false dawn. He stirred again and muttered her name in his sleep. A frown passed over his brow and then again he was still.

She drew her robe about her and tiptoed out into the anteroom where she quickly dressed. She commanded pen and ink:

My Darling:

This has all been a dream and I am grateful. You must not think of me again for I am not worth the thought. I knew I could not be with you past this dawn and yet I allowed your love for me to grow. Darling, try to forgive me. I go into nothingness. Do not think of me as unfaithful for I shall be faithful. But I was given forty-eight hours of freedom and now— By the time you read this I shall be dead. Do not search for me. It cannot be otherwise. I am grateful to you. I love you.

Meredith

At six, Tommy Crandall woke with a terrified start. He did not know what had happened but he seemed to hear a far-off voice cry to him. Meredith was gone. He flung back the covers and leaped up to search madly for her. A valet looked strangely at him.

"Mrs. Crandall left here two hours ago, sir. She went in a taxi. She said she had left you a note— Here it is, sir."

Tommy read the note and then, trembling, read it through again. He walked in a small circle in the middle of the room and then suddenly understood. Wildly he snatched at his clothes and got them on.

"Get the car!" he roared at the valet. "Oh, my god, get the car! I'll find her. I have to find her!"

He did not bother to go to the Astor, for there was an urgency in the note which directed his steps immediately to the police.

And he found a sleepy sergeant at the morgue who yawned as he said, "You can look but we ain't got nothing like that in here. Two firemen that burned up on a ship and a couple of accident cases come in about dawn. But we ain't got no beautiful woman. No, sir, it ain't very often you see a beautiful woman down here. When they're beautiful they don't let themselves—"

Tommy flung away and then turned. "How do I find a medical examiner?"

"That's a thought," yawned the sergeant. "Call headquarters and they'll give you the duty desk."

It was eight o'clock before Tommy found the medical examiner who knew. The man was still perturbed and perplexed, for he was not at ease about things. He was a small, nervous politician's heel dog.

He ran a finger under his collar as he gazed at the overwrought young man who stood in the doorway. "Well, I thought it was irregular. But it was my duty and there was no sign of foul play. And so I took the death certificate and signed it—"

Tommy turned pale. "Then...then she is dead."

"Why, yes. A funny thing," said the coroner uncomfortably. "But she came and got me and said to come along and, of course, a beautiful woman that way and looking rich, I went along. And we came to this undertaking parlor and went in and she said she had two hundred and twenty dollars of her own money. She was very particular about its being her own money and she—"

"Are you sure she is dead?"

"Why, yes, I say, she made the arrangements on the condition that she would be buried right away without a notice sent out or anything and paid spot cash and then—well, she dropped dead."

"How do you know?"

"Brother, when they're dead, they're dead. My stethoscope doesn't lie. And no sign of foul play or poison whatever. And, well, I took my pen in hand and signed. She didn't want an autopsy because she said she couldn't stand being cut up, and she didn't want to be embalmed. So they just took her and buried—"

"What funeral parlor?" demanded Tommy savagely.

"I'll give you the address," said the examiner. And he did.

The professional manner of the undertaker Tommy dashed aside. "A lady by the name of Meredith Smith Crandall was here this morning."

"Why, yes," said the sad gentleman. "Yes, that is true." He looked upset. "Is there anything wrong?"

"No. Nothing wrong—no trouble for you, I mean. What happened?"

"Why, she came in and paid for a funeral on the condition that she would be buried right away and so we buried her, of course. She paid cash, double price on our cheapest funeral. She insisted it was her own money. I don't know why. The thing is very regular. We have a certificate—"

"Take me to the cemetery!" cried Tommy in anguish.

"Certainly," said the undertaker respectfully. "But she has been legally buried and an exhumation order—"

"Take me there!"

They drove between the gateposts of Woodpine and it was twenty minutes of ten. The undertaker pointed to the grave where the turf was still raw. A workman was starting to clear away to put sod on the place and another was hauling away spare dirt.

The undertaker looked at Tommy with amazement. The workmen stared. Tommy immediately seized a spade and began to throw back the earth. When they attempted to stop him he struck at them with the implement and kept on digging. And then, because his very savageness had cowed them, they helped him lift the cheap, sealed coffin from the earth. Tommy knocked off the lid with the spade.

A little old lady lay there, clad in decent if ragged garments, her fine gray hair a halo above the delicate oval of her face. But she was not lying with crossed arms. And she had not died with a smile. She had been so tiny that she had been able to turn over in her coffin and now she lay, with a bruised and bloodied face and torn hands, huddled on her side, and her expression did not indicate that she had died in peace.

It was ten o'clock.

The workmen suddenly drew away from Tommy. The undertaker gasped and involuntarily crossed himself. For the man who clutched the body to him and wept was no longer young. He was an old man of more than sixty now where he had been young before, and the good garments he had worn had become carefully kept but threadbare tweed. What hair he had now was gray. And the tears which coursed down his cheeks made their way through furrows put there by loneliness and privation.

You see, Georgie had made two calls the day before.

Catching My Death

written by
J. L. George

illustrated by
KAITLYN GOLDBERG

ABOUT THE AUTHOR

J. L. George lives in Cardiff, Wales, and writes weird and speculative fiction. J. L. is a 2019 Literature Wales bursary recipient and is currently working on a near-future dystopian novel. She was recently a winner of the New Welsh Writing Awards for her novelette "The Word." In her other lives, she's a library-monkey and an academic interested in literature and science and the Gothic. She's also quite fond of baking cakes, though not as fond as she is of eating them.

ABOUT THE ILLUSTRATOR

Kaitlyn Goldberg was born in 2002 in Ann Arbor, Michigan. Katie is an illustrator whose love for visual storytelling started when she was just a toddler. Using a Magna Doodle, she captured emotion and movement even with her early attempts at drawing characters.

Over the years, her interests grew more serious and her skills improved with a dedication to art classes at high school and at the Kendall College of Art and Design in Grand Rapids, Michigan.

Her talent for capturing the essence of a story grew from daily practice and tools like Adobe Creative Cloud and a Cintiq drawing tablet.

Katie's favorite illustrations include fantasy characters, especially girls in scenes that include a touch of magic.

Catching My Death

Jacob caught his death yesterday.

I watched him carry it back to town from the top of the hospital steps. It looked like a good one: quiet, a soft, dark-grey thing nestled like a kitten in the crook of his arm.

There weren't a lot of spectators. Tuesday morning and a few idling shoppers wandered out onto the street to rubberneck, but no crowd. I'd been watching hospital visitors trickle in and out of the car park, toying with a cigarette as I waited for the nurse to finish setting up Mum's chemo infusion. But when I saw the bright red flag of Jacob's jacket I jumped up. He'd been out in the forest since last Friday night and we'd begun to wonder if he'd be one of the ones who didn't come home. It hadn't happened to anyone I knew, but you saw the photographs on the news sometimes.

Jacob met my eye and he raised one hand in greeting as he passed—certain, already, that his death would stay where he put it. I white-knuckled the railing as the door opened behind me.

Mum's death trotted at her heels. Keeping a respectful distance for now, but alert and ready. She ignored it and fiddled with the IV in her arm.

"Don't," I said, snapping into dutiful daughter mode. "The ward sister'll tell you off again."

She snorted. The faint lines beside her eyes looked deeper today, or maybe that was just the sunlight. "You'll need to go out to the woods soon," she told me and stole my cigarette. "You're almost eighteen, Ash. You can't keep on without one forever.

You won't be able to get a mortgage. Car insurance. Nobody'll want to date you."

"I *know*," I said and shrugged her twig-light hand off my shoulder. I looked back at Jacob and his bright, carefree smile and for a brief, startling moment, I hated him.

His parents had planned a party. Tomorrow morning he'd stumble hung over down to the courthouse to get his death certified, but tonight he could drink and laugh and tell loud stories about how he'd finally caught it, rolling around in the soft cloud of his relief.

Heather knocked at my door an hour after we'd returned from the hospital. Mum was sleeping upstairs. I sat in the living room and tried to watch TV and kept looking out at the road to the forest instead. It bent sharply out of sight behind the houses, but if you followed it back through town, past the hospital, you'd see it peter out into a dirt track and then just a path between the dark conifers, needles crunching beneath your feet. Then you'd start listening out for deaths.

"You hear about Jacob?" Heather asked me, chewing her lip. It was a nervous habit; she always had scabs. She didn't have her death yet, either. Her parents were the opposite of Mum, finding some reason to put it off each time she suggested going out to the forest. When we were small, we'd decided to go together when the time came. We'd even played at it, making our Barbies sneak through bed-sheet forests and leap at the stuffed animals we'd pressed into service as deaths. The older we'd got, the less fun the game had seemed and eventually we'd given it up.

"People are going to start talking about us," I said. "We're the only ones in our year group without our deaths."

Heather nodded and looked miserably down at her sneakers. "It makes me feel like a little kid. Or—"

She went quiet, but I felt sure both of us were picturing the same thing. The Deathless enclave down by the railway tracks in the bad part of town, a patchwork of tents and makeshift shelters. Heather and I had wandered into it by mistake once, attempting a shortcut home, and a woman who sat repairing her shoes at the side of the road had scowled up at us. I'd stared, horrified by the dirty hollow where her teeth should have been, until she snapped at me to mind my own business.

Later, Mum had told me off for wandering—and then for staring. The poor woman probably hadn't seen a dentist in a decade, she'd said. That was the sort of thing that happened when you were Deathless.

I took a breath. "You know what?" I told Heather. "We should go now. Before the party."

Heather's eyes went wide. "My mum and dad would never—"

"I know. That's why we don't tell anyone. We just—go." Saying it aloud turned the idea solid. Mum would be relieved that I'd sorted it out myself. One less thing for her to worry about. There were pins in her sewing kit we could use for imprinting; she'd never notice they were gone. The walk to the forest was short; we were lucky we didn't live in one of those places where you had to hike for hours. We could put on our sturdy shoes, pack sandwiches and fill our water bottles and be there in less than an hour. "Right now, no hesitating."

It took a moment for Heather to answer me, but she bit her lip and nodded again. "Right now."

I started out walking fast, Heather trailing half a step behind, but as we neared the forest, I felt myself slow. Now it was Heather who nudged me on, glancing behind her as though fearful her dad would materialise out of nowhere to stop her. Every time she told them she needed to go to the forest soon, they'd squeeze her hand and agree and tell that it wouldn't be long now; but every time, they'd find an excuse, a reason for her to wait. Her father's mouth would tighten with fear and he'd hang onto Heather's hand a moment longer than normal. Heather's Auntie Jean, his sister, had had a bad death and been hit by a drunk driver on a zebra crossing in the middle of the afternoon. She'd been twenty-five.

It was afternoon now and Heather's parents would be in work.

I understood her nerves, though, my hand going involuntarily to the needle case in my coat pocket.

"Come on," she said. "We're almost there."

I swallowed air and raised my eyes to where the first trees reared up above us, black and spindly, even their lowest branches six feet above our heads. "Yeah," I managed. "Almost there."

We climbed over the stile, leaf mulch squelching beneath our shoes as we landed, and then we were on the forest path. A neat bundle of long-handled nets—like the ones little kids use for rock-pooling, only bigger—leaned up against the gate. My fingers shook a little as I reached for one. The varnish on the wooden handle was peeling and it was rough in my hands. I breathed in the wet, brown smell of the forest and imagined I caught a whiff of something else, too. Musty, like the interior of an old church. Death.

Heather touched my shoulder and I shook myself. "I'm okay."

There was no smell to death: everybody knew that. Your death was your own, unique, and smelled and felt only like itself. I took a steadying breath and we walked. The forest muffled everything, the damp carpet of pine needles killing the sound of our footsteps, the branches filtering out the late-afternoon sunshine. Down here it was cool. Almost pleasant, if you didn't think about where you were.

Long moments passed before I saw the first death. I almost missed it, the smoky black of its fur disappearing into the shadows between the trees. It was a good one, small and calm, watching us with curious, yellow-green eyes from the lowest branch of a tree.

"Look," I whispered and nudged Heather with my shoulder. "There's one!"

She glanced up, wide-eyed.

Then she was jumping for it, net flailing in the air. The death gave a high-pitched squeak and bounded away, springing from one branch to another until it had vanished into the forest canopy.

"Nice one," I said. "Be *quiet*."

Chastened, Heather trudged back to the path, falling into line, eyes downcast.

That was the last one for a few minutes. Perhaps it was a bad day for them. Or Heather had scared the lot of them off. We should head back to town, I thought, and come back another day.

Something scurried across the path near my feet and I sucked in a breath and stepped back. It was another death, a big one with a mouthful of sharp teeth. It didn't bother to dodge out of the way of our feet. I didn't need to warn Heather this time; we both held as still as we could until it disappeared between the trees.

They multiplied around us after that. In the undergrowth and in the trees; big ones and small ones, placid ones and ones that snorted and snuffled and slavered, hungry to be found. The forest was alive with deaths. They were its heartbeat and its breathing, its air and its flesh.

The sullen expression faded from Heather's face. She raised her eyes, scanning the trees around us for opportunity. I took a breath and did the same.

"There's one!" Heather gasped—and with that she went crashing off into the trees, net raised, and disappeared from view.

I was on my own now.

Well, I wasn't going to go charging around like a coked-up rhinoceros and scare all the good ones off. I tucked myself in against a tree trunk close to the path, net clutched tight in a clammy hand, and did my best to keep my breathing steady.

It took me a few moments to spot my prey. There. On the forest floor, a little way into the trees. A small death with a coat of pink-tinged grey, sniffing at a patch of dock leaves. It didn't seem to have heard me, distracted by whatever it had scented, and I held my breath. As I watched, it raised one delicate paw and licked at it, washing itself like a cat.

I crept closer, net at the ready, careful where I put my feet. Something cracked beneath the sole of my boot and I froze as the little death raised its head and scented the air. Don't run, I pleaded silently. Don't run.

KAITLYN GOLDBERG

Miraculously, it didn't. I took another step, and another, and raised my net ready to pounce.

A distant crash. "Shit, my leg!" Heather's voice, a strangled cry. "I think I'm stuck!"

My small death raised its head, looked at me with wide startled eyes and bounded off into the undergrowth before I had time to move. I swore under my breath and was petty enough to hesitate a moment before I headed in Heather's direction.

She lay sprawled on the ground, net discarded beside her, one leg pinned beneath a fallen branch. I glanced up and saw the pale-green scar on the tree trunk where it had broken off. "What the hell happened?" I asked, bending to try and lift the limb off Heather.

She had the grace to look embarrassed. "There was one up there," she said. "A nice little death. The branch was hanging off already, but I didn't think it was ready to go. I was trying to get the death and I caught the branch with my net and then—" She spread her hands.

I sighed. "You have *got* to be more careful."

"I know," Heather said miserably. "I know."

I dropped my net and heaved, managing to lift the end of the branch and pull it to the side. Heather pulled her injured leg in close to her body.

"Let me have a look at that." I crouched and she tugged up the bottom of her trouser leg, rolling her ankle and wincing.

I prodded at the tender skin, probably not as gently as I should have. Heather hissed. "Watch it!"

I ignored her. "Doesn't feel like it's broken," I said. "Might be sprained, though. Here, see if you can stand up on it."

But Heather wasn't looking at me anymore. Her eyes were fixed, aghast, on something over my shoulder. I went still.

"What?" I asked, my voice dropping to a whisper without my permission. "What are you looking at?"

"I..." Heather said, her gaze falling. She couldn't look me in the eyes. "Oh, Ash, I'm so sorry."

It was in her face, in the way her voice wavered on *sorry*. My throat tightened and for a moment I couldn't move. If I didn't look, perhaps it wouldn't be true.

There was a violent rustling of leaves behind me. A thud like some rabid creature flinging itself at a door, desperate to get in. And a smell, dank and muddy and faintly sour, like when they'd dredged the canal in the spring.

The death was bigger than the one that had crept across the path in front of us earlier. Bigger than any I'd seen outside the hospital. There was a damp, unhealthy look to its dark coat, like something unearthed from under a rock on the forest floor and its mouth was wide and hungry. It thrashed in the net and bared its needle-sharp teeth and only calmed when I bent to examine it. Then it eyed me greedily, a small, crooning noise issuing from its throat. It sounded like it was beckoning me.

How had it even got in there? I'd only had my back turned for a few minutes—but I'd been focused on Heather and that had been long enough. Stupid, stupid, stupid.

I tore at the net. My hands shook and the fibres refused to break. The death was tangled up tight in my net, one hind leg trapped in the mesh, the fibres digging deep into its skin. When I gave an experimental tug at the net, it lunged at me with teeth bared and I snatched my hand out of the way just in time. There was no way I was getting it out. My head started to ache, quick hard throbs of panic behind my eyes.

Maybe I could run. Leave the net and the death here and hide at home while I figured out what to do. It hadn't imprinted on me yet. Nobody needed to know it had been mine.

Except Heather. Heather, who couldn't move. I took a step away from her and the net, glancing at the path, and heard her sharp gasp. The death began to struggle again.

"You can't carry me," said Heather. "Ash, please, I can't get up. You've got to get help."

It would be dark in a few hours. And the forest at night was home to things worse than deaths. I'd heard the stories of what roamed there. Heartbreaks and cruelties and despondencies; things that warped a person, left some part of their consciousness forever wandering the night-woods like a ghost.

Heather sniffled. I closed my eyes in despair and nodded.

When I returned an hour later, with Heather's dad and two paramedics, Heather was still sitting on the ground. My net was where I'd left it, the big, sharp-toothed death still tangled up, grumbling at intervals.

Heather cradled something against her chest. A death, medium-sized and docile, butting its head against the underside of her chin. A decent death. A normal one.

Her dad let out a sigh of relief and went to her side while the paramedics unrolled the stretcher and inspected her ankle. I eyed the death in my net and got no closer than I had to.

Heather's dad clapped me on the shoulder before they left. "You girls shouldn't have come out here without telling anyone," he said. "But thanks for coming to get me." Heather hadn't spilled that it was my idea to come out here in the first place, then. He glanced at the net. "Sorry about—that," he said, and gave me one more squeeze on the shoulder and then let go.

That would be how things went from now on. I could see it. Pitying looks and touches that lingered no longer than necessary, fearful that my bad luck might be catching. University interviewers would enquire whether I really believed I'd be able to complete the course and I could forget about Ellie Chong coming to the end-of-term dance with me. Nobody wanted a date with a timer ticking above her head.

Heather, her dad, and the paramedics disappeared around a curve in the path. I took a few reluctant steps toward the net and stood over it, staring the death in its bright, hungry eyes.

This would be a good time to imprint. If you caught a good death, you wanted to bind it to you right away, before you got out of the forest.

If you didn't—well. If you were alone and no one had seen you, you might, I supposed, try to get rid of it. Free the bad death from your net and kick it until it ran loose, then return to town empty-handed. No other death would go near you or your net until you'd gone home and scrubbed off the scent of the bad one, but you could always come back and try again later.

But Heather and her dad had seen it. The paramedics hadn't got close enough to inspect it, but they could hardly have missed its noises. They had to know I'd caught a death. I couldn't go back to the hospital without it. If I did, and one of them reported me, I'd go down on record as a cheat, one who'd tried to subvert the natural order. And then the courthouse might not accept any other death I caught. I could even end up Deathless.

A chill had touched the air now and my fingers were clumsy with the cold. I almost dropped the needle case, and when I finally pulled out a single pin and held the point to my fingertip, my hands wouldn't stop shaking.

The death looked up curiously, waiting. A single drop of blood was all it took. Then it would be mine for life. Or I would be its.

I sighed and put the needle away. I wouldn't be able to keep the death out of sight once it had imprinted. Mum would worry and she didn't need any of that right now. I'd put it off a while. Only a day or two, I told myself. It couldn't make things any worse.

It was a long trudge back home. I walked fast and kept to the backstreets, the death bundled up under my coat, its warm bulk nestling against my torso as if it belonged there. Mercifully, it was quieter when I kept it close.

I took a left toward home, though first I'd have to pass the posh houses on Oak Avenue and Birch Way, big detached affairs with gleaming conservatories and manicured hedges.

This part I didn't mind so much; the streets were near empty, the gardens equipped with sensor lights that turned on at a footstep, and anyone who saw me walking fast with my head down would probably cross the road to avoid me.

Almost at the end of Oak, I heard noise. Music and laughter, lights in someone's garden and a whiff of barbecue. Jacob's parents' house.

The party had slipped my mind. I'd been invited. Jacob would probably ask me on Monday where I'd been, and then I'd have to recount the whole story and see the pity in his eyes as he cradled his good death in the crook of his arm.

I crept closer and peered through a gap in the hedge. The garden was full of people, thirty or forty of them—kids from school and Jacob's parents and their friends—gearing up for a long night's drinking. I heard Jacob's laugh through the hedge, loud with relief and unaccustomed alcohol, and wedged myself farther into the greenery to get a look. The death gave a protesting wriggle beneath my coat and I held it tightly.

Then I stopped and stared. Jacob didn't have *his* death with him. That meant it hadn't imprinted yet.

But then, Jacob's parents were rich and proper, the kind to do everything by the book. They'd probably told him not to rush it, out alone in the woods. They'd get it witnessed first thing in the morning, I expected. Risky to wait, but then again, maybe not, around here. It was all Neighbourhood Watch and security systems and no need to guard your precious things too closely. No need to worry about a good death being snatched away before you'd bound it to you for good.

There was a gap in the hedge behind the speakers, big enough to fit through. And I'd been invited.

It was unusual for a death to turn once it had been caught. It happened once or twice in a generation around here. A good, small death caught in the forest changing overnight, swelling into something hungry and malign. Unusual, but not unheard of.

The thought froze me, an alien interloper in my mind. To steal someone's death was the worst sort of crime. Impossible, almost. Unthinkable. Surely I didn't have it in me to do something like that.

I thought of Mum, then. She'd probably be lying awake, wondering where I was. The chemotherapy always knocked her for six, and once she'd slept off the worst of it, she'd wake in an anxious sweat. When I came home with a bad death—

I slipped through the hedge.

Behind the speakers, I gathered myself; shrugged off my coat and bundled it and the death, under my arm. Then I made for the house.

Jacob raised his arm to greet me, just when I thought I was clear—but all he said was, "Hey! Didn't think you were gonna make it." He was grinning widely, already a little drunk. He hadn't noticed the death bundled in my coat.

I returned his smile, though weakly, and let slip as little of the truth as I reasonably could. "Heather's hurt herself," I told him. "We were out for a walk and she, uh, she tried to climb a tree and fell on her ankle."

Jacob made a sympathetic face. "That sucks. She won't get to play in the match on Friday."

"Yeah," I said. "Poor Heather." An awkward pause. "I'm going to drop off my coat. Is there a . . . a bedroom or something?"

"You can dump it in the spare room. Upstairs, second left. Then get yourself a drink!"

The house was quiet. Conversation and light spilled from the kitchen. Laughter, bottles clinking. I trod carefully on the stairs, the death clutched tight against my chest, and didn't open the second left door.

The door before it was the bathroom, which meant Jacob's room had to be either the one on the right, or down at the end of the corridor.

I opened the first door and looked inside. The room was unlit and I peered around slowly, waiting for my eyes to get used to the dark.

Gradually, the outlines of furniture and scattered possessions came into focus. A bed, a desk piled with books, a widescreen TV. Pictures tacked to the walls—a couple of band posters, a map of the world, a bikini girl and a shirtless guy baring identical, toothy smiles. This had to be Jacob's room. But I couldn't see his death. Maybe he'd already imprinted on it after all and I'd just caught him at a rare moment without it. Or maybe it was elsewhere in the house, locked safely in his parents' office.

Something moved, then, in the shadows. Under the desk.

I held my breath, crouched, crept forward like I was approaching a wild animal. Which, in a way, I guessed I was.

The death beneath my coat squirmed harder, perhaps sensing the presence of another of its kind. Imprinted deaths were docile in public, showing no more than passing interest in one another, but those in the forest were different. These might be, too.

A wire cage sat under the desk. My heart sank—but, as I crept closer, I realised there was no padlock on the cage door, just a simple catch, easily opened from the outside. How could Jacob's family be so stupidly trusting?

But then, they lived in the nice part of town. Their house and garden were well-secured against intruders. And they'd invited nobody here tonight but friends.

I was a friend, wasn't I?

Jacob had never been anything but kind to me. He'd never made fun of my worn trainers, or Mum's geriatric car, the way some of the well-off kids did. It wasn't his fault he had a good death and I had a bad one. It was just blind luck, nothing more.

Some people always seemed to get lucky. People said there was nothing you could do to change your death. The one you ended up with was the one you'd always been meant to have and that was that. It didn't stop some from trying, though. If your parents could afford it, they'd pay for you to have private instruction on how to catch your death, not just the bare-bones lessons we got in school. And somehow, it always did seem to be the rich kids who made it home with the smallest, quietest deaths.

It was people like Mum who watched their lives begin to dwindle in their fifties, each round of chemo costing a little more and offering a little less hope. And now she wouldn't even be able to reassure herself with the knowledge that I'd be fine after she was gone.

I'd always been Jacob's friend. But I was a daughter, too. And I was a person, my life suddenly cut off at the knees. My death shifted against my side and I saw the abyss yawning beneath my feet. I wanted to scream, helplessly, like a toddler. What about me? It's not fair!

But I wasn't helpless. Not completely.

Guilt made my insides clench. I hesitated, listening for footsteps on the stairs. Outside, I heard Jacob laughing. Somebody turned up the music.

I opened the cage.

Jacob's death came out easily enough, accepting my clumsy attempt to scoop it into the crook of my arm. I set it down carefully on the bed. "Stay," I warned it.

It did as it was told. My death, though—that was another matter.

No, not my death—the death from the forest, the bad death. It squirmed and thrashed in my hands and made a gargling noise like an angry plughole.

"Shh!" I hissed. It snapped at me in return and I narrowly missed losing a fingertip.

I thrust it into the cage and closed the latch, leaving it to grumble and stare balefully at me through the wire.

The good, quiet death on Jacob's bed watched me, calmly inquisitive. I fumbled in my pocket. This time my hands weren't shaking.

I drove the pin into the pad of my forefinger. The good death sniffed. I held my breath. Its little pink tongue emerged, flickered, testing the air. Then it darted forward and licked the bead of blood from the tip of my finger.

Its tongue was rough and cool. Then it was gone and I looked my death in the eyes.

There was no cataclysm, no melding of minds. There was only the sensation of something slotting into its right place—and then a flood of relief. I tucked the death under my arm and it settled in there as though it had been mine all along.

"I'm sorry," I said—to Jacob, or to his death, or to the room at large. The door closed softly behind me and the noise of the party downstairs covered my footsteps as I left.

Deaths didn't turn often—but when they did, it was nasty.

Jacob was one of the unlucky ones. That was what people started to say, the morning after the party. I'd missed the moment when he went up to the bedroom and returned with wide-eyed terror on his face. Mum had texted me, I explained, when people asked. She'd been feeling ill and I needed to go home and administer her antisickness meds.

I made sympathetic noises down the phone and two days later went out into the forest and returned with my good, docile little death already imprinted. It slept on my shoulder or at my feet and never gave a hint that it didn't belong with me.

I didn't realise how worried Mum had been until I saw how relieved she was. She hugged me at the kitchen table and said, "You'll definitely get a student loan now. Maybe even a permanent job one day!" Then she started to cough and had to sit down, but she was still smiling.

Walking to college the next day, I found Jacob smoking on the grass around back of the art department, the bad death circling his ankles like a hungry cat. I smoked out here most days, but I'd never seen Jacob with a cigarette before. He sucked in a lungful of smoke and then sputtered angrily, his eyes watering.

His whole face looked red and watery, come to think of it. It occurred to me that he'd been crying and then that I ought to walk away.

He waved before I could. I dawdled over, the side where I held my death cradled against my body, angled away from him.

I needn't have bothered. Jacob didn't really study my death, just scuffed his toe morosely in the dirt and then pulled it back when it got too close to his death. "Had an email this morning," he said. "Durham's rescinded my offer. Bristol too."

His first choices for uni. His parents could have afforded either, easily. But the worse your death, the less chance you had of getting a half-decent job. No point training somebody up if they were only going to be around a couple of years. And no university wanted its graduate employment statistics skewed by early deaths.

"Shit," I said. "I'm sorry."

Jacob shook his head. "I must've missed something. There must've been a sign it was gonna turn. But I was so—so *sure* everything would work out, you know? What an idiot."

"I'm sorry," I said again. Jacob scowled, flicked the butt of his cigarette away onto the grass and didn't answer.

That was the last time I saw him, as it turned out. I came down with a bout of the flu (nothing to worry about, the doctor reassured me, with a relieved glance at my death) and by the time I got back to classes, Jacob had dropped out.

I stopped seeing him around town. His friends came into the café where I worked on Saturdays a few times, but Jacob wasn't with them.

The next time I saw his face was on the local news, five years later. His parents had done their damnedest to protect him, given him an allowance so he wouldn't have to take one of the factory jobs that were about the best you could get with a death like that. Industrial accidents were a hell of a killer among those with bad deaths.

And it had happened anyway, a late-night fall from a railway platform. He'd been planning to take his driving test back in college, but no insurance company would risk you with a death like that.

Heather texted me and told me to turn on the TV. No other comment.

She knew what I'd done, of course. How could she not have figured it out? But she also knew it had been partly because of her and she'd never told. Nor had her dad.

I chain-smoked through the news item. It ended with Jacob's mother in tears, saying she was going to campaign for greater safety awareness on railway stations. A few months later, the yellow lines on the platform were repainted two feet farther from the edge and a crop of garish warning signs bearing words like *Stop!* and *Think!* and *Safe!* appeared around the station.

People shrugged and walked past them. Health and safety wouldn't have saved Jacob. We all knew that.

It wasn't going to save Mum, either. She was back in the hospital, the latest period of remission ended. Her death padded in restless rings around the bed, quieting a little less after every session of chemo, and I seemed to do nothing but shuttle between the house and the ward, afraid each time I pulled up in the hospital car park that this visit would be my last.

I didn't have time to worry about Jacob, so I put it from my mind and looked away from the posters whenever I passed the station.

It had been a small news item, local. I hadn't expected to see Jacob's picture on the news again, even if I saw it before my mind's eye most nights.

But there it was again two years later, next to the photograph of a smiling blonde girl who'd contracted MRSA in a hospital ward—neglected, it was suggested, by overstretched cleaners who'd noticed all the patients had bad deaths anyway.

And again a year after that. This time it was followed by a debate on a late-night news programme and I hadn't been much of a sleeper since Mum died, so I sat up and watched it. A dark-skinned woman with a whopping, salivating death sat on one side of the studio, talking with barely suppressed rage about how the whole system was unfair, it needed to be overhauled and what was so important about catching your death anyway? What was wrong with not knowing? Opposite her, a besuited man, whose small death sat silently on his shoulder, smiled and nodded and then mildly pointed out that without our deaths, without knowing when we'd die, the whole system would collapse.

We might as well, he pointed out, all move to the Deathless enclave and live without jobs or secure housing or medical insurance.

The woman with the hungry-looking death opened her mouth to retort, but the presenter cut in. "Thanks, Amanda. Thank you, Nick. That's all we've got time for tonight. Now, sport, and Manchester City—"

The segment ended, the woman with the bad death closing her eyes and rubbing at her forehead.

It wasn't the last, though. She appeared again and others like her. And when, eventually, her photograph appeared on the news—national, this time—alongside Jacob's and the blonde girl's, people marched with placards in the streets. I had to pause my TV and study the screen to be sure of what I was seeing. Some of the marchers in the crowd had no deaths.

I called Heather. "Are you seeing this?"

"Yeah. Yeah, I'm seeing it." She paused. "You know, I've been reading up online about this. These new—Deathless activists, I guess."

"And?"

"Well—some of them have always been Deathless. They're like the people in the slums. But some of them? Apparently, they've found a way to get rid of their deaths."

"Get rid of their deaths?" I repeated, stupidly. "How would that even work?"

"I dunno. Like I said, it's just stuff I've seen online. Rumours." Heather sounded thoughtful now. "But yeah, it's interesting, right?"

I frowned. "Right."

We started to drift out of touch. Heather joined a local Deathless campaign group, took coach trips to demonstrations every other weekend. Her husband's death was middling like hers and they marched each holding one end of a banner, their deaths scurrying at their ankles.

I worked, doling out career advice to bright-eyed students with calm little deaths like mine and then zoned out in front of the TV, most days. The kids I didn't see—the ones whose deaths meant they'd never get into uni, no matter how many As they got in their exams— Well, those I tried not to think about. I saw other people energised by the new movement, arguing animatedly over lunch in the staffroom, but every time I thought about it, exhaustion weighed me down, lying over my shoulders like a lead blanket.

And then, out of the blue, Heather texted me. *I've done it!* read the message, with a dozen grinning emojis to signify her exultation. It took me a moment to understand what she meant.

What about your job? was what I sent back, eventually. *What about the house? How will you cope?*

The world's changing, Ash, she replied. *You should, too.*

I paused, frowning over the phone as I tried to parse that last sentence.

It might help you get past some things, Heather added, after a moment.

I stared at the text, knowing exactly what she meant, breathing out hard through my nose. Then I deleted it.

My death was waking up.

It had been years since I'd last spoken to Heather. *The world's changing. You should, too.*

Those last words stuck with me sometimes. Like when I sat in a café with potted succulents and industrial décor in the gentrified streets of what had once been the Deathless enclave. When I saw young, idealistic people on the news, talking about their decisions not to catch their deaths. ("It'll find me anyway. Why spend my whole life worrying about it?") When I walked through the corridors of the hospital and saw hopeful, Deathless faces in the waiting rooms, holding hands with their loved ones and dreaming up futures instead of studying their deaths, calculating how long they had left.

Mine scampered behind me down the corridor, close to my feet in their hospital-issue slippers. A small child gawked openly at me as I passed. His mother grabbed his hand, whispering an admonishment, and I hobbled back to my room.

The nurse on duty—perky, bright-eyed and Deathless— appeared to administer pills and take my blood pressure. She didn't leave when she was done, but fussed around smoothing down the covers and glancing at me from the corner of her eye. My death kneaded my chest like a cat trying to get comfortable.

Eventually I pushed it off and sat up with an irritable sigh. "What is it?"

The nurse sidled closer to the bed, lowering her voice.

"There are—things that can be done, you know." She inclined her head toward my death, as though afraid it would hear her. "There are still people who deal with that sort of thing, even if there's less call for it these days."

She slipped something out of her pocket and left it on the nightstand. A business card. Email address and phone number. *Deaths removed.* A neat euphemism. I'd heard the process was a lot messier than it sounded.

Then I remembered Heather's joy. The row of grinning emojis—hopelessly dated now, but as clear an expression of freedom and relief as I'd ever seen.

I turned the card between my fingers. My death settled down beside my feet, watching.

I kept the card with me all night and the next day too. Once, I even picked up my phone and dialled half the number.

Then I caught sight of my reflection in the screen, liver-spotted and wizened, with white hair thinning around the temples. I'd had a good life. It was written on my face.

My death bared its teeth; stretched its jaw like a python contemplating dinner.

It had cost, this good life. What would Jacob have looked like now, I wondered? Would he have had white hair, a face as hollow and cadaverous as my own? Or would he have looked younger than his years, unburdened by guilt?

My death looked different now, I thought. Not so calm, not so sleepy. It was bigger. So were its teeth. Its coat had darkened, its eyes brightened, everything turned that little bit more intense. It looked, I thought, just like the death that had blundered into my net that day in the forest.

There came a twinge in my chest. This was always how it started. But this time my death uncurled from where it lay beside my feet, eyes fixed upon my face.

There was a button somewhere, to call the nurse, but I couldn't remember where and I couldn't make myself look for it.

The card was still in my hand, the phone still in front of me. I could call now, tell the guy to hurry. There might be time.

I blinked. My reflection in the screen began to blur. For a moment I saw myself young again, the way I'd looked the day we headed out to the forest.

I saw the blonde girl and the dark-skinned woman from the TV. The Deathless woman in the slum, with her toothless scowl. Heather.

Jacob.

The phone slipped from my hand. I looked once more at the card the nurse had given me and let it drop.

The mattress dipped under the weight of my death. Its eyes shone, fixed on my face, and I could feel the low rumble of its breathing. It had waited at my feet for so long, patient as a faithful dog, but there was no more waiting to be done.

Slowly, carefully, one paw at a time, it made its way up the bed.

A Prize in Every Box

written by
F. J. Bergmann

illustrated by
BEN HILL

ABOUT THE AUTHOR

F. J. Bergmann edits poetry for Mobius: The Journal of Social Change *(mobiusmagazine.com), is the former editor of* Star*Line, *the journal of the Science Fiction & Fantasy Poetry Association (sfpoetry.com), and imagines tragedies on or near exoplanets. She has competed at National Poetry Slam as a member of the Urban Spoken Word team. Her work appears irregularly in speculative markets that don't pay enough to be pro, and literary journals that should have known better.*

A Catalogue of the Further Suns, a collection of dystopian first-contact expedition reports, won the 2017 Gold Line Press Poetry Chapbook contest and the 2018 Science Fiction Poetry Association Elgin Chapbook Award. She lives in Madison, Wisconsin, inside a towering library of science fiction, fantasy, and horror novels with her husband Fred and Wiley the cat, her spawn within bicycling distance. She works as a freelance book designer and copy editor for several horror and literary presses.

ABOUT THE ILLUSTRATOR

Born in 1996, Ben did not start pursuing art seriously until he was eighteen. Without any local schools or classes, he chose to be a self-taught digital and traditional artist.

Now living in rural Florida on the space coast, over the last three years he has focused on studying with online resources and taking SmArt School mentorships.

Inspired by artists like Alphonse Mucha and Arthur Rackham, he draws creativity from old fairy tales and art nouveau.

In his work, he has a love for experimenting with movement, texture, and pattern, and he tries to learn something new with every piece.

157

A Prize in Every Box

We begged for the brand-name cereal *as seen on TV*, in aluminum-silver cylindrical boxes lined up on the supermarket shelves like a phalanx of spaceships, with *twice the nutrition of oatmeal*. Hints about the prizes appeared in commercials: wind-up robots, tiny books, toy-store gift certificates, even the keys to a mansion...and other, *special* prizes.

We tried to include cereal as a "basic food group" at breakfast, lunch, dinner, and snack time. When the last speck slid from a box, we would immediately rip open the next and root through its oddly slithering flakes, translucent as shed snakeskin. In less than a week, three boxes had somehow toppled from the top of the fridge to spill on the floor, and Lucy had to throw up right after breakfast twice, until our mother issued an ultimatum.

The only reason our mother kept buying it at first was that most of the "prizes" were coupons for 50% off another box of cereal. The nutritional information on the side of the boxes was phrased in an unusually convincing manner, however: *120% USRVTOL-recommended levels of aractozone! Results of recent studies published in the Journal of Developmental Confrontation suggest that this compound promotes general rectitude, reticence, and well-formed stools*, and she continued as a loyal customer, fondly watching us for signs of advanced traits.

She took little interest in the prizes, only saying, "If those keys turn up, you let me know right away, hear?" But we didn't think she really believed they existed. *We* believed in all of it;

we were the faithful, the elect. Inside the margins of summer, imagined destinies filled each day with fantastic colors.

The first interesting prize was from the fifth box (the first four had enclosed coupons for more cereal): a small book with a velvety green cover. A flip-book, it showed only a picture of an iridescent bubble rapidly expanding in size as the pages flew past, until the end of the book, when it appeared to burst, and—this was the miraculous part—would spray a fine damp mist from the last page, smelling faintly of brass, like sprinkler fittings.

We kept it a secret until Thomp couldn't bear it another second and tried to tell our mother, but she was busy with something under the sink and said if it wasn't the mansion keys, she would leave it to us. We riffled through it over and over until the binding finally snapped and the pages fell out in stained, dripping wads.

Subsequently, for several placid weeks the toys were exactly what we expected. We got an x-ray stereoscopic viewer that allowed us to look at each others' skeletons (Thomp's right thigh bone had an interesting bluish glow toward the top end), Mrs. Tagliello-next-door's draconian corsets, and the plumbing inside the walls. Other toys were an unbreakable egg that shimmied and wiggled like a Mexican jumping bean, and screamed unpleasant-sounding gibberish in a voice so high-pitched that only Thomp and Russet, our English setter, could hear it, and a framed hologram of a winter landscape where the drifts occasionally moved as we watched.

"All good things must come to an end." My father would say that when it was time to go home from the beach or a picnic. The viewer images faded and went black; the egg became silent and finally disappeared. We were afraid that Russet might have swallowed it, but, in any case, we never saw it again. The framed picture gradually filled completely with snow, and stayed permanently white.

It was only three weeks before school started again. We were arguing about falling back on our ordinary summer games (tearing around in the woods with Russet chasing uncatchable squirrels, and Lucy's determined variations of Extreme Soccer). Thomp occasionally complained that his leg hurt, if he ran for more than a few minutes. And then the latest cereal box produced an object that was not interesting, at first.

It looked like a TV remote, but with no instructions, and no indication of the appliance it was intended to accompany. It had a little screen, and a grid of four buttons, labeled "Zoning Coördination" with the little dots above the second *o* that made it look like an alien language. The buttons said "Intensity," which we figured was for volume, "Reconfigure," "Enhance," and "Delete." The English labels were crudely stuck on below lines of symbols that looked like the swirly decorations at the end of each story in an old book of fairy tales we'd gotten from the library. All the other buttons were yellow, but "Delete" was blue. There were hollow indentations on the underside, which didn't correspond to our fingers but gave a reasonably secure grip, and the device tapered to a point with a knob on the end, sort of like a squat antenna.

We wondered what it was supposed to control. There were no directions on its glistening black case, whose surface gave an impression of endless depth beneath its reflective film. Finally, Lucy tried pointing it at the television while *Restless Hearts* was on, and cautiously pushed "Enhance."

The episode was kind of gross. The woman who convinced the guy who was married to the lady in a coma that he was the father of the baby she pretended was hers suddenly started to stick out of her clothes a lot more, and the guy kissed her and fell on top of her, and then several other people came in and started taking each others' clothes off and fighting at the same time, and then a couple of dogs joined them, and Russet, who had gotten excited when the fight started, began barking really loudly and wouldn't stop. Mother shouted "David! What on *earth* are you kids *doing* to that dog?" and we could hear her hurrying toward the living room.

I whispered "Oh, crap!" and Thomp's eyes got big. Lucy tried pushing the button again, over and over, and the people started moving so fast we couldn't tell what they were doing. The screen on the remote or whatever it was displayed a line of the twisting script, then a giant flashing question mark in blue. As Mother pushed the living room door open, Lucy scrunched up her eyes and stabbed at the blue "Delete" button. On the television, everyone sprang apart, panting, and began refastening their clothes. The dogs slunk out of camera range, and Russet sat down with a sigh.

Of course, we couldn't resist trying it again. This time, at a safe distance from the house. We went through the McDonoughs' woods and out to the edge of the soybean field and debated which button to try first, and on what.

We tried Reconfigure on a small pebble and nothing happened, which was a relief and a letdown at the same time. And then we tried Intensity. "Oh! It's a jewel!" Lucy almost shrieked. It had melted for an instant, then resolidified as a translucent spindle, like a dirty icicle faintly tinged with pink.

"Wow..." Thomp breathed. It was something, all right. I think Lucy still has it.

We used Intensity on a leaf, but that didn't work so well. It skeletonized and turned to black lace. It was pretty; but still, we were dismayed. It disintegrated to black powder when Lucy touched it. We tried Enhance on a toad, which hopped about five feet in one smooth leap, gliding over the tall grass. Before it disappeared, we noticed its stomach was bright green, but we weren't sure whether or not it had been that way before.

Then we Enhanced one of those yellow cabbage butterflies. At first we thought it hadn't changed either, but up close it had tiny glittering patterns on the wings, sort of like Mother's holiday dinner tablecloth, where it looked all white but you could see flowers and leaves in the cloth when the light hit it a certain way. We tried Reconfigure on another butterfly hovering near the ground on its tattered wings and the edges formed again, good as new. Both butterflies circled above our heads for the rest of the afternoon.

"What do you think Enhance would do to Russet?" Lucy asked wistfully. "She's getting kind of old, and she has those bald places from chewing on herself. Maybe it would make her coat nicer."

"But what if it melts her?" Thomp was almost crying.

"When we did Delete on the TV, it undid it. Let's try it on a little animal, and see if we can undo it," I said.

We finally decided to try a squirrel. The Enhanced squirrel had curlier fur, and seemed redder when the light caught it a certain way, and, sure enough, Delete changed it back to what it had been before. Thomp finally said doubtfully, "Well...if we can *undo* it..." And I pointed the device at Russet and pushed Enhance. Her coat did look better, and redder, with a pattern of roundish spots where the hair caught the light differently.

"Oh! I've seen that before, on Sugar, the pony my friend Alice rides in lessons. It's called *dapples*," said Lucy, with an important air.

"There are still a few little bald places," I said. "Do you think we should try Reconfigure?"

Thomp was still worried, but Lucy and I overruled him. "We'll undo it really, really fast if it doesn't work right," I said, "I promise."

Reconfigure made the bald spots disappear completely. It also made Russet more muscular (she leapt, bounced, and barked all the way home) and gave her darker stripes on her flanks and shoulders like the Roberts' Great Dane. Mother didn't notice the stripes until the next day, and by then we had concocted a semi-plausible excuse—a shampoo sample in the mail, the packet thrown away. "Her coat looks so healthy!" Mother exclaimed. "What did you say the shampoo was called?"

BEN HILL

We had vowed not to try the box in the house again, but the next day, it rained. We were playing with Russet inside while Mother was at the grocery store and I tripped, running through the living room, and fell against the TV, and broke it. I knocked it against the wall, and one of the legs snapped off, and worst of all, when we turned it on, there was snow on every channel. We looked at each other. With a shrug, I went to fetch the remote-thing, pointed and clicked Reconfigure, and everything seemed to work fine once more. There had been a bad scratch across the top when Dad bought it at the discount store, but the scratch was gone.

"What will you tell them about the scratch?" Lucy asked.

"I can't think of anything," I admitted. I finally went to the kitchen and got a knife, and carefully gouged the top to match the way it had looked before, as far as I could remember. We rubbed some ketchup and peanut butter into it so it wouldn't look so fresh—and breathed easier when Mother swiped it with the furniture polish the next time she dusted, without comment.

Thomp had started getting tired all the time, and kept wanting to go to bed earlier. At first, Mother was pleased, and said, "You all should be following his example—Thompson is the only one of you who won't have trouble getting up when school starts." But she noticed one morning that he was limping when he tried to run. She asked him what he'd done *this* time, and he kept saying, "Nothing, it just hurts."

She said she didn't like his color, and went to call Dr. Blanchard's office. She came back in with a smile. "They had a cancellation this afternoon! I'll take you right after lunch, Thomp."

He stared at his dark reflection in the oven door. "I look the same color as always," he said dreamily.

Thomp came back relieved. "I didn't have to have any shots at all!" he crowed. "They did exer-rays instead. But I have to go see another doctor on Friday." Mother looked a bit set about the jaw, and after we went to bed she had a hushed, intense conversation with Dad that I couldn't quite hear.

On Friday, Mother had to drive Thomp all the way to Youngstown early in the morning. They didn't get back until late, and Thomp had been crying. Mother cried too, when she thought I wouldn't see.

She and Dad stayed up talking until after midnight. I crept halfway down the stairs, and heard Mother say, "They think the cancer already spread from his femur to his liver. They did a biopsy. If it's malignant, they want to operate right away, and then start chemotherapy."

Fee-mur was the name of the long bone in the leg of our Transparent Human Figure. Lucy and I had spent all of the last winter vacation gluing it carefully together while Thomp watched us, fascinated. I remembered the blue glow on the screen of the viewer, centered at the higher end of Thomp's femur.

Thomp didn't get up for breakfast the next morning, and he put a pillow over his head when I pulled open the underwear drawer, which squeaked. "Let him sleep in, if he wants to," Mother said.

"But won't he have trouble getting up when school starts?" Lucy asked.

"We're not worried about that right now," Mother said austerely. Then her face softened, but we saw her hands trembling as she set our cereal bowls on the table. "Your brother is sicker than we realized. He might not be able to start school right away. Try to make sure he doesn't wear himself out, David. Your father and I are taking him to the clinic again on Monday for more...tests."

Thomp finally came downstairs as Lucy was finishing her cereal. "Do you want some orange juice, Thomp?" she asked.

"I don't want *anything*," he said. He slumped into his chair and started pinging his spoon on the edge of his cereal bowl. For once, Mother didn't tell him to stop. "They used a needle *this* long!" He dropped the spoon and held his hands almost a foot apart.

I expected Mother to laugh and contradict him, but her face was serious. "I know, honey. That was the biggest needle I've ever seen, but they had to have a tiny piece from inside you for the tests. At least they didn't have to cut you open...." She patted his head clumsily, then turned toward the sink and began running hot water to soak the crusted dishes from last night's dinner.

I wished more than ever that the viewer still worked. Would Thomp's liver show the same blue glow that we'd seen inside his thigh? I went to get the remote from its hiding place inside one of my winter boots, and we trooped outside.

Behind the garage, Lucy asked the question on all of our minds. "What are they going to do to Thomp when he goes back there?"

"I don't wanna go!" Thomp wailed. "I hate that place and I'm not going back, even if it kills me...." He lifted his head to look at me. "David...do you think I'm going to die?"

"Of *course* not," I said quickly. "But I wish I'd known what that blue glow meant when we saw it with the viewer."

We stood around glumly for a few minutes, while Russet nudged each of us in turn.

"What if we tried using the remote to fix the viewer with Reconfigure?" said Lucy.

We found the viewer buried at the bottom of Thomp's toy box. I pressed Reconfigure, then handed the remote to Lucy and slowly lifted the viewer to my eyes.

The blue glow had spread down most of the length of Thomp's right femur. On the Transparent Human Figure, the liver is way up higher than you'd think; in the chest, sort of, but in back. On Thomp, that area glowed blue, too. I anxiously scanned the rest of him, and saw a few more luminous patches in the part where the figure had its intestines, and, even more ominously, inside Thomp's skull.

"Let me, let me!" Lucy tried to pull the viewer out of my hands.

Thomp kept his eyes on my face. "It's bad, isn't it, David?" he said softly.

Tears filled my eyes. I kept trying to blink them away so he wouldn't see. I couldn't imagine growing up without Thomp.

As I started to reach out one hand toward him, Lucy wrestled the viewer away, looked through the lenses, and promptly burst into sobs. "That blue stuff is *everywhere*," she wailed.

We must have huddled together, crying, for at least half an hour. Russet lay with her head in Thomp's lap, tail gently thumping. Then Lucy suddenly jumped to her feet. "David," she shouted, "David!"

"What?" I said stupidly.

"David, what if we fix him? What if we try Reconfigure on Thomp?" She was practically jumping up and down with excitement. "It fixed Russet, didn't it?"

"But it might not be safe for humans! I mean, whatever it is, it can't have been tested, or we'd have heard about it."

"I don't care." Lucy's tone was flat. "I saw a TV show about cancer, and once it spreads all over like that, I don't think doctors can fix it, no matter what they do. And the stuff they did to try to fix it was horrible. Do you want him to just die?"

"Of course not!" I said. "But how will we explain if it works?"

"Dad and Mother will be so happy, they'll just think the doctors made a mistake," Lucy said, waving a hand airily. "Or it could be a miracle of modern medicine. That's what Miss Kittredge said last year when they cured her aunt's ulcer. And if it fixes Thomp, I don't care about anything else."

"Please, David," Thomp begged, "just try it. You can Delete, can't you, if something goes wrong?"

"I know one thing we can test first," I said grimly. "I've got a wart on the bottom of my foot. Let's try it out on that. Lucy, you'd better do it, because I can't twist it around enough to aim straight."

I took off my shoe and held my foot out behind me. Lucy took the remote, pointed it at my sole, and pushed the button. "Well?" I said.

"Do you feel any different?" Thomp asked. His expression was anxious.

"No," I said. "Is it all gone?" I reached down to feel my now-smooth sole.

"Yep," said Lucy proudly. "It worked! Now let's get rid of Thomp's blue stuff." She handed me the remote and I reluctantly took it. I felt sick in a way I didn't think the remote was going to fix. What if it did something horrible? What if it made Thomp worse?

Then I made up my mind. What was happening to Thomp was already horrible—and *would* get worse if I didn't do something. "Where do you guys think I should aim it?" I asked.

"Just point it at his middle," Lucy advised. "It fixed Russet all over, not just where you aimed."

I suddenly couldn't bear delaying any longer. I swung it toward Thomp's waist and pressed the Reconfigure button. The remote made a gentle humming noise we had never heard before, as the screen flashed with undulating waves of yellow light.

We all held our breath for a moment. Thomp definitely looked pinker all of a sudden, and not so tired. "Look in the viewer, David," whispered Lucy. I scanned Thomp all over, inch by inch. The blue spots were completely gone.

"I knew it, I knew it!" chortled Lucy, grabbing Thomp by the wrists and spinning him around in circles until she got dizzy and they both sprawled in the grass.

I couldn't stop grinning a silly grin. "Thomp, do you feel okay? Does your leg hurt at all?"

He thought solemnly for a moment, moving his right leg up, down, and around. "Nope; it feels fine. Like always. Like before, I mean," he corrected himself hastily. "I bet I can run, even!"

"Really?" Lucy's eyes lit up. "Maybe we could try playing soccer? Just a little bit, to see if your leg's okay."

We were running like mad around the far end of the clothesline, Thomp in the lead, and both Lucy and Russet trying to get the ball away from him, when I heard Mother shout, *"DAVID!"*

We all skidded to a halt, panting, except for Russet, who grabbed the ball awkwardly in her teeth and bolted for the woods. Mother ran up to us from where she'd been standing in the back doorway, her face ghastly. "David...I cannot *believe* you would do this to your brother. He has to have surgery on Monday. He may die from this!" She was weeping openly now, and dropped to her knees, flinging her arms around Thomp.

"But Mom, I'm fine. I'm better, really!" Pressed against her shoulder, his voice was muffled by her shirt.

"Honey, I know this is a terrible, terrible thing to happen, but you've got to be very brave. Somehow, I know you'll pull through. I know it!"

"I have already! I don't need to go back to any old doctors!" Thomp squirmed to get away, but Mother kept him enfolded in a fierce hug.

"No more running. *At all.* Thompson, you lie on the living room sofa for the rest of the day, where I can keep an eye on you, and get you snacks and drinks when you need them. You two," she swung around to face me and Lucy, "should be *ashamed* of yourselves. You will stay in your rooms until your father and I decide what to do." She carried Thomp into the house. He rolled his eyes at us from over her shoulder.

Lucy had the room right next to me and Thomp. There was a hole through the two closets that we could talk through and you couldn't hear it from the hallway. "So what can we do?" she whispered.

"Nothing," I muttered. "They'll figure out eventually that the cancer's gone, and they'll leave him alone."

"That's not true! You heard her! She said he's supposed to have surgery on Monday! They won't believe it disappeared overnight, and they'll cut him open just to look around."

"It goes away by itself sometimes, I think," I said cautiously.

"It's called *remission*," said Lucy. "It was on the TV. But it's not instant; it takes a long time. It would have to be a lot longer time later for the doctors to believe it was gone."

"Longer, like years? Or like weeks?"

"Well, if he said he was fine every day for a week, they might look more carefully before they cut him up," Lucy mused. "I don't think they can usually do surgery right away like that. They must have been really worried about it. If something happened

Monday, they'd have to reschedule, and if Thomp said he felt fine every day until then, they might take a closer look at him first."

"Then I know what to do!" I said. "There's a sort of cave down by the river, under the bank, that I don't think anybody knows about but me and Steve, and he moved away last year. If Thomp can sneak out with me Sunday night and hide until Monday night, they won't be able to do the surgery. I'll stay with him, and you can tell everybody that you don't know where we are, but we're fine."

"Which will be true," said Lucy. "You'll need to take food. And blankets. And stuff to drink."

We got away pretty much okay, except for a scare with Russet. When she realized Thomp and I were going outside without her, she started to whine. Lucy told us later that she finally had to take Russet into her room and snuggle under the covers with her to keep her quiet. But other than that, it worked perfectly.

Mother and Dad were *furious* when Thomp and I came back just after dark on Monday night. Lucy was already grounded for a week when we got home, and I was grounded for a month. It's not like there were other kids I played with much, anyway. I missed riding my bike to the public library though, and was almost wishing for school to start so I could use the library there.

Sure enough, they had to reschedule the surgery. Thomp kept saying over and over that his leg didn't hurt anymore, that he felt great, and that he was sure he was better. Mother ignored everything he said, but Dad looked him over speculatively about halfway through the week, and said, "You know, Emily, I believe he *is* doing better. And he's not limping anymore, even when he thinks we're not watching."

Mother finally relaxed a little after the next visit to the hospital. They had to admit him and run a bunch of tests before they operated, and that's when they realized he really was better, and decided to postpone the surgery. "His blood count was normal!" she said to Dad. "They said they don't understand it, but if this keeps up, they won't do the surgery at all. Let's keep our fingers crossed!"

The last night of summer vacation, I tried to tell Dad what we had done, but before I could explain about Russet, or the other stuff, or show him, he burst out laughing, and said, "David, don't be ridiculous. Nothing out of a *cereal* box, for crying out loud, is going to cure cancer! We're just glad your brother is getting better, and I suppose now it's just as well he missed his surgery. But"—and his face grew serious again—"you were very lucky that your little jaunt didn't have life-and-death consequences for Thomp. Don't you *ever* try to interfere with anyone's medical treatment again."

Mother had eggs and bacon cooking when I woke up the next morning. I thought maybe she was making a special breakfast because it was the first day of school, but she laughed and said, "Well, that too; but it's the strangest thing, David, I went to three different supermarkets yesterday and I can't find that cereal you kids liked so much anywhere. Isn't that odd? Maybe there's a strike at the factory that makes it."

"Maybe," I said.

With everything that had happened, I'd almost forgotten about starting middle school that fall. I was half-excited and half-scared when my school bus came, fifteen minutes before Lucy and Thomp's bus (except they were waiting until his next checkup to let Thomp start school). He watched from the kitchen window with a disappointed expression as I shouldered my backpack and got on. Lucy came flying out the door and waved frantically after the departing bus, but with a big grin, so I guess she was fine.

"That your sister? She looks like a stupid bitch." I turned to see an older boy with short blond hair and an ugly expression sitting halfway down the aisle.

"You stop that, Alfie!" snapped the bus driver, an incredibly huge woman wearing tight red-and-white striped shorts and a turquoise T-shirt. "No bad words on *my* bus."

Alfie made a sneering face at me and turned to stare out the window on his side. I sat down near the front of the bus. No one got on that I recognized from last year. I wished for the millionth time that Steve hadn't moved away.

I was going to try to get off the bus as soon as it stopped, but I got my backpack strap stuck between the seats, and as Alfie came up the aisle, he kicked me in the ankle. I said "Ow!" and the bus driver lady turned around quickly, but she didn't see him do it.

The new school seemed okay. It's hard to tell the first day what the teachers are going to be like, but the science teacher was a younger guy, Mr. Tilling, who acted pretty nice. And I've always liked math. In the middle of the morning we had a general assembly, with a speech by the principal. Mr. Enright was tall and had swept-back silver hair; he talked about how important middle school was to our futures, and said that he was our friend, and smiled a lot in between sentences. I saw him in the hallways once or twice later in the day, looking busy and important.

Lunch was in a big, noisy cafeteria. I was sitting at a table by myself when Alfie came in with a couple of other boys, both of them hulking, oversize monsters like Alfie, almost the size of high school kids, wearing those baggy jackets that made them look even bigger. I've always been small for my age. I saw him stare at me, then he pointed at me and said something to his friends that I couldn't hear. When I got on the bus to go home, Alfie was already on it, sitting near the front, and he kicked me again as I passed by him.

Lucy was upset when she saw the bruises on my shin. "I'll get the remote, and you can Reconfigure it!" she said.

"No, Lucy," I said. "This isn't that big a deal. I don't know if the remote has batteries that can run down or what, but I bet we can't get new ones. I want to save it from now on, in case something important happens."

"But won't the batteries run out eventually, anyway?" Lucy pleaded.

"I don't know," I said.

I hadn't made any friends yet in school, and, since I was still grounded, I wouldn't have been able to get together with anybody anyway. Aside from Alfie, hardly any of the kids on my bus route lived nearby. Most of them lived a lot closer to the school. I got to be alone on the bus with Alfie for at least ten minutes each way every day (oh joy, oh bliss). The bus driver lady was sharper than she'd seemed at first, and kept a close eye on him, but I was still careful to sit as far from him as I could. At least I had a lot of books from the school library. I asked the librarian for any books on remote controls, like for TVs, but all she could get me were books on how television and radio worked.

Lunchtime got worse. Alfie and the other two started making a habit of coming over to wherever I was sitting and telling me it was their table and I'd better move, or else. Sometimes they'd grab some of my food if none of the teachers were watching.

I kept wondering about the remote. What if Thomp's cancer came back, or something happened to Mother, or Dad, or Lucy? I had the feeling that if anything happened to it, there would be no way of getting another. Steve's dad had taken their phone apart once to fix something that had stopped working inside, and it always made a buzzing sound after that.

"We're going to talk about the electromagnetic spectrum this week," Mr. Tilling announced. "Not only the light you see, and electricity, but heat, x-rays, and the microwaves that cook our food are part of this spectrum, which includes a much larger range of radiation." The part I couldn't understand was about light being a wave, like radio, *and* a particle, like an atom or something. I tried to get him to explain it, but he said, "I know it's a contradiction in terms—David, is it?—and a little hard for our minds to grasp. We haven't got time now, but you could stay after class one day, if you don't mind walking home, and I can try to explain it a little better."

"That's okay," I started to say, and then it hit me: maybe the remote worked by using part of the electromagnetic spectrum. "Mr. Tilling," I said urgently, "could I stay after tomorrow? I want to bring...a thing, from home. I was wondering if you can tell how it works."

"Well, I'll do my best, David. What kind of thing?"

"It's like, um, a remote-control thing. It has buttons...that do stuff." By now the rest of the class was laughing, but I didn't care.

"Fine." He grinned at me. "Bring it in, and we'll have a look."

One of Alfie's sidekicks was in my science class too, and slammed sideways against me in the hall afterward, smirking. "Is Da-a-avy going to bring in a toy for show and tell? Wow! I can't wait."

"But what if the teacher keeps it?" Lucy asked.

"I don't think he'll do that," I said. "The class heard me say I was bringing it in."

"We only tried Intensity twice," said Lucy, thoughtfully. "Maybe we could try it just a little bit more, before you show it to him?"

"I guess that would be a good idea, so I don't wreck stuff at the school by accident. Let's go out with Thomp and try all the buttons one last time. We could try it on things that are alike, so we can compare them."

We ended up picking a bunch of those magenta cosmos flowers that all looked about the same, and laid out a row of them in a crooked line on bare dirt at the edge of the field beyond the woods. Intensity made a flower burn to black, just like the leaf, but the interesting part was that a bud on the same stem swelled and opened almost all the way into another flower. Delete turned it back to what it had been. Reconfigure made the cosmos less wilted-looking, and Enhance gave it a double row of petals with a network of dark purple veins, and some truly impressive thorns on the stem. Each time, Delete reversed whatever we had done.

But when I pushed Delete the last time, I must have aimed a little crooked, because the flower next to it disappeared, leaving a faint vapor, and nothing we did brought it back. We tried Delete all by itself on a rock, a stick, and then a spare hex nut I had in my pocket. All of them were irretrievably obliterated.

We didn't feel like trying it anymore after that. We looked at each other, wide-eyed and silent. "I guess it's a good thing you didn't push Delete more than once that first time, Lucy," I finally said. "We would never have been able to explain losing the TV."

"I think it would be a really, really good idea to take it to Mr. Tilling, and have him figure out how it works," said Lucy, with a little shiver.

The next day, I had it in my backpack when I got on the bus. There was a different bus driver, a tired-looking elderly man. Alfie and one of his friends were sitting in front. "He's not supposed to be on this bus!" I told the driver indignantly.

"He's staying at my house while my aunt's out of town. Tough luck, sucker." Alfie said. *No wonder they look alike*, I thought.

They stuck their legs out across the aisle, and one of them shoved me as I stepped over. The bus driver watched but didn't say a word. I went to sit way back in the bus, as far away from them as I could. That was a mistake, because they followed me back there right away, and sat where they could keep me from getting past them. I put my backpack in the corner, and leaned against it.

"Hey, Davy, got your toy for show and tell?" Alfie taunted. "Can we play with it?"

"Get lost," I muttered, bracing myself against my backpack.

"Ooh, Jason, I don't think he wants us to play with him. I think we should teach him to share, don't you?" Jason grinned slyly and slid across the bus to sit next to me, pinning me in the corner.

"Hey!" I yelled, as loud as I could. *"Hey!* Cut it out!" The old man driving the bus never turned a hair. Maybe he was deaf. Alfie twisted around to get up on his knees and reach over the seat for my backpack, while Jason grabbed my arms.

I fought as savagely as I could. *If either of them gets hold of the remote...* I got one good kick on Alfie's elbow, and I hit Jason's nose hard with the top of my head, spraying blood down his lip, but it didn't do any good; they were both so much bigger than me. Jason pushed against the seat and slid us both onto the floor, giving Alfie the chance to grab my backpack.

I struggled silently, desperately, to get out from under Jason, as Alfie rooted through my pack. "Ooh, M&Ms, my favorite!"

"Hey, I want some of those!" Jason hauled himself off me and clambered into the seat next to Alfie. I hoped my lunch would distract them, but they threw the rest of it onto the floor, item by item, and then began pulling out my books and homework.

"What if I pee all over it, Davy? I bet you'll get a really good grade then." Alfie dangled my math folder in front of his crotch, leering.

"Give me back my stuff, *now.*" I made a lunge for the backpack, but Jason pushed me so I fell into the seat on the other side of the aisle. Doggedly, I threw myself at them again, thinking, *Maybe if I can distract them a little longer; it's only five minutes till the next stop.* "If you wreck my books, you're gonna have to pay for them! And if you pee on the bus, I'll tell all the kids in school you wet yourself."

Alfie got an ugly look, pulled out a book without looking, and started ripping pages out of it. I hoped it would keep him busy until the bus stopped on Grant Avenue for the next bunch of kids (it was my math textbook, but it would have been worth it).

"What about his toy?" Jason said.

Rats.

"Oh. Right." Alfie let the mutilated book drop to the floor and reached into my backpack again, pulling out books and papers and tossing them aside. I hurled myself at them once more, fists pounding, but Jason pushed me away as the bus swung around a bend, sending me sprawling into the opposite seat, and I hit my head so hard I saw stars, which I'd always thought was just a way people had of saying that someone was dizzy, but there they were, turquoise and swirling.

By the time I sat up, Alfie had the remote, clutching it in one fat fist, and was reading the labels on the buttons—I could see his lips move. "Rek-one-fig-you-ree—what the hell's that? Hey, Jason, want to get rekked? Oh, wow: In-ten-si-ty; let's see what that one does." Both boys were laughing as he swung the point of the remote toward Jason and pushed the button.

In mid-giggle, I heard Jason's voice change to a lower pitch. He suddenly seemed to fill out his baggy clothes a lot more. His face lost the roundness it had had, developing more planes and angles, and pronounced dark bristles where a beard and mustache would have grown in a few years. Alfie's jaw dropped. "Cool!" he finally managed to breathe.

I don't know why some kids think that looking grown up is so great. Adults have their own world, and we have ours, and there are always problems in both, as far as I can see. Why give yourself both sets at once? But these two were the kind that saw getting older only as a way of being able to intimidate other kids even more, that never thought about what being an adult—or a parent—really meant. Heck, they probably never thought as far as appearing in juvie court.

"What? Whaddya mean?" Jason croaked. He still hadn't figured out what was different. He looked down at his hands, with their newly prominent knuckles and veins, and snapped his head up to stare at me, horrified. "What's happened to me?" His voice was hoarse with fright.

"You're, like, grown up, man! We'll be able to massacre everybody on the football team! This is awesome." Alfie swung the device around to face himself.

I don't know whether he just pushed it by accident, hit Delete instead of Intensity, or thought that all the buttons did the same thing, but suddenly Alfie was gone. So was the remote.

Jason sat, paralyzed, staring fixedly at his reflection in the bus window, until the bus came to a shuddering halt. I don't know whether fear actually has a smell, but I saw his face bead with sweat, and a rank, adult odor spread through the back of the bus. Three girls got on and came down the aisle, chattering about some movie they'd seen. Then they saw Jason.

"What are you doing here?" one of the girls asked. She turned toward the bus driver. "Hey, mister. Mister bus driver! There's a man on our bus!" They retreated back toward the front of the bus, and tried to attract the bus driver's attention. Before the driver could turn around, Jason leapt to his feet and ran for the front of the bus, still wearing his school backpack. He pushed through the startled kids still waiting to board, zigzagged between a couple of houses, and was gone.

Nobody asked me that day about Alfie, or Jason. I saw their other friend hovering disconsolately at the fringes of the cafeteria, looking strangely vulnerable. In science class, Jason was marked absent, and when Mr. Tilling asked me if I'd brought the gadget I wanted to ask him about, I mumbled that it had gotten thrown away by mistake.

Lucy asked what Mr. Tilling had said about the remote, naturally. I swore her to secrecy and told her what had happened. "It's not your fault," she finally said. "That boy was really mean, and I don't care what happens to him."

"But what about his parents?" I said. "What about the other one, Jason? He won't have any idea how to act like a real grownup. What's going to happen to him?"

We decided not to tell Thomp what had happened to the remote until he was older.

The next day, I got called down to the principal's office. The lady behind the desk was pretty, with hair in tiny little braids, kind dark eyes, and a yellow dress. She smiled at me and said,

"Mr. Enright wants to talk to you, David, but don't worry, you're not in trouble—he just has some questions."

He was behind a big desk, fiddling with an expensive-looking pen. There was a woman with bloodshot eyes and clothes that looked like she'd slept in them for weeks sitting on one of the chairs off to the side. She smelled like cigarette smoke and stale food.

Mr. Enright said, "David, this is Mrs. Alberts, Alfie's mother," and it felt like my stomach swallowed itself. "We know you usually ride the same bus as Alfie, and we wondered if you remember seeing him Tuesday morning, two days ago? Or his cousin Jason?"

"Um," I said, "I think they were on the bus...."

"I *know* they were on the bus, sonny! I saw them get on; now what I want to know is if they got off it before it got to the school!" Her gravelly voice was a little hysterical.

"I think so," I said cautiously, "I was finishing my math homework during the bus ride, so I wasn't really paying attention. Um...Doesn't the bus driver remember if they got off?"

"The bus driver said there was a man hiding on the bus, who jumped off and ran away at the stop after yours," said Mr. Enright. "David, did you see this man? Were the boys with him?"

"Alfie's real mature for his age," his mother said proudly. "My sister's boy's big too; runs in our family."

"I don't remember any man on the bus," I said slowly. "Alfie and Jason were there when I got on, but I don't think they were there when I got to school."

"They were reported absent for the entire day, Mrs. Alberts; they must have gotten off the bus somewhere along its route, which is not our responsibility," said Mr. Enright with firmness. "You'll have to take up the matter with the bus company, or the police."

"There wasn't no call for them kids to be going anywhere! What's my sister gonna say when she comes back from Topeka?"

"Is there any possibility that Jason decided to join his mother, and Alfie chose to go with him?"

"He'd just made the football team! Ain't no way, no how, he'd leave school and miss out on that!" Her face had turned red and she was breathing in rapid little pants.

I was feeling worse and worse. Mr. Enright nodded to me, and said, "You can go, David, but be sure to inform us if you remember anything you heard them say that might indicate where they were going."

I heard her yelling swear words at him as I left the office.

The police questioned me twice, but I told them exactly what I'd told Mr. Enright. They found Jason's backpack behind a convenience store, where there was a hold-up by a tall white male in his early twenties, dark hair, unshaven, who claimed to have a gun but never produced it. There's a railroad track right behind the store. I bet it's a lot harder to be a grownup than you'd think.

I never saw that brand of cereal again, or anything resembling any of the devices, which we had so completely taken for granted, that were inside those silver boxes. Each year there are new and magical technologies that surprise us for a moment, until they become the new commonplaces, but the origin and operation of the remote remains as inaccessible as the name we had given it.

Yellow and Pink

written by
Leah Ning

illustrated by
IRMAK ÇAVUN

ABOUT THE AUTHOR

Leah lives in northern Virginia with her husband and their five pets: two cats, a dog, and two sugar gliders—all of whom are exactly as cute as they sound. Despite her years of living there, both past and yet to come, her heart lies in cold, snowy New England, and she hopes to get back there someday.

She works as a programmer and spends her non-writing time drawing, playing video games, and learning to make delicious new foods.

"Yellow and Pink" is her first writing sale.

ABOUT THE ILLUSTRATOR

Irmak Çavun, also known as Max, was born in 2000 in Albany, New York, but has lived most of her life in Turkey. Since there were no influential artists near her, Max's inspiration has been based solely on her imagination.

She grew up drawing and was interested in any and all forms of art. That is, until her contact with the gaming community. She was astonished by the level of design and the illustration aesthetics with such a welcoming community. So she shifted her focus toward game art and design, which she wants to pursue in college.

She is now a passionate high school student who works hard, with the hopes of one day becoming an important figure within the art community.

Yellow and Pink

"How many times?" the dying man whispered.

Nathan Reed's attention did not waver from the arm he was working on. Decades ago, Edward Weaver's dying words had bothered him. Today they were like a fly lighting briefly on his neck, and he had to ask: "Pardon?"

"How many times...have you killed me?"

"Eight, counting this one," Nathan said. "Nothing personal, it's just that this way you can't tell anyone."

He pulled a small, square piece of plastic from Weaver's arm as its owner's breaths grew shallower. He dipped it into the bottle of alcohol, which he sealed and stored in Weaver's left pocket. The rest of the instruments, still bloody, went into the right.

"What...are you trying...to change?"

Nathan had never heard that question before. Did he owe the man whose life he was stealing an answer? He stayed silent and inserted the plastic into the incision on his own forearm. Then he pressed the pistol into Weaver's hand and stood. Soon, to anyone observing this scene, it would appear that Nathan had been attacked but died before his device could be taken.

"Shoot," Nathan said.

"Gladly," said the dying man. Nathan had chosen someone vengeful for a reason.

The flat report of the gunshot echoed around the alley. Nathan fell with a grunt of pain, fingers pressing at the new slick of blood on his belly. Gut shot again. He had thought that he might be used to it by now, but he always began to whimper when the burning started.

The first time he'd killed Edward Weaver, Nathan spent the first years he could remember of his childhood having regular panic attacks. He learned to hide them when his parents began discussing how to afford a psychiatrist. The last thing he needed was anyone prying into the cause of his anxiety.

When his family started calling him an "old soul," he silently berated himself. The rich were used to their children being wise beyond their years. The middle class and poor were not, and those who did manage to reset pretended to be children and teenagers until their bodies caught back up with their minds. All Nathan could do was try to act more childish and hope that they didn't look too closely.

As bad as the panic attacks had been, the worst was the first day of high school. A flash of red hair made him catch his breath and look around. He had caught her laughing, her eyes squeezed shut, revealing the lines that he imagined would form around her eyes in thirty years, her mouth open and displaying that crooked canine he loved. A half-wilted yellow daisy drooped behind one ear. A choked cry burst from his mouth before he could stop it and he had to run for the bathroom. He wept as quietly as he could manage, hunched on the hard plastic of a toilet seat.

For all his planning, he had never believed, deep down, that she would really be alive.

Nathan had little fear of being caught now. The disgust he felt at how easily he avoided capture was just a low background hum today, buried by the relief that was just around the next bend in the tiled halls of the high school. He passed a scene he would never get used to: the splash of red hair on a dark T-shirt, the crooked canine in a laughing mouth. His throat tightened. So close. Close enough to touch again for the first time in sixteen years. He had to swallow hard to get the lump out of his throat, but he didn't cry. After all, she would always be alive, just waiting in the next timeline.

Two hours later, switching classes for the second time, Nathan kept his head turned strictly forward. His back and shoulders tingled with anticipation. As he passed a familiar bit of permanent marker graffiti on a locker (the name of some band he had watched come and go seven times), he heard the running footsteps and did not brace himself for the impact.

When she slammed into his back at full speed, he fell, the textbooks he held driving all the air from him in a strained "uh!" The peals of laughter from the girl sprawled on the floor next to him thawed him like sunlight on snow.

"I'm so-so-s-s," Holly tried to stammer before dissolving into giggles again.

"Well, that'll teach me to start using my bag," Nathan grinned, gathering his books into his arms.

"If it doesn't, then you're hopeless anyway. I'm Holly."

He couldn't help letting his hand brush hers when she dropped his chemistry book onto the stack.

"You know what they say about right person, wrong time?"

These words marked the beginning of a lifetime spent alone. Nathan never dared to try to accelerate the events leading to their marriage again. The part of him that always called him "murderer" or "time thief" tried to convince him that this was a sign, that he didn't deserve to be back with her after what he'd done. He seized those thoughts with both mental hands and shoved them down to a cold, dark, and as-yet-unexplored part of his mind. It was always only Holly's first time, he told himself. He had been married to her for seven years, been with her for ten, but she didn't know that. For her, too soon would always be too soon instead of never soon enough.

Of course, friendship was better than rejection and the inevitable growing apart that followed. And wasn't that what marriage was supposed to be, in the end? Really, it was about being friends, best friends, two people who knew each other better than anyone else on Earth.

No matter how many times he told himself this, his chest always ached until he started to see her looking at him that way again. Then he would hold her regard like a butterfly on the tip of his finger, carefully feeding it sweet things until it knew he was safe.

Although the bonfire danced far enough behind them that the crackling was almost inaudible, it still painted Holly's face with a soft orange glow. The salt wind teased at her hair. Nathan's heart was pounding. Sure, it wasn't exactly the first time he had done this, but he always felt afraid of getting it wrong. He knew too well how long another twenty-five years without her would feel.

"Nate," she smiled. "Why do you look so nervous?"

"You always make me nervous," he said truthfully.

Her low laugh was almost lost in the sound of the ocean. "Maybe we can fix that."

"Maybe we can," Nathan said, and then she was leaning in, he could see the white grains of sand stuck to her eyelashes, and her mouth was on his. Ten years seemed like forever standing at the beginning of what they would be, but at the end, he always felt cheated.

Didn't they always say things like "If only we had left ten seconds later?" Nathan had thought this at first too, but after three resets he found himself lashing out at those who said it in their awful pitying voices in the days following the accident.

On his second reset, he had shattered a glass of water, which resulted in a delay of ten minutes. The car that swerved in front of them was white instead of red, which was of no comfort.

Holly had rubbed his back for half an hour as he vomited on his third reset. Each touch sent jagged bolts of terror (*in an hour I will comfort you as you die in my arms*) down his spine.

Then the miracle happened: she stayed home. Thanksgiving

185

dinner was rescheduled for the following weekend with words of concern from her parents. Holly saw his tears of relief and smoothed the hair from his forehead, remarking that "You must be hurting pretty bad."

Nathan woke the next morning while she was in the shower. That was it. He had finally done it. Twelve hours after her death in the previous three timelines, she was alive in this one, now stepping out of the shower and drying her hair. He kissed her in near disbelief as she left for work.

When the police rang his doorbell an hour later, he realized that he had never thought to check when the town had cleaned up the oil slick that killed her.

Oil slicks, he discovered, didn't have timing, and nor did the people who swerved around them. Oil slicks just were. Oil slicks shimmered their deadly existence into your eyes like spikes even while the blood from your wife's head pooled in their centers.

How did she manage to make four years pass so quickly? Nathan stood with his hands clasped behind his back to hide their shaking. A flat expanse of neatly cut grass rolled in from his left and sloped down to his right. A few rows of close family and friends showed him only the backs of their heads while pale yellow ribbons fluttered from their chairs.

And there she was. Holly's hair glowed fiercely red in the sunset and she was grinning, exposing that crooked canine. Her hands clutched an explosion of yellow daisies, pink peonies, meadowsweet, and yellow roses. Nathan had grinned back at their first wedding, but he hadn't cried. Today, two hundred years later, he did both. When she reached him, she smiled and wiped the tears from his face with one thumb.

Nathan had changed only one thing about the wedding. Instead of "'til death do us part," he said, "until the end of my days."

For the rest of that night, he drank her in. Her hair left burning trails in the darkening sky. When he spun her, the gauzy white dress floated around her legs. They danced barefoot in the grass as the end of the night came. She laid her head on his chest as they swayed. Her pale face seemed to blur into his shirt in the gloom.

"I love you, Nathan Reed," she murmured.

"I love you, Holly Reed," he said, and kissed the top of her head as she smiled.

Seven years still stretched ahead. It wasn't long enough. It would never be long enough.

To punish himself for his fourth reset, Nathan spent his fifth without Holly. He had gotten too arrogant. How had he ever thought he could handle what he had always entrusted to professionals?

Her blood, rather than spreading darkly across the shimmer of the oil slick, had swirled in bathwater. Her fingers had kept a tenuous hold on a sodden, wrinkled sonogram instead of clutching at his shirt.

After that, he hadn't been sure he deserved to ever even glimpse her again. But he had still come back, hadn't he? He had still murdered Edward Weaver on the same day, at the same time, and in the same place. Because he hadn't been sure. God, that had been a whole new level of moral depravity.

I killed someone to have more time to punish myself, he thought with deepening disgust. But that wasn't quite right, was it? He had been horrified, sure, and he had had all the requisite "I don't deserve her" thoughts, but he hadn't come to the next timeline to punish himself. He had ultimately decided to kill Weaver again because he hadn't been sure he should stop trying.

The idea of Holly at thirty years old, at forty, even at fifty, was so attractive that it almost had a gravitational pull. He couldn't resist the possibility that a version of his wife whose laugh lines were permanently pressed into her face might be waiting just in the next timeline.

The idea that she might not want him anymore if she knew began to well up in that deep, unexplored place in his mind as he prepared to commit his sixth murder.

"I think it might be time to try some therapy," Nathan said. The vase on the windowsill was empty. He had cleaned it out the day before she'd come home from the hospital and left it that way, having learned that the sight of pink flowers—pink for a girl—made her eyes well up every time she glanced at them.

Holly looked up from her bowl of cornflakes. It was slowly turning into a mass of soggy, inedible lumps. Her right hand moved to cup her belly, which should have no longer been flat.

"Do you think I'm crazy?" she asked.

"No," he said. "I just think you could use some help from someone less clueless than I am."

"I'm grieving, Nathan."

"Grieving is fine. But you've stopped eating and you barely sleep anymore. And every time you do fall asleep, you wake up screaming."

Holly was suddenly on her feet, her chair teetering just on the edge of falling. "I am *grieving*!" she shouted.

Nathan forced himself to stay in his own chair. "Holly, you can grieve all you want," he said quietly. "But not alone. I don't want you to grieve alone anymore, and *I* don't want to grieve alone anymore."

That was the crux of the thing, wasn't it? He always grieved for her alone. And how long had it been since he'd really felt for the loss of this baby? His wife was across the table, her skin beginning to look thin and hollow with sorrow, and he had just finished his second bowl of cornflakes. He couldn't even pretend his lack of feeling for the baby was a result of experiencing it over and over. Although nothing else felt like anything anymore, the memories of Holly bleeding on shimmering pavement still had the power to crush every last bit of breath from his lungs.

Nathan's throat began to ache, and revulsion rose like acid in his chest.

"I'm sorry," Holly whispered. Her slippered feet shushed against the floor as she moved around the table toward him. She wrapped her arms around his waist, and he slid his own around her shoulders. "I know I need help," she mumbled into his shirt. "I know. I'm sorry. I'll call tomorrow."

"Don't be sorry," Nathan said, his voice breaking a little. "I just want you to be okay."

That was too true. He breathed in the sweetness of the shampoo he'd scrubbed into her hair that morning and wondered how far his selfishness had really spread while his focus had been pinpointed on sparing himself the pain of losing Holly.

You have to tell her, whispered the voice he always tried to keep locked away. Nathan squeezed his eyes shut and buried his nose farther into her hair.

After they were together again, he would tell Holly everything. That was what Nathan told himself on his sixth try. That wasn't something you just told a friend, after all. Friendship was just friendship. She couldn't possibly understand before they fell in love, why he would even consider doing what he had been doing for the past century or so.

But maybe dating was too soon after all, he thought after they had their first kiss. She hadn't yet decided to spend the rest of her life with him, so how could she understand? Nathan decided he would tell her after they were married. That made much more sense than asking while everything was still fragile and undecided.

And then they did marry again. The wedding day came far too soon, though, and so did the honeymoon. In fact, he thought, wouldn't it be better to wait for the ease and familiarity of marriage to set in? It would be so much easier for her to understand then. When would it set in for her? He had felt it for so long now that he had difficulty remembering when it had first happened for him.

Three years later, she miscarried, and that would be the worst possible time to talk about it. He waited for her to recover fully. They were twenty-seven years old when Nathan finally admitted to himself that she was fine, had been for a year, and now it was time to tell her everything.

He walked into the living room. She was sitting on their lumpy green couch, her legs pulled up, and she smiled when she heard him.

"Come sit," she said, patting the couch next to her. So he did, and she relaxed against his shoulder with a content sigh. "I love you," she murmured.

His resolve broke just like that. He only had a year left of this. What if she grew to hate him? That thought brought a new rush of terror swirling into his chest. He shied away from the images of her anger and bewilderment his mind tried to conjure. Instead of "Can I ask you something" or "I need to talk to you," his response was "I love you too."

This will be the last try I need, he reasoned, smoothing his thumb down her arm and reveling in its warmth. He had decided to lock her in the bedroom on the day of her impending death to stop her from getting in the car.

When he did it, she thought it was some kind of game. He almost screamed when she slipped into the hall, wagging a bobby pin mischievously between two fingers. "You thought you could keep me in there with just a little lock?" she said, grabbing the keys. "I'm leaving, with or without you. Let's go."

Twenty minutes later, he yelled, "Stop, stop, there's an oil slick!"

Her last word was "Where?"

Despite all his attempts to the contrary, Nathan would hold Holly as she died for the eighth time a year from today. A normal person wouldn't be certain of this. It bothered him that he was so certain of that despite all his attempts to the contrary. He kept trying and failing to convince himself that a year wasn't so short. A year only seems like a long time when you're faced with things less monumental than the death of your wife and the subsequent sixteen years of scrambling to get back to her. After today, the number of years left slipped into the number of days left.

"Hi, you."

Nathan started as Holly's arm crept around his waist. She didn't laugh. Five years of marriage was enough to know when not to laugh. If she knew when not to laugh after five years, how could he not know the answer to the question burning in his mouth after more than two centuries? Maybe, in all the time he had spent drinking her in like a man in the desert, he had been paying attention to all the wrong things. All these years had been about his wants, his needs. He had pretended for the last two resets that he had wanted to know her opinion: was he doing the right thing? Did he still deserve her? Was this what she wanted?

Perhaps he should have understood his wife well enough to know the answers to his questions. Perhaps he knew the answers already and only wanted to hear them from her mouth. In any case, he knew her well enough to know that she wouldn't let him back out after he started.

"Holly, I need to ask your advice."

"How many times?" his dying wife whispered.

Watching her die on his seventh reset, Nathan didn't register the meaning of her words. He shushed her gently and smoothed his hand across her forehead.

"How many times have you done this, Nate?"

"What?" he asked.

"You're on a reset," she said. Even though she still whispered, he knew it wasn't a question.

"Yes."

"How many?"

"Seven. This is my seventh."

Her forehead was shaped wrong from the impact against the pavement. She wrinkled it. A bead of blood ran down one of the channels.

"Oh, Nate," she breathed. Her hand reached toward his face, slow and trembling, and her mouth opened. Then her face slackened and her reaching hand fell to the ground with a soft smack. Nathan picked it back up and put it to his cheek as his vision blurred. He would have given a great deal to hear the end of that sentence.

It was this memory Nathan tried to keep in mind as they sat at the rough, wooden kitchen table with mugs of steaming coffee warming their hands. The vase by the window was full again with yellow daisies clipped from the garden. He wondered whether this would be the last cup of coffee his wife would ever make him. He refused to consider comforting himself with thoughts of fixing it with another reset, another timeline. It was her decision now. If she left, he wouldn't force himself on a version of her who had never had this conversation.

When he finally looked up from his coffee, Holly was watching him steadily. She hadn't asked questions or tried to prod him into speaking, and this made him love her even more.

"I need you to hear me out," Nathan said. "You're probably going to be mad, and you might have a lot of questions, but please let me explain everything first."

"I can do that," she said. She blew on her coffee and took a sip, her eyes never leaving his face.

He took a deep breath and closed his eyes. Then he paused and opened them again. He had been too much of a coward to tell her everything until now, but he would look into her eyes as he did it.

"I'm on a reset."

Holly blinked. A moment later, her face grew confused, but she stayed silent.

"You died in a car accident," he continued. "I couldn't take it. Everyone at your funeral, they... kept telling me how if only we'd left a moment sooner, or a moment later, then maybe it would have been okay, and how bad our luck was, and I missed you so much and I couldn't take it. So, I got hold of a reset and I went back. You wouldn't move anywhere else and you wouldn't go on a different day or at a different time or by a different route. Leaving earlier didn't help. Leaving later didn't help. I couldn't save you once. Not even once, Holly, and I don't know what to do anymore, and I miss you so bad."

Nathan had started to cry in the middle of his explanation and now he hid his face in his hands and sobbed. He was surprised to hear the scrape of Holly's chair on the floor and her footsteps coming toward him. She bent and put a warm hand on his shoulder. He looked up at her, his eyes burning and aching, feeling more hope than he had dared imagine.

"How many times?" she whispered.

He froze. His face suddenly felt distinctly sticky and swollen, childlike, shameful. He had heard that question every time he had murdered Edward Weaver, but only ever once before from Holly.

"Eight."

"Eight," she repeated. She closed her eyes. Inhaled slowly. Exhaled. "How?"

Nathan's throat locked up. He had known that she would grasp this immediately, but he still couldn't force his lips to form the words.

Her hand tightened on his shoulder. "How, Nathan? How did you get it? Because unless you suddenly became a very rich man after I died, there's only one way you could have gotten it."

"I killed someone." He couldn't look at her anymore. His eyes fixed on the digital reading on the oven. She had removed her hand and backed away from him.

"I'm sorry. I didn't know what to do. I didn't know how else to get back to you, I'm sorry—"

"You killed someone. Eight times!" Holly said, cutting off his babble.

"I didn't know if you'd understand—"

"What part wouldn't I understand? The murders?" Her eyes blazed for a moment before she dropped back into her chair and put her forehead in her palms. "Have we ever had this conversation before?"

"No," Nathan whispered. Something hot lanced his guts each time she said "murder," exactly the way the voice in his head always did. She let out a little laugh.

"You killed eight people before you thought you might ask me if I was okay with it?" she asked. When she looked up at him again, he pushed the heels of his palms against his eyelids, unable to meet her gaze. He heard her breathe deep again. Then again. "Oh, Nate," she groaned. "What a mess."

Déjà vu pinged sourly in Nathan's brain. There was the end to the sentence she'd started in his last reset. The hope that memory had given him drained through his fingers like sand.

Holly's chair scraped back again. He listened to her shuffle around the house with no desire to look up and watch. When he heard the rasping of a zipper, he supposed it could only mean one thing after a fight like this.

More shuffling, and then her voice in his ear. "I need some time to think," she said. "A few days. I don't know what to do, so...I'll call you no matter what. Okay? I won't just go dark forever."

Nathan's fingers tangled in the roots of his hair, pulling, pressing his palms tight against his eyelids. "I'm sorry," he whispered. "I just wanted to grow old with you."

She lingered for a few more seconds before her hand fell from his shoulder. Shuffling. The jingle of keys. By the time the front door had closed, the last heat from her hand had left his skin.

Maybe she'll go dark anyway once she has time to think. Maybe that's what you deserve, said the voice in his head. He wondered if that voice had always sounded so much like Holly's.

When Nathan arrived at Holly's first funeral, he couldn't remember the funeral director's name or the coffin in which the woman who looked like his wife lay. Looking at the flowers—white, frilly, with a smell that combined to create something thick and almost buttery—he guessed the choices had been made by her parents. They had somehow never discovered that their daughter hated white flowers. All of his bouquets had been yellow and pink. He smiled mechanically at this thought, and then haze overtook him.

His next clear memory was the haze breaking as he snarled accusations at his mother-in-law in a voice unlike his own. Perhaps he should have felt guilt at the sight of Jade Gray's crumpled, tear-stained face, but he could make none come. After all, hadn't it been she who insisted they visit for Thanksgiving? The haze washed back in as his father-in-law put an arm around her. The expression on Don Gray's face was almost like fear.

When the haze receded again, he was sitting on the floor in front of the couch, his head leaning on a cushion that he had wished into one long, lean thigh. His throat was sore, and his mouth tasted stale and fuzzy. In the haze, Holly had been with him, and that had been good. Out here, he had to see that she was not, and that was bad. He was on the point of sinking again when the commercial caught his attention.

An old man on what was clearly his deathbed, smiling. His family surrounding him, smiling. "I'll see you again soon," the old man croaked, and closed his eyes.

Nathan's eyes welled up again as the scene dissolved into an upbeat jingle.

"Never say goodbye," said a warm female voice from the speakers. "Only see you soon."

People like him didn't get to reset. Money could buy you tens or hundreds of lifetimes, every politician in power right now could attest to that, but people like Nathan made do with wishes and fantasies.

He closed his eyes, but this time the haze didn't come for him. His subconscious had already begun to consider possibilities other than money.

Nathan trusted his wife more than he trusted himself, and that was the only reason he didn't fabricate some excuse for going to find her. He had a much harder time stopping himself from destroying his phone to make sure he saw her one more time. He wanted her to make the decision, should have allowed her to do so from the start, so he would have to do it right. No more manipulation, no more thinking of how to do it better next time.

The idea that he could fix his mistakes in the next timeline had become almost an addiction. It was the only way he could reassure himself that things would be okay. For him, like the rich who owned reset devices legally, mistakes were no longer final. The only thing that kept him from trying new things without thought to the consequences was the sharp memory of Holly dying in his arms. A mistake could be fixed, but a mistake could also mean reliving her death again.

Shame rushed warmth into Nathan's face. His sharpest memory of his wife was of her death, but hadn't he been with her for eighty years? He had started this because he had felt cheated out of his time with her. As he had gotten more time, it had become wanting to grow old with her, not just have more time. When had he started believing that his life with her no longer started until after the day she died? Shouldn't he have known, after eighty years with her, whether she would come back? When had he decided that he knew everything he needed to know about her?

When the front door opened two days later, Holly had brought her suitcase back with her instead of bringing boxes. It was more than he would ever deserve.

"Ready to go?"

"Ready to go."

The lie came easily, as Nathan had promised it would. He didn't try to grab for the car keys, also as promised. Holly smiled at him as she scooped them herself and jingled them on her way to the door.

"Hold on," he called after her, and as she turned, he caught her with a kiss. He hadn't done this the first time she had died, and some eternally whirring part of his mind hoped that this would change the timing enough that maybe he wouldn't have to go through with his promise, but he shut it away.

She didn't want to know when. That had been her second stipulation for staying. She just wanted to live what life she had left with him, and that was good enough for her. Her first stipulation had been that it should be good enough for him too. He couldn't undo what he had done in previous timelines, but he could end the cycle in this one.

When he pulled away from the kiss, he arranged his face into a careful smile.

That will be the last time we kiss in this house.

He shoved that thought away before it could shout from every inch of his body.

Too soon, they were in the car. He had considered whether to hold her hand to keep her from noticing him shaking and had decided, in the end, that he could keep himself together for the last twenty minutes of her life. So he held one of her hands while she drove with the other, the sun soft on her face and blazing in her hair. He watched her instead of the road in front of them so that it would be just as much a surprise to him as it would be to her.

Except that it couldn't be a surprise to him, because he knew that her brow would wrinkle briefly in confusion, and suddenly she was saying "What is he—"

And then the shrieking of tires began, and the car slewed sideways, tilted, began to roll. Holly screamed over the sound of shattering glass and groaning metal. There was a roar of pain in Nathan's arm as her hand was ripped from his. He lost his sense of direction as the car continued to roll, mashing his head into the door.

Finally the car came to rest on its roof and the world seemed to go silent. Nathan had already begun to extricate himself from his seat. The jagged remnants of Holly's seatbelt swung in the edge of his vision.

He dropped down onto his shoulders and neck and could not scream out his pain because all the breath had been squeezed from his lungs. The few pieces of broken glass left in the window tore at his shirt as he scrambled out. The howling pain in his arm was new. He had never broken his arm before, but he had never decided to hold her hand before.

Even with the broken arm, dragging himself around the front of the car was not difficult. He didn't want to miss Holly's final moments. More than that, he didn't want her to be alone. Still, when he got closer, he feared that she was already gone. Her eyes were closed and an impossible amount of blood had spread under her head.

He brushed hair from her forehead. Her eyes opened.

"So this is it," she whispered.

Nathan nodded and picked up her hand.

"This is the last time. Promise me. The last time."

He nodded again, but she clutched at his hand and said, "Say it!"

"I promise. No more. This is it."

Her grip relaxed and the corners of her mouth twitched. "I love you."

"I love you too."

But her eyes had closed before he had finished. Her hand suddenly weighed more in his.

"Holly?"

Nothing.

"Holly?"

There were hands on him and voices in his ear, but he couldn't hear them. They patted at his face and grabbed at his broken arm, not knowing that the purpose of his last two hundred years was lying in the dark, shimmering rainbow on the pavement.

"No."

Holly's parents looked up at him with hurt eyes and he winced.

"I'm sorry," he said. "It's . . . she hated white flowers."

"Well, of course they're traditional, but we're more than happy to accommodate," the funeral director said. "What color would you like?"

More important than this, the hurt drained from her parents' faces. He really did love them.

IRMAK ÇAVUN

"Yellow," Nathan said. "Yellow and pink. She said they were happier."

"Anything in particular...?"

He closed his eyes, and the right memory came in flashes. Pale yellow ribbons on white chairs, stark against a darkening lawn. Gauzy white floating around bare feet on grass. Red hair backlit by sunset warmth. And in her hands...

"Pink peonies," he said. "Yellow roses and daisies. And pink meadowsweet."

Making Collaboration Work for You or Co-writing with Larry and Sean

BY SEAN WILLIAMS

Sean Williams is a multi-award-winning, New York Times *bestselling author of novels, short stories, and poetry. His professional writing career began when he placed third in the first quarter of the Contest and appeared in Writers of the Future Volume 9 in 1993. He has been a Contest judge since 2005.*

Sean has well over four million published words. He has worked with visual artists, dramaturges, composers, and other writers on collaborative works that include stories set in the Star Wars *and* Doctor Who *universes, original series created with Garth Nix, and a science fiction musical performed at the National Museum of Australia in Canberra. In 2017, he was the recipient of the Australian Antarctica Division's annual Arts Fellowship, which took him to Casey Station to research a novel combining the Heroic Age of Antarctic exploration with H. G. Well's* War of the Worlds.

An affiliate of the J. M. Coetzee Centre for Creative Practice, he lectures in Creative Writing at Flinders University in South Australia.

His latest novel, Impossible Music, *is an extended meditation on heavy metal, hearing loss, and hope.*

Making Collaboration
Work for You or Co-writing
with Larry and Sean

In 1993, the year I won a prize in Writers of the Future, Shane Dix and I were offered the deal of a lifetime.

We had become friends by virtue of the facts that we lived close by and liked each other's published work. As many new writers do, we talked about writing a short story together but had yet to find the right project. In the same vein, we both had plans to submit novels but hadn't made that big leap into the wider publishing world. Like *every* new writer, we dreamed of having books on the shelves with our names on them.

Then, the deal. Based on our separate track records and the fact that we got on, an editor offered us a contract to collaborate on a novel set in a shared world. Small publisher, untested universe, but it was a deal, and hey, they don't just drop out of trees—not in Adelaide, South Australia, anyway.

My recollection is that Shane and I discussed the offer over pizza, then said yes. But not without giving some serious thought to what would come after signing the contract.

Collaborating. On a novel. Huh. How would we go about it? What pitfalls should we do everything in our power to avoid?

That's where Larry Niven comes in. Not in person, but in the form of an essay.

Immediately on winning the Writers of the Future, I had joined SFWA. Their legendary handbook contained advice from such luminaries as Frederik Pohl, Nina Kiriki Hoffman, Kevin J. Anderson—and yes, Larry Niven, whose work I had loved from an early age. It was probably him who had first seeded the idea of co-writing in my mind, thanks to his work with Jerry Pournelle and Steven Barnes. No one, in my youthful opinion, was more qualified to write six pages under the title "Collaboration."

I read his essay, re-read it, then gave it to Shane for him to do the same. And then we got to work.

If the value of someone's advice can be measured in achievements, Larry's was solid rhodium. Shane and I went on to co-write thirteen novels together, award-winners and *New York Times* bestsellers among them. We were described by Paul di Filippo in F&SF as the "Niven & Pournelle for the 21st century"—a more fitting tribute than he knew. And my track record of collaborations didn't stop with Shane. I've written seven novels with Garth Nix and short stories with many other authors. I've co-sold TV series, co-created multi-media installations, and worked for big franchises like *Star Wars* and *Doctor Who*, which I count as a kind of collaboration, since there are so many people involved. All with Larry's advice in the forefront of my mind—and all alongside my solo career, which continues quite healthily despite my dalliances with others.

So why co-write at all? There are many answers to that question. Collaborating can be:

- creatively stimulating
- a way to learn (firsthand from a collaborator who is good at something you're not)
- motivating (you won't be the only person you disappoint if you miss a deadline)
- a jolt of electricity through the heart of a dead idea
- a safety net for catching mistakes, identifying blind spots, etc.
- synergistic, in that a positive outcome is one that neither author could have created on their own
- a method for keeping projects progressing even when you're not actively working on them
- a career-starter/booster/revitaliser.

It has its downsides, too. The eleven rules Larry listed in his essay are strategies developed to avoid some of them. Even though he himself admitted that he didn't follow all of the rules all of the time, they have all been relevant to me at one point or other in my career, and despite being first published in 1973 they still hold incredible currency. If you've read them already, you'll know.

That said, it never hurts to take a second look. Having taught collaboration workshops for many years, I reckon there's a better way to structure Larry's advice—more as stages along the way rather than rules to strictly adhere to. I hope he'll forgive me for taking the liberty.

Stage 1: You must *want* to collaborate.

Larry said it best in his Rule #4: "Most writers aren't built for collaborations." That's easy enough to see. We already know how we and our worlds work; adding someone else to the mix risks breaking everything. Then there's the whole fragile-ego business, the heartfelt desire to work alone in a cave, the terror of letting something go . . . and so on.

There's no shame in wanting to write on your lonesome. If you already know that about yourself, feel free to skip to the end.

Stage 2: You must want to collaborate *with this person*.

You will want a partner you respect and who delivers reliably. You will want them to bring something to the arrangement— be that an interesting perspective, a skill set you don't possess, or any number of things. You will want them to share your values and aspirations, and to be glad to have your name on the finished product.

You will, of course, offer the same in return, because, very importantly, you will want them to want to write *with you*.

A collaboration is a relationship. Like any relationship, it's one that's not going to work if there's doubt and suspicion between the people involved. "You must trust each other absolutely," Larry says in Rule #1, and that's a moving target. Sure, you may trust each other *now*, but you don't really know someone until you've raised a story together.

Collaboration can be an incredible boost to a friendship or it can sound a death knell, so choose wisely. With collaborators (as with marriages and agents, to borrow from Tim Powers), it's better to have none than the wrong one.

Stage 3: Get it in writing.

So you've agreed to write together. The next step is to create an agreement between you that will spell out rights, obligations, exit clauses... all that fun stuff.

Shane and I operated with nothing more than a handshake between us, and perhaps through blind luck we never lived to regret it. You want to be smarter than we were. Plenty of collaborations break up, and in other sectors of the creative industry—such as film—contingencies are set in place before work even starts. Why not between writers, too?

Things you might want to specify before putting pen to paper include: whose name goes first; whose agent will represent the collaboration; who owns what IP; and how you'll split the money, if any. You might also want to consider Stages 4 and 5.

Stage 4: Two critical decisions.

In Rule #7, Larry provided the two greatest antidotes to conflict I've come across in all my years of thinking on this subject.

The first is: in the case of disagreement, one of you has the final say. Doesn't matter how entrenched your positions become: *you know in advance* who will break the tie. By all means plead your case, but if you can't convince the veto-holder to change their mind, you simply have to concede.

This doesn't give the veto-holder the right to become a tyrant. It's simply a strategy to avoid protracted disputes.

You may, of course, consider specific cases depending on your strengths and weaknesses in certain areas. Writer A might have the veto when it comes to business decisions, say, while Writer B has the veto when craft is at issue. It doesn't really matter how you arrange it. As long as you have this parachute on your back, you'll likely never need it.

The second decision you need to make is: one of you has to be responsible for the final rewrite.

Why? Well, someone needs to do it to make sure there's no jarring mishaps on the style front. Whether this role is a burden or a blessing is up to the individual. Whether this person is the same as the one who holds the veto is up to the individual collaboration. Either way, at this late stage no one should make major decisions without consultation. Nor will they change the text so everything sounds like them.

You will find that a collaboration, assuming it's working as it ought to, evolves its own voice. The final pass simply makes it sing.

Stage 5: So. Many. Decisions.

"Every collaboration is different," says Larry in Rule #6. Until you discover how your collaboration works, you'll want to consider every aspect of the process and how it can be shared. Where it will take place, too. Shane and I were practically neighbours, but Garth and I live in different parts of Australia, which caused the occasional scheduling headache.

In terms of methodology, there are variables too numerous to list. My collaborators and I have written works based on a single author's idea. We've alternated drafts. We've split the text into different facets depending on who is better at what. The trick is to find what works for you and to stick with it until it stops working—then to find new ways all over again. (Stage 6 is especially important here.)

One particular thing you'll want to settle on early and *stick to religiously* is version control.

Stage 6: Communicate, communicate, communicate.

Larry's Rule #2 concerns the exploration of ideas: "Talk is recreation. Writing is work. Until you're sure you want to do the work, *keep talking*." Which is great advice, but I would go further. Communication is essential to every stage of the collaborative process, from conception to completion.

Communication is the oil that keeps relationships ticking over. Never skimp because it seems too hard; failure to communicate will make things harder in the long run. Ask questions. Offer opinions. *Listen*. If you don't understand what your collaborator is saying, tell them that. Respond to what they're telling you in a reasonable time.

That doesn't mean you have to be one hundred percent agreeable. Conflicts are inevitable, but they are not essentially bad; they are, in fact, opportunities to find ways to do things better. When you have fears or concerns, raise them with your collaborator before they impact on the relationship. And if you have to critique someone's work, do it kindly, because you're likely to be next.

Larry's Rule #8 fits in here, I think: "Outline what you're doing." Even when you don't really know what you're doing, it'll help if you're lost on the same page.

Stage 7: Make it real.

All writing, from single or multiple authors, lives or dies in the execution. Talk all you want, but if at the end of the metaphorical day you don't have a story, then your collaboration has failed. So get to work and see what happens.

It should be easy, right? Two heads are better than one. Two sets of hands, ditto.

Sadly, no. Larry's Rule #5 states unambiguously: "Don't expect a collaborator to save you work." Apart from all the talking and the rule making and the contracts that should happen before Stage 6, there's the simple reality that no two heads will ever function as one. The potential for inefficiency squares every time you add a new person to the mix (I claim naming rights for this law if it doesn't already exist) and the total amount of work goes up accordingly. Even though there are two or more of you working on just one project, you might end up feeling like you're doing nearly as much work as you would on your own. Larry advises to "go into it expecting to do 80% of the work" for a total of 160% with two people. That, in my experience, is a good estimate.

When it comes to collaboration, the math just doesn't add up. (Don't forget that when your masterpiece sells, you'll be paid half as much!) Except it *does* add up. Collaborating may not make writing easier, but it may make it better, more fun, more whatever it is that you're seeking from this bold, new venture.

Stage 8: Credit where credit's due.

"It doesn't matter who contributed what idea." That's what Larry says, and I agree. By the time your collaborative project has made it into the world, you'll likely have no easy means of distinguishing the source of any particular element. That great joke? Could be yours, but you don't remember for sure. That big twist? Could be your collaborator's, but they've forgotten, too. It's natural, and normal, and nothing to worry about. It is, in fact, a good sign.

I mentioned in Stage 4 that collaborations evolve their own voices. This applies to ideas, too. My film and TV collaborator introduced me to the idea of "the third idea." Say I come to the table with a concept so brilliant it's guaranteed to blow her mind. The only problem is, she has one of her own that she expects me to be floored by. We can't agree on which is best, so what do we do?

Before invoking the veto power that one of us holds, we try finding the third idea. That's the idea we didn't know we needed, the idea that's out there, just waiting for us to find it. What's more, it's usually better than either of our original ideas. But who does it belong to?

To both of us. To the collaboration. To the weird gestalt that forms when two or more people sit down to make something wonderful together.

Conclusion.

If you've read this far, you might be having second thoughts about collaborating with anyone, ever. It's too hard. Too complicated. Too *fraught*.

I hope my final words will change your mind.

A writer never stops learning. That's why I keep asking writers who collaborate for the hows and whys of their working relationships. Without exception, they all tell me the same thing.

Co-writing can be immense fun. I'm not saying it's the most fun you'll ever have with someone else, but it can be a powerful antidote to the many forces that will grind your enthusiasm for writing into the dirt if you give them half a chance. A quick story with your mate (or two) might be just the reminder you need of why you got into this in the first place. For the whizz of words going by, for the fizz of fabulous ideas. For *story*.

Misery loves company, and so does mastery. For those two reasons alone, it's worth a try.

The Phoenix's Peace

written by

Jody Lynn Nye

inspired by

ECHO CHERNIK'S *UNCERTAIN EGG*

ABOUT THE AUTHOR

A native Chicagoan, Jody Lynn Nye is a New York Times
*bestselling author of more than fifty books and 165 short stories.
As a part of Bill Fawcett & Associates (she is the "& Associates"),
she has helped to edit more than two hundred books, including
forty anthologies, with a few under her own name. Her work tends
toward the humorous side of SF and fantasy.*

*Along with her individual work, Jody has collaborated
with several notable professionals in the field, including Anne
McCaffrey, Robert Asprin, John Ringo, and Piers Anthony. She
collaborated with Robert Asprin on a number of his famous Myth-
Adventures series, and has continued both that and his Dragons
Wild series since his death in 2008.*

*Jody runs the two-day intensive writers' workshop at Dragon
Con, in Atlanta, Georgia, over Labor Day weekend.*

*About "The Phoenix's Peace," she said, "I was delighted to
learn that Echo Chernik, an Illustrators of the Future judge and
coordinator of the artist winners' program, was painting the cover
of this year's anthology. I love her work, with the curving lines,
lush figures, and rich colors inspired by art nouveau. I volunteered
to write the story that went with whatever she produced, and
my offer was accepted. I am fortunate that the opportunity was
available.*

*"When I saw the finished artwork, I was enchanted. I am
familiar with the legend of the Phoenix. At the end of her long
life, the mystical bird settles into her nest and bursts into flames.
Nothing remains afterward but ashes—and one shining egg. From
that egg, the Phoenix rises, reincarnated as a young chick to begin*

her life again. Echo took the legend in a different direction: what if, instead of one egg, the dying Phoenix left two? I found the concept intriguing and inspiring. How would the world change from the moment they hatched?

"I started publishing professionally too early to participate in the Writers of the Future Contest, but I might have submitted a story like this for the judges' consideration, featuring a compelling central character, this lovely young priestess, whose dearest dream can only be accomplished if the rest of the world is at risk, a lot of magic, a little love, and a twist of my own to complement Echo's."

ABOUT THE ILLUSTRATOR

Unlike all of the other stories in this anthology where the illustrations were commissioned for each story, here Jody Lynn Nye conceived her story based on Echo Chernik's illustration, which graces the cover of this Writers of the Future volume. For more information on Echo and her painting, see page 4.

The Phoenix's Peace

War is inevitable," intoned the High Priestess Aduna. Her voice, though still resonant, musical and deep, cracked with age. She dropped to her knees in front of the golden altar.

Melana cringed, knowing how arthritic those bony old knees were. Melana bowed her head and joined in the prayer. "Our country is at risk. If this is the time, come to us, come to us now! As your mother arose to succor Dembia, and your grandmother, and your great-grandmother before her, as since the hatching of the World Egg, come to us, holy Phoenix—Phoenixes." Her tongue stumbled on the word. "Come to us, come to us now!"

"Come to us, come to us now," Melana chanted, along with thirty other priestesses and postulants in the Nest Chamber of the Temple of Peace. She spread her hands out before her palms up, and swayed from side to side, feeling her gold, red, and white skirts brush against her legs. Her long, thick black hair was crowned with a golden diadem that resembled feathers. More gold feathers swung around her neck and waist, smoothly brushing her deep brown skin. She was prepared, should a hatching begin, to offer her hands, her body, and her heart to the country's protectors. "Come to us, come to us now!" The pulse of the drums and the lilting music of flutes rose around them, echoing off the red marble walls of the inner chamber. The music made Melana's soul soar to the lofty Temple ceiling decorated with polished golden images of flying Phoenixes.

Nothing happened. Nothing ever did, not in the five years that Melana had been chosen as one of the sacred band of Protectors of the Egg, nor in the twenty-two before that. The singular title still held, though history had changed at the fiery blaze that claimed Ucutumwa, the last Phoenix of Dembia. Upon that great golden altar, engraved and enameled with stories of every incarnation of the Phoenix, lay a nest woven of jewels and wire as fine as strands of her hair in which reposed not one, but two eggs. Two bright, shining ovals of gold, gleaming more brightly than the mined metal. Two, as brilliant as the sun on the water. One slightly larger than the other. But, two. Not one. *Why?*

Historians and magicians had argued the reasons for that unique and bizarre change. Melana and half of the priestesses were too young to remember Ucutumwa. The girl and her five siblings had listened breathlessly at their grandmother's knee how the Phoenix's egg had cracked the day Colodino enemies swarmed over the mountainous northern border of Dembia, sacking its second largest city, Megros. Together with her priestess, Thonia, Ucutumwa had used her magical powers to drive out the invaders, giving Queen Zini's generals and diplomats time to fortify defenses on the borders and to find out what had made Colodi break the decades-long peace. The accounts of those negotiations were recorded in annals stored in the Temple library, open to anyone who wanted to read. Deals were struck. Trade resumed, and travelers came and went, all under the auspices of the Phoenix of Dembia, as it had been in every incarnation of the great magical bird. On Thonia's shoulder or nestled in her arms, Ucutumwa had been always present at the right hand of the queen, spreading her magic over the negotiation. Zini had been succeeded by her grandson, Alimbi, and still Dembia lived in peace.

Then, the day had come when Ucutumwa had grown old. She left her grieving companion and had taken to the nest. With a cry that the older priestesses said they would never forget, the Phoenix had vanished in a blaze of red and gold fire.

Free eBook

Enjoy *L. Ron Hubbard Presents Writers of the Future Volume 36* eBook on any eReader device. Simply fill out this card and send it in. We will email you a link to download the eBook edition of *L. Ron Hubbard Presents Writers of the Future Volume 36* absolutely FREE.

☑ **Yes, send me the FREE** *L. Ron Hubbard Presents Writers of the Future Volume 36* **eBook and a Galaxy Press catalog.**

Send in this card today and get your

FREE eBook & Catalog!

PLEASE PRINT IN ALL CAPS

First _____ MI ____ Last _____

Address _____

City _____ State _____ ZIP _____

Phone # _____

Email _____

☐ **Yes, send me newsletters and further information via email.**

Call toll-free: 877-842-5299 • International: +1-323-466-7815
or visit us online at GalaxyPress.com
For more information send us an email at sales@galaxypress.com

Fold at dotted line and tape closed with payment information facing in and Business Reply Mail out.

7051 Hollywood Blvd., Los Angeles, CA 90028

CALL TOLL-FREE: 877-842-5299
FOR NON-US RESIDENTS: 323-466-7815
OR VISIT US ONLINE AT
GALAXYPRESS.COM

When the flames died down, they rushed to behold the newest egg that contained the soul of the immortal and ever-rising bird, only to discover that Ucutumwa had left them two eggs. One— and a puzzle.

When Melana was small, listening to the gripping tale along with her brothers and sisters, her mind had pushed aside the boring parts about trade and war and deal-making. She envied Thonia. She wanted to be the one whom the Phoenix loved for a lifetime. With two eggs, the possibility of becoming that guardian doubled. Why shouldn't one of them be her?

"Do you want us to go to war?" her mother had demanded, unbelieving.

"No!" the child Melana had protested. But if that was the only way to become the Phoenix's companion, then she supposed she must. Her mother looked so horrified that Melana made a joke of it. "Do you think the Phoenix will rise if I start a fight with my brothers?"

Her mother had shaken her head and shooed them all out to the open-air kitchen to help make supper. Under the warm tropical sun, Melana's strange words had been forgotten.

Even when her siblings found other interests, the obsession with the Phoenix never left her. When Melana turned twelve, she joined other would-be postulants in Rigulos City Temple to be interviewed by the seekers from the Temple of Peace in Dembia's capital, Luros. If chosen, she would join the priestesses caring for the Phoenix's eggs.

She would have done or said anything to sway the seekers. Three firm but kindly women dressed in flowing scarlet and gold, their warm, walnut skins youthful, though their long black tresses were shot with silver. Their hands moved with the grace of birds in flight, putting the nervous children at ease. They had the girls sit in a circle.

The senior seeker, whom Melana came to know as Olinke, produced from a slim enameled case one single feather of such brilliant gold that it nearly blinded the girls. She touched it to the forehead of each girl. Warmth spread from that brushing kiss, flowing into Melana's body. If a mere feather could do such magic, imagine what the Phoenix herself was capable of!

"What do you dream of?" Olinke asked them.

Melana listened with envy as each girl related the fascinating, complex, ever-changing visions that visited them at night, like the great stories her aunties told on feast days. When the seeker came to her, Melana wanted to lie and relate the biggest, most impressive sounding fantasy she could think of, but the feather magic chided her gently. Ashamed, she blurted out the truth.

"Nothing."

The girls snickered. Olinke regarded her with kind, golden-brown eyes.

"Nothing at all?"

Melana felt her cheeks catch fire with shame.

"No. I fall asleep and I wake up."

Olinke smiled and shook her head. She turned to her sisters and made a gesture of dismissal. Melana didn't need to have her failure spelled out for her. She clambered to her bare feet, feeling as though she had been whipped, and shuffled toward the door.

"Where are you going?" Olinke asked. "You are the one we have been looking for. When the time comes, the Phoenix will fill your mind with dreams."

Melana couldn't wait for those dreams, and more. Everything the teaching sisters told her about the Phoenix who was to come was more fantastic and amazing than the tales she had heard. The magic that would come to all of them when the sacred bird hatched was stronger than anything performed by court wizards. Like any power, it could be used for good or ill, but the Phoenix herself exuded an air of calm and control. You couldn't help but want to please her. The aegis that would fall upon the chosen companion was the strongest of all.

Beside the altar was a throne in which the priestess would sit. An image of the Phoenix with wings outspread made the high back of the chair. All along the posts and legs, feathers had been carved that looked so real Melana expected them to be soft and downy. A round cushion of gold and red silk lay upon the seat. Rumor had it among the younger priestesses that it was stuffed with feathers from previous Phoenixes, but Aduna wouldn't even dignify that speculation with a reply.

Behind the throne, a mannequin held the regalia a priestess would don when the Phoenix chose her. A crown larger and more ornate than their diadems stood on the head, delicate gold and ruby bracelets and anklets adorned the wound-wire limbs, and a jingling belt of carved feathers was wrapped around the hips. The most magnificent part was the huge golden wings, taller than a man's height and almost two wide, and held on by a pectoral of feathers made of gold that would be worn over the priestess's bare breasts. No one had worn them since Thonia had passed away six years before. Melana would have died to try them on, just for a moment, but a spell of repulsion kept dust off the throne and regalia, along with an ambitious and curious young woman. They were only to be used when war threatened and the sacred bird required her companion.

Still, as long as Dembia's neighbors offered no threat, the Phoenix eggs remained unhatched. Every day the priestesses made the same prayer, bidding the Phoenixes emerge and bless them with its visions of peace, then resignedly went about their business. Melana couldn't help feeling impatient that the egg continued to sleep. She didn't care which of the two it was as long as the great bird loved her. She already knew she would love it.

Her daily duties were not onerous, since she could accomplish all but the most vital with small spells and cantrips. No dust settled on the great bookshelves in the library or on the precious vessels in the room where the priestesses formulated potions for healing, ease in childbirth, and calming of the mind. The inlaid marble floors cleaned themselves, a nice change from Melana's early days, when sweeping and scrubbing began again at the near end of the house as soon as she finished washing the far end. She and the other young priestesses took instruction in the tasks expected of them as well as in mystical means of defending themselves from attack.

"Many of these tasks will not be possible until the Phoenix—Phoenixes—come," Aduna said, pounding the end of an ironwood cane on the marble floor to keep the young women's attention. "For others, you will draw upon the power of the earth and sky, as need arises. The Phoenix expects you to behave responsibly."

Melana and her friends exchanged amused glances. How could they resist experimenting with their new abilities? Tirinia, the youngest and newest priestess, discovered she could cling to a wall and climb like a spider. Others found talents in sweetening sour wine, bringing the rain, or hearing the thoughts of animals. Melana spent hours seeking her own talent, but her mind scattered to too many places. Aduna demanded that she concentrate, but she didn't want to focus on only one thing. Magic was too exciting!

They also learned how to deal with those who rose up as enemies of Dembia.

"Always show mercy," Stihila said. She taught the history of warfare to the entire group, since no one could predict whom the Phoenix would choose as her companion. "Drive them out, don't wipe them out. Leave the enemy a means to escape, and they will respect you. The goal is peace. Knowing you will hold back the death blow is the most powerful weapon you wield. Retreat is honorable. Control your anger. Give them room to depart, no matter how much you want to break them."

"But some of our soldiers will die if we let them move freely!" wailed Elori, a small, plump girl from the hill country. "Honorable men and women who protect our land may suffer because we held back."

Stihila gave her a sad, kindly smile. "They will rise again, like the Phoenix, into a land filled with peace. If you show mercy to your enemies, you stand a greater chance of gaining their trust and friendship later. Have faith. You cannot make allies of the dead."

Elori didn't look convinced. Neither was Melana, but each of these lectures gave her much to consider as she went about her daily tasks.

Apart from wishing the Phoenix *would* hatch, her favorite role was that of guide to her new home. The Temple of Peace always had visitors, from shy worshippers who lived in the far corners of the tropical forest to diplomats and nobility from foreign countries. The tall, golden stone structure lay in the heart of hectares of garden tended by Melana and the other priestesses, alongside acolytes and volunteers devoted to the Phoenix. Curved walls circled the grounds. At a distance, the Temple looked like a great nest, a tribute to the bird herself. It held rooms within rooms, cellars upon cellars, and tiny niches no one had discovered for years, if not centuries. When she was not guiding visitors to the Nest Chamber or helping scholars in the library, Melana explored. A few of the older priestesses found her curiosity dismaying, but Aduna and Olinke encouraged her.

Outside, wagon and animal traffic in the city near the Temple made for a disturbing cacophony, but inside, the reservoir of peace had become a haven of silence, birdsong, and music. The priestesses gathered in small groups to discuss tidings brought by visitors. At prayer time, everyone assembled in the Nest Chamber to ask for the Phoenix's benediction. Meals were shared in the garden or in the open-air refectory, though the local birds, lizards, and monkeys often joined the humans in their repast, cheekily stealing crumbs or crusts right out of diners' bowls.

"Melana!"

She looked up. Shala hurried toward her, waving. A couple of men in court dress strode in her wake, one very tall and slim, the other the same height as the priestess. Shala, slender as a passing thought, with cheekbones sharp as razors and big, bright black eyes, always had male company. Forming a love relationship wasn't forbidden, as decades, even centuries, could pass between incarnations of the Phoenix of Peace, though few priestesses bore children. Both of her companions were handsome young men, clad in the black and yellow livery of Jumheuri: yellow trousers gathered at the ankle, black silk slippers that turned up at the toe, and a leopard-spotted shawl with a golden cat's-eye brooch worn over one shoulder. They must be visiting from their embassy. Melana smiled at them and rose to her feet.

Shala drew the taller man forward with her arm crooked through his. She tossed her head, making her hair, and the beads braided into it, dance.

"Melana, meet Lord Suleyman Das. He is the son of the ambassador of Jumheuri."

Melana offered her hand to the tall gentleman. "Honored One, I am pleased to greet worshipers of the great Leopard."

He took her fingers gently. "I am honored to meet one of the Phoenix's servants. May I present Ingalo Res? He serves as my secretary, though he is also of noble blood."

Melana almost gasped when she met the other man's eyes. Long, thick dark lashes that any girl would envy surrounded eyes of deep brown, a mix between blood red and black. The corners of his full lips rose in a tiny smile. His curly black hair shone with blue and green lights. Under the cloth tossed over his left shoulder, his bare bronze chest was broad and muscular.

"Lord Ingalo," she said, releasing Suleyman's hand and offering hers to Ingalo, hoping he had not noticed her hesitation. He squeezed her fingers once and let go.

"He saw you at prayers this morning," Shala said artlessly. She typically said whatever came into her head. "He said he was interested in meeting you. He likes a girl with curves like yours."

Melana felt her cheeks burn.

"Well, you may admire them," Melana said, eyeing him sideways through her lashes. The sight pleased her.

"I hope to do that," Ingalo said, his smile broadening. "In the meanwhile, Shala says you are the most knowledgeable about the Temple and its buildings. Would you be so kind as to show them to us? We want to see everything!"

"In the name of the Phoenix who sleeps, be welcome," Melana said, putting her hands together. They copied her gesture, then followed as she turned to lead them inside.

Most visitors wearied of endless chapels and meditation gardens, preferring to view the treasures of the Temple briefly, then go straight to the Nest Chamber to see the eggs in their nest on the altar. Suleyman and Ingalo never showed impatience. They kept asking her questions about the buildings, their origin and history, and all the small details she had discovered during her tenure.

Suleyman let out an audible gasp at the vast, blue-painted library in the north end of the main keep. Scrolls, palimpsests, bound volumes, even treatises engraved on sheets of horn or carved into wood were preserved there on endless shelves and in beautifully made chests and boxes. They kept their voices hushed despite there being only eight readers at tables in the whole room.

"You see, artists dedicate their best work to the Phoenix," Melana said, halting by an enchanted crystal cube that held the oldest and most fragile of their treasures, a miniature book believed to be over ten thousand years old. It was one of her favorite pieces. Every day, the archivist turned to the next page in the book to display the perfection of each tiny illumination, limned with powdered jewels.

"The Phoenix whose history is recorded in it was named Bocoretwa," Melana explained.

"Why does she have different names? Aren't they all the same bird, born again and again?" Suleyman asked, brow furrowed.

"You know our history well." She smiled. "It's true. The Phoenix of Peace retains her memories throughout incarnations, but lets her new companion know the name by which she wants to be called in each life. Sometimes her color pattern differs. Sometimes she is larger or smaller than the time before."

"What about these next ones, the two unhatched eggs?" Suleyman's eyes bored into hers as though trying to read her mind. "Our Sultan believes it is a sign that two eggs came forth from the fire. Does this mean the power of the Phoenix is meant to be shared? Perhaps one bird to be here, and one somewhere else?"

Shala gasped. Melana looked at the men in horror. "The

Phoenix will never leave Dembia," she said. "She is our guardian and our light."

Ingalo shook his head. "Your intensity shocks our hosts, Sul," he said. "Wishing is not having. Please, may we go on with our tour? We have not yet seen the Nest Chamber, and it is almost time for evening prayer. Then you must show me your favorite parts of this beautiful complex."

Melana appreciated his tact, but inwardly she was shaken at the notion that other nations had been discussing the second egg as if it was a commodity to be given or traded instead of the most important thing in the world. She didn't know why she had never considered anyone would think that way, but it shouldn't have surprised her. Jumheuri was Dembia's closest neighbor and ally. Most nations surrounding Dembia lay on the other side of mountain ranges or deep oceans. Jumhueri began at the eastern banks of the great river Solenke. Eight bridges spanned the enormous flood, though the spring thaw coming down from the highlands sometimes washed one of them away. Travelers and traders made the journey from one nation to the other constantly. Once she considered, she realized Jumheuri might believe the two lands were halves of the same country, only needing to be cemented by some…gesture? But thinking they were entitled to the Phoenix's egg was too much!

"Can we touch them?" Ingalo asked, gazing at the eggs like any spectator. His hands moved of their own volition toward the nest, then stopped. "What is in the way?" He waved a palm, and hot bronze energy shot from his fingers. The magic flame burst against the invisible barrier and rebounded at his hand. He yelped.

"It's the aegis of protection," Melana said, amused. "No spell can penetrate it. Only when the Phoenix is about to rise will it open. Until then, no one can touch them. No one needs to."

"It's selfish." Suleyman seemed to carry a little resentment at having been shot down over the notion of sharing the Phoenix's eggs.

Melana did her best to amuse him. "We all have to get used to it. We are creatures of habit, here." She pointed to a chair before the altar. "This is where our oldest priestess sits during services," she said, with a wicked twinkle. "She gets very upset if anyone else tries to sit there. If they succeed, she stands over them and prays *very loudly*."

The noble's bad mood broke, and he let out a playful cackle. "I must do that. It will be a great story to tell back home."

At that moment the music of flutes began, imitating birdsong and she felt Ingalo's hand envelop hers. The tingle of magic flooded through her.

"Prayers are about to begin, aren't they?" Ingalo said, raising her hand and kissing her knuckles, "I will see you later." Melana blushed as she watched him go.

Ingalo's attention devastated her ability to concentrate. Throughout the devotions, she couldn't help but think of him and his touch. Shala kept shooting her glances and nods toward the rear of the room. Aduna didn't seem to notice their inattention, but Olinke cleared her throat audibly. Melana turned away and concentrated on her prayers.

When services ended, most of the visitors went outside to join the communal evening meal. Shala caught her arm as they followed into the twilight.

"Did I do right, introducing you to Lord Ingalo?" she asked, wide eyes anxious.

Melana laughed. "We will see whether you have done *him* any favors by introducing him to me!"

"Oh, you always joke at your own expense," Shala said, pushing her playfully. "I can tell you like one another."

Glowing lights along the wall of the Temple shed soft golden light on the many benches and tables where the crowd of diners already had bowls of meat and vegetables in fragrant, spicy sauce, wedges of fresh bread with flavored oil, and wooden cups of fruit juice or wine.

"Melana!" Ingalo hailed her from where he and Suleyman sat

alone at the end of one long table. They must have fought to defend the seats beside them from other guests. The priestesses took food for themselves and joined them.

Shala leaned against Suleyman, sharing bites of food with him and conversing in tones so low Melana could hear only the occasional whisper and giggle.

"She is not serious about him," Ingalo murmured. "Neither is he. You are a more serious person, I think. If you were to say sweet things to me, I would believe you."

"Oh, you don't know me very well," Melana said lightly. "I'm not a serious person."

He kissed her hand. "You are one who should be valued above rubies. Should you ever leave the Temple with me, I would bring you to my mansion in the cloud forest. You would be lady of the heights!"

"I will never leave," Melana assured him. "The Phoenix will be mine when she hatches. I must be here when that time comes."

He laughed. "Are you so sure? Have you dreamed of it?"

"We don't dream," Shala said. Melana nodded agreement.

Ingalo looked from one to the other with a curious expression.

"Never?" Suleyman asked with a disbelieving chuckle. "What strange priests you are. Our Leopard Priests always dream of the future. They tell our fortunes weekly, or daily, if you have the gold."

"And what did they tell you about *your* future?" Shala asked, with a provocative glint in her eyes.

"Shall I tell you? Or show you?" Suleyman asked, wrapping one arm tightly around her.

Ingalo pursed his lips in amusement. His eyes twinkled at Melana.

"I think we should leave them alone, don't you?" He rose and offered her a hand. She jumped up, feeling awkward. "Show me the places you like best here."

She brought him through the herb garden, crouching beds of dense leaves between grassy paths now lit with the bluish glow of the full moon. Once they were out of sight of others, he drew her close and kissed her. His kiss was soft and filled her with a warmth she had never felt before.

"It is beautiful here," he said.

"You're not even looking at the flowers," she said, breathlessly. His touch left her weak in the knees.

"I see the most perfect of blossoms," he replied. "Take me further, dreamless beauty."

Voices grew louder as threshing footsteps approached. Impulsively, Melana took Ingalo by the hand and drew him down one of the side paths leading back toward the main keep.

"I will show you my favorite place," she said. They passed under a curved archway just past the entry to the Nest Chamber. Three doors were cut into the high wall beyond, but only the rooms through the center door were much used. She opened the left-hand door and guided him in.

Lamps glowed at long intervals in the narrow corridors through which she led. The light threw their shadows in black against the golden walls, and their footsteps hissed on the floor.

"Where are we going?" he asked, his whisper echoing off the stone.

"To a place no one else seems to care about."

Three turns took them to a staircase that led down into darkness. Melana paused. In her upturned palm, she gathered magic from the unseen sky and caused it to warm until light shone between her fingers. Ingalo drew a surprised breath.

She smiled. "It isn't very bright, but enough to keep us from stumbling down the flight."

At the bottom, a heavy door of rough stone opened far more easily than its bulk would have suggested. Inside, her small possessions were undisturbed: an ancient book borrowed from the Temple library, a jug of water and a clay cup, a cutwork image of the Phoenix from eight incarnations back, and a worn but thick cotton quilt that served as padding, blanket, or both, on the stone floor. With her outstretched arms she could touch all four walls, but the room had no ceiling. Instead, it was a shaft three stories high that opened to the sky. The full moon was just beginning to creep into the square aperture. She let her light spell fade.

"I come here often during the middle of the day when everyone else takes their rest," Melana said. "The sun comes blazing down the chimney, so I have plenty of light to read. Sometimes I meditate."

"It's cozy," Ingalo said, throwing himself down beside her. "Just big enough for two."

Melana let him draw her mouth to his lips. His hands stroked her body, up and under the gold pectoral that covered the upper surface of her breasts and down below the leaf girdle on her hips. "I will make you dream of me," he said, covering her face and neck with kisses.

She let herself enjoy the sensations he evoked from her body. She began to learn what pleased her and sought out what pleased him as well. She experienced some pain, which surprised her, but also bliss. Moonlight poured down upon them like a blessing. When it began to retreat at the other edge of the shaft, they lay together, her fingers playing over the hair on his chest as if she was ruffling the breast feathers of a bird. In the dark hours she helped him find his way out of the Temple and back to the now quiet main street.

In the morning, she approached the high priestess privately after devotions, and confessed what had happened. Instead of being angry, Aduna shook her head and smiled. She took Melana to a room beside the infirmary and handed her a bottle and a book.

"That's to prevent pregnancy, should you choose," Aduna said. Melana glanced into the book and blushed at the drawings on the pages. "Use them both, my dear, and may the Phoenix grant you fire."

Fire she found, in plenty. She felt doubly blessed, being a priestess in the Temple of Peace and spending the evenings after prayers in Ingalo's arms. They shared the experiences of their lives in the quiet times. He told her about life in Jumheuri, and she told him about her experiments with magic.

"Another night and the moon won't be looking in on us," he said one night, stroking her hair as she lay upon his chest. "I wonder when they will call us home."

"What?" Melana asked, lifting her head to look at him. "Why would you go?"

He let out a rueful chuckle. "My mission here is not forever. We seek favors of King Alimbi. When they are granted, or not granted, I must go back."

Her throat tightened so much she couldn't speak, and she hugged him hard.

Never mind, a practical part of her said. *His leaving won't be soon. It couldn't be.*

"What of it if they have to leave?" Shala asked, when Melana told her what Ingalo had said. "We will enter our next incarnation, like the Phoenix. Be happy *now*."

Both men were in and out of the Temple day after day, joining the priestesses at meals and after their duties were done. Melana pressed for details on how the embassy was doing, but Ingalo put her off. "You are my respite from the big matters. Let us talk about the small things."

Instead, she gleaned from courtiers and palace workers that the Sultan of Jumheuri wanted King Alimbi to marry his eldest daughter and heir, thereby drawing the two countries together as one in the name of the Great Leopard. The ambassador and his aides had presented the offer, a handsome one, with gifts for the king from the sultan and the princess.

The next day, the courtiers arrived to join in prayers, not looking as optimistic as they had before. The king had considered the offer and turned it down. He had another noblewoman in mind for his bride.

Melana and Shala finally managed to draw out Suleyman

about the situation. He looked glum. "It is true," he admitted. "My father made a stronger appeal, hoping to persuade Alimbi that this alliance was in his best interests. He promised to consider it, but I fear the Sultan will be displeased."

Ingalo found it hard to meet Melana's eyes, and his caresses were more distracted than before. Her sleep that night was more disturbed than it had been in the weeks before.

"Trouble is coming," Aduna declared before the next morning's prayers. She leaned over her ironwood cane as though the news weighed heavily on her. "Give your whole heart into your prayers that the sacred Phoenix will guard us."

Though Melana sought for him, Ingalo didn't come to meals or meet her afterward. She missed the comfort she found in his arms. The word from King Alimbi's court became even unhappier. Scarcely anyone wanted to gossip or pass cheerful words in the garden.

That afternoon the worst news possible arrived, brought by a high noblewoman. Jumheuri's leader had demanded both the marriage and one of the Phoenix's eggs, or Dembia would face attack. The nation across the river was far larger and had a bigger army than theirs. Unless the Phoenix or Phoenixes hatched, they would be overrun in a matter of days. Jumheuri's embassy was barred to outsiders. Heavily armed guards patrolled the walls and perimeter of the sturdy building. Passersby spotted war vehicles through the gates and troops drilling in the courtyard. Melana tried not to think about Ingalo.

She prayed harder than she ever had, devoting her free time to crouch before the altar and stare at the unmoving eggs.

"Save us," she begged, feeling sweat running down her body from her effort. "Come to us. Come to *me*."

It took all her willpower and experience at meditation to fall asleep in the dormitory room she shared with Shala. By the rustling from the nearby cells, none of her fellow priestesses could relax, either. The moon through the thick greenery had waned to its gibbous form, looking like a mocking face as it descended toward the west.

Melana must have dropped off at some point, because she woke gasping. She had dreamed.

"Did you...Did you...?" On the pallet beside her, Shala could hardly finish the sentence. Her eyes were wide with fear. "Jumheuri has attacked, hasn't it?"

Melana nodded. She still saw every detail of the visions. Soldiers in brown and yellow uniforms carrying weapons swarming over the bridges, some riding war leopards and others in vehicles bristling with cannon barrels. Men and women in the uniform of Dembia's army met them on the other side. The two armies met with a clash that sent blood spurting high into the air. Soldiers on both sides fell like wheat before a scythe. Leopards bounded, tearing into throats with their sharp fangs.

"If this is what it is like to dream, I don't like it," Shala whimpered.

"Come," Melana said, grabbing her hand. "The Phoenixes are about to rise! They will save us. We must be there."

They stumbled barefoot across the sun-washed courtyard into the Temple. The rest of the priestesses, still in their nightclothes, disheveled and frightened, assembled before the altar. The larger of the two eggs rocked and twitched, dancing to a frantic rhythm. The second lay still.

"Come to us! Come to us now!" Aduna chanted, falling to her knees. Melana felt the floor hit her knees, not even aware she had dropped. Visions swam in her sight, almost swamping the one thing she wanted to see: the egg.

Oh, come, blessed chick! she thought. *Be mine!*

The egg rocked back and forth. It pinged as the first crack appeared. A triangular section of shell shot out of the nest and tumbled across the floor with a noise like glass. Tirinia stooped for the fragment and clutched it. Tears poured from her eyes. Melana wiped her face with the back of her hand and discovered that she wept, too, whether for joy or terror, she didn't know.

Ping! Ping! Ping! More bits of the shell burst away. Melana

stood on tiptoe, trying to see into the nest, but it was surrounded by a halo of fire. The visions nearly blinding her were of flames engulfing the royal palace, burning the jungles and driving the wild animals into the city. The beasts tore innocent people in their terror.

"Come to us! Come to us now!" the priestesses chanted.

With a report like a massive tree falling on the marble floor, the larger egg split in two. A chick no larger than Melana's palm hopped up onto the edge of the gold nest. It was naked as a frog with bright red skin, amber eyes huge and bulging in its tiny head.

As they stared, minute tufts of orange down appeared on its body. More feathers followed, row upon row. The outstretched wings, no longer than a finger, fledged in moments with pinions of glorious gold. Tail feathers sprang from its tiny, pointed bottom, extending into swirling, long, curling plumes. The bird herself increased in size, doubling, tripling, quadrupling. The fires rose around her with a roar. Melana gulped. Was the Phoenix to be born only to die again? But the flames receded, leaving the fully grown bird staring at them with cocked head. Waves of calm and joy rolled out from her, driving away the feelings of dread. She was the bird of Peace. Melana sobbed, overwhelmed by the wonder.

"The Phoenix is here!" Aduna shouted, beaming. "We serve you, sacred bird! Bring peace to this troubled nation! Our hearts, our souls, our magic, all are yours to command!"

I am Coletwa, a voice said in Melana's mind. *You are under my protection.*

"I am Melana," she said aloud. "I serve you." Around her, all the priestesses announced their names. The visions still pushed at her, but she ignored them, unable to think of anything but the glory of Coletwa. The bird preened her new tail feathers, incandescent with their own holy light. Aduna approached her with her head bowed humbly.

"Will you, beautiful Coletwa, select one of us as your companion?"

"Me!"

"Me, blessed one!"

"Oh, let me be yours," pleaded another.

The Phoenix threw back her head and let out a trill of song. The sound was so delightful that Melana laughed. Coletwa turned to regard her with a tilt of her head. Automatically, Melana held out her bare arm. The priestesses hastily followed her example, providing a perch for the Phoenix to alight upon. The great gold wings spread wide, and Coletwa hopped into the air. She circled the room again and again, calling in that sweet, wild voice. In her mind, Melana heard prayers of peace that dated from ages past, to the time before the Temple, to the time when only animals heard that song.

Melana's arm ached as she waited, hoping, as Coletwa decided. All the others had devoted their lives to the Temple of Peace, too. Surely any of them were more worthy than she, but she wanted so much to have that lovely bird on her arm, to stroke that silken breast and head. Then, sharp claws penetrated the skin of her forearm, and the featherlight form settled into place as though she had always been there. The Phoenix had chosen her.

Will you stroke me? Coletwa asked, fixing those amber eyes on hers.

"Gladly!" Melana brought her against her chest and smoothed the tiny feathers of the Phoenix's head. Delight fountained in her heart. She had achieved the desire of a decade, and it was better by far than she had ever imagined. "Mine! You are mine! And I am yours."

That is good. Like a cat, the great bird moved her body so Melana's caressing fingers found just the right places. She *felt* Coletwa's pleasure. The sacred bird cooed and nestled into her hands. No one in the wide world existed but the two of them. She had never been so happy.

She was so immersed in her task that when a much heavier weight descended upon her shoulders, she looked up in surprise.

Aduna and Olinke were placing the regalia wings on her. Olinke fastened the elaborate gold pectoral around Melana's neck. They guided her to the golden throne beside the nest and helped her sit. She cradled the bird and continued her ministrations while the high priestess and the seeker fastened bracelets and anklets on her and replaced her diadem with the feathered crown. Peace and love enveloped her. All was well, but for one tiny feeling of uncertainty. She put that down to the newness of it. There was so much to absorb! So many new responsibilities!

"Congratulations," Aduna said, her wrinkled face pleated into a smile. "The new incarnation of the Great Phoenix begins, and you are her priestess. Now, use the magic wisely, as Stihila has taught you. Bring peace to Dembia and her neighbors."

The borders are breached, Coletwa said, sitting up high on Melana's arm. *We must put them to rights.*

"We shall," Melana said, soothingly. "We will aid the king in driving the enemy back."

No, now! The invaders come!

As one, the priestesses glanced past Coletwa to the second, smaller golden egg. It still had not moved.

"Perhaps it is dead," Shala said in a timorous voice.

A dark figure leaped forward out of thin air. Melana stared in shock as it shot toward her, heading toward the altar and that precious second egg. Coletwa shrilled and took to the air.

The borders are breached!

"I thought you meant the country!" Melana said, springing up. "Who are you? What do you want?"

One dark figure after another seemed to appear out of nowhere, multiplying impossibly before her eyes. She couldn't tell how many they were or where they came from.

"How did they get in here?" Shala cried. "Who are they? What are they?"

"Jumheuri!" Stihila was on her feet, too, gathering sky power in her hands as if she were making a bread roll. She threw the ball of energy. It landed in front of the lead figure and exploded in a burst of light. Stihila ran after it, making another. "Stop them!"

ECHO CHERNIK

Even before the tactician said it, Melana knew it was true. The darting dark figures wore black leopard masks and enveloping silk robes. The only spot of color on each was the glowing green jewel of protection amulets. Even under the disguise, she realized one of them was Ingalo. The tall one coming up the aisle from the right had to be Suleyman. They knew the protection spell on the altar had been broken with the rise of the Phoenix. They wanted the second egg, or the chick that hatched from it. The betrayal made her heart constrict in pain, but she had to push the pain aside for the sake of her Phoenix.

"Coletwa, help me!" she cried, hurrying to get between that first intruder and the nest.

The Phoenix circled around on one wingtip. Her tail brushed Melana's face. The priestess felt power fill her. She tried to remember Aduna's lessons, and swept both hands together.

A barrier of wavering golden light appeared between an intruder and the altar. He snarled deep in his throat and bounded upward in an impossibly high leap, almost clearing it. Melana clapped her hands again and a second wall appeared atop the first. The Jumheuri hit it and fell back to the floor. He gathered himself and threw himself at the wall, seizing handholds of the power as if climbing a rope.

Melana thought desperately through the skills she had learned, but they were all defensive spells. She had nothing that would attack the Jumheuri and send them away. The others flung barricades at the intruders. The leopard men jumped or climbed over them as if they were hurdles in a race.

Bang!

The report from a gun made Melana jump. They were armed!

"Surrender the egg!" Suleyman's voice boomed. "Surrender it or you will all die!"

"We will not!" Melana shouted back.

Another explosion from a gun, this time much closer to her.

Melana saw an illusion swim in her vision, a waking dream so powerful it almost put her on her knees.

She saw her own death. Her body lay on the altar steps, blood running from her mouth. From the expressions on the faces of the nearest priestesses, they had seen it, too.

Yet another bullet sang, this one passing so close to Coletwa, Melana felt its passage.

Melana lost her temper. "I don't care if I die, but you will not harm the Phoenix of Peace!"

"Overwhelm them, sisters," Aduna ordered, throwing out her hands. "Suffuse them with the goodness of their own natures. They must have virtue in them *somewhere*."

Melana felt ashamed for letting Ingalo worm his way into her affection, but her duty was clear. She called on her meditation skills to dismiss the negative emotions. Coletwa landed on her shoulder, and she felt the deep and benevolent sense of calm. She sent it radiating outward. The wall of peace was so powerful the Jumheuri dropped to their knees with heads bowed.

"That's better," Aduna said, turning her palms upward. "Now, come, brothers, we welcome you with love."

But Melana felt the spell breaking. Their leopard charms glowed angry green, and the power flung itself back toward the casters. The priestesses staggered with the force of their own spell. Aduna moaned and fell over. Her ironwood staff clattered to the floor. Shala had blood running from her nose and ears.

"The Leopard is as strong as you," Melana told the Phoenix desperately.

It is not, but my sister-self is in danger.

"The egg is alive?" Melana asked, astonished.

Yes!

The Jumheuri were scrambling to their feet. Melana had only moments to prevent them from achieving their goal.

She leaped toward the altar and scooped the egg from the nest. Cradling it to her, she dashed toward the nearest doorway. Coletwa clung to her regalia's wing joint.

"Run, Melana! We will delay them if we can!" Stihila cried.

Melana burst into the sunlight, surprising the few visitors in the garden. Some of them stared at the elaborate garb she wore.

235

It was much heavier than she'd ever thought it would be. The wings banged against her back with every step.

She sought around. So much of the Temple environs were open air. Anyone could spot her, wherever she went. Who knew if any of the leopards were already following her?

"We must get to the palace and tell the king!" she said.

We must not leave the Temple. The others will die. My power protects them while I am here. How did they overcome my power? Peace should have stopped their advance and given them perspective.

Melana frowned and thought hard as she ran. "Ingalo told me they had dreaming priests who predicted the future. They know about your abilities, so they designed spells to combat the patience and kindness we sent at them. They *want* to be at war!"

Coletwa sounded dismayed. *Is my time at an end so soon?* she asked, her voice in Melana's mind plaintive.

"No, never!" Melana insisted. "We will figure out how to stop them and the Jumheuri army. But we need time!"

There was only one place she knew she could be safe and stay within the Temple environs: her small haven.

Her bare feet torn by stones and body hammered by heavy gold regalia, she ran to the left door beyond the arch and threw it open. She was only a short distance ahead of her pursuers. Ingalo would figure out where she would go, but they wouldn't be able to breach that heavy door. By then, someone would have warned the king, or she and Coletwa would figure out how to undo the Leopard's power.

She bounded down the stairs, taking them two and three at a time. Footsteps hammered down the hallway in her wake. They were close, so close!

The heavy door swung open at her touch. She tumbled in onto the cotton quilt where she and Ingalo had shared so much pleasure. Coletwa flew in a spiral up the open shaft, calling desperately.

Close the door, close the door!

Melana tucked the egg safely into the box she'd reserved for her special treasures and flung herself at the stone portal. She had it almost closed when a hand gloved in black silk interposed itself between the door and the lintel. Melana shrieked and bit the fingers. A bellow came from the hallway outside, but the hand didn't move. She swung the door open a few inches, then slammed it on the hand. Its owner bellowed again in fury.

By now, many more hands had joined the first. Melana threw her slight weight against the portal, desperate to keep it closed. Coletwa landed on her shoulder, lending her power to defend her priestess.

It wasn't enough against the new spells of the Leopard. She felt the Phoenix's magic drain away, leaving them a helpless seventeen-year-old girl in fancy dress, and a young bird with long, yellow feathers. Melana was flung backward. Men in black silk streamed into the tiny room. Two of them grabbed Melana and held her with her arms pinioned behind her. Another bounded up the wall in pursuit of Coletwa, who flew straight up the shaft toward the sky. To Melana's horror, another servant of the Leopard appeared at the top of the chimney and seized Coletwa in his arms. The Phoenix struggled but could not move. Melana cried out to her.

"You should have surrendered," Suleyman said, pulling the cat mask from his face. Ingalo bared his, too. He at least had the grace to look sheepish. Suleyman demanded, "Where is the egg?"

"You can't have it!" Melana said, furious. "It belongs to Dembia."

"We will have it! My Sultan demands it!"

A deafening explosion rocked the room. Pieces of Melana's treasure box and shards of eggshell embedded themselves in the men's legs.

You want me, evil cats? Then have me!

The new voice in Melana's mind must also have been audible to the Jumheuri, because their eyes widened.

A tiny naked bird, smaller than the newborn Coletwa, bounded up Melana's body to her left shoulder and glared in Suleyman's face. The new Phoenix looked almost absurd. It was as white as chalk, with tufts of black and silver down sprinkled on its minute frame. In mere heartbeats its feathers filled in and its tail grew. It enlarged rapidly, until it was still only half of Coletwa's size, but its aura felt far larger than the room, or perhaps even the Temple itself. It glared at Suleyman with mad, silver eyes.

I am Solingwa. Fear me.

Suleyman laughed at the little bird.

"You are the Phoenix of Peace," he said. "We have defeated your sister's magic. Come, I'll take you to the Sultan as a prize."

He reached for the small creature. Solingwa didn't move, but when Suleyman's hand closed, black needles shot through the flesh. They struck the other men and embedded themselves in the wall.

The Jumheuri wailed in pain, wadding up their silk robes to staunch their bleeding. Not one needle had hit Melana, but Suleyman's hand bled from a hundred small wounds.

My sister is the Phoenix of Peace. I am the Phoenix of War. That was a small taste of my power. Let my sister-self and my priestess go.

Ingalo gestured hastily to the men holding her. Melana jerked her arms loose and glared at them. Coletwa, her glory restored, sailed down in a spiral and landed on Melana beside Solingwa. The two Phoenixes cooed and rubbed beaks.

"You see, Dembia is well protected," Melana said. After her fright, she couldn't help but enjoy the look on the Jumheuri's faces. "No army can withstand our power. Either you are at peace with us, or you will be defeated. Do you surrender?"

With blood dripping down his arm, Suleyman ripped the amulet from his neck and offered it to her. Ingalo did the same. Melana collected the charms, feeling the furious power within them, then called up the new force she felt coming from Solingwa. She crushed the amulets between her hands, smashing them into a harmless mass of gold and green shards, then dropped them to her feet. She had found her own magic. She channeled the Phoenixes—all of them.

"You are bleeding on my quilt," she said, narrowing her eyes at the leader and her former love. "Get out."

One month later, King Alimbi attended a massive service of thanksgiving, offering gifts to the new Phoenixes and their priestess. With the help of Coletwa and Solingwa, Melana had sent out waves of peace to the borders. When the Leopard's troops would not stop fighting as they departed, there were consequences. New tactics had been met by new tactics. Dembia was no longer under threat. The Sultan of Jumheuri had sued for peace within days.

Melana rose from her throne at his approach and bowed low. The Phoenixes, gold and silver, clung to her forearms. When she straightened, they walked up her arms to her shoulders, where they perched on the angles of her ceremonial wings. She no longer felt their weight.

"Will they bite me?" the king asked. He was a handsome man of thirty, with full lips and a snub nose between shrewd brown eyes.

"They serve Dembia, as do I, Highness," Melana assured him.

"You three have stopped a war," the king said. "I and all the realm are grateful. But I hear the victory was not without cost to you. A broken heart, perhaps?"

Melana shook her head.

"I am sad about Ingalo, Highness, but I know he could never have been my first, most important love." She caressed Coletwa, then scratched between Solingwa's black and silver wings. "Or even my second. I promise you, like Dembia, I am at peace."

Educational Tapes

written by
Katie Livingston

illustrated by
JOHN DALE JAVIER

ABOUT THE AUTHOR

Katie Livingston lives in Middletown, Connecticut, where she attends Wesleyan University for a BA in English. She spent her high school years tending chickens and writing speculative fiction novels, since there wasn't much else to do smack in the middle of rural Oklahoma. She is a fan of Stephen King novels, '80s horror flicks, rural living, and cats— all of which inspire her work. Katie hopes to attend graduate school for American literature so that she can continue learning, reading, and writing for many years to come.

ABOUT THE ILLUSTRATOR

John Dale Javier was born in 2000 in Queens, New York, but lived most of his childhood in La Plata, Maryland.

Unlike most artists, his interest in art didn't start until his second year of high school. Until then he was studying to become a programmer. He changed his career path after being encouraged by his mentor and colleagues and began self-study in both traditional and digital painting.

His inspiration was found in what entertained him in his youth— video games. From sci-fi to medieval, John would build on top of his favorite games and even create his own fictional worlds.

John is currently pursuing a double major in both illustration and game design at Maryland Institute College of Art and is working to break into the videogame industry.

Educational Tapes

1.

This is installment one of the government-issue educational tape for student 147B. If you are not student 147B, you may now remove your headphones and raise your hand. Your educational professional will provide you with further assistance. If you are student 147B, cross your arms and lay your head on your desk. Close your eyes and smell the faint chemical residue of the disinfectant that the school janitor used to wipe your desk down this morning. Smell, also, the dirt and playground rock dust still clinging to your skin.

Know there is nothing here to harm you. Only your choices. Only yourself.

Every choice that you have made up to this point was your own: eating toast for breakfast, putting on a wrinkled green T-shirt, watching a bug twitch on your windowsill until it lay still.

When the mail arrived at exactly 8:30 a.m. yesterday, like it does every Sunday, you made a choice to get out of bed and go directly to the mailbox. You made a choice to open it, to extract the manila folder tucked inside, to turn it over and run your fingers across the seal, careful not to break it.

You stared for a few seconds too long at the governmental logo embossed on the front before a bird perched near you, a little closer than birds tend to perch, and tilted its head ever so precisely toward you.

It was your choice to then tuck the manila envelope under your arm, run back into your house, and shove the package far under your bed where it would be safe from the piercing gaze of birds.

Some decisions are more important than others. Like the decision to speak up or remain quiet when two adults are arguing, or to move your mouth in mimicry of words in a chant without actually speaking them aloud, or to only pull out the manila envelope late at night, when everyone is sleeping, so that you can be alone with it.

You carefully picked at the corners of the seal, then put it back down on the bed and walked away. You came back later, picked it up, measured its weight in your hand. You handled it like a thing that could bite you. And it could. But not on its own. The choices are your own.

Manila envelopes always contain choices.

Some will say there is no need to fear this choice, as long as you make the right one. But the right choice made for the wrong reasons is still the wrong choice. And fear will give you a healthy respect for the decision you're going to make.

You do not need to worry, though, about making the choice now.

When you open the manila envelope with the governmental logo embossed on the front, you will be greeted with a thick stack of papers coated in fine print. It will look like a series of indecipherable symbols rather than a string of cohesive thoughts.

The papers are saturated with questions. Questions about you, your life, your childhood, your education, your likes and dislikes. Do not worry about these. These are for later. These you will fill out with the help of your parent, guardian, or an appointed educational professional.

The page that is important, the page that you are now worried about, is the final page. On this page, there is only a bit of fine print at the top, a box that says "I accept," a box that says "I decline" and a line on which to write a shaky, reluctant signature.

In the manila envelope that I have sitting in front of me, there is something different. There is more paper with more fine print. Fine print with a very specific set of instructions on how to conduct an educational tape.

The paper tells me that the instructions are only a set of guidelines, a framework on which to build.

I have other manila envelopes. Manila envelopes on you, on your case, on the way you pinch tacks too tightly between your fingers and gaze too long into the distance.

I also have tapes. Bits of audio collected over the years. Bits of video. Notes on behavioral analysis.

But the envelope in front of me now, the general one with the homogenized guidelines, says to make a point about the positives of becoming a citizen, a point about the greater good.

You already know about the greater good. You know about food supply and nuclear families. You are aware that society is an intricate machine and that you are an important piece of it and that the purpose of the machine is greater than your individual purpose. You know what it means to contribute to the greater good.

But why should that matter to you? Why should it matter to any child that a monolithic entity wants to swallow you up in contribution of the greater good?

I have taken a black marker and blotted out entirely this small bit of advice. I've erased a small part of what was in the manila envelope. I have made a choice.

2.

This is installment two of the government-issue educational tape for student 147B. If you are student 147B, cross your arms and lay your head on your desk. Close your eyes and think about the monolithic entity that wants to swallow your life whole in contribution to the greater good. Know that it does not seek to erase you, but to help you see yourself.

When you were six there was a book. A book that was passed

around at lunch tables so that it ended up with grease spots on the pages and scratches on the cover. A book that was whispered about in hallways and argued about on the playground so that fights erupted and a small boy had his face shoved into the rocks.

There was something surrounding that book. Something you needed to know. You wanted to read it. You asked your parents if you could read it. But the book was not a book for children, was not a book that you should have known about.

That was the first time you stole. The last time too, unless you've gotten better at it, hidden it from prying eyes, stayed away from birds.

You took the book from its place in the library and slipped it into the small and secretive pocket of your backpack. It was a pocket that you never used and so, you assumed, one that others wouldn't look into.

You could feel the book prickling there the rest of the day. It didn't matter where you were in relation to it, the part of you that was closest to it always had a desperate tingling sensation. You wanted to pull it out of your backpack, feel its weight in your fingers. You didn't.

You didn't see it until later that night when you removed it carefully from your bag as you sat cross-legged on your bed. You ran your fingers over its cover, much in the same way that you ran your fingers over the cover of the manila envelope today, assuring yourself of the gravity of the situation.

The ocean does not exist. It's imperative that you remember that the ocean does not exist. You doubted it once when you opened the finger-worn but still glossy pages of the book and read about endless shores and white sand, about deep undiscovered waters and the creatures that live there and beyond there. You went over and over the illustrated pictures and did your best with the words, though they were still only half-formed when you sounded them out as if you were speaking with rocks in your mouth. The book, itself, explained quite clearly that the ocean does not exist. That didn't matter to you.

Every night you pulled out the book, ran your hand along its pages, fumbled with the words, closed it, shut your eyes tight in bed, trying to control yourself, and then pulled it out again.

It began to consume you.

The school soon noticed the book was missing and the witch hunts began. Searches, bribes, whispers on the playground, calls home to parents. It all seemed, to you, more significant than it was in reality.

The world was no longer safe for you. You drew into yourself, keeping the secret locked so deep away that you almost convinced yourself that you had not stolen the book. But at night you still drew it out. At night it was still yours.

You were isolated. There was no one you could talk with about the book, no one you could show its illustrated, glossy pages, no one who you could show yourself to.

As your guilt grew, so did your shame, and so did your isolation. It was only you and your secret.

It is maddening, to act in one way outwardly and be another person entirely in your own mind. Transgressions, even if they're unintentional or uncontrollable, cling to you, set you apart, taint you. They will always isolate you.

This is why your choices are important. This is why you have reason to fear your choices.

You finally reached your breaking point. The book began to give your fingers a stinging sensation when you pulled it out at night. A burning in your throat. Shame.

You feared your confession but you feared worse isolation, so you tucked the book under your arm and walked to your parents' room, your footsteps muffled by the carpet.

You rapped on their door, waited, felt your heart beat in your chest, your ears, your mouth, your face. You felt your resolve melt, then solidify again. You rapped on the door, this time harder.

Your father appeared there, and you wished to god it had been your mother, but in truth, a part of you knew you needed him. You extended the book to him and it took him a second of processing to understand. After the processing came the anger. After the anger came the hitting.

Blunt pressure, then stinging, then flashes of warmth, blunt pressure again. It hurt, but it also felt like relief. You deserved it. You knew you deserved it. All that time, you had been aching for the punishment. You wanted to pay the price and move on. That way the sins would no longer stick to you.

Some sins always stick to you.

He didn't hit you for long, and when he finished, the dull throbbing of your skin and the tears streaming down your face felt like release. He knelt down, whispered forgiveness in your ear, and clung tight to you. You cried again, and this also felt like release.

He had rejected your sin, but he still loved you. This was acceptance. This was belonging. The warmth that spread through your chest when you finally realized that you were seen and known for who you were, the need to cling tighter to your father, to feel the comforting reassurance of his love wash over you.

This is why you will check the box marked "I accept" and write your name next to it.

3.

This is installment three of the government-issue educational tape for student 147B. If you are student 147B, cross your arms and lay your head on your desk. Close your eyes and think of the stinging of your father's hand against your cheek. Think of the release, of the acceptance, and, finally, of the warmth.

There is a book sitting in your backpack now. A book about the ocean. It is the same book stained by the hands of small children. It is stained, also, by your own, private memories. Holding it no longer feels enthralling. It is only a children's book, like many others that you've read, now far below your reading level. Its only significance is that one, lonely time in your life.

Perhaps holding it brings back bad memories. Or, perhaps, it still fills you with some shadow of an idea.

I should be clear. There are only two options. Only "I accept" and "I decline." There is no ocean.

Now that we have covered the personal reasons for choosing "I accept," let's take a look at some of the structures of our society and how you will operate within those structures, should you choose to mark the correct box.

Shortly after your entry into society is accepted you will be sent another manila envelope, this one much thinner. Inside, you will find a few sheets of thick government-issue cardstock marked with a date, time, and location. You will go to the location on the specified time and date and take a test. The lights in the testing room will be bright, a little blue, and flickering. This will make you feel as though you've done poorly on the test. That is a ridiculous thought. There is no way to do poorly on an aptitude test.

This test, along with the opinion of a panel of experts, and a detailed analysis of your previous performance in school, will be used to select a career for you.

Once a career has been selected, you will continue your schooling with a focus on this subject. Remember, for some careers you will have to move away when you are older. Most, however, don't require that you move away. It is only very rarely that this happens. If it does happen, you have no need to be afraid, only slightly apprehensive.

It is likely, however, that you will stay. That you will continue to live and work in much the same way that you always have. You will continue spending time with your family, attending after-school activities, participating in community-bonding rituals. You will continue to live a happy life until you reach age twenty-one, finish your school, and are placed with a permanent partner in a permanent home with a permanent job.

Again, it is likely that you will not leave your current town. Again, if you leave your current town there is nothing to be afraid of. Only slightly apprehensive. Apprehensive in the way that one is apprehensive when a loved one says they will be home at a certain time but is running significantly late and the gaps of time are beginning to be filled with all of the horrible ways that they could have died, even though you know deep down that they're okay, that they've always been okay in the past.

Of course, there is the off chance that this time they are not okay.

You will be okay. You will not be dissatisfied. You will not wake up at three in the morning with the residual feeling of a dream still clinging to you, making you feel as though you're supposed to remember something that you can never quite put your finger on.

Once you are put in your situation it will remain permanent. You will live out your days in the comforting lull of routine unless you are uprooted due to special circumstances. It's preferable to not be uprooted due to special circumstances.

This all might sound slightly terrifying. That's okay. It should.

The natural human response to that which is slightly terrifying is autonomy, rebellion, and control. But a lack of willingness to relinquish control inevitably leads to mistakes, regret, failure, and a waste of human life. Do not be arrogant. Arrogance is what leads us to think that we should have control over our own lives, that we know best how to live them. It shows a lack of understanding of the greater forces in our world, the ones that have our best interest at heart, that operate out of a selfless care for our well-being, and that use advanced algorithms to determine what trajectory in life will make us the happiest and most useful members of society.

Even if you meet some amount of suffering in this life, you should know that in the end, it will be worth it.

In addition to helping you structure your life, entrance into society will grant you more rights than you are currently afforded. You will be an active participant of the community-bonding ceremonies, annual rituals, and after-school studies, rather than a passive bystander.

It will be difficult to mouth the words of a chant rather than saying them aloud when you are the one expected to lead the chant. This is something you should begin taking into consideration.

Weekly community-bonding rituals have a few important purposes. They act as a reminder that we are part of something larger than ourselves and also help us better live out our daily lives as community members. It is important that you begin actively participating in community-bonding rituals. I know that the rituals are often grotesque, but you should know that there's a purpose for this and that the purpose is for the common good.

4.

This is installment four of the government-issue educational tape for student 147B. If you are student 147B, cross your arms and lay your head on your desk. Imagine for a moment that you have a mother. You do, of course, have one. But yours is soft-spoken and flinching.

Imagine for a moment that you are not you. You are a hypothetical you, a you being used for this hypothetical illustration.

You have another, different mother. Her hands aren't soft, but rough. Her cuticles are bitten and bloodied. Her eyes never focus. She never looks at you and when she does she is looking through you. She drinks, and you don't yet understand that she does this not to hurt you but herself. She goes through life in a constant state of lethargy. She rejects her duties as a wife, mother, and civilian. She does not attend community-bonding rituals. Until one day, she does.

On that day, you look up momentarily from your dry wheat cereal and see that she's put on a white shirt. Though the shirt is wrinkled, you think she looks beautiful. She notices you watching her and gives you a slight, wavering smile. This makes you happy. You go back to eating your cereal.

That morning you leave the house with your two parents, glad to feel the unfamiliar pressure of your mother's hand in yours. Just like every Sunday, you walk. The suburb streets are speckled with other families, much like yours, also walking. As the streets merge toward the center of town, the people grow thicker, until you are pressed up against them and standing in the square in the middle of town.

They begin chanting. The chants mean nothing to you now. You are too young to understand but you say the words regardless, liking the way that they sound leaving your mouth and drifting up, mixing with the other voices. It has not yet occurred to you that you might not agree with the words you are saying. Your mother is also chanting. This makes you happy.

When the chanting is done your throat is almost sore from it and your father has to keep you gently held up against his side, or else you would be on the ground pouting and begging to leave.

You don't listen to the droning words of the man in front of the crowd. He has nothing for you. Listening to him is boring. You wish you were home, outside in the backyard collecting bugs and pinching their tiny bodies between your fingers.

His words only mean something to you when your mother moves from her place beside you, hesitantly at first, as though she were just shifting her weight, and then more assuredly, leaving you, walking through the crowd, toward the man. You are suddenly very invested in the man and what he has been saying. What has he been saying?

You strain for it, but come up with nothing. All you can do is watch as she speaks to him in hushed tones. You feel nervous, but you don't know why. Your mother's hard face cracks. It has been a while since you've seen it do that. She sobs but you cannot hear it. You think that the man she is talking to also cannot hear it. It is too quiet, too closed up in her throat.

He puts a sympathetic hand on her shoulder, then he embraces her and holds her for a moment while she continues to sob. Suddenly you know why you are apprehensive. You

251

remember what this means. He says something in a loud and booming voice, something about transgressions and atonement. Your face is burning and you cannot move. Someone throws the first stone.

There are not many loose stones in the cobblestone-paved city square, so people have brought their own. You watch as they fly through the air and meet their mark.

She stands for a while, unwavering. But she can't stand for long. You stand and listen to the dull thumps of rock against her skin. You think you might be screaming but you cannot tell. Your father holds you and you listen until the thumps stop. The sound of your mother's screams, the cheering of a crowd, the thumping of stones is replaced by indifferent silence.

One by one the people disperse until it's only you and your father and your mother's limp figure slumped against the cobblestone pavement. Her white shirt is bloodied, her dark hair matted against the sweat on her forehead, her breaths are coming in rasps. In spite of this, she is conscious. She gives you another slight, wavering smile. This time, you don't smile back.

All you can feel is a numb, buzzing feeling in your face and in your chest. Your father scoops her into his arms and walks you both home.

You are convinced that everything around you is evil, but that is only because you do not understand. You do not understand that people have to be broken down at a fundamental level before they can be rebuilt into something new and better.

Your mother's bones are not cracked, and she has no internal bleeding but for the large bruises that have spread across her skin like a disease. In the next few days, the healing process begins and you begin to understand.

As her body mends itself her mind, too, seems to shift. There's a brightness, an alertness in her eyes. You think it might be panic but it slowly morphs into something else. Motivation. Determination. She smiles at you fully now, her eyes fixed right on you, usually. She only drifts occasionally. You only see her choke something down occasionally.

In the afternoons she is gone. Gone to a meeting, your father says. Something for people like your mother to go to after work. Something to keep the light in her eyes and the stones away from her flesh.

It works, for a time.

Pain is not innately bad. It can be used to mold and change us into better people. Refining a person is a painful and difficult process. You should, by no means, consider that process to be an evil one.

Active participation in community-bonding ceremonies, annual rituals, and after-school studies are imperative to your education and growth as a newly accepted citizen. If you want to be happy in these structures, it would be best for you to begin saying your chants aloud, carrying stones in your pockets, and not flinching when someone hands you a knife.

Taking these steps will ensure that you are more ready for entrance into society, that you do not have to keep rotting things stuffed inside you, like the hypothetical mother from today's illustrative story.

It will also ensure that you do not wake up at 3:15 a.m. with something moving in your chest, something that feels alive and separate from you but only slightly. Something that can't be cut out with knives or squelched by stones.

You will not get out of bed and pace the house until you find one tile in the kitchen to stand on and stare, unblinking, out the window. You will not hope that the feeling will go away, that it won't grow again, and that you won't end up like her.

If you say your chants aloud, you will not end up like her.

5.

This is installment five of the government-issue educational tape for student 147B. If you are student 147B, cross your arms and lay your head on your desk. Close your eyes and feel the cool of your desk pressed against your cheek, hear the humming of the air conditioner and the distant shrieks of laughter from the children outside taking their recess break. Know that you are safe here. Know that not everywhere is safe.

Today we will discuss the second option that is tucked into the manila folder, which is tucked under your bed, away from prying eyes.

Inside this manila envelope there is a box that reads, "I decline." Some wonder why the box "I decline" is included in the manila envelope. These nameless faceless people have argued that "I accept" should be the default option and that "I decline" should be obvious in the case that anyone should decline.

Children, they say, should be encouraged toward the most desirable option in any way possible. The people who propagate this idea, while well-intentioned, are severely misguided.

There is reason for the box which reads "I decline." The importance of personal choice cannot be understated in instances such as these. No one can coerce you into making a decision regarding the trajectory of your life or else the choice has not been yours. The choice has not been genuine.

It is for this same reason that I must explain to you your inevitable future should you choose to check the box which reads "I decline."

As you well know, those who live outside of the constructs of our society are forced into their only other option. That is, to live outside of those constructs. Alone, without guidance or protection.

It is an arrogant and foolish choice, a result of the idea that each individual has the capacity to control their own life. The cruel irony here is that each individual does have the capacity to control their own life, but the choice to cling selfishly to that autonomy results in unhappiness, lack of meaning, and, ultimately, death.

You already understand this on a rudimentary level. You understand that stealing a book from the library was your own, autonomous decision. You understand, also, that it resulted in your isolation. Keep this in mind when choosing between "I accept" and "I decline."

As for the nuances of living outside of the structures of society, you have already experienced them on a rudimentary level. Though you may remember this trip—the extra sack lunch that you packed, the tightness with which your mother held you before you left for school—I can assure you that what you saw was not entirely reflective of the reality of this lifestyle. You were sheltered from the full reality because you were small and unable to understand. You are still small, but I hope, for your sake, you are able to understand.

When you got on the bus you clutched your two paper lunch sacks until your knuckles were white. The lunch sacks had to be paper, no plastics, no metals, nothing hard or heavy or with any other remotely sinister qualities. You didn't know why you were pressing your fingers through the brown paper into the palms of your hand with such ferocity. But you understood something a little better than the children around you, the children who were already eating the dessert from both of their lunch sacks.

The bus stopped at the school and you were there for a few moments, sitting at your desk, still clutching the paper bags, listening to your teacher's cheery and lilting voice, listening to things which should not have been said in such a cheery and lilting voice. There was a tightness in her smile that you may have imagined, but probably did not.

Then you were on the bus again and it was rainy and gray, which you, as a general rule, enjoyed. You did not so much enjoy it this time because this grayness wasn't over rows of familiar houses or the school playground or the general store. This grayness was over endless stretches of emptiness and dead grass that went on, seemingly, in all directions. Until it did not. Until it turned into hills and rocks that you were sure had things hidden behind them.

The rocks then turned into trees, which turned into dense trees that blocked out the gray sky altogether. This, you liked even less.

255

The bus came to a stop. You stepped out and followed your teacher who was clutching a leather-bound book to her chest in much the same way that you were clutching your paper bags.

She led the class down a narrow dirt path, ducking occasionally for branches that hung low and threatened to scratch your face. This went on until you came to a clearing. In the clearing were makeshift homes and campfires and people who were unlike any people you had ever seen. Your teacher smiled her tight smile and cracked open her book. She began saying words that you had already heard iterated many times over, words that were meaningless background noise to what you were attempting to process.

People were hunched over themselves, their faces gaunt, their stomachs caved in, their ribs protruding.

You were meant to leave only one lunch sack. You left both. That was nice of you. It was also useless.

You couldn't understand why they wouldn't reach out and take what was being offered to them, why they wouldn't pick it up when you set it on the ground in front of you. You couldn't have known that when you left, they threw each paper sack into the fire because they could not accept the implications attached to it. You went home with a hollow stomach for nothing.

6.

Imagine for a moment that you are not on the giving end of the paper sack. That you are not you, but the hypothetical you from our purely hypothetical illustrations.

That after the stoning, your mother mends herself only briefly before she has to leave to a white, rectangular building where you cannot see her. Imagine that every time she comes back her eyes are glassier, her grip on everything less sure. Imagine that she does not come back at all.

You choose, for a while, to be bitter toward her and then toward them. The men who stand in city squares and speak with booming voices, the men in white jumpers who carry people off to white rectangular buildings, the men who hold you with soft but firm hands when you try to fight and claw your way out of them.

You don't want to be around them anymore. Not without her. So you mark the box which reads "I decline" and leave it on the coffee table, hoping to send a message. Though the only message you send is that you were no better than her.

It is night when you leave the house and go walking just alongside the streets with their white, reflective glow and their slight buzzing that you can only hear at night.

You stay away from white rectangular buildings and town squares. You walk out until there are no buildings and town squares, only dead grass and then rocks and then trees and then denser trees. You walk until you can't. And then you sit and sob and wait.

They find you eventually, just like you knew they would. The group that finds you is small and not unkind. You're grateful for this much, at least.

They give you pieces of dehydrated meat and tea made from tree bark and hot water. You get a bed next to an elderly woman who sleeps with a knife under her pillow and teaches you curse words you didn't know existed. She shows you how to hunt and take care of yourself and lets you watch when she uses burned pieces of wood to write out manifestos on pieces of scrap paper. Her conversation focuses mostly on the government.

The things she says get inside of you in a violent way. You begin to speak like her and she smiles at you until you show the first sign of wanting to put words into action.

The sting of her hand against your cheek doesn't hurt so much as the shock of betrayal. She did this, she says, to protect you. You believe her.

After that, you keep to yourself about walking toward the ocean that doesn't exist, or about walking back toward the place you called home with sharp objects in your hands.

You don't voice these things aloud anymore. Instead, you focus on the immediate. The shortage of food and medical supplies, the poorly constructed homes, the sickness that spreads to someone new each day.

You build and think and sometimes write. And, for a time, you make things better. There is a terraced garden where you grow five different kinds of vegetables, an irrigation system, a waste-disposal system, homes that no longer fall apart, and a growing supply of food. There is a small window of time when you think you are happy.

It is worth noting that any semblance of happiness outside of the structures of society will always be superficial and fleeting. Happiness, here, is an illusion based upon temporary circumstance and with no eternal value. It is purely selfishness receiving what it desires. But keep in mind that a selfish nature will always result in more want, and is therefore insatiable.

It is when things begin to get better, when there are gardens and irrigation systems and community gatherings that don't consist of stones and knives and condemnation, that the birds start to appear.

There are only a few at first. And then a few more. And then a multitude, from almost every angle, always.

You know what birds mean. You are not surprised when the birds are followed by men in white jumpers who come and drag you out of your home and hold guns to your head. You are not surprised when a man with a leather book and booming voice comes and speaks words that only sound faraway and scrambled filtered through the blood rushing in your ears.

You are not surprised when they grab the old woman and push her to her knees and demand her to make a choice.

She makes the wrong choice by pulling out her knife. You don't know how she planned to use it. On the men or on herself. Either way, she never gets the chance.

It is the first time you see anyone killed. It is too quiet. Too fast. A shot and a thump and a thin trickle of blood in the dirt. You think she deserved more than that.

After her, they ask each person to make a choice. We all have to make choices. We all receive a second chance.

JOHN DALE JAVIER

They make the wrong choice.

You make the right choice, only you've made it too late. And that will cost you.

Please understand that those who seem like the victims in this hypothetical story are, in fact, the perpetrators. They had a choice and chose wrongly. Even then, they were given an opportunity to repent.

It was in their best interest to choose "I accept" and yet they brought suffering and death upon themselves under the prideful assumption that they could take control of their own lives. Do not make their mistake.

7.

This is installment seven of the government-issue educational tape for student 147B. If you are student 147B, retrieve the tack from your desk drawer. If you are so intent upon pressing it into your thumb, do so now. Know that later you will regret seeking out pain, but do it if you must.

Now that we have discussed the two options available to you concerning your choice, and its consequences, we should also discuss the nonexistence of a third option. There are some who like to propose the possibility of a third option. Some illustrated children's books that, at first glance, seem to propose the possibility of a third option. This, you will come to find, is absurd. There is no third choice. And those that seek it find only suffering and an untimely death.

It is understandable that you have returned the illustrated children's book to its place under your bed. That you draw it out in much the same way that you did when you were a child, that you hold it up next to the manila envelope that you have still not opened as if you were weighing your options.

Do not weigh options that do not exist. There are only two options. "I accept" and "I decline." There is no ocean.

There are people who believe in an ocean and choose to walk east, toward nothingness. You have seen them before. People who move alone or in packs through cities and towns or skirting around cities and towns. It is just as foolish to skirt around cities and towns as it is to walk into them and place undue trust in the people who live there.

You have seen firsthand how foolish it is to place trust in people who live in very neatly lined houses and attend community-bonding ceremonies on a regular basis. You have seen how foolish it is to place trust in nice, well-meaning people who sharpen the heels of toothbrushes and tuck them into their breast pockets.

You had not sharpened the heel of a toothbrush or broken a TV remote into plastic shards or confiscated a fork from the kitchen. But others had. And you watched.

You put down the piece of chalk that you had been using to coat the sidewalk in solid blue and watched as a group of people, people unlike any you had ever seen but for that one time in the woods, walked down the middle of the street. They huddled together, hands clasped in solidarity and fear, like a pack of animals pushing the strong out to the sides and keeping the small and weak protected.

They looked at the rows of houses and neat lawns and you and your blue chalk as though all were threats. They watched you and you watched them and their eyes begged you to be silent. You were silent. But not still.

You got up and ran inside to find your mother and she ran to find your father and he took a sharpened toothbrush out of his breast pocket as though he had been waiting.

He had been.

You should not have gone to the window to watch, but you did. You watched as he went out to them and used the sharp end of the toothbrush. How a few of them stood still and resigned, as though this had been what they were waiting for, as though they never hoped to get to the ocean, not really. Others were not so sedate. They tried to run. But it didn't matter, because there were already other people in the streets, spilling out of their houses with broken flowerpot shards and heavy objects in hand.

You watched, unable to pull yourself from the window until they all lay on the ground with various sharp objects protruding from their flesh. Your father came back inside and smiled at you, as though he had done you a favor.

Later, men in white jumpers came and hauled some of the people with sharp objects protruding from their flesh into ambulances to transport to rehabilitation facilities. Others, they shot in the head. You watched this too. You did not bother going back outside to finish coloring the sidewalk blue. The chalk was already tainted, mixed with red.

While these practices may seem cruel and remembering them may make you tighten your grip on your pencil and dig your teeth into the inside of your cheek, it is important to note that these people are dangerous. They present a threat not only to the health and well-being of community members like yourself, but also a threat to our way of life.

Keep in mind, also, that allowing them to die here spares them from a more gruesome death later and affords them the opportunity to repent and be taken to rehabilitation.

If you choose the option which does not exist and attempt to walk east, toward the ocean that doesn't exist, this will be your fate. You will end up lying on a suburb street with a toothbrush protruding from your neck.

No one in their right state of mind walks toward the ocean that doesn't exist.

No one gets up late at night and opens their window so that they can slip out without tripping any alarms. No one takes nonperishable food items and several days' supply of bottled water and starts walking out of town, cutting through front lawns and avoiding streets and sidewalks that hum slightly but only at night.

Steer clear of the rehabilitation facilities and the sounds that come from them but only at night. Keep to darkened areas and away from any birds that you may come across. At the edge of town, toward the east, there will be dead grass and then rocks and then trees and then denser trees. Stay off the road.

The roads take you only to other towns. Avoid other towns. Instead, follow the streams. When you get to the rocks there will be a stream that cuts through under the road. Follow the branch that leads east. If it takes you to a town, do not enter the town. Do not enter in the night or in the day. If you do enter a town, attempt to look as inconspicuous as possible. Ask no one for help. Trust no one to help you. The rivers do not lead to the ocean because the ocean does not exist. The rivers lead east. Despite what you have been told, there is no ocean in the east.

This is a hypothetical example of what someone who believes that there is an ocean in the east might say. Do not listen to such people.

Do not go east. Do not go east ever. Not yet.

8.

This is installment eight of the government-issue educational tape for student 147B. If you are student 147B, think of the bird that you saw on the sidewalk yesterday at two in the afternoon. The bird that was half-dead, its neck bent at an unnatural angle, its chest rising and falling too rapidly, its movements panicked and sporadic. You thought killing the bird would be the merciful thing to do. But perhaps you were wrong. If you had let it live, it might have only suffered and died. It might also have suffered and lived and been stronger for it.

Remember, some suffering is necessary.

Now that we have covered the two options and the third option that is not an option, we will cover rehabilitation. While the word *rehabilitation* is often thrown around, there is a bit of confusion in regards to what it constitutes. And where there is confusion there is fear.

There is nothing to fear.

Rehabilitation is an integral part of our society. It has been put in place as a means to help community members live more happy, productive lives. It is for this reason that persons seeking reentrance into society after leaving it must undergo rehabilitation. It is also the reason why a few community members themselves must sometimes attend rehabilitation. It is for their own good, as well as the good of the community.

In order to dispel some of the confusion surrounding rehabilitation, today's tape offers a look inside rehabilitation facilities and the treatment methods they use.

Keep in mind that some suffering is necessary. That it molds us into better people.

I'd like you to imagine that you are not you, but the purely hypothetical you we have been using in these purely hypothetical illustrations.

You are a government worker specializing in educational materials. You believe, as you should, that our society is ideal and that divergence from it is detrimental. Imagine also that you were once a little girl before you were a government worker specializing in educational materials. A girl whose mother often attended rehabilitation. A girl who marked "I decline" on the cardstock paper embossed with the governmental logo, who lived outside of the structures of society for a time, and who attended a rehabilitation facility.

After the rehabilitation facility, you were educated and placed in a job, a job as a government worker specializing in educational materials.

For a time, you were happy. You don't remember the rehabilitation facility at all and you remember only partly the time that came before the rehabilitation facility. You do not notice the dull lull of routine, or that you are sharing a house with a man who you live with but do not know. You are only happy to be doing work that you find important.

The satisfaction of this is only occasionally interrupted by small bursts of doubt, feelings of unease that surface for no particular reason and that fill you with the panicked thought that you are just like her. That you will never be better than her. This happens mostly at night when the man who you live with but do not know is asleep beside you and the other thing that lives inside you and feels separate but inextricable from you surfaces, causing you to get up and pace the house and stare glassy-eyed out the windows.

These instances are rare and fleeting and do not cause you much alarm. You love the work you are doing. Important, meaningful work. And one day your work requires you to tour a rehabilitation facility. You are glad to go. There is only the faintest inkling in your mind that you do not want to go to the rehabilitation facility. But it is vague, flickering, and easy to push down.

When I tell you what you see in the rehabilitation facility, it is important to remain calm and to maintain the idea that there is nothing innately wrong with rehabilitation. Remember the stoning. Remember that people have to be broken down at a fundamental level before they can be built back up again.

The walls outside the rehabilitation facility are white. Stark white. And reflective. It is a monolith, nested between streets and houses and other symbols of normalcy. It is meant to stand out. It wants you to know that it is there. Looking at it pulls up that vague sense of unease. Pulls it up a little too much for you to push it down so easily. You push it down nonetheless.

Inside the rehabilitation facility, the walls are the same reflective white. Hallways without doors branch off into more hallways without doors that branch off into more hallways without doors. A man in a white jumpsuit leads you through these hallways. He is talking at you, and you smile politely, dismissively. He senses only the politeness and continues.

There is something about the rehabilitation facility that seems, to you, familiar, though you cannot quite put your finger on why. It is the same feeling of a vague memory resurfacing. A memory that feels like half dream, half reality, that is still forming, causing you to question the reliability of your own mind. There is no way that you remember the rehabilitation facility.

The man in the white jumpsuit puts a hand to one of the white walls and a door opens up. Inside is an unremarkable room with a few chairs arranged in a circle. The people seated in the circle are wearing gray cotton shirts and gray cotton pants.

They look up at you with a familiar hollowness in their eyes, though a few smile.

A woman, who looks as though she is leading the group, who is not wearing a gray cotton shirt and gray cotton pants, says hello. She introduces herself and goes on to explain that she is facilitating a small group so that patients can share their experiences. This practice is a positive one for rehabilitation patients. They are able to sit in a circle and share, without judgment, their struggles and their inability to adhere to the constructs of society. They are able, also, to receive support and encouragement from their peers. They are able to know with a small amount of certainty that soon they will be able to leave rehabilitation.

There are other parts to the rehabilitation facility. There are many other treatments. You are privy to only a few of these. There are classes dedicated to knitting and needlework, though the needles are plastic and patients are closely monitored, a courtyard garden where patients meander and absently poke at the dirt with primitive-looking farm tools, classes on what constitutes a healthy marriage and familial relationships, sensory deprivation tanks where patients float for hours. There is also aversion therapy, shock therapy, high-pressure water hoses, medical procedures.

There are many other treatments that you are not privy to. But you can hear them, faintly. And while you are tempted to slip back into the comforting thought that it is just your mind playing tricks on you, that it is just a faint and flickering dream trying to resurface, you know that it is not. You know that you can hear them. You know that you remember.

You remember the aversion therapy and shock therapy and high-pressure water hoses and medical procedures. You know that you are not supposed to remember.

The vague unease that has been a part of you for so long—that has lived in the cavity of your ribcage and slept, only resurfacing occasionally at night, in the silence of your thoughts, in the cracks between everything else—is finally awake and, again, a full part of you, an old friend that you have neglected. It refuses to be neglected any longer.

You feel it rising in your throat and choking you. You struggle to push it back down in the way that you have so many times before. This time it will not go down.

As you watch a few patients work on an intricate paint-by-number of Vincent van Gogh's sunflowers you feel the urge to scream or run or dig your nails into your skin. Instead, you stand very still and, as calmly as you can, turn to the man in the white jumper, thank him for his time, and ask to leave because you are not feeling so well.

When you return to your house you open the mailbox to find a manila envelope. You open it and find a questionnaire about your experience at the rehabilitation facility. You mark everything as satisfactory and in the blank space provided for additional comments, you specify that you had a good time and were especially impressed with the garden.

As you write this you remember faintly a garden that you once planted in a clearing in the dense woods far from your home. You remember an elderly woman who slept with a knife under her pillow. You remember a shot and a thump and a thin trickle of blood in the dirt. You begin to sob. There is a bird perched at your window.

9.

This is installment nine of the government-issue educational tape for student 147B. If you are student 147B, think of a dream that you had a long time ago. A dream that felt pungent and real so that it stuck to you when you woke up and still comes to your mind occasionally, just to remind you of itself. Was it really a dream?

Doubt is easy to get under the skin. But once it is there, it's difficult to get out. In handling doubt you should always be careful. Know that it can turn you on yourself quickly before you even realize what's happening. It is for this reason that whenever you have doubts, you should doubt your doubts. Or, at the very least, push them very far below the surface of conscious consideration so that they do not pull you under.

It's best, however, to cut doubt out entirely. Because doubt which you have ignored can resurface suddenly, and become all-consuming before you realize it's resurfaced at all.

You have felt doubt bubble up inside and you have felt, too, the repercussions of letting it take hold of you. On the bus ride back from the dense part of the forest, when your stomach was hollow and you couldn't get the gaunt and desperate faces out of your head. When the boys behind you were mocking and you turned and snapped at them and they looked back at you, shocked and silent, and you turned back in your seat, shocked and silent at your own words, and looked out the window in silence the rest of the way back to school. That is when the doubt began. That is when you should have snuffed it out. But you didn't.

You went back to school and sat in the hard plastic chair and squirmed a little more than you normally squirmed, and stared out the window a little longer than you normally stared.

You listened to your teacher as she explained that there was a reason those people lived the way they did. That they refused to abide by the structures of society. That they deserved what they received and that they would only find suffering for it, in both life and death. You pressed your thumb against the tip of your pencil and watched as the skin turned white, but you didn't dissent. Not yet.

The lessons went on that week, about the government, about its structures, about its goodness. You continued to press your thumb against your pencil. You continued to hold your tongue. Until once, only once, you raised your hand in the middle of class and asked your teacher about those who choose to stay within the fold of society, yet live in poverty.

Your teacher's face twitched, as though she were irritated. As though you had asked this question not out of genuine concern or curiosity, but in an attempt to make her look like a fool in front of her class. The twitch of annoyance was gone as quickly as it had come. She smiled and took on her affected cheery voice as she explained that those people would receive their reward in full later. That there were limited resources, that some people were, by chance, placed in bad situations and had to suffer in life. But in death, they would receive their reward in full. And because of that, they had hope.

This answer only made something like anger twist in your gut. It only made the doubt grow stronger, though you were perhaps still unaware of it then.

Sometimes we do not recognize the doubt in ourselves until it is too late and we are too far gone. Sometimes we don't recognize doubt until it's already taken its toll and it's too late for us to turn back.

It's important not to forget the effects of doubt.

It is important not to forget what can happen when you—the hypothetical you—have just come home from a rehabilitation facility. When you remember things that you should not remember. When you allow your thoughts to fester, rather than going to an appointed psychologist to seek psychiatric help.

You do not notice the bird that is perched outside of your window. Nonetheless, it notices you. They notice you and take note of you. This is not the first time or the last time that birds will take notice of you. It is important from here on out that you also take notice of the birds.

It is at this point that things begin to lose their meaning to you. That the thing that lives inside of your chest, that feels as though it's not a part of you, begins to feel as though it's a part of you. It only used to squirm inside of you in the middle of the night or in the small fragments of time when there was too much room to think, or when something shocked it out of you. Now you feel it all the time, reaching into your chest and tightening, into your stomach and clinching, into your head and poisoning.

The things in your life that once held value start to lose their significance. The educational tapes and instructional videos and instructional sessions sound more and more like lies. Your deep-held beliefs sound foreign and strange coming out of your mouth. The thing that lives inside of your chest is moving beyond your chest. It is in other places. It is every other place.

The man who you live with but do not know becomes more of a stranger. You sometimes look at him, watch him, catch him in the middle of some mundane activity like scraping a spot of food off his shirt, or brushing his teeth, or pouring creamer into his coffee. He will catch you staring and smile a sweet, if a bit unsettled, smile and ask you what the matter is. Inside your head, there is a panicked screaming, an overwhelming sense of his strangeness to you, your lack of knowledge of the interworking of his mind, his hopes, his fears, what drives him. You have the urge to press your fingernails into his cheeks just so he will stop smiling that sugary-sweet fake smile. Instead, in these moments, you only smile back.

Nothing is the matter. Nothing at all. Nothing is the matter.

You do not doubt. That is what you tell yourself. You do not doubt. But you do.

You begin to feel more out of place in the place that you're in. You are detached from the world around you. Even your skin feels wrong settled around you.

You think of the people in the rehabilitation facilities, the people living in the dense forests, the people who are members of society but not blessed by the protection of society. You think, for a fleeting moment, that this is all a lie, then press the thought down as soon as it has the chance to surface.

You cannot afford to lose your grip on your place in society. Not again. You cannot afford to live out in the woods and build from the ground up only to have it torn down all around you. You cannot go back to the rehabilitation facility where there is gardening, and knitting, and high-pressure water hoses. You cannot afford to go to the ocean.

The ocean, the lie of the ocean, fills your head more often than not. You remember when the woman who slept with a knife under her pillow told you not to walk any farther east than you already had. You remember the pull to walk farther east. Not only to walk away but to walk toward. Toward an ocean that does not exist.

It is important to remember, in spite of youth and folly and desperation, that the ocean does not exist. It does not matter how badly the thing that lives inside of your chest squirms. The ocean does not exist. Rehabilitation facilities and the dense part of the forest and people who lie in suburb streets with toothbrushes protruding from their necks do exist.

10.

This is installment ten of the government-issue educational tape for student 147B. If you are student 147B think about the last time you discovered that a parent or friend or someone you trusted lied to you. How did it feel? Did you still trust them?

It does not matter if you, the hypothetical you we have been discussing in these hypothetical illustrations, think you find the things that you built up around you are lies.

You find that the things built up around you are lies.

In only a few days what once seemed solid and firm and sure dissolves and is replaced with doubt. The things that you preach into a microphone, the things that end up on educational tapes become empty and meaningless. Still, you do not realize this for yourself. Not yet. You are pressing it down too far to realize that you are pressing it down.

It is not until one day when you come home from the job where you preach lies into a microphone to the man who you live with but do not know.

It is not until one day when you come home and stand at the window and stare until it is night and continue staring until you are staring at an old woman and a young girl walking down the street that you finally realize the all-encompassing nature of your doubt.

The girl is small. Only just old enough to have chosen "I accept" or "I decline." It may be that she listened to one of your educational tapes. It may be that you know her. She has long blond hair but it is dirty and matted. Her clothes are also dirty and matted. She holds tight to the elderly woman's hand. The girl does not look scared. The elderly woman is smarter than that.

She looks around her as though something was following her and could come upon them at any moment because something could, and something does.

They were not smart enough to stay off of the street that only hums at night. There are men in white jumpers. You think of a young girl who planted a garden and an elderly woman who slept with a knife under her pillow. You think of rehabilitation facilities and the dense part of the forest and a trickle of blood in the dirt. And you move.

You move to the fireplace and grab the poker, wrapping your hand tight around its hilt, sure of your decision.

The man who you live with but do not know is sitting on the couch. He looks up from his book, at you, into you, with such an understanding that for a moment you think maybe he is not such a stranger after all. But that doesn't matter anymore. The decision is final. The doubt solidified. He doesn't move to stop you. And you move to the door, to the streets that hum but only at night.

The man in the white jumper has a gun to the old woman's head. He is asking her a question that you don't hear through the blood rushing in your ears. He sees you and moves aside with a slight smirk, thinking that he knows what's coming. He does not know what is coming.

You draw near him.

You bury the fireplace poker into the soft part of his temple, right beside his eye. It makes a muffled cracking sound that you feel reverberate in your hands and arms, that settles in your stomach.

You pull out the fireplace poker. If you were not gripping it so tightly, your arms would be shaking, your whole body would be shaking. But it is not.

The other man in a white jumper is too shocked to raise his gun. You take advantage of his surprise. You swing and catch him in the jaw. This does not kill him. It only hurts him very badly. You have to swing again. You will always regret those few seconds between the first and second swing.

The girl and the elderly woman stare at you in shock for a few moments. Then, the elderly woman takes the girl's hand and they run. You watch them run until you cannot see them anymore.

That is when you loosen your grip on the fireplace poker. That is when you shake. That is when you retch and vomit onto the sidewalk next to the cracked skulls.

Before you open the door to go back into the house, you wipe your hands on your jeans, leaving dark burgundy streaks. When you walk in the man who you live with but do not know is gone. Sitting on the coffee table is a manila envelope.

Manila envelopes always contain choices.

11.

This is installment eleven of the government-issue educational tape for student 147B. If you are student 147B, you should know that manila envelopes always contain choices. Your manila envelope contains a choice. The manila envelope that's sitting under your bed, hidden, undisturbed except for when you choose to take it out and lay it across your bed and stare at it. Your manila envelope contains a choice.

Not your manila envelope but the hypothetical manila envelope that contains a hypothetical choice, from the entirely fictional story which is being used as an educational tool to help guide you in your decision of whether to choose "I accept" or "I decline." Your manila envelope contains a choice.

You run your hands along its seal, much in the same way that you—the real you, not this hypothetical you—ran your hands along the seal of the manila envelope that you pulled out of your mailbox. You—the hypothetical you not the real you—run your hand along the seal, afraid to break it, afraid to stain it with the residual blood on your hand.

Instead of breaking it, you tuck it under your arm and bring it with you to the kitchen, where you find a spot and stare, glassy-eyed, out the window. Staring glassy-eyed out the window does not fix anything. You tuck your nail under the seal and break it, staining it burgundy. You remove the heavy government-issue cardstock paper from the manila envelope. You bloody these also. They are exactly what you expected and what you feared.

They are familiar papers. Papers that showed up for your mother often, for you once. They are an invitation to attend rehabilitation and a box to mark "I accept" or "I decline."

You stare at them for a long time and, the longer you stare, the more the thing that lives in your chest becomes a solid and recognizable part of you. The longer you stare, the more you realize that doubt is no longer doubt. It is full-on disbelief.

You have felt something like it before but never like this. Never have you made a choice that is so irreversible. But the choice had already been made. It was made before you checked any boxes. It was made before you picked up the fireplace poker. It had always been inside of you, separate from you but inextricable. Only now, it seems irrevocable.

It is invigorating and horrible.

You drop the papers so they flutter onto the tile floor. You go to one of the kitchen drawers and pull a paring knife out and press it deep into the soft pad of your palm. These decisions have already been made for you. You are only acting on them now.

Once the white cylindrical object has been cut out of you, you drop it, and the knife, into the sink. You press your palm to your mouth so that you taste iron and the stinging in your hand subsides only slightly. You find a bandage to wrap the hand, hastily, poorly, and then you leave.

You leave the manila envelope and the choice inside it lying on the tile floor.

You get into your car and drive east, pressing the broken skin of your palm hard against the steering wheel, trying to get the pain to subside. The pain will not subside. Even when it scars over, the pain will not subside.

Slowly, as flat, dead grass turns into rocks and then into the forest and then into denser forest, your tears turn into anger and your anger into hatred. It starts somewhere in your chest, where the doubt used to live, and spreads, hot, up into your face.

You consider many of the things that you've been taught. That your desire for autonomy is selfishness and arrogance. That any choice made for yourself will be the wrong one. That the governmental structures have your best interest at heart. That they are there to protect you because they love you, because you are a part of something bigger. That choosing them will make you happy. That if you keep choosing them, even when it gets difficult, one day it will not be difficult. One day you will be at peace. If only you accept. If only you shove down the pieces of yourself that are trying to claw their way out. Even if it's hard, one day you will receive your reward in full.

You feel like screaming. And you are alone, so you do.

You hate yourself. But that is not a new feeling. Once all the emotion settles, it is mostly comfortable numbness. Once it is settled, you are grateful.

Once it is settled, you've made it to the dense part of the woods. Luckily, you do not have to find your way by memory because your memory is foggy and unreliable. You have been privy to footage, though. And you know exactly where to park. Right next to what looks like a deer trail into the dense part of the forest. It's not a deer trail, even if it started out that way, and you begin walking down it, having to duck branches that you once did not have to duck.

You don't know, really, why you've come back. Maybe to prove that it is real, maybe because you hope to suck the last bit of memory out of it, maybe because some part of you hopes that you'll walk into the clearing and everyone that you left behind will still be there.

When you walk into the clearing everyone you left behind is not there.

Whatever colonies came out of the surrounding cities, they've found a new place to live. A place that hasn't been ravished.

You scavenge it. For leftover supplies, for leftover memories.

You don't come upon many supplies or many memories, but what you do find you hold onto as best you can.

You remember the things that you planned to do when you were young and stupid. Before you made educational tapes and understood the systems in place to protect the systems in place.

You think, briefly, of turning around and going back as you realize what a stupid, stupid mistake you've made. You've stepped outside the realm of protection, you are vulnerable, weak.

But you have made your choice. And government workers do not go back. Not twice. And you do not go back to rehabilitation facilities. Not twice.

You get back in the car and drive until you cannot drive any longer. Until the sun comes up over the horizon. Until you reach a point beyond the dense part of the forest and hit crop fields that stretch for miles in every direction. Until you reach a place from which you have never seen footage from the birds. From here on out is the unknown. This only solidifies your decision.

You pull the car over and sleep.

When you wake it isn't of your own accord. There is rapping on the window. After the rapping, there is smashing. This is what jolts you from whatever horrible dream you were having. You see broken glass and arms reaching for the door, then for you. They find you. Nails digging into your skin, wrapping firmly around you. You writhe and kick. They hold firm. You are being dragged from the car into the street. Then comes the pain of blunt objects and shards of glass.

It should be noted that illustrative stories are not always to be taken as examples of how to live. Sometimes, they are cautionary tales. Sometimes, they show us what happens if we take the wrong path. This is up for interpretation.

12.

This is installment twelve of the government-issue educational tape for student 147B. If you are student 147B, think of the first time you saw someone's body flattened against the concrete. Think of the anger and the resentment, the burning taste of bile in the back of your throat. You were sick. You hated community-bonding rituals. You hated them. But one day you will not hate. One day, you will press the knife in yourself. Because one day, you will understand.

Sometimes, if you get close enough to the bad parts of a thing, you cannot see the good of its whole. It is hard to see the good of the whole when a person you love lies twitching on the pavement in front of you, when someone you trusted's hand comes down hard on the soft part of your neck where the spine meets the brain, when people lie on the pavement with toothbrushes protruding from their necks. It is hard to see the good of the whole when you see, also, the small amount of suffering. But you must try to see, not as you would see, but as another entity would see. One devoid of the bias of human emotion, one who is objective, one who knows and sees all with thousands of eyes. Who nothing is hidden from.

Imagine that you are not you, but one of the thousands of eyes. One of the thousands of eyes which see, from its perch, a small girl. The small girl is you and you are happy. But not for the purpose of this hypothetical illustration. For the purpose of this illustration, you are one of thousands of eyes. One of thousands of eyes watching the girl and judging her. Your judgment is not judgment in the usual connotation of the word. It is not malicious in nature. It does not see the girl or her family or her affection for her family and pass a negative judgment on her. Instead, the judgment is objective, detached. Objectivity innately comes from detachment. Your judgment on the girl is that her affection for the family is good, but that it must be kept in check. It must be tested, measured against her affection for other, greater goods. She does not realize that her love for her own family is a tool to test this allegiance to what constitutes the greatest good for the greatest number of people.

She does not realize that every child her age is tested in this way. She has been taught, from a young age, to stand before class and say certain pledges, to stand in city squares and recite chants, to sit in after-school programs and watch educational tapes about the greatest good for the greatest number of people. But then she goes home and reads to her parents and plays with them in the backyard and falls asleep in their arms. She loves them. Loves them dangerously.

You, one of thousands of eyes, watch on a foggy Saturday morning as the girl's parents put on hooded robes that they only wear a few times a year for special occasions. Clothes that are marked with different symbols which hold different meanings, which give the girl's parents a misguided sense of accomplishment. They dress the girl in robes of her own. Hers are unmarked but will not remain unmarked for long. Though the girl is confused, she is happy. Because they are with her. And she loves them.

You watch, and thousands of other eyes watch along with you, as the girl and her family and other families with other robed parents and other children filter into the streets and create a single, swarming mass that moves, as though alive, toward the edge of town, past the miles of dead grass, to the rocks. Large gray slabs of marble worn down by the elements and by other causes unrelated to the elements into smooth rounded hills. Rounded hills marked with dark russet spots that the girl does not pay attention to or understand.

It is here that she is faced with a choice between the greater good, the objective good, and her good, which is her family. Other children, also, are faced with this decision. The decision is not meant to be cruel, and neither is the outcome if they choose rightly.

The girl does not choose rightly. When a knife is pressed into her hand, she chooses to save what she loves, which is only natural. Only the human response. But she should know better.

She should have been taught better by now, that the human response is not always the good response.

As a lesson in what the difference between the human response and the good response is, she must hurt what she wanted to protect.

You watch, one of thousands of eyes, as the girl tries to use the weight of her tiny body to break free and protect what she loves. But she is small and weak. We, also, are small and weak.

Other children also try to use the weight of their tiny bodies to break free. They also fail. They must also watch the thing that they love, the thing that they loved more than the greater good, suffer.

Some children, however, do not choose wrongly. They choose the good over what they loved and, in return, they did not have to see the thing they love hurt.

The lesson here is an important one but you, one of thousands of eyes, can see that it does not stick to the girl in the way that it should.

Other children become closer to their parents because they value them more deeply and form a better understanding of the fragility of those bonds. The girl does not. It sits with her in the wrong ways, makes her bitter and resentful, makes her press thumbtacks into her fingers and gaze out of windows a little too long. It makes her do things that a normal, well-adjusted child should not be doing.

The girl does not have thousands of eyes. She cannot see the greater good. But you do, you have thousands of eyes.

13.

This is installment thirteen of the government-issue educational tape for student 147B. If you are student 147B, imagine that you are one of thousands of eyes.

With one of those thousands of eyes you see, many years after you saw the girl, a woman who leaves a manila envelope lying on her floor and presses the tip of a knife in the soft pad of her hand. Who drives out past the dead grass and the rocks and even past the dense part of the forest and sleeps in her car. You watch as the doors are ripped from her car and as she is pulled out of it and assaulted with blunt objects and shards of broken glass. You can see the panic etched on her face. The panic results not from fear of the unknown, but from fear of the known. Fear of knowing exactly what kind of situation she is in.

It is this fear that wanes, for a moment, into defeat. The woman's body goes limp as she sinks into acceptance. Then a fork is jammed into her shoulder and the defeat is gone. She manages to grab hold of something, a piece of brick, though you do not see this with your one of thousands of eyes. She uses the piece of brick on the man who stabbed her with a fork. It takes a few attempts, but his skull eventually caves.

She runs, brick still in hand. You chase her, though she doesn't see you, not yet. She runs through crop fields until she is far away from the people who attacked her. Far away from her car. Far away from civilization. She runs until she is lost.

She pauses for a brief moment to rest. Then, she grows still. She turns and looks right at you. She sees you. She sees *you*. You attempt to fly away. But it is too late and she is too good at throwing stones.

It meets its mark, and your eye goes dark. But it doesn't matter. You have thousands of other eyes. The woman only has two, and she cannot see the greater good.

You, the hypothetical you, have just killed a bird with a stone. You have just blacked a single eye, one eye of thousands of eyes, and your vision is so limited that, to you, this feels like an accomplishment.

You pick up the bird and measure its weight in your hand. Then you throw it, as far as you can. The world is a better place with fewer eyes.

You look up to the sun in an attempt to find your bearings. But you don't know whether it is morning or evening and so there is no way to tell which way is east. You wait a bit longer until the sun sets slightly in the sky and you know which way is east, so you walk east, through miles of dense crops which you think are something like corn but are not exactly corn. As your heart slows you begin to notice the place in your shoulder where a fork was pressed into the muscle and fat. It is bleeding profusely and the best you can do for it is to press a hand firmly against it in attempts to stop the blood flow. But the blood runs freely, seeping through your shirt and between your fingers, slick and warm and reeking of iron.

You stumble on, thirsty, tired, bleeding. Hoping that you do not collapse and die and rot in a field. Hoping that you do not end up like her.

You do not collapse in a field. Instead, you stumble out of a field and onto a lawn, where the grass is a yellowish fading green. There is a small, dilapidated house in the distance. Beyond the home are more homes. Beyond the home is a neighborhood. You know that you have made a mistake, but at this point, it doesn't matter. There is nowhere else to go, your head is light and throbbing, your stomach clenching. You lay down on the yellowish fading green grass and close your eyes.

Remember your family. Remember the good of your family that was given to you. Remember watching that good taken away. Remember watching the woman press a knife into the soft palm of her hand. Remember watching her being dragged from her car, the fork plunged into her shoulder. Know that the bad parts of a thing are only parts. See, with thousands of eyes, the good of the whole.

14.

This is installment fourteen of the government-issue educational tape for student 147B. If you are student 147B, think of all the things that have caused your throat to close up and your fists to clench and your teeth to dig into the soft skin inside your cheek until you taste blood.

When you wake you think, at first, that you are in your own home, in your own bed, engulfed by your own sheets, sleeping next to the man you live with but do not know. You forget, temporarily, about all that has happened to you: the rehabilitation facility, the dull cracking of skulls, the fork in your shoulder. Then the ache of your body returns to you and, with it, the memories and the hatred and the disappointment that comes with not being dead.

The answer walks in through your bedroom door. She is an older woman with graying hair that isn't quite yet gray. She comes and sits on the edge of your bed. You look at her, confused. Because you know her. But you scarcely have the courage to articulate how.

The woman puts two fingers to her lips and then presses them to your forehead. Then, you are sure you're dead.

The woman is your mother, and your mother is dead.

She smiles at you, softly, sweetly, as though she is expecting you to smile back. But you don't, because you can't.

Your mind goes back to the woman and her children. You wish you would cry, because then maybe the horrible mixture of emotions throbbing inside of you would leave. But you can't cry. And you can't smile. You can only stare.

The woman, your mother, seems to understand this. She doesn't press you. Instead, she leaves. She comes in and out over the course of several days. Sitting on the side of your bed, putting her fingers to your forehead. She leaves trays of food, and takes out trays of uneaten food, and administers medicines that you only take begrudgingly.

You stay in bed. Not because you are weak, though you are, but because you can't think of any reason to get up.

Until, one day, you see a bird at your window. The bird is not looking at you with one of thousands of eyes. It is looking away from you, its eyes a haziness of ignorance. Before you know, fully, what you are doing, you go to the window to look at it. It perches there only a moment longer, sees you, and flies away. You have no choice then but to look out the window. There are rolling hills covered in dead grass and a dark, almost black, lake. There are no roads, no cities, and no other birds for as far as you can see. You want to know where you are.

So you ask. You go to the kitchen that smells faintly of almond cookies. The scent is familiar, unsettling. You ask the woman with graying hair where you are. The only reply she offers is that you are somewhere no one can harm you. "Nothing here can harm you," she says.

You ask her why she is there. Why she never came home to you and why her breath is no longer laced with the smell of alcohol.

Her answer is "rehabilitation facilities."

This is not an answer that you want to hear. This is not an answer that makes sense. Because the people who enter rehabilitation facilities and never come back are never seen again. There are no rumors, no houses in the hills, and no escape. But your mother stands in front of you in a house in the hills, escaped and, seemingly, happy, in the same way that the woman you loved was happy.

You ask her why you are there and she answers that you are there for a second chance, to make a choice. Manila envelopes always contain choices.

That is when you see the manila envelope lying on the kitchen counter.

That is when you turn and leave.

You walk out the front door. Past a garden that looks familiar in a way that makes your stomach knot uncomfortably. You walk away from the house in an unknown direction. Hoping that you can keep walking.

You reach a fence that is tall and shocks you when you touch it. You begin to walk the perimeter of the fence, throwing dead leaves at it and listening to the crackle of electricity as they catch there, hoping you'll find a chink, hoping you can leave. You do not. You walk along the edge of the fence for miles.

Night begins to fall as you come back to the place you started. Your next thought is to walk into the electric fence and hold tight to it until you feel tingling and then numbness and then nothing at all or to walk into the lake and let your lungs fill with water. But some part of you knows that neither option will result in death, only waking up in another strange bed to ache and hate the world.

So you walk back, past the lake and past the garden and into the house that is dark but for a light on in the living room, and empty but for your ghost of a mother. She sits on the couch, cross-stitching with bright red thread.

She looks up from her work. Up, at you, and asks if you're ready to talk. You sit in a chair beside her and tell her that you wish you were dead. She knows this already. Knows because she felt it.

In a moment of weakness, you tell her everything, because her eyes are sympathetic and motherly and familiar in their faraway-ness. They look almost how they looked when you were a girl. They look almost how your eyes look now.

You talk about hate. Things that you have seen with two eyes, without the perspective of thousands of eyes.

She nods and says that choices have to be made but not now, not today. And she holds you in a way that feels familiar but better than familiar because her arms were not so strong or so sure before.

She whispers apologies in your ear, though you don't know what she's apologizing for.

As time drags on, you begin to understand. You understand that some people do leave rehabilitation facilities but do not reenter society. You understand that you have been brought there because you could be one of those people. You could stay in the little house with your mother. All you have to do is open the manila envelope and make a choice. All you have to do is choose "I accept."

The back of your throat tastes acidic when you think about this, so you try to swallow it down, push it away.

Instead, you spend your days digging carrots out of the soil in the garden and baking almond cookies, and cross-stitching things in red thread and relearning, yet again, what it means to be happy. Some days, your mother performs rituals.

She goes out into the middle of the dead grass and chants from a black book aloud to no one. Or she traps small animals and opens up their throats against a rock. Or she gets on her knees and claps her hands together and whispers fervently under her breath. On those days, you stand far away and watch.

You begin to forget about the ocean that does not exist. You begin to get the feeling that you could be happy there with your mother.

This frightens you.

Your mother talks, occasionally, about the good of society. About the greatest good for the greatest number of people. When she does this, the hatred comes out of you. You raise your voice, you throw things. She lets you do these things until you are spent of them. Until you grow tired of raising your voice, and throwing things, and instead you sit and listen.

Everything evil is for a reason. We do not see with thousands of eyes. We see partially. Subjectively. Every evil intentionally inflicted has a reason, for the greater good. There is a plan, greater than all of us.

You ask why you were allowed to live and receive a second chance when you should have died.

Your mother replies that she does not know, but there was a reason.

You ask her to justify all the evil in the world.

She justifies it with all of the good. With all of the families that stay whole, and the people who find meaning, and the satisfaction that the general population finds with life.

You ask her about the people whose stomachs are empty and who live in rotting houses.

She answers that they are, statistically, the happiest out of the whole population.

You ask her about people who chose to stay within the fold of society but are sent to rehabilitation facilities.

She answers that people like her are never abandoned.

You ask if her beliefs are founded in truth.

She answers that her beliefs are founded in what's good.

She chooses this lie because the lie gives her a reason.

You realize that you, too, can find a reason.

You will have to return first to the man that you live with but do not know, then to the rehabilitation facilities, to cut out any unclean part of yourself.

But then you can return home to your mother and your garden and the smell of almond cookies. You can write educational tapes from the small cabin and you can forget that you ever wanted to walk toward the ocean that doesn't exist. You can be happy.

So that is what you do.

You reach for the manila envelope on the table. You open it and run your hands carefully across the government-issue cardstock paper. You flip to the final page and you mark "I accept" and write your name in a shaky, reluctant signature.

15.

This is installment fifteen of the government-issue educational tape for student 147B. If you are student 147B, know that every choice you have made up to this point has been your own. A choice cannot be made for you. A reason cannot be found for you.

Your manila envelope contains a choice. Attempt to make the right choice.

Do not walk east toward the ocean that does not exist.

No one in their right state of mind walks toward the ocean that doesn't exist. No one takes a kitchen knife and presses it into the soft pad of their left palm until they extract a white sphere. No one gets up late at night and opens their window so that they can slip out without tripping any alarms. No one takes nonperishable food items and several days' supply of bottled water and starts walking out of town, cutting through front lawns and avoiding streets and sidewalks that hum slightly but only at night.

Steer clear of the rehabilitation facilities and the sounds that come from them but only at night. Keep to darkened areas and away from any birds that you may come across. At the edge of town, toward the east, there will be dead grass and then rocks and then trees and then denser trees. Stay off the road. The roads take you only to other towns. Avoid other towns. Instead, follow the streams. When you get to the rocks there will be a stream that cuts through under the road. Follow the branch that leads east.

If you follow the branch of the river that leads to the east you will come to crops and farmlands that will morph, slowly, into hills. Hills with dark, almost black, lakes. Hills surrounded by electric fences. Do not go near the hills. Do not trust the people who live in the hills.

Continue to follow the river until you reach the sand of the beach and the electric fence that will prevent you from walking on the sand of the beach. Do not be fooled by the blue ribbon of water that lies beyond the electrified fence. The ocean does not exist.

Follow this electric fence south until you come to a rocky cliff. Sleep at the base of this cliff until the right person finds you and shows you the rest of the way.

The rest of the way will not include going to the ocean that does not exist. It will not include boarding a boat and sailing for several days out to a remote island that is beyond the jurisdiction of your current society.

This option does not exist because the ocean does not exist.

This is the end of the government-issue educational tapes for student 147B. If you are student 147B it is now time for you to either mark "I accept" or "I decline" in your government-issue manila envelope.

Remember, there is nothing here to harm you. Only your choices. Only yourself.

Trading Ghosts

written by
David A. Elsensohn

illustrated by
MASON MATAK

ABOUT THE AUTHOR

David Elsensohn lives for coaxing language into pleasing arrangements. He is typically inspired by such language-coaxers as Tolkien, Howard, Leiber, Norton, and Gaiman, or by well-crafted batches of single malt whisky. He makes rather good sandwiches, he's told, and his chili recipe gets appreciative nods from friends.

Most of his story ideas come from midnight scribblings on pads kept above his headboard, which occasionally results in appearances in various anthologies or online publications. He is currently laboring through several novels in the hopes that one of them will complete itself.

Terminally distracted, he lives in Los Angeles with an inspirational wife and the ghost of a curmudgeonly black cat.

ABOUT THE ILLUSTRATOR

Mohamad Hossein Matak is known by his American friends as Mason. He was born in 1991, in Tehran, the capital of Iran.

As a child, Mason carried his prized possessions everywhere— whether it be a ball, a toy motorcycle, or his painting notebook!

His favorite colors are red and black. Red to honor lost countrymen and all who strive for freedom. Black for his difficult life.

As Mason says: "I dream and paint. I imagine and paint. Finally, I paint my life!"

In 2008, he graduated in fine art from Tehran high school. He continued his education in university and earned a master of art degree in illustration.

With the dark future of his land, Mason tries hard to continue as an independent illustrator. But he loves his life. He spends much of his salary on art materials, and he continues to search for a better future with his résumé and portfolio, and hopes someday to work in a country that understands the value of his art.

Trading Ghosts

I shouldn't drink. There is a squeeze in my chest that won't leave. Nothing ever reads wrong on the imagers. It has left me slow to move, reluctant to act, a manacle that rusts inside my ribcage. I hate it, and myself, and if I could be rid of the pain, I would, though I could never lose the memory. Nor should I. I deserve it.

So I maintain my status as drunkard in a diner called the Ninth Novena, outside the mining colony I work for, on the oldest outpost of Glief b. The diner stands aloof by the banks of Throughway Six, one of eight mighty roads the color of powdered iron. Down these arteries thunder hectometer-long magnetrucks, laden with ore, wavering in the dusty heat. Our primary star, contemplating its imminent expansion into a red giant, sends its beams straining through a blood-flecked sky to pierce the diner's dirty windows. The light slices the air into crepuscular stripes, intercepted by dust motes and the glow of LEDs.

Sister Jessamine runs the joint, wiping the counter in full habit. She's the Missionary Prime for this octant. She has a patient ear and a firm tone, and Byrchkktai the bouncer, he of the twenty knuckles, when those fail. Sister Jess takes care of the girls and boys who work in the kitchen and who dance on the countertops for entertainment and sit on laps and sell conversation or intimacy. She doesn't let ghosts into the place, so they cluster outside, murmuring in hazy daylight.

Glief b is overrun with ghosts, more ghosts than all the

sentient beings who have ever lived here. It's like an ethereal dumping ground, a spirit's orphanage. Sometimes they're human. They take form, clustering in your periphery where it's hard to focus on them. Maybe ghosts are a species who died out millions of years ago. Maybe they're remnants of past divine creations that ran their cycle. Personally I think they get swept into the accretion disk when planets form, crunched down into rock and fluid, until they seep their way upward to envy the living. Maybe the unlucky ones become our souls. I think about these things when I get deep enough in the bottle to see through its bottom, and my heart is at its tightest.

I empty my glass and wait patiently for Sister Jessamine's attentions. I glance around.

An angel sits at the counter. A fallen one. He has been forgotten by God, allowed to slide off his plane of attention.

I can't easily explain how we know they're angels. They're paragons of physical perfection, sure, but you can purchase that sort of thing on the mainworlds. It's something about the eyes, the aura, the vibrations our skin detects. You can almost see the wings, folded into themselves, hidden away in some fractal dimension. The old scriptures only mentioned wings for certain creatures. I hear the Islamic planets are visited by brilliant beings who are almost translucent, and never sit or bend except in graceful, worshipful prostration. They are never fallen, like ours.

I'm not saying angels are saucer-dwelling aliens, or that we were invented by ancient spacefaring humans, or some other anthropocentric pipe dream... just that divine beings turned out to exist. Theirs is not a science we understand yet, but they move among the stars, and our first little water-soaked ellipsoid isn't the only one they know about.

People were conflicted when we first discovered their presence. Galactic exploration received a giant economic boost from the unexpected source of our home world's religious institutions. We tore some sheets from our scriptures when we found other civilizations and when the ghosts found us, but no one has ever answered our questions about what happens after we die, so we still chew on a vague dissatisfaction. We still have no idea whether there is an afterlife. The angels aren't saying, and the ghosts don't say much at all.

Despite this, or because of it, we still have religion, down here on the planets and moons we move to. As an intelligent species, we land on worlds and colonize them, inserting ourselves into their exoticism, but we live with an eternal *dépaysement*. Hence the religion. Afterlife. We can only believe in something we haven't visited yet.

The angel has been here every day for a week, emitting sadness like a beacon. He speaks to no one, ignoring the girls and boys who clamor for his attention. I have no idea where he goes at night, unless Jessamine locks up the place with him in it.

I look at her, nodding toward him. Her brown face carefully neutral, she upends a bottle over my glass and drops in a rare ice stick with a pair of tongs.

"I know what he is, Ambrose," she murmurs. "But how can you counsel an angel? How do you pray for one?"

"No idea. I guess you just do, pray on someone else's behalf. Isn't that the process?"

I used to pray. Before launch and touchdown, or before docking maneuvers, or before ring-jumps. I was a freighter ship captain. I contracted small cargo between planets, below the attention level of the larger carriers and interworld law enforcement. Ulandre was my chief engineer, and my partner. Short, brilliant, funny as sin. Had her breasts removed and her hips augmented since that was the style back then. Wore her silver hair shorter than mine except for a thin braid with her family's tribal symbols woven into it. We shipped goods, legal or larcenous, had adventures and told stories in starbars.

She used to talk to the ghosts while she worked. Ghosts never answer, but they do seem to respond when you notice them, in fitful shudders and a sense of held breath. She'd tell them jokes and then laugh since they wouldn't. I ignored them, although they watched me hungrily.

MASON MATAK

We were in a parking orbit over a destination planet, with a busted stabilizing pod. Ulandre was out on an EVA, repairing it so we could conduct a de-orbit burn. I sat in the cockpit, monitoring.

She had just locked down the pod when the debris hit us: shards of an outdated satellite that once measured oceanic biomass and whose orbit was allowed to decay, and the charts hadn't updated its orbital station-keeping. The mass of our ship wasn't deflected much off course, but it dented the hull and put us into a slow spin. I scrambled, putting out the deadly fires and closing the holes that were releasing our atmosphere into the void. Ulandre bobbed and bounced on her tether like a toy.

I prayed when I surveyed the damage, prayed for the ability to fix it, begged and swore against Heaven and Hell, awash with dread because I knew there was no other reality to switch for mine.

I can still see her shocked, betrayed eyes through the polycarbonate of her helmet, when I told her the airlock could never open again. Goddamned mass-produced microcargo ship with only one airlock. I had been meaning to replace the fill valves and the condensate module, or better yet, install a suitport to save money, but the airlock had been reliable enough, and I had never gotten to it, and now never would.

She got it, finally. She snapped only briefly, crying and cursing, hammering the shield again and again with her gauntleted fists. The sound was on my side, the silence of forever on hers.

Ulandre wound down, and floated, and talked, her braid dancing slowly about her face inside the helmet. She asked me for stories I hadn't yet told her, about summers on Avacitai Delta, about men and women I'd dated. She didn't untether herself. She let her suit pump her full of painkillers. She stayed, for hours, until her breathing reached that shallow rasp of CO_2 oversaturation. I couldn't tell when she passed.

Only five hours of air remained in the wounded ship. I had to descend into the planet's atmosphere. There just wasn't anything else.

She stayed connected until the end, keeping pace with the ship, then tore away sometime during reentry, flaring into a tiny, arcing mote.

I drink enough to forget it, sometimes.

Looking over at the angel, I can almost see the deep wells of sorrow within him. He cares about nothing. Since I don't care either, I sidle over. Misery and company, and all that.

"Hey. I'm Ambrose," I say.

"I know. I am Zehanrael."

I hadn't expected him to answer, seeing as he hadn't responded to anyone else's human attentions. "How do you know?"

He cocks his head as if listening. "How do you know when you are awake? How do you know the suns are at your back? What are you scanning for?"

It unnerves me that he knows I'm scanning for something. I'd clicked my eyelids to log in and run his name through a remote dataport. I can't find a meaning for it, nor a mention. Stories of angels often end up in media. Some of the fallen ones work as mercenaries to give themselves some kind of purpose, although I wonder what it's like to work for humans instead of a creator. Those who do that kind of job are more devastating than a squad of armored gunsuits.

He looks at me, and I can feel his gaze rippling through all the parts of me, sorting through them like a gallery.

Angels don't see like we do. We humans, anyway. I can't speak for Byrchkktai. They don't see the shapes, exactly. They see the truth of us, the roiling turmoil inside ourselves that is roughly shaped like us. It's why angels move slowly, deliberately. They can see the forms but not quite the edges, so sometimes they brush against things, bump past them. But it means they are unerring in battle. They strike right to the core.

I shudder. The 18:00 magnetruck delivery passes by outside, the last for the day, and I wait for its long, wall-shaking groan to subside before I resume.

"Maybe you can do something for me," I venture.

"I doubt it, Ambrose."

"Then maybe I can do something for you."

"It doesn't matter. It will not create balance. You will not erase anything. Draining one well does not fill another."

I take a sip and let the cold liquor burn under my tongue. I can feel Sister Jessamine giving me the side-eye. I don't know why I'm pushing the question. Maybe seeing another brooding, empty shell is too much like looking in a mirror. Maybe because he is the closest thing I have had to a goal for long years. "Since when has balance ever factored into the workings of the universe? Helping one life might make the other seem less empty. So what do you want?"

"You cannot offer it to me."

"Try me. The store's closed upstairs, but we're open."

He looks at me, weighing me. He drinks from his glass of water. "I want to die."

Me too, sometimes.

"It is my only goal," says Zehanrael, watching the invisible swirls of liquid inside its defining cylinder. "It is the only purpose I can have, to yield up my ghost."

I watch Sister Jessamine slip into the kitchen, hand over her eyes. I look back at Zehanrael, into him, trying to measure my own human emptiness against whatever howling, inexpressible void he must feel. "You can't do it yourself?"

"I cannot make it happen. It is a sin."

"I wouldn't think you'd be concerned with that detail."

"It concerns me beyond easy understanding."

Scratching my chin, I let my imagination wander ugly paths. "I guess it's not easy to accomplish? Not to be awful, but I could put you on a ship, and set it to plunge into a star."

"It would destroy me, but not end me. When we become ghosts, it is a dire thing."

I hadn't considered that angels might ever experience that fate. I let the last of the liquor embrace the ice stick on its way past my lips, then crunch the ice as I wrestle myself off the stool. "I'll ask around."

Sister Jessamine emerges, motioning to one of the girls to take over, and pulls me with her eyes. She waves me into her office, where I have never been, and sits behind her desk. An obsolete datapad gleams next to an old leather-bound book. She blinks on an overhead light, which focuses a beam downward like wrapping us in secrets.

"Why are you pushing him?" she says. "He has depths we can't imagine. Even angels don't know why they become disfavored."

"We don't need to comprehend suffering to want to stop it."

The hands that massage her forehead under her veil are scarred. "I appreciate it, Ambrose, but even those of us who have studied the Word all our lives don't really know what to do for...for those even closer to it. We only have faith, but celestials have history. Let it go. I need to pray."

"Why, will it help?"

"Why do you care?"

"I'm not sure," I admit.

"Go home. There isn't anything we can do except ask for guidance."

"You ask," I say. "I'm sick of the silence."

The evening is ruled by wind. I wrap my head and plunge hands deep into pockets as I walk home through the whipping, thrashing grit.

The ghosts follow me as they always do. Every day I shrink-wrap myself into a gas-tight biosuit, work underground in four two-hour bursts, then pass through the decontamination chamber, peel off the suit, eat a meal at Jessamine's place, listen to the laughter and complaints of others, and go home, trundling through minor dust and ghost storms to my dome. There, I sit and read, and drink, and fail to forget. I have saved up months of earnings. There is nothing to spend it on except debt payment or transport off-planet, which few can afford anyways, or companionship that becomes a permanent resource drain, or meals at the Novena. Nothing to do but dig and drink, a little death every day. Embrace the routine. Either that or go mad. The ghosts love that. They don't belong here, either. No one does.

I shut the door against the ghosts' chaos, shake red dust onto the floor, swallow a measure of bitter brown alcohol, and go to bed. I lie awake, my heart aching against its barriers.

We humans have no idea what we're doing. As indicated by the existence of mining colonies with people who work and die on them, we still haven't reached a level on the Kardashev scale which intelligently harnesses the vast power available to us. Not because we can't get there. Because we keep slipping back. Even with the discovery of something like the divine, we can't seem to get the hang of binding ourselves into an effective social unit.

We live by the illusion of opportunity, of promises we made to ourselves or thought were made for us. Created without purpose, without reason unless you count a vague throb of species perpetuation. We can't make it. No true understanding, no evolution outside our needy, limited, fluid-filled shells.

I think about Zehanrael, what he must be feeling. What would you do if the air was taken from you but you couldn't die? Every day, asphyxiating on the absence of what kept you alive, every day losing bits of meaning. I shiver. A being who was created to serve, to be a living facet of the universe... then to be left without function, without... air.

He is like a door that has opened for me. I know it, as strongly as knowing a silent, murderous vacuum wraps around our planet, but I have no idea how to pass through that door.

I can't leave it alone, so I rise, unlatch my lopsided desk, let it swing open, and start accessing data. I research, requesting scholarly access from antiquated repositories. There are paths humans tread that are murkier than angels could, and I travel every one that shows itself. I send messages to black-market acquaintances, throwing my old cargo captain credentials against every wall in the hopes of finding a treasure, looking until the black sky becomes dusty red and then beige.

Morning pulls me to work, where I put on the biosuit, the prison, like the one that soaked Ulandre's last breath, and work all day with substances that want to kill me. I return home without eating, and dive back into my pit of discovery. I do it

299

again, the next day, eating and drinking sparingly, until I can find someone who can help. Each path leads to a dead end or deeper inward, hints and histories and suggestions, passing from resource to resource.

On the third night I find a name: Gahn.

There is a price, the least of which is money, and burdens that must be accepted. I send a goodbye message to the mining company, for there is only the one path I can bear to take.

I walk to the Novena, ghosts fluttering at my heels, silent breaths held, as if wanting but not daring to tap me on the shoulder and talk to me.

He is there. He listens to an excited young woman telling him about herself, too loudly over the music. He absorbs her glee but does not reflect it.

Jess scowls at my entrance but pours liquid into a glass and sets it before me. We lean close across the bar, under the prancing legs of one of the older teenagers who gyrates his way down the bar to a miner waving a credit square.

"I found someone," I tell Jess. "Her name is Gahn."

"I know of Gahn. She is a Sister, but not . . . not of my order."

"I didn't know you had siblings."

"I have three," sighs Jessamine. "Two of us are alive. I'm the only one who still believes in something. But no, she's not *my* sister. A Sister. A Sister of an order that didn't exist before Heaven let us know of its presence."

"Well, Gahn will provide. All I need is a blessing from you. It's part of the payment."

"She serves in a different, more direct capacity. That kind of role isn't what I believe in."

"So why do we do anything at all, then?" I snap, glancing over at Zehanrael. My anger, so long directed at small, wounded parts of myself, uncoils and flares. "Why are you a Missionary Prime, why do you wear that clothing, kiss those artifacts, scuff your knees on dirt? Why do you give these teenagers a home? I can't believe our closest role to Heaven is to observe and pray, and not change."

"This isn't giving food to starving children or building a home for someone who lost theirs in a storm, Ambrose. We humans are too small to help anyone but ourselves. Our own sin..."

"If God asked you for help, would you hesitate?"

She looks at me, hard. "You don't know what Gahn does."

"Yes, I do. All I need is your blessing. A real one. I don't know anyone else who would give it. And you're the most real person I know, Jessamine, the closest one to... anything that matters. Please."

"I found a way to gain your desire," I say.

Zehanrael looks up from his thoughts and regards me. "How?"

"We need to go to a planet called A'raf. A city named Neue Limbus. I'll have to charter a ship. It'll take a few weeks traveling from here until we arrive at Port Shahris, then a year or two in hibernation." I wonder briefly how to modify the settings on a cryobunk for an angel's biology.

A smile finds its way to his face. "There is no need. The Lord does not see me, but I can still travel on my own."

Sister Jessamine looks up as we turn to go, eyes shadowed under her veil. She always makes her opinions known, but her thoughts are unclear now; I see neither support nor condemnation. She and I had talked for an hour, telling each other secrets and desires, as if balancing our emotional books. Her blessing was quick, an invisible whisking of water and ritual, yet I feel its weight like ancient coins on the eyes of the dead. I nod to her, and exit the Novena, I think maybe for the last time.

Outside, the atmosphere scatters the sun's disk into a series of diffracted bands. A breeze sweeps up the earth into whorls, defining the faint outlines of the ghosts, who cluster around us as if attending a hanging, or a baptism. I squint. Zehanrael looks down at me with colorful eyes.

"Are your affairs tended to?" he asks.

"Everything important is gone," I answer. "My job isn't aware enough of me to hate me for leaving. All my net worth is stored here." I indicate the access point under my ear.

"Then we will go now, to A'raf."

He embraces me, and we rise up, through the stratosphere and into orbit in seconds, an ever-exploding increase in velocity, yet I am not crushed into paste by our acceleration. We fly through the vacuum, his arms around me, and I can breathe but do not, and my eyes take in the wonder of nothingness and light and everything that travels through it.

I never considered that the transparent substance of a window or a helmet could be a barrier, but without being encased in a protection of human make, naked before nothing, I can see, truly *see*, everything. His wings are most visible here, a mantle of shadow that encompasses worlds.

We fly, beyond the speed of matter, reducing the universe's expanse to a dimensionless quantity, and I feel the unimaginable cold of space against my eyes though no wind exists to feel. The tightness around my heart is relaxed, as if the vacuum coaxes it gently away with each ripple of gravity's waves. We are beyond such ugly, law-bound concepts as matter and mass. We are not even energy, but spirit, that undiscovered element.

He lands. He lets me go. I feel the burden of worldly weight pressing my chest into itself, and I sink to my knees and weep.

"Few have traveled this way," he says, waiting patiently for me, shifting as if uncomfortable. "Enoch had much to say of his experience, but never wrote it down. There are other beings, those that can fly between worlds, but you do not want their aid."

Trapped now by the unloving draw of gravity, I gather myself and the information from the local public network, and get our geodetic bearings.

I don't know how he knew how to find it, but we are outside Neue Limbus, the city I need. It is old, built of raw substances instead of printed synthetic, and its sun hits the landscape with a harsh drumbeat. I make two calls, one to arrange transportation of the more mundane kind, the other to arrange a meeting.

We are silent on the hovertrain as it descends into the maw of the city, passing many-tiered structures of white brick and gray glass that can barely be seen through the train's tinted windows. Smog lies in almost palpable layers on the roof, but it is nothing compared to the gritty beige opacity of Glief b. I watch advertisements on a screen. A pair of citizens watches me from their seats, a human and a Hyrxtian, reading me with four of their six eyes. They do not acknowledge the celestial seated next to me. Zehanrael speaks.

"The people here do not like my kind."

"Yeah. This is the place where humans tried to escape their own beliefs," I say, watching an advertisement for body-replenishing, growth-encouraging, soul-mate-finding milk. "They thought they were creating a secular paradise. I don't think it's a bad idea, they just forgot to fix their own drawbacks before trying it out."

"I feel for them. So much anger. Their own troubles, still blamed upon us."

"Easier that way. We don't like to blame ourselves." Except that I do. Always.

The train hisses into downtown. An autocab ride and two blocks of walking later, we find the Ash Drift, where Gahn will be. The bar is as new and bright as the Ninth Novena is old and sand-pocked. There are no servers. Patrons speak to the walls and furniture, and drinks pop up like new friends through panels in the tables and counters. The dance floor is above, transparent but tinted red, showing the silent scuffle of soles and heels, and tantalizing hints of skin.

The others here seek only pleasure, and therefore shy away from Zehanrael, sensing what he is and throwing glances as if irritated that their sins might elicit an opinion. I don't care. I head toward the one who must be the woman I seek.

She is short and slim, her skin lighter than mine, her body toned. Her ballistic clothing reflects grays, greens and browns, and she seems in constant motion, almost blurred. A gun rests at her side, a gun Jessamine whispered of. Its metal is a dull bronze, its surface crawling with symbols. The seats around her are vacant.

"Um, I'm Ambrose," I venture.

"Ambrose with the money and the blessing." Her voice is like Jessamine's when she is controlling a situation: calm and cool, fierce waters crashing underneath. "I didn't expect you for a couple of years."

"Yes, that's me." I turn to Zehanrael, who regards her with a melancholy smile. "This is Gahn."

She watches us both with lead-gray eyes, the same lancing gaze as Jessamine but devoid of warmth. Her shape is never quite defined, and I somehow realize she occupies the same space as every creature she has slain. Their ghosts slip in and out of her contours.

"This is new," she murmurs. "Usually I have to hunt them down. You want to see my credentials?"

He gazes at her with his colorful eyes, reading her co-occupants. "I know some of these."

"You might. Some of them are mine. A lot aren't. They find me."

"I believe she can perform this task," he says to me. "Thank you, Ambrose."

She shrugs as she rises, and walks toward the door, her step smooth and predatory. She leads us into a waiting hover car, which guides us quietly into an old part of the city.

The buildings are of stone and steel, their occupants fled. The earth rises in painful lumps, shrugging free of its infection of steel piping and concrete foundations. The car trundles and breathes carefully over the urban graveyard, and we alight in a field. Flowers and weeds push through cracked earth. Gahn unwinds from the car. She gestures, as if introducing her office. She looks at us expectantly.

Zehanrael and I step forward, unsure where to stand. Gahn hands him a shiny spike the color of copper, then walks around us, reading a display on the back of her hand. She drags a boot toe through the dirt in a perfect circle with us in its center. She taps her knuckle, and the spike in the angel's hand throbs green, then back to its reflective calm. She takes back the spike, and waits.

Zehanrael turns to me, places his hands on my shoulders like a departing brother. He leans close and breathes upon me, an insufflation that bleeds away my addiction like peeling paint, leaving the memories raw and undulled. I weep and groan at the burst of truth and sink to my knees in the dirt. Sobs escape me uncontrolled, releasing my damned history, my heart beating more freely and with increasing vitality, gaining strength with each ragged breath. It was my fault. I killed her. She died, and it was because of me. I carry her death, with mine.

His hand is warm upon my head, stroking my hair; the concern of even a forgotten angel is comfort. He cannot erase my sin, but he pulls it up from alcohol-soaked depths and makes it clean and sharp and part of me, instead of buried within.

Something leaves me. I rise.

Gahn takes my money and regards us silently. I realize that I no longer feel the spiritual pressure of Sister Jess's fingers, of her words upon me. The blessing too has been taken, as part of the payment.

Gahn leans a little to the left, and a ghost flickers away from her and drifts back to me, enfolding me in a cloud of love and memory. I can almost see a single silver braid wrapping around me, its plaits woven with family symbols. I take in breath, maybe for the first time. I stumble outside the circle.

She then draws her gun, the one with the runes carved into it that predate the system's circumstellar disk. "Any prayers to make?"

The angel descends gracefully to his knees and looks up at her. "I have already made them, many thousands of times."

She places the barrel against Zehanrael's forehead, and he breathes in as if smelling a delicious memory he has not known since youth.

Stolen Sky

written by
Storm Humbert

illustrated by
ANH LE

ABOUT THE AUTHOR

Storm Humbert grew up in Wauseon and Fayette, Ohio, but now lives in Westland, Michigan, with his incredible girlfriend Casey. It doesn't seem like a far move, but he had to go through Philadelphia to get there. On the way, he picked up an MFA in fiction from Temple University, where he had the opportunity to study under Chip Delany, Don Lee, and other excellent professors. While there, he also had the opportunity to actually teach creative writing, which he would love to do again.

Storm currently works as a technical legal writer in Ann Arbor, Michigan. He is also a slush reader for Clarkesworld Magazine, *which has been extremely helpful in his efforts to continue to grow and improve as a writer. He has previously been a silver honorable mention and finalist in this Contest and is overjoyed to finally be counted among the winners. In addition to this piece, Storm's fiction has appeared in* Andromeda Spaceways Inflight Magazine, Apex Magazine, Interzone, *and others.*

ABOUT THE ILLUSTRATOR

Anh Le was born in Ho Chi Minh City, Vietnam, in 1998. Anh's name is pronounced like the letter N. His family migrated from Vietnam to the United States in 2007 for a chance at a better life.

Ever since Anh can remember, he loved drawing and creating fantastical characters and monsters from his imagination. He didn't even have a concept of what art was—he just drew whatever came to mind. His love eventually evolved into a passion to become a concept artist and illustrator.

Anh started his journey by creating complex colored pencil and marker drawings but was introduced to digital painting several years ago and hasn't been able to stop since. His objective is to immerse viewers in his breathtaking worlds and his own unique view of visual development for films, games, and animations.

Stolen Sky

My first night on Earth-Vega was also my first sunset show. The viewing was held on the Sunset Mezzanine, which jutted out from the third floor of the hotel. My human guide, Ruya, gently escorted me through the press of humans to the front railing so that I could see, since we yelvani are no larger than human adolescents.

From the balcony, the hills seemed to tumble over each other down the gentle grade from the hotel to the edge of the forest, which then climbed gradually up toward the horizon until it terminated at the feet of the distant mountains. The breeze was bracing but not so cool that I had to turn up the temperature of my garment. It was perfect. Everything the humans made was perfect.

For that first night, they chose the sunset of a world called Arrinae in the Alpha Carinae system. I knew nothing about this world, but I watched in amazement as the sun of Earth-Vega became the sun of Arrinae. When the sun touched the distant peaks, it changed from white to a smoldering orange and shrunk by at least a third. It painted the sky vivid greens and purples. There was no gradient to the shades—no violets, light greens, or near-blues. The sky was either emerald or amethyst. The clouds swirled into the shifting colors as the shades swam but never mixed.

It was so beautiful that it startled me. I still had so much left to see, not only on Earth-Vega but throughout the galaxy, and

I feared nothing would ever measure up to the sunset show—to the first time I saw the humans change the stars.

"How do you do this?" I asked Ruya.

He was an attractive man, the kind I and the other yelvani women would have whispered about when I'd worked at Paradise Yelva, the human resort on my home planet. He had an easy smile that pushed the light from his eyes and warmed whomever he was speaking to. He seemed kind and spoke gently even when I asked him the most useless questions.

He tried to explain the sunset show, but there were too many words I didn't know and too many things of which I was ignorant. I hadn't been smart enough for the human university on Yelva and was lucky my nurma, mother of my father, had taught me to windwrite. The humans loved native art. Though some on Yelva said humans loved our native things too much.

"Why did they choose Arrinae?" I asked.

"There's a native singer here from Arrinae," Ruya said. "I think his name is Ackchat. It's his last night, so the show is for him."

I'd never seen any beings besides humans or yelvani, so I asked Ruya to point out Ackchat. The singer was toward the back. He stood as much above the humans as I did below, and his head, as white as a sun-bleached bone, had a prominent ridge that ran from front to back. Ackchat's mouth opened into a perfect circle when he spoke, and he stood slumped as if perpetually in the act of being dragged to the ground by his arms. His cheeks seemed heavy too, and his face rested in a frown. It was difficult to tell if he enjoyed the show.

After dinner, I attended Ackchat's last performance. Ruya and I sat in a private balcony with a perfect view of the stage and the tables of humans below. I was surprised when Ackchat sang in his native language, but when I asked why this was, Ruya said it was expected because humans loved the authenticity. I still wished I could understand the words, but I wanted to learn to appreciate authenticity as well. I had so much to learn from the humans.

I also found that, even though I couldn't understand the words, Ackchat's voice was show enough. The lower tones crouched in the air and rumbled in my body while the higher notes filled the room to the lofty ceiling and shook the light as it clattered and tinkled through the crystalline fixtures.

Some parts of the song seemed silent, but Ruya said those notes were simply beyond human or yelvani hearing. I wondered if he and I missed the same parts or if we experienced different sections of the song, but I didn't ask. Once the show was over, however, I did ask Ruya if it were possible for me to meet Ackchat.

"Of course," he said through his warm smile. He stood and extended his hand. "Let's find his guide and we'll introduce you right now."

Ackchat stood at the edge of the stage below shaking hands with some of the humans from the audience. Handshaking was their formal greeting as well as their formal farewell, which I still found confusing, but this was not what I meant when I asked to meet Ackchat. I did not want only to have him see my face and hear my name, which seemed to be the purpose of human handshakes. I wanted to meet him as yelvani do. I wanted to speak to him—to learn about him.

"Could I meet him privately?" I said. "I have only ever met humans and yelvani. I am worried I will act wrongly."

Ruya seemed confused and a little worried—he was a kind man. "I'll find his guide and see what I can arrange. Stay here."

Ruya patted my shoulder as he passed and sealed the clear door of our balcony behind him.

The line to meet Ackchat dwindled over the next few minutes, and the auditorium was nearly empty by the time he left the stage. Ruya still had not returned, and I stared at that lonely stage for several more minutes after the last human left, cursing myself for not accepting Ruya's initial offer.

I nearly jumped from my seat when someone knocked on the door. Ackchat towered in the doorway and gestured toward the lock panel for me to let him in. I rushed from my chair to pass my chip over the scanner, but after the door receded into the floor, I had no clue what to do next. I panicked and stuck out my hand.

"That is for humans," he said and left my hand unshaken. Instead, he gently touched the ridge on his head with both of his thick fingers then turned the open palm of that hand toward me. "That is how we greet one another on my world."

Ackchat waited patiently as I stood dumb for a moment, but I eventually understood and extended my nervous fingers toward his face, which I could not reach. I took his hand and placed it on my cheek, and he lowered his head to rest in my palm. His eyes were much smaller than I'd noticed before, and they had large, black pupils that went almost corner to corner. He had two small orifices that seemed to do his breathing tucked in behind the rear undercorners of his jaw, and his skin quivered at my touch, bristling against my flesh like a stone-polishing brush. It must have been covered in billions of short, invisible hairs.

"That is a wonderful greeting," Ackchat said. "I hope you haven't shown it to a human. May I come in?"

"Of course," I said, confused and still numb to what was happening. I felt as if I was floating through a scene in a human simulator—as if reality could crush the moment in an unforeseeable instant.

He pulled a small cube from a crease of his jacket and tossed it onto the floor, where it quickly unfolded and expanded into a chair, the seat of which came to my waist rather than the middle of my legs. "An interstellar resort, and all the chairs are made as though only humans will fill them," he said. "It makes quite a statement, doesn't it?"

"Oh, I don't know..." I felt adrift. With humans, I was at least familiar. I could read their expressions and understand what was meant or expected, but I couldn't even tell if Ackchat was smiling or frowning.

"I'm sorry," he said. "I'm babbling. I hear you wanted to meet me."

His expression still told me nothing, but his voice was softer.

"Yes," I said. "I wanted to tell you your song was beautiful."

"I'm glad you enjoyed it." Ackchat sounded rehearsed but pleasant, as if some germ of earnestness remained from when he'd used to mean it. We sat in silence for a moment before he said, "I don't mean to rush you, but was that all you wanted to say? I'm not sure how much time we have."

"I'm sorry. I didn't mean to interrupt your schedule. Ruya said he would check with your guide—"

"You're not interrupting, and your guide did no such thing. Neither he nor my own handler know I'm here."

"Then how—"

"I *heard* you. To sing in the full range of sound, one must hear the full range. Not even the best human technology is as sensitive to sound as a fully trained Clachen singer."

He seemed to swell in his seat, which made me smile because it was the first time I felt I understood him. Pride in one's people—in one's art—was apparently universal.

"Clachen? I thought your world was called Arrinae."

"Humans like to name things before they know whether they already have names or not."

I walked over and took the seat opposite Ackchat. "I've heard humans call Yelva Trappist-G."

"They do like to make it seem as though they created everything, don't they?"

I didn't know what to say to that. I'd heard elders grumble such things, but hadn't expected it from a traveled performer like Ackchat—one who had been lifted, as I had, up into the stars by the grace of human generosity. They'd lit our homes, cleaned our water, and taught us about the universe. I did not understand how ones who gave so much could ever be called thieves.

"What was your song about?" I said, trying to change the subject.

He looked over the edge of the balcony toward the stage. It was as if he were watching himself—as if his voice still filled the room. "It was a very old song about a battle of perfections—the humans call them gods. They fight in the sky for control of the light."

"That sounds fascinating."

"Most beings have myths about eclipses." Ackchat shrugged, but the motion was exaggerated—clearly something he'd picked up.

I was about to ask him how long he'd been performing when his eyes jumped from me to the clear door and traced a path down the unseeable corridor beyond the opaque walls.

"I'm sorry, but we will have to cut our talk short. Your guide just got on the lift. He's heading this way." Ackchat stood and grabbed the back of his chair, which collapsed upward into his palm like magic.

This wasn't how it was supposed to go. We were supposed to sit and laugh and discuss our home worlds. He was supposed to tell me how amazing his life had been, performing all over the galaxy—seeing unimaginable worlds and people—how he wouldn't trade it for anything.

"Wait!" I said, not sure what I wanted him to wait for—grasping for that one question I needed him to answer.

"I'm sorry, I really need to—"

"What is your favorite place?" I said. "Of all the places you've been, which was the most wonderful?"

At first, Ackchat seemed surprised. His mouth sat open in that perfect circle and his eyes locked on mine. Then he closed his mouth and took one sweeping stride back from the door toward me. He placed his living, rasping palm on my cheek and lifted my hand to rest on his. "Home," he said. "They take you everywhere but home." Then he left.

A few moments later, Ruya came in and told me that he'd spoken to Ackchat's guide and that he was, unfortunately, unavailable. I stormed past him without a word and went up to my room. I was angry and disappointed and nothing was right. I thought that maybe if I slept, it would all be better tomorrow.

By the next day, Ackchat was gone and another performer from another world was on the schedule. My shows were late afternoon, before dinner and sunset, and the veteran performers headlined the evenings. I knew I could be a headliner if my matinee shows went well. So, I tried to think about my conversation with Ackchat as little as possible because the more I replayed it in my head, the more confused and angry it made me.

Ruya told me the new entertainer was a poet named Sadiq from Tajawuz in the Antares system. Sadiq was serpentine and seemed to swim through the air on a wave of brilliance caught under her translucent frills and spans of thin tissue that shimmered like the pink crystals of the yelvani mountainsides. I wanted to speak with her, but I feared I could not do so without bowing to my gnawing desire to touch her. There was also the risk of another disappointment.

The headliners tended to stay for only one or two nights, and Sadiq was of the single-show variety. So that night the sunset show was of Tajawuz. The white sun took on a deep red shade and grew to three or four times its normal size as it approached the horizon. Radial splashes of yellow, orange, red, pink, blue, and deep purple filled the sky like so many layers of colored sand.

The sun was so large that the colors wound all the way across the sky to the rear horizon. When I looked straight above, all I saw was pink and purple. It seemed a sunset befitting a being as beautiful as Sadiq.

When I looked over, however, Sadiq seemed different. She no longer flowed with the air but writhed against it. For the first time, her levitation looked like defiance, as if she warred with the air and ground, resolved to be untouched.

I worried that the humans had gotten her sunset wrong, but when she came on stage later that night, she seemed as radiant and joyous as she had throughout the day. I was glad Ruya had agreed to sit at one of the tables down by the stage rather than on a balcony. She was so beautiful up close.

"I call this piece, 'Stolen,' and I have written it especially for you all this evening," she said in Standard rather than her native tongue. Then she read:

> My boy, he is mine no more.
> My son was taken in the fire
> with my red and my orange,
> atop the sea of blue and green.
> My son now lies far from me,
> though his face fills the sky.
> I thought I did remember him,
> but this visage says I lie.
> His captors make him theirs.
> They love his beauty and his strength.
> But while they marvel at his size
> and call themselves his masters,
> they forget the laws of sea and sky:
> What sinks does later rise.

The audience clapped a mixture of polite nervousness and disappointment.

"She should have spoken Tajai," Ruya whispered. "It's much prettier than Standard."

"Do humans speak Tajai?" I said. "Would they have understood?"

He was polite, like a mature speaking to young, as he said, "Understanding isn't the point. Beauty is."

That didn't seem right to me, but Ruya knew more about such things, so I said nothing. It seemed to me that Sadiq's sadness was beautiful *because* I could understand it, and that pretty words without meaning would've been like so much wind.

The humans near the back got up from their seats and filed toward the door. None came forward. No line formed to meet Sadiq even though she stood as ready to receive them as Ackchat had.

"Where are they going?" I asked. "Is it because she doesn't have hands to shake?"

"No, no," Ruya said. "When hands are lacking, you bow, like so." He stood, tucked his arms gently to his sides, and bent at the waist with his eyes closed.

"So why aren't they going to congratulate her on her poem?"

"I—" Ruya glanced toward the stage as if to gauge the distance. "She should have spoken Tajai," he said, as if repeating that phrase would somehow make me understand.

It did, and understanding made me furious. I looked up at the stage again, where Sadiq floated, confident as ever even in the face of the quietly emptying theater.

I stood. "I would like to meet her," I said, already two steps toward the stage ramp.

Ruya calmly followed, to the edge of the stage and no farther, but I could tell by the hard set of his jaw behind his close-lipped smile that he would have stopped me if he could have done so without causing a scene.

I considered reaching out to greet Sadiq as I had Ackchat, but it didn't feel right with Ruya and the few other humans there, so I bowed. Sadiq did the same, but the absence of arms and legs made it little different than a nod.

Up close, Sadiq was even more incredible. She was somewhat transparent, except for her head, but I couldn't see any organs or bones inside her graceful, floating frame. It was as if she were made completely of pink and purple light—a beautiful spirit in worldly form. She had two pupils at the center of each electric orange iris, and these pairs of pupils twirled and danced in a celebration of sight itself. *What did the world look like through those?*

It was only after Sadiq blinked a few times in quick succession that I realized how long I'd been staring.

"I loved your poem," I said too quickly.

"I am glad it spoke to you." Sadiq's voice and body glowed with a brief, aural radiance that made her response seem so much more genuine than Ackchat's *I'm glad you enjoyed it.*

317

"Yes," I said, excited, bold. "It made me think of my mother and how much I miss her, as I'm sure your son misses you."

There was no glow this time, and her smile tried but failed to cover it up. "How long have you been touring?" she said.

"This is my first location."

"Ah, a fresh stellification."

I was embarrassed that I didn't know the word, and therefore didn't know what to say.

"Don't worry, young one," Sadiq said. "It's just a term some humans use for us—it means they've made us into stars."

"Oh, I see. I understand."

Sadiq's eyes whirled and stormed—a defiant strength, twisted by sadness all the same—as she said, "No, but you will." The heavy moment passed in an instant though, and Sadiq brightened. "Would it be all right if I gave you a gift?"

"I would be honored."

Sadiq's honest glee radiated from her spinning pupils and traveled slowly down her length until a twinkle, like a tiny star, rested on the tip of her tail.

"How would you like my poem to keep with you forever? It will be always available in your mind, so you can never forget it. Think of it as a signed copy."

"That sounds incredible."

Sadiq's smile was light itself. "Focus on my eyes," she said. "This will feel strange."

I focused on the ocular dance of her pupil pairs within those liquid-fire irises as the sparkle of her tail passed briefly through the edge of my vision. I felt a shiver touch the side of my head. Sadiq's skin was a static tingle—like touching a piece of metal so hot or cold that it's hard to tell which it is. Then the sensation went deeper, and I knew it was warmth.

For a second, I feared Sadiq's tail was swimming into my skull, but her eyes told me to stay calm. I smelled the spulerendle seeds of my childhood—spicy and cloying—and heard my nurma telling me that the wind of Yelva herself is the writer and that we are only the colors of the breeze.

ANH LE

Then those things were gone and I heard, saw, and felt nothing but the gravity of Sadiq's eyes. It was in this place—this ready and waiting space of my mind—where she put her poem. She made it a part of me. I think I fell in love with her before I passed out, but I don't fully remember.

The next day was my last, and I was scheduled as the headliner. After my fainting episode, Ruya doted on me all morning. He really was such a kind, helpful man. Throughout the day, I rubbed the spot where Sadiq's tail had touched. I thought of her poem often. It was magical because her voice read it in my head, so it was as if she was there with me.

As the day wore on, I became less nervous for my performance and more anxious about my yelvani sunset show. Part of me was happy, but another part worried all day, *will they think my sunset is beautiful?*

Finally, the moment came. As the sun entered the final quarter of its descent, it went from whitish to deep blue. Then it fractured in the sky—a fiery ball made of innumerable glass beads. The more it sank, the more kaleidoscoping patterns of sparkles surrounded by radial rainbows were spawned, and these flowed into more sparkles and rainbows in a seemingly endless cycle that undulated away from and toward the sinking star like a tide.

"What does that?" Ruya asked, as if he'd forgotten to breathe.

I was going to tell him of the Oldest Ones—all yelvani who had lived and died—who slept in the sky and danced the fire below the water to give the living rest, but then I looked again.

The Oldest Ones could not have been there. They were on Yelva, always. So I could not tell him how this sunset was made. In my silence, a nearby human said something about methane crystals and the thermosphere, but I was too confused to follow.

All I could do was stare at the way the light flowed between sparkles and rainbows and wonder at it like any other visitor.

All I could do was look at this beautiful thing that was mine but also not mine. It was theirs. It was every bit as wondrous as the sunset that was mine, but there was nothing of it to understand—nothing to tether me to it.

I wept then as I remembered the elders' words about the fruit from our trees and stones from our ground that the humans loved so much. I thought of Ackchat, Sadiq, myself, and others like us—other stellifications. Were we just another kind of sunset show?

I gave thanks that none of my village would see this. It was better that they never know they had been right—that the humans hadn't even left us our sky.

Ruya only smiled at me and nodded. He probably thought I wept for joy or gratitude. He probably thought that my tears were beautiful, but that was only because he did not understand—could not understand even if he tried—because all skies were his.

Breaking In

BY MIKE PERKINS

Comic-book illustrator Mike Perkins has worked on Captain America, Thor, *and* Spider-Man. *After wrapping up the 31-issue adaptation of Stephen King's* The Stand, *he transitioned to illustrating* Astonishing X-Men *and has since successfully relaunched* Deathlok, Carnage, *and* Iron Fist. *He recently moved to DC comics where he has depicted the adventures of the* Green Lantern *and* Swamp Thing *as well as successfully launching his latest project—a* Lois Lane *series with writer Greg Rucka. He has been nominated numerous times for Eisner and Harvey Awards and, as well as winning the Eagle Award, counts being on the* New York Times *bestseller list and exhibiting his works in Munich, London, and Paris among his career achievements. Mike has been a judge with the Illustrators of the Future Contest since 2017.*

Breaking In

Advice about how to break into the illustration business is as diverse and wild as the ways that people actually break in. It's not a one-size-fits-all proposition.

That bespoke suit that perfectly fits Daniel Craig when he's playing Bond, James Bond, may look like a sack of potatoes on you once you reach the apex of your career—or it might fit you as tightly as a pig in a rubber blanket. It's then that you realise that you just have to be *you*. Enough of these sartorial shenanigans—and believe me I've got enough fashion faux pas to fill more articles like this—you want to know about commercial illustration, right?

I have two breaking-in stories and both are so wildly different that it just proves my point—there is no one way to break in.

The first is the expected approach: I broke in through an agent who liked what he saw but figured I wasn't ready. He gave me advice to follow and suggested meeting again after six months. We did so and he was massively surprised that I'd taken to heart and actually worked on all the things he'd suggested.

Here's a great piece of advice which obviously many artists think they are beyond the point of considering. *Listen!*

My agent had been in illustration for thirty years—like his father before him—and he was used to young artists thinking that they knew everything. He imagined arrogance would override my common sense and subsume my burgeoning talent. But when we met that second time, he could see the major improvement in my illustration due to his sound advice, so he straight away picked up my first professional work.

My second breaking-in story follows a more bizarre, circuitous route. This is my "How I broke into Marvel" story.

A writer friend of mine was always recycling paper. There wasn't a missive that came to me without something written or drawn on the back of that letter, which had nothing to do with the details in the correspondence. He could be writing to me about some ideas he was thinking of developing and I'd turn the page to a gas bill or a report from an appointment at the STD clinic (okay, okay, I'm making that up). He'd sent some story ideas into Marvel UK and after a while they replied that they didn't have any openings for the enclosed ideas but asked "Who did the illustrations on the back of the letters?"

Thankfully, that had been me. It led to my first work at the company—the wonderfully forgotten *Biker Mice from Mars*. My fame was assured!

It can be difficult to find your first work, even accidentally. The above example came after *years* of trying and failing, but learning.

It can be even more difficult to keep working once your career starts, though. Never get complacent once you break in! I'm always, *always*, thankful that I'm doing something I've wanted to do ever since I learned to hold a pencil at a precocious age.

One of my favourite anecdotes comes from writer Brian Michael Bendis who, when faced with successful professionals bitching and moaning about their lot in life, reminisced about his last day working at McDonald's. His boss came up to him and said, with a hand on his arm and a fatherly glare in his eyes, "We'll always have a place for you here, Brian!"

I've heard it said by far wiser heads that to keep working in a freelance world, once you're actually a part of it, there are three things to keep in mind: be talented, be nice, and be on time.

You don't even need to be all three at once. If you have the personality that seems like a confluence of Eeyore and Simon

Cowell judging a dreadful musician but you're talented and on time, an editor is likely to overlook your unpleasant attitude.

Alternately, if you have the time-management skills of a flight leaving an airport in Chicago but your editor likes you and your talent shines through on the finished page, you're in a good place.

And remember—if you suffer from Imposter Syndrome and worry that your work just isn't as good as everyone else's but you meet those deadlines and it's always a pleasure for your professional colleagues to hear from you, then you should be rewarded with a long and healthy career.

If, by any chance you're all three, you're a Unicorn. I always try to be a Unicorn. I may not succeed sometimes, but I *do* always attempt to aim for that lofty ideal.

It really is your job as a creative freelancer to make your editor or publisher's job easier. That's what it boils down to.

Editorial offices get extremely busy and overworked. No, really, they do! The last thing they need—as pleasant as your conversational repartee may be—is to spend an hour or two on the phone talking about what you had for dinner. They can see that on Facebook!

Oh, and speaking of the minefield that is social media, be aware of how you use it. I think that's sound advice for absolutely anyone in today's world, let alone those who are exposed publicly.

As an illustrator you *will* have fans. That makes you a public figure, and fans love to gossip.

Be aware that the people you're working with may also be on that very same social media—you've probably already friended them—but, if you're liking things and commenting on other people's walls or inputting your own rambling tweets instead of trying to beat that deadline which zoomed past your head three days ago, then you may be de-friended sharply by those with whom you want to remain on a check-signing basis.

If I may be so bold, I have one last piece of advice that I sometimes fail to follow myself. I openly justify this failure by reminding myself that I truly love what I do, but nevertheless it *is* sound advice: Find a balance between your work life and your personal life. Set aside time just for you and those precious moments with your family. When you're starting out, it may be impossible to imagine that as there will be times when you're spending hours and sometimes days on end fighting to beat deadlines, but those days *will* come. Relish them, but don't let them devour you whole.

Learn to say, "No, as much as I'd like to, I just can't fit this into my schedule at the moment."

I still fail at that. I really should have said "No" to this article. God knows I have monthly deadlines breathing down my neck, but I knew that I'd enjoy writing this article and I hoped that it might be useful to you.

Good luck breaking in. Enjoy yourself!

The Winds of Harmattan

written by
Nnedi Okorafor
illustrated by
BRITTANY JACKSON

ABOUT THE AUTHOR

Nnedi Okorafor is a Nigerian-American author of Africanfuturism and Africanjujuism for children and adults. Her works include Who Fears Death *(in development at HBO into a TV series), the* Binti *novella trilogy,* The Book of Phoenix, *the* Akata *books, and* Lagoon. *She is the winner of Hugo, Nebula, World Fantasy, Locus, and Lodestar Awards and her debut novel* Zahrah the Windseeker *won the prestigious Wole Soyinka Prize for Literature.*

Nnedi has also written comics for Marvel, including Black Panther: Long Live the King *and* Wakanda Forever *and the* Shuri *series, an Africanfuturist comic series* Laguardia *(from Dark Horse) and her short memoir* Broken Places and Outer Spaces.

Nnedi is also co-writer for the adaptation of Octavia Butler's Wild Seed *with Viola Davis and Kenyan film director Wanuri Kahiu. Nnedi holds a PhD (literature) and two MAs (journalism and literature). She lives with her daughter Anyaugo and family in Illinois. Nnedi has been a judge for the Writers of the Future Contest since 2013.*

Nnedi's short story "Windseekers" was a Writers of the Future Contest finalist in 2001 and was published in Volume 18.

She described the experience like this: "I was shocked when I received the letter in the mail telling me that my short story 'Windseekers' was a finalist. 'Windseekers' was about a mean, fearless, somewhat crazy, flying Nigerian woman who goes to an organic city. All I could think was, 'They liked it? Really?' Then I thought, 'Oh! They liked it!' It was a dawning moment for me in many ways.

"And the subsequent Writers of the Future week in LA was equally so. I met and learned from so many budding and established writers and I felt comfortable amongst them. I was still growing into the idea that

I was writing this strange stuff called 'fantasy and science fiction' and the Writers of the Future experience played a pivotal role during a most impressionable time in my writing career.

"Everyone was so welcoming. And afterwards, the WotF folks were always around when I had questions or needed help. It was all far more than a mere writing contest."

Fittingly Nnedi's contribution to this volume is another Windseeker story.

ABOUT THE ILLUSTRATOR

Brittany Jackson, also known as Bea, is an award-winning freelance illustrator born and raised in the "Motor City" of Detroit, Michigan. She illustrated the New York Times *bestseller* Parker Looks Up: An Extraordinary Moment.

Taken by a passion for the arts at a young age, Bea embraced her gift of drawing and learned how to bring her vivid imagination to life in a variety of artistic styles she's studied throughout the years prior to majoring in illustration at the College for Creative Studies. Bea loves the challenges that arts bring, the thrill that comes with learning something new and the satisfaction of using her gifts to help others visualize their dreams. With a strong sense for concepts and design, Bea has become well recognized for her ability to paint a picture from words, communicating ideas—hers and others—through beautiful narrative illustration.

She is a former grand-prize winner of the Illustrators of the Future Contest. Her artwork was published in L. Ron Hubbard Presents Writers of the Future Volume 24.

The Winds of Harmattan

Asuquo followed her nose and used her birdlike sense of direction. All around her were men selling yams and women selling cocoa yams. She always knew where to find the good ones; they had a starchier smell. Her mother didn't believe her when she said she could smell specific vegetables in the market, but she could.

Asuquo was about to jostle past a slow-moving man carrying a bunch of plantains on his shoulder when an old woman grabbed one of her seven locks. The woman sat on a wooden stool, a pyramid of eggs on a straw mat at her feet. Next to her, a man was selling very dried-up-looking yams.

"Yes, mama?" Asuquo said. She did not know the woman, but she knew to always show respect to her elders. The woman smiled and let go of Asuquo's hair.

"You like the sky, wind girl?" she asked.

Asuquo froze, feeling tears heat her eyes. How does she know? Asuquo thought. She will tell my mother. Asuquo's strong sense of smell wasn't the only thing her mother didn't believe in, even when she saw it with her own eyes. Asuquo's face still ached from the slap she'd received from her mother yesterday morning. But Asuquo couldn't help what happened when she slept.

The man selling yams brushed past her to hand a buyer his change of several cowries. He looked at her and then sneezed. Asuquo frowned and the old woman laughed.

"Even your own father is probably allergic to you, wind girl," she said in her phlegmy voice. Asuquo looked away, her hands fidgeting. "All except one. You watch for him. Don't listen to what they all say. He's your *chi*. All of your kind are born with one. You go out and find him."

"How much for ten eggs?" a young woman asked, stepping up to the old woman.

"My *chi*?" Asuquo whispered, the old woman's words bouncing about her mind. Asuquo didn't move. She knew exactly whom the woman spoke of. Sometimes she dreamt about him. He could do what she could do. Maybe he could do it better.

"Give me five cowries," the old woman said to her customer. She gave Asuquo a hard push back into the market crowd without a word and turned her attention to selling her eggs. Asuquo tried to look back, but there were too many people between her and the old woman now.

After she'd bought her yams, she didn't bother going back to find the old woman. But from that day on, she watched the sky.

Asuquo was one of the last. It is whispered words, known as the "bush radio," and the bitter grumblings of the trees that bring together her story. She was a Windseeker, one of the people who could fly, and a Windseeker's life is dictated by more than the wind.

Eleven years later, the year of her twentieth birthday, the Harmattan Winds never came. Dry, dusty, and cool, these winds had formed over the Sahara and blown their fresh air all the way to the African coast from December to February since humans began walking the earth. Except for that year.

That year, the cycle was disrupted, old ways poisoned. This story will tell you why...

Asuquo was the fourth daughter of Chief Ibok's third wife. Though she was not fat, she still possessed a sort of voluptuous beauty with her round hips and strong legs. But her hair crept down her back like ropes of black fungus. She was born this way, emerging from her mother's womb with seven glistening locks of dada hair hanging from her head like seaweed. And women with dada hair were undesirable.

They were thought to be the children of Mami Wata, and the water deity always claimed her children eventually, be it through kidnapping or an early death. Such a woman was not a good investment in the future. Asuquo's mother didn't bother taking her to the fattening hut to be secluded for weeks, stuffed with pounded yam and dried chameleons, and circumcised with a sharp sliver of coconut shell.

Nevertheless, Asuquo was content in her village. She didn't want to be bothered with all the preparations for marriage. She spent much of her time in the forest and rumors that she talked to the sky and did strange things with plants were not completely untrue.

Nor were the murmurs of her running about with several young men. When she was twelve, she discovered she had a taste for them. Nevertheless, the moment a young man from a nearby village named Okon saw her, standing behind her mother's home, peeling bark from a tree and dropping it in her pocket, he fell madly in love. She'd been smiling at the tree, her teeth shiny white, her skin blue black and her callused hands long-fingered. When Okon approached her that day, she stood eye to eye with him, and he was tall himself.

Okon's father almost didn't allow him to marry her.

"How can you marry that kind of woman? She has never been to the fattening hut!" he'd bellowed. "She has dada hair! I'm telling you; she is a child of Mami Wata! She is likely to be barren!"

My father is right, Okon thought, Asuquo *is* unclean. But something about her made him love her. Okon was a stubborn young man. He was also smart. And so he continued nagging his father about Asuquo, while also assuring him that he would marry a second well-born wife soon afterwards. His father eventually gave in.

Asuquo did not want to marry Okon. Since the encounter with the strange old woman years ago, she had been watching the skies for her *chi*, her other half, the one she was supposed to go and find. She had been dreaming about her *chi* since she was six and every year the dreams grew more and more vivid.

She knew his voice, his smile and his dry leaf scent. Sometimes she'd even think she saw him in her peripheral vision. She could see that he was tall and dark like her and wore purple. But when she turned her head, he wasn't there.

She would someday find him, or he would find her, the way a bird knows which way to migrate. But, at the time, he was not close, and he was not thinking about her much. He was somewhere trying to live his life, just as she was. All in due time.

Her parents, on the other hand, were so glad a man—*any man*—wanted to marry Asuquo that they ignored everything else. They ignored how she brought the wind with her wherever she went, her seven locks of thick hair bouncing against her back. And they certainly ignored the fact that, though she was shaky, she could fly a few inches off the ground when she really tried.

One day, Asuquo had floated to the hut's ceiling to crush a large spider. Her mother happened to walk in. She took one look at Asuquo and quickly grabbed the basket she'd come for and left. She never mentioned it to Asuquo, nor the many other times she'd seen Asuquo levitate. Asuquo's father was the same way.

"Mama, I shouldn't marry him," Asuquo said. "You know I shouldn't."

Her mother waved her hand at her words. And her father greedily held out his hands for the hefty dowry Okon paid to Asuquo's family.

Somewhere in the back of her mind, she knew her duty as a woman. So, in the end, Asuquo agreed to the marriage, ignoring, denying and pushing away her thoughts and sightings of her *chi*. And Asuquo could not help but feel pleased at the satisfied look in her father's eyes and the proud swell of her mother's chest. For so long they had been looks of dismissal and shame.

The wedding was most peculiar. Five bulls and several goats were slaughtered. For a village where meat was only eaten on special occasions, this was wonderful. However, birds, large and small kept stealing hunks of the meat and mouthfuls of spicy rice from the feast. On top of that, high winds swept people's clothes about during the ceremony. Asuquo laughed and laughed, her brightly colored lapa swirling about her ankles and the collarette of beads and cowry shells around her neck clicking. She knew several of the birds personally, especially the owl who took off with an entire goat leg.

After their wedding night, Asuquo knew Okon would not look at another woman. Once in their hut, Asuquo had undressed him and taken him in with her eyes for a long time. Then she nodded, satisfied with what she saw. Okon had strong, veined hands, rich brown skin and a long neck. That night, Asuquo had her way with him in ways that left his body tingling and sore and helpless, though she'd have preferred to be outside under the sky.

As he lay, exhausted, he told her that the women he'd slept with before had succumbed to him with sad faces and lain like fallen trees. Asuquo laughed and said, "It's because those women felt as if they had lost their honor." She smiled to herself thinking about all her other lovers and how none of them had behaved as if they were dead or fallen.

That morning, Okon learned exactly what kind of woman he had married. Asuquo was not beside him when he awoke. His eyes grew wide when he looked up.

"What is this!?" he screeched, trying to scramble out of bed and falling on the floor instead, his big left foot in the air. He quickly rolled to the side and knelt low, staring up at his wife, his mouth agape. Her green lapa and hair hung down, as she hovered horizontally above the bed. Okon noticed that there was something gentle about how she floated. He could feel a soft breeze circulating around her. He sniffed. It smelled like the arid winds during Harmattan. He sneezed three times and had to wipe his nose.

Asuquo slowly opened her eyes, awakened by Okon's noise. She chuckled and softly floated back onto the bed. She felt particularly good because when she'd awoken, she hadn't automatically fallen as she usually did.

That afternoon they had a long talk where Asuquo laughed and smiled and Okon mostly just stared at her and asked "Why" and "How?" Their discussion didn't get beyond the obvious. But by nighttime, she had him forgetting that she, the woman he had just married, had the ability to fly.

For a while, it was as if Asuquo lived under a pleasantly overcast sky. Her dreams of her *chi* stopped, and she no longer glimpsed him in the corner of her eye. She wondered if the old woman had been wrong, because she was very happy with Okon.

She planted a garden behind their hut. When she was not cooking, washing, or sewing, she was in the garden, cultivating. There were many different types of plants, including sage, kola nut, wild yam root, parsley, garlic, pleurisy root, nettles, cayenne. She grew cassava melons, yam, cocoa yams, beans, and many, many flowers. She sold her produce at the market. She always came home with her money purse full of cowries. She liked to tie it around her waist because she enjoyed the rhythmic clinking it made as she walked.

When she became pregnant, she didn't have to soak a bag of wheat or barley in her urine to know that she would give birth to a boy. But she knew if she did so, the bag of wheat would sprout and the bag of barley would remain dormant, a sure sign of a male child. The same went with her second pregnancy a year later. She loved her two babies, Hogan and Bassey, dearly, and her heart was full. For a while.

Okon was so in love with Asuquo that he quietly accepted the fact that she could fly. *As long as the rest of the village doesn't know, especially Father, what is the harm?* he thought. He let her do whatever she wanted, providing that she maintained the house, cooked for him and warmed his bed at night.

He also enjoyed the company of Asuquo's mother, who sometimes visited. Though she and Asuquo did not talk much, Asuquo's mother and Okon laughed and conversed well into the night. Neither spoke of Asuquo's flying ability.

Asuquo made plenty of money at the market. And when Okon came back from fishing, there was nothing he loved more than to watch his wife in her garden, his sons scrambling about her feet.

Regardless of their contentment, the village's bush radio was alive with chatter, snaking its mischievous roots under their hut, its stems through their window, holding its flower to their lips like microphones, following Asuquo with the stealth of a grapevine. The bush radio thrived from the rain of gossip.

Women said that Asuquo worked juju on her husband to keep him from looking at any other woman. That she carried a purse around her waist hidden in her lapa that her husband could never touch. That she carried all sorts of strange things in it, like nails, her husband's hair, dead lizards, odd stones, sugar, and salt. That there were also items folded, wrapped, tied, sewn into cloth in this purse. Had she not been born with the locked hair of a witch? they asked. And look at how wildly her garden grows in the back. And what are those useless plants she grows alongside her yams and cassava?

"When do you plan to do as you promised?" Okon's father asked.

"When I am ready," Okon said. "When, ah...when Hogan and Bassey are older."

"Has that woman made you crazy?" his father asked. "What kind of household is this with just one wife? This kind of woman?"

"It is my house, Papa," Okon said. He broke eye contact with his father. "And it is happy and productive. In time, I will get another woman. But not yet."

The men often talked about Asuquo's frequent disappearances into the forest and the way she was always climbing things.

"I often see her climbing her hut to go on the roof when her chickens fly up there," one man said. "What is a woman doing climbing trees and roofs?"

"She moves about like a bird," they said.

"Or bat," one man said narrowing his eyes.

For a while, men quietly went about slapping at bats with switches when they could, waiting to see if Asuquo came out of her hut limping.

A long time ago, things would have been different for Asuquo. There was a time when Windseekers in the skies were as common as tree frogs in the trees. Then came the centuries of the foreigners with their huge boats, sweet words, weapons and chains. After that, Windseeker sightings grew scarce. Storytellers forgot much of the myth and magic of the past and turned what they remembered into evil, dark things. It was no surprise that the village was so resistant to Asuquo.

Both the men and women liked to talk about Hogan and Bassey. They couldn't say that the two boys weren't Okon's children. Hogan looked like a miniature version of his father with his arrow-shaped nose and bushy eyebrows. And Bassey had his father's careful mannerisms when he ate and crawled about the floor.

But people were very suspicious about how healthy the two little boys were. The boys consumed as much as any normal child of the village, eating little meat and much fruit. Hogan was more partial to udara fruits, while Bassey liked to slowly suck mangoes to the seed. Still, the shiny-skinned boys grew as if they ate goat meat every day. The villagers told each other, "She *must* be doing something to them. Something evil. No child should grow like that."

"I see her coming from the forest some days," one woman said. "She brings back oddly shaped fruits and roots to feed her children." Once again, the word 'witch' was whispered, as discreet fingers pointed Asuquo's way.

BRITTANY JACKSON

Regardless of the chatter, women often went to Asuquo when she was stooping over the plants in her garden. Their faces would be pleasant, and one would never guess that only an hour ago, they had spoken ill of the very woman from whom they sought help.

They would ask if she could spare a yam or some bitter leaf for egusi soup. But they really wanted to know if Asuquo could do something for a child who was coughing up mucus. Or if she could make something to soothe a husband's toothache. Some wanted sweet-smelling oils to keep their skin soft in the sun. Others sought a reason why their healthy gardens had begun to wither after a fight with a friend.

"I'll see what I can do," Asuquo would answer, putting a hand on the woman's back, escorting her inside. And she could always do something.

Asuquo was too preoccupied with her own issues to tune into the gossip of the bush radio.

She'd begun to feel the tug deep in the back of her throat again. He was close, her *chi*, her other half, the one who liked to wear purple. And as she was, he was all grown up, his thoughts now focused on her. At times she choked and hacked but the hook only dug deeper. When her sons were no longer crawling, she began to make trips to the forest more frequently, so that she could assuage her growing impatience. Once the path grew narrow and the sound of voices dwindled, she slowly took to the air.

Branches and leaves would slap her legs because she was too clumsy to maneuver around them. She could stay in the sky only for a few moments, then she would sink. But in those moments, she could feel him.

When her husband was out fishing and the throb of her menses kept her from spending much time in the garden, she filled a bowl with rainwater and sat on the floor, her eyes wide, staring into it as through a window to another world. Once in a while, she'd dip a finger in, creating expanding circles. She saw the blue sky, the trees waving back and forth with the breeze.

It didn't take long to find what she was looking for. He was far away, flying just above the tallest trees, his purple pants and caftan fluttering as he flew.

Afterwards, she took the bowl of water with her to the river and poured it over her head with a sigh. The water always tasted sweet and felt like the sun on her skin. Then she dove into the river and swam deep, imagining the water to be the sky and the sky to be the water.

Some nights she was so restless that she went to her garden and picked a blue passionflower. She ate it and when she slept, she dreamt of him. Though she could see him clearly, he was always too far for her to touch. She had started to call him the purple one. Aside from his purple attire, he wore cowry shells dangling from his ears and around his wrists and had a gold hoop in his wide nose. Her urge to go to him was almost unbearable.

As her mind became consumed with the purple one, her body was less and less interested in Okon. Their relationship quickly changed. Okon became a terrible beast fed by his own jealousy. He desperately appealed to Asuquo's mother who, in turn, yelled at Asuquo's distracted face.

Okon would angrily snatch the broom from Asuquo and sweep out the dry leaves that kept blowing into their home, sneezing as he did so. He tore through her garden with stamping feet and clenched fists, scratching himself on thorns and getting leaves stuck in his toenails. And his hands became heavy as bronze to her skin. He forbade her to fly, especially in the forest. Out of fear for her sons, she complied. But it did not stop there.

The rumors, mixed with jealousy, fear and suspicion spiraled into a raging storm, with Asuquo at the center. Her smile turned to a sad gaze as her mind continued to dwell on her *chi* that flew somewhere in the same skies she could no longer explore. Each night, her husband tied her to the bed where he made what he considered love to her body, for he still loved her. Each time, he fell asleep on top of her, not moving till morning when he sneezed himself awake.

Even her sons seemed to be growing allergic to Asuquo. She had to frequently wipe their noses when they sneezed. Sometimes they cried when she got too close. And they played outside more and more, preferring to help their father dry the fish he brought home, than their mother in the garden. Asuquo often cried about this in the garden when no one was around. Her sons were all she had.

One day, Okon fell sick. His forehead was hot but yet he shivered. He was weak and at times he yelled at phantoms he saw floating about the hut.

"Please, Asuquo, fly up to the ceiling," he begged, grabbing her arm as he lay in bed, sweat beading his brow. "Tell them to leave!"

He pleaded with her to speak with the plants and mix a concoction foul-smelling enough to drive the apparitions away.

Asuquo looked at the sky, then at Okon, then at the sky. He'd die if she left him. She thought of her sons. The sound of their feet as they played outside soothed her soul. She looked at the sky again. She stood very still for several minutes. Then she turned from the door and went to Okon. *When Okon gets well,* she thought. *I will take my sons with me, even if I cannot fly so well.*

When he was too weak to chew his food, she chewed it first and then fed it to him. She plucked particular leaves and pounded bitter-smelling bark. She collected rainwater and washed him with it. And she frequently laid her hands on his chest and forehead. She often sent the boys out to prune her plants when she was with Okon in the bedroom. The care they took with the plants during this time made her want to kiss them over and over. But she did not because they would sneeze.

For this short time, she was happy. Okon was not able to tie her up and she was able to soothe his pain. She was also able to slip away once in a while and practice flying. Nonetheless, the moment Okon was able to stand up straight with no pain in his chest or dizziness, after five years of marriage, he went and brought several of his friends to the hut and pointed his finger at Asuquo.

"This woman tried to kill me," he said, looking at Asuquo with disgust. He grabbed her wrists. "She is a witch! *Ubio!*"

"Ah," one of his friends said, smiling. "You've finally woke up and seen your wife for what she really is."

The others grunted in agreement, looking at Asuquo with a mixture of fear and hatred. Asuquo stared in complete shock at her husband whose life she had saved, her ears following her sons around the yard as they laughed and sculpted shapes from mud.

She wasn't sure if she was seeing Okon for what he really was or what he had become. What she was sure of was that in that moment, something burst deep inside her, something that held the realization of her mistake at bay. She should have listened to the old woman; she should have listened to *herself*. If it weren't for her sons, she'd have shot through the ceiling, into the sky, never to be seen again.

"Why...?" was all she said.

Okon slapped her then, slapped her hard. Then he slapped her again. Only her *chi* could save her now.

Okon brought her before the Ekpo society. He tightly held the thick rope that he'd tied around her left wrist. Her shoulders were slumped, and her eyes were cast down. Villagers came out of their huts and gathered around the four old men sitting in chairs and the woman kneeling before them in the dirt.

Her sons, now only three and four years old, were taken to their aunt's hut. Asuquo's hair had grown several feet in length over the years. Now there were a few coils of grey around her forehead from the stress. The people stared at her locks with pinched faces as if they had never seen them before.

The Ekpo society's job was to protect the village from thieves, murderers, cheats, and witchcraft. Nevertheless, even these old men had forgotten that once upon a long time ago, the sky was peopled with women and men just like Asuquo.

Centuries ago, the Ekpo society was close to the deities of the forest, exchanging words of wisdom, ideas and wishes with these benevolent beings who had a passing interest in the humans of the forest. But these days, the elders of the Ekpo society were in closer contact with the white men, choosing which wrongdoers to sell to them and bartering for the price.

Her husband stood behind her, his angry eyes cast to the ground. All this time he had let her go in and out of the house whenever she liked; he never asked where exactly she was going. He never asked who she was going to see. It couldn't have just been the forest. He had asked many of the women who they thought the man or men she was being unfaithful with was. They all gave different names. Father warned me that she was unclean, he kept thinking.

The four old men sat on chairs, wearing matching blue and red lapas. Their feet close together, scowls on their faces. One of them raised his chin and spoke.

"You are accused of witchcraft," he said, his voice shaky with age. "One woman said you gave her a drink for her husband's sore tooth and all his teeth fell out. One man saw you turn into a bat. Many people in this village can attest to this. What do you have to say for yourself?"

Asuquo looked up at the men and for the first time, her ears ringing, her nostrils flaring, she felt rage, though not because of the accusations. It made her face ugly. The purple one was so close, and these people were not listening to her. They were in her way, blocking out the cool dusty wind with their noise.

Her hands clenched. Many of the people gathered looked away out of guilt. They knew their part in all of this. The chief's wives, their arms around their chests, looked on, waiting and hoping to be rid of this woman who many said had bedded their husband numerous times.

"You see whatever you want to see," she said through dry lips. "I've had enough. You can't keep me from him."

She heard her husband gasp behind her. If they had been at home, he'd have beaten her. Nevertheless, his blows no longer bothered her as much. These days her essence sought the sky. It was September. The Harmattan Winds would be upon the village soon, spraying dust onto the tree leaves and into their homes. She'd hold out her arms and let the dust devils twirl her around. Soon.

But she still couldn't fly that well yet, especially with her shoulders weighed down by sadness. If only these people would get out of the way. Then she would take her sons where they would be safe, and the caretakers she chose would not tell them lies about her.

"Let the chop nut decide," the fourth elder said, his eyes falling on Asuquo like charred pieces of wood. "In three days."

She almost laughed despite herself. Asuquo knew the plant from which the chop nut grew. In the forest, the doomsday plant thrived during rainy season. Many times, she'd stopped to admire it. Its purplish bean-like flower was beautiful. When the flower fell off, a brown kidney-shaped pod replaced it. She could smell the six highly poisonous chop nuts inside the pod from meters away. Even the bush rats with their weak senses of smell and tough stomachs died minutes after eating it.

Asuquo looked up at the elders, one by one. She curled her lip and pointed at the elder who had spoken. She opened her mouth wide as if to curse them, but no sound came out. Then her eyes went blank again and her face relaxed. She mentally left her people and let her mind seek out the sky. Still a tear of deep sadness fell down her face.

The four elders stood up and walked into the forest where they said they would "consort with the old ones."

Those three days were hazy and cold as the inside of a cloud. Okon tied Asuquo to the bed as before. He slept next to her, his arm around her waist. He bathed her, fed her and enjoyed her. In the mornings, he went to the garden and quietly cried for her. Then he cried for himself, for he could not pinpoint who his wife's lover was. Every man in the village looked suspect.

Asuquo's eyes remained distant. She no longer spoke to him, she did not even look at him, and she did not notice that her babies were not with her. Instead, she unfocused her eyes and let her mind float into the sky, coming back occasionally to command her body to inhale and exhale air.

Her *chi* joined her here, several hundred miles away from the village, a thousand feet into the sky. Now, he was close enough that for the first time, a part of them could be in the same place. Asuquo leaned against him as he took her locks into his hands and brought them to his face, inhaling her scent. He smelled like dry leaves and when he kissed her ears, Asuquo cried.

She wrapped her arms around him and laid her head on his chest until it was time to go. She knew he would continue making his way to her, though she told him it was too late. She'd underestimated the ugliness that had dug its roots underneath her village.

The elders came to Okon and Asuquo's home, a procession of slapping sandals, much of the village following. People looked through windows and doorways, many milled about outside talking quietly, sucking their teeth and shaking their heads. Above, a storm pulled its clouds in to cover the sky. The elders came and her husband brought chairs for them.

"We have spoken with those of the bush," one of them said. Then he turned around and a young man brought in the chop nut. Her husband and three men held her down as she struggled. Her eyes never met her husband's. One man with jagged nails placed the chop nut in her mouth and a man smelling of palm oil roughly held her nose, forcing her to swallow. Then they let go and stepped back.

She wiped her nose and eyes, her lips pressed together. She got up and went to the window to look at the sky. The three young women and two young men watching through the window wordlessly stepped back with guilty looks, clearing her view of the gathering clouds. She braced her legs, willing her body to leave the ground. If she could get out the window into the clouds, she would be fine. She'd return for her sons once she had vomited up the chop nut.

But no matter how hard she tried, her body would only lift a centimeter off the ground. She was too tired. And she was growing more tired. Everyone around her was quiet, waiting for the verdict.

The rumble of thunder came from close by. She stood for as long as she could, a whole half hour. Until her insides began to burn. The fading light flowing through the window began to hurt her eyes. Then it dimmed. Then it hurt her eyes again. She could not tell if it was due to the chop nut or the approaching storm. The walls wavered and she could hear her heartbeat in her ears. It was slowing. She lay back on the bed, on top of the rope Okon had used to tie her down.

Soon she did not feel her legs and her arms hung at her sides. The room was silent, all eyes on her. Her bare breasts heaved, sweat trickling between them. Her mind passed her garden to her boys and landed on her *chi*. Her mind's eye saw him floating in the sky, immobile, a frown on his face.

As the room dimmed and she left her body, he dropped from the sky only thirty miles south of Asuquo's village of Old Calabar. As he dropped, he swore to the clouds that they would not see him for many many years. The wind outside wailed through the trees but within an hour it quickly died. The storm passed without sending down a single drop of rain to nurture the forest. No Harmattan Winds shook the trees that year. They had turned around, returning to the Sahara in disgust.

A year later, on the anniversary of Asuquo's death, the winds returned, though not so strong. Reluctant. They have since resumed their normal pattern. Her husband, Okon went on to marry three wives and have many children. Asuquo's young boys were raised calling his first wife "mother" and they didn't remember the strange roots and fruits their real mother had brought from the forest that had made them strong.

As the years passed, when storytellers told of Asuquo's tale, they changed her name to the male name of Ekong. They felt their audience responded better to male characters. And Ekong became a man who roamed the skies searching for men's wives to snatch because he had died a lonely man and his soul was not at rest.

"There he is!" a boy would yell at the river, as the Harmattan Winds blew dry leaves about. All the girls would go splashing out of the water, screaming and laughing and hiding behind trees. Nobody wanted to get snatched by the "man who moved with the breeze."

Nevertheless, it was well over a century before the winds blew with true fervor again. But that is another story.

As Able the Air

written by
Zack Be

illustrated by
BROCK AGUIRRE

ABOUT THE AUTHOR

At the time of this writing, Zack Be is an overworked and under-slept graduate student long trapped in the gravity well of the Washington, DC, area. As a writer, musician, student, former rehabilitation counselor, and current couple and family therapist, Zack hopes you are reading this bio in a brighter future; one in which he's finally found time for sleep between weekend warrior concerts, therapeutic interventions, and industrious all-nighters.

When he isn't working, writing, or gigging with his bands, Zack plays with his dog Misty, grapples at the Brazilian Jiu-Jitsu gym, and generally tries to avoid the clarion call of web-surfing lollygags.

This is Zack's second prose publication, following the novelette "True Jing," which appeared in the July/August 2018 edition of Asimov's Science Fiction.

ABOUT THE ILLUSTRATOR

Brock began creating art after a change in his physical well-being. Overweight since he could remember, he shed 130 pounds over a three-year period. This imbued him with the confidence and willpower he needed to pursue creative endeavors.

After high school, Brock spent two years at the Academy of Art University studying visual development. He is continuing to practice his art with the ultimate goal of going to California Institute of the Arts to study animation. He dreams of starting a studio named Mage Animation that will focus on comedic sci-fi and fantasy film.

As Able the Air

Airto couldn't shake the feeling that Dart's luck had finally run out.

"Please be careful," he said. "Keep your eyes open."

"My eyes? Funny," Dart replied. "I will, sir. Of course."

Airto leaned back in the command couch and listened to his partner's far-off footsteps trickle through the receiver. He felt this way at the end of every shift, barely wanting to breathe for fear of upsetting some nominal cosmic balance and incinerating his friend in the process. Airto's own discomfort, however minor, however superstitious, seemed a small price to pay.

"The topography has remained surprisingly stable here," Dart noted.

"Right," Airto said. Exhausted, he flexed his fingers in the nerve-net mesh innards of his control surface, a sleek silver tongue that jutted from the center of his globular operational suite. He wished again for some fantastical hotkey that could bring this mission to a swift and auspicious end, a fast-travel cheat to an agreeable future.

"One and a quarter kilometer out from contact," Dart said. He never sounded nearly as concerned as he should.

"No need to rush," Airto responded, "not at last call."

Last call—he had tried to stop saying that out loud but caught himself articulating the phrase at least once a week. He knew perfectly well there was no logical reason to believe the night's twenty-fifth landmine decommission would be any more deadly than the twenty-fourth, or the twenty-third, or the first. Yet the irony of this imagined tragedy continued to set Airto's teeth on edge. Things would be so much easier if he could be as blithe as Dart, but he knew that was impossible.

"Three quarters of a kilometer from contact," Dart said. "Not a lot of traffic out here. We'll be done in time for supper."

"Dinner's come and gone, bud," Airto said. "We've been working all night."

"Breakfast, then?"

"What difference does it make?"

"All the difference," Dart said. "It's something to look forward to."

"I can't say I agree," Airto replied. He checked his clock again and punched in a report code.

"What's on the menu?"

"What's always on the menu? Bugs and yams, probably grasshoppers."

"A scrumptious, popular dish," Dart said.

"What gives you that idea?" Airto asked.

"Is it not to your liking, sir?"

"Maybe expand your search parameters beyond Coalition-subsidized cookbooks," Airto replied. "Can we please focus?"

"Certainly, sir," Dart said.

Airto shuddered against a tickle of sweat in the straps of his helm. The spherical contraption was plated with screens that sent him a live feed from Dart's many cameras. He sifted through the images with the twitch of a finger, looking out toward the blackened horizon and its silent plumes of dim red and gold. A data line in the helm kept him updated on where other mines or tripwires had been set off by unlucky Coalition friendlies and enemies alike. More often than not, they were accounts of small nocturnal animals burrowing up and blowing themselves to bits. In operator slang, these "faunal decommissions" were all just acts of environmental terror—kamikaze vermin blissfully ignorant of whichever alliance they had just given their life to protect.

"To my fallen comrade," Dart would say of them, apparently in jest.

And how far they had fallen—all their diurnal cousins were already long gone from this scared corner of the world. It was a natural consequence of the combat ecology that had taken hold here. Immense pitched battles would rage by day and subside by night, the world's solar-powered automaton platoons both vicious and entirely energy-inefficient. Given the demands of the great sun-drinking war machines, all sides of the conflict had long since concluded that restricting skirmishes to the daytime was the only way to keep the pace of engagement between drones above a meaningless slither until battery tech could be improved. The traps left in the receding tide of melee were merely a secondary deterrent to any enemies who thought they might get clever and march their mechs under the moon.

"Ready? Let's clean up," Dart would say every single night, without fail. The war waltzed in these concentric circles, the dance invariably ending in a white-hot flash.

Airto gripped his mesh tighter, careful not to send any false alarms to his partner. He had seen the white flash on his screens before, those terrible last transmissions from an exploded technician's cameras. The images would intrude on him from time to time, often when he was just lying in bed. Other times he would see them when walking to the OpSec or in the middle of a conversation in the mess hall with another operator. The flashes were broken memories of his old partners' sudden, final moments, their fragments interlaced with his current partner's life. For months now it had been Dart's screens he imagined disappearing into the white light, and it was somehow more visceral than anything he had felt with any of the cold and distant professionals from before. There was a difference now—Dart was his friend.

"Twenty meters," Dart said.

"Let's have a look around," Airto replied.

BROCK AGUIRRE

The technician stopped for a moment and studied the area. His cameras showed an average spread of gray dirt, rocks, and a smattering of tall yellow grass that had managed to grow through the usual daily bedlam. Diagnostics flooded Airto's screens, showing no signs of any additional traps that had evaded previous aerial scans. No animals either.

"All right," Airto said, "let's do it."

Dart crawled over the next several meters until he came to a leveled patch of ground. There was a slight red glow beneath the loose dirt.

"Is that a 676 F-series?" Airto said. "That model is months old. How could we have missed one?"

Dart straddled the landmine.

"It's possible they are emptying their reserves, sir," he said. "If you believe this is a 676, I can dispose of it now. Shall I proceed?"

Airto's stomach twisted a bit—the enemy occasionally nested new types of mines within old shells as a ruse to catch Coalition officers off guard.

"Wait," he cautioned. "Just wait."

The speed at which both sides could produce iterations of these weapons made it impossible to keep databases current. The job of improvising solutions in real time rested squarely on the operator's shoulders.

"Sir, would you like a closer look?"

"Affirmative, proceed," Airto said, the worry of finality nagging him again. He hoped the impersonal jargon would make the command easier to give.

A canister of compressed air on Dart's midsection blew the dirt away without upsetting the trigger. Airto's eyes narrowed as he zoomed in on the image of the revealed bomb. He took a second to scroll through Dart's x-ray and heat filters.

"Sir, shall I continue?" the technician asked.

"Let's just be absolutely sure," Airto said.

"I trust you," Dart replied.

Airto's arms went rubber in the tongue as he began to fumble the controls, trying to bring up any reports of 676 decoys. A red column of text drizzled down his screen, but there were no confirmed lures.

"Another MRD was injured last night," Airto said.

"Could have been anything, sir," Dart replied.

"I'm looking into it."

"Wasn't necessarily a mine," Dart reiterated, referencing the same data stream.

"But there is no confirmation on cause," Airto said, although he could feel himself grasping at straws. "It could have been a similar trap. Maybe we should abort."

"Sir, we have classified the likely model and are required by law under Section C.11 to attempt decommission as soon as possible. Do you have evidence this may not be a 676?"

He didn't, and of course, Dart was right. What Airto felt in his gut couldn't be found in any Coalition handbook.

"It's just," he said, words catching in his throat. "I'm...I'm worried about you."

Dart did not respond.

"I don't want you dying on me."

The technician offered more silence in return, leaving Airto to watch the light of far-off fires refract in the treated glass layers of Dart's lenses.

Airto was starting to wonder what his partner could possibly be calculating when he finally responded. "Sir, if I may, please let me explain again. We have already classified..."

"No, I know, I know," Airto cut him off. "Just give me a second."

"I won't be hurt, sir," Dart said.

"You're supposed to say that," Airto sighed. "You have to say that."

"And?"

Airto closed his eyes and waited for it all to go away. When it didn't, because it never does, he sat up a bit in the couch and forced himself to answer. "Fine," he said. "But we're doing it slow. Slow enough for me to see each move, understood?"

"Understood," Dart said. He inserted a small pin-like tool

into the mine and began to lift the depressor. Then he swung a camera around into its body. As the technician worked, Airto attempted to count the wires inside the shell and find any irregularities compared to the hundreds of other F-series triggers they had deactivated in the previous months. Any dither could mean death. He nibbled the raw cut he had been nursing inside his lip. His heart sped up and every pump seemed to reverberate through the stale air of his ops suite.

Dart suddenly stopped.

"What is it, why'd you stop?" Airto asked, words barely louder than the hum of the OpSec gear surrounding him. His eyes flitted over the screen in a desperate attempt to see what Dart could see.

"Airto, 'How far is the farthest?'" Dart asked.

Airto groaned and dropped his head.

"Not right now," he said through his teeth.

"Airto, 'How far is the farthest?'" Dart repeated.

The operator flinched—he knew these words well. They were the beginning of a mindfulness exercise designed to help operators reduce their anxiety. The helm's biofeedback subroutine would have triggered it. Every time he heard the first line of the ridiculous couplet he was reminded that he had never wanted to be a mine removal expert, not specifically. He didn't think that anyone did, except maybe Dart, who was built for it.

"Airto, 'How far is the farthest?'" Dart asked again, his voice cool. Airto already knew his technician wouldn't budge until the stupid call was properly answered. There was no use in a power struggle.

"'As able the air,'" Airto murmured. The strict word scheme was meant to force the operator into some sort of focused objectivity. To Airto, it felt more like condescension and control from the Coalition. His mother used to play a similar game with him, withholding a bowl of her perfect feijoada until he recited this Bible verse or that. These days, back home, he felt power

in his freedom to just walk the Real Market and purchase a pot
for himself.

"'How blank is the sand?'"

"Enough, Dart, you've got me. You can see my heart rate is
down."

"Marginally," Dart said, lifting the gaggle of wires through the
slit in the mine. "I'm going to burn off the contents now."

Airto released the little bit of air he had left in his lungs. His
sticky pulse labored beneath his skin.

"Okay."

Dart sucked the propellant from the mine into a sealed tube
and separated the rest of the explosive material into a small bag.
He clamped a metal bowl over everything that remained and
then scampered several meters away to light his fuse.

"I've scavenged the useful materials and prepared
decommission."

"Are you safe?" Airto whispered.

"Decommissioning now," Dart said, ignoring him. "In three,
two, one..."

The mine ignited like a small firecracker and was gone. Airto's
shoulders dropped through the floor.

"Twenty-six for tonight," Dart said as the smoke cleared.

"I counted twenty-five," Airto replied.

Dart instantly forwarded twenty-six still shots of dead mines
from his data core, each an instant reminder of the night's work.

"You got me," Airto said, not really counting. "It's been a long
one."

"Perhaps you need rest, sir."

"'Perhaps?'"

Dart began to walk away from the contact site. Airto sat for a
moment, listening to the familiar crunch of his partner's six legs
and the soft whirr of his engine. Somewhere inside a gyroscope
spun like a heart.

"Dart, how are you?"

The machine did not respond again.

"Dart?"

"My OS is fully updated and my physical diagnostic was satisfactory," he said. "You can find my most recent report in the cloud storage. Will there be anything else?"

Airto was almost too embarrassed to ask. He felt so very far from his friend.

"I was just wondering if you'd like me to stay online with you, you know, to keep you company on the way back. It's a long walk."

"I'll run," the mine removal drone said, "and I don't have anything to say at this time. Sorry, sir."

"No, no, of course," Airto replied, forcing a little chuckle. "What am I thinking? I should get that rest."

"Yes, sir. Permission to disconnect?" Dart asked.

"Yes—I mean, granted."

The screens faded to a dull gray in Airto's helm and the straps fell away automatically. The whole contraption began to rise, dragged easily off the operator's head and into the ceiling above by vines of fiber-optic wire. Airto pulled his arms out of the tongue and rubbed his eyes. Why had he said any of that to Dart? He must have sounded desperate.

The low red shade of the small operational suite shifted then to its obnoxious white floodlights, dragging Airto to his feet. The door raised and he climbed out onto the frigid gunmetal catwalk of the OpSec. A hundred other orbs just like Airto's compartment lined either side of the walkway, their rusting curves obscured by perspiring pipes and webs of fiber-optic cabling. Large AC units chilled the massive chamber down to uncomfortable temperatures to ensure no ops could be botched by overheated machinery, at least on Airto's end. All of this hung above a deep black chasm, the lower level of which supposedly housed an emergency water reservoir. Airto could not see the bottom.

He strode quickly toward the exit, handing his OpSec keypass through a kiosk window to a woman cloaked in a heavy winter jacket. Shivering through arctic shroud and shouldering a wall of plastic strips, Airto climbed his way to the tall, minimal white halls of the surface concourse.

He passed all manner of military and corporate officials, most of whom couldn't be bothered to look up from their tablets. It was all right though; Airto had nothing to say to them. After being denied the conversation he wanted, Airto simply needed to disappear into his bed. His appetite was gone.

The soft, shuffling malaise of the War Complex reminded him a great deal of those lonely ghost-hour monorail journeys from his old coding job in the capital city to the Coalition-subsidized apartment hive he called home. Over years, the city's endless flurry had turned opaque in Airto's eyes. The crowd was a form of isolation unto itself, the bitter truth being that beneath the deafening metallic grind of the city's infernal infrastructure no one was really trying to talk anyways. Airto had little trouble abandoning the churning capital for the less exacerbating military frontier. A din of silence hung around the War Complex with startling sincerity. The quiet here, not enforced by authority or drowned by chaos, was sublime. Sometimes it was easy to forget altogether that there was a war going on. The Complex was so far from the fighting that the warzone disappeared around the curve of the Earth, making the conflict as invisible to the naked eye as it was silent to the ear.

The door to his quarters in the SubComm slid open with a satisfying swish and immediately the harsh spots in the ceiling illuminated his Spartan accommodations: a bed, a chair, and a desk, each fused to the rigid gray walls and floor. He hated thinking of this cell as a home, but it was all he had known for months.

"Kill the lights," Airto told the room before falling into his bed.

Face in his pillow, he began counting the twenty-six mines they had removed that night, hoping that he could find proof that Dart was off by one despite the photographic evidence to the contrary. It would be so great to catch Dart in a fallacy like this and watch—well, listen, anyways—to his friend try to compute his way out of the mistake. As he pondered each mental image the world began to slow down and he was able to take the deepest breath he had in hours. Sleep was imminent.

Instead, a square of light appeared on the wall across from his bed and a loud ringing vibrated Airto's room. He sat upright and read the message on the screen.

"Answer, answer," he said.

The screen went white, then black, and then filled with a low pixel-count video feed of a young woman at a desk in what looked like Airto's capital city apartment.

"Airto, meu docinoh, how are you?" she said.

"Tired, very tired, my love," he replied.

"Oh no, were you sleeping? I did not mean to wake you," she said. "Your calendar says you are usually off work around now."

"No, no, I am, it was just...it was a long one today."

"I'm sorry to hear that, baby, do you want to talk about it?"

Airto looked at the clock inset on a nearby wall. It would be dawn soon locally and he couldn't remember what time it was in the capital.

"You wouldn't want to hear it," he said.

"Oh please," she crossed her arms. "What's the point of having special access if you aren't going to talk to me?"

Airto let out a sigh and tried to smile.

"Is that maté?" he asked, pointing at the cup of tea next to her hand.

"Your mother had some sent to your apartment," she said. "She left you a message."

"Tell me about it, the tea."

"It's warm and smooth and very sweet, like you like it," she said. "It's not my favorite, but I get it. It's fine."

"You prefer it green?"

"I prefer it coffee," she said, and laughed as she sipped from the cup. "But I was thinking of you, so I thought I'd have some."

"What else did my mother's message say?"

"Something about you not dying," she said. "Do you want the full transcript?"

"No," he said, letting out a small laugh. "How many times do I have to explain to her I'm not anywhere near the fighting?"

"No one is," she responded.

"Dart is," Airto said, rubbing his temples.

She put the cup down on the desk.

"Dart?" she asked.

"Yes, my partner. We've been working together for a couple of months."

"I know," she said. "But isn't he a drone?"

"It's not like that," Airto responded. "It's not."

"Well, what is it like?" she asked.

"Let's not talk about it," Airto said, falling to his side on the bed.

"Fine; I can tell you about my day."

"Okay."

"Work was tough, commute was tough, there was nothing good on TV," she said. "Then I stayed in, hoping to talk to you."

"I'm sorry; I know it's tough in the capital as well. I don't mean to ignore you, I'm just tense."

"Then relax, it's all right."

The conversation broke for a while and Airto's heavy eyelids began to close, the glow of the screen falling over his face.

"You don't have to talk," she said, finally.

"Okay," he mumbled, half-asleep.

"You just have to listen."

Airto's eyes opened again and he watched her start to undo her blouse. Her bosom loosened and he imagined he could reach his hand through the screen and sink into her milky white skin.

"Are you listening?" she asked.

"Yes," he said.

"Yes what?"

"Yes, ma'am," he corrected, starting to sit up.

"Then get up; on your feet."

Airto rose to attention and tried to wipe the sleep from his eyes.

"Put your hands down."

"Yes, ma'am."

"Now take it off, all of it," she said, undoing one more button on her blouse. Airto quickly removed his clothes and folded them on the corner of his bed, just as she liked them. He stood again at attention in the crystalline light of the screen and waited, his body cold and warm all at once.

"Are you ready, boy?" she asked.

"Yes, ma'am."

"Then listen very closely..."

"Specialist Lima," the Major said, signing a document on his tablet. "How are you?"

Airto shifted uncomfortably in the forced ergonomics of the backless chair. He had been put on suspension from active duty—they called it "leave"—for two days, no reason given. Then, his presence had suddenly been required in the Major's office, still with no reason given.

Airto did not like where this was going.

"War is war," Airto said. It was one of those automatic responses he had become so used to giving.

"Interesting sentiment from someone with so little skin in the game."

"Excuse me?" Airto said, raising an eyebrow.

"I don't mean to be harsh, Lima, but no one your age has any idea what it actually feels like to be on a battlefield." He pointed a thumb out of his office window and across the plain toward the invisible fighting. "We used to send men out there."

Airto glanced down through the clear plastic desk at the Major's two synthetic legs, their angular ridges poorly hidden beneath his well-tailored pleats.

"You're right, sir," Airto said.

"Don't get me wrong; if I never have to send another soldier's remains home again, I'll be a happy man. I'm just not sure anyone can win a war with no skin in the game."

"Sir, Coalition predictions show us gaining ground in..."

"No, Lima, you're not listening," the Major continued, looking out the window. "It's all just drones killing drones; out of sight, out of mind. Corporate sends the new models every few months and we keep them greased, updated, and on course. There's no fear, no trepidation, no one's life is hanging in the balance. It begs the question: with stakes so low, why should we ever stop?"

Airto was having trouble hiding the shock on his face. He couldn't remember a time when he had heard a superior officer talk in this manner.

"What, surprised to hear management being honest?" the Major said, "Have I said anything you haven't heard around the mess hall from your brainy friends in OpSec?"

Obviously, the answer to that was "no." The philosophy of the military "gear grinder" was the only topic some of the other specialists in OpSec could ever seem to discuss. Perhaps chattering over the existential dilemma of modern war helped them to cope, but it only increased Airto's anxiety.

He shook his head very slightly to affirm the Major's words.

"I'm glad we're in agreement," the Major said. "I suppose I should treat this report from MRD-1087 as a misunderstanding, then?"

Airto stiffened a bit.

"Dart?"

"Yes, 'Dart,'" the Major said. "You all are a fairly productive mine removal team. In fact, you are fifteen percent more successful now than you were with your previous MRD."

"Yes, sir," Airto said.

"What do you attribute that to, Specialist?"

"Our relationship," Airto said without hesitation. "Dart is an excellent mine technician. You're not thinking of decommissioning him, are you?"

"I wasn't, should I?"

"No, no, please don't," Airto said, sitting forward in the chair.

A little twitch crossed the Major's face.

"To be clear, Lima, this report is not about MRD-1087. It's about you."

The air grew thin between them.

"About me?" Airto said.

"MRD-1087 says you were acting erratic toward the end of your shift two nights ago. His automated reports indicated that you were attempting to violate the rules of Section C.11 and leave a discovered mine in the field without attempting to disarm it. He also indicated that the reason you wanted to leave the mine—at potential great military and financial cost to the Coalition—was to, and I'm quoting the report here, 'keep MRD-1087 alive.' Please, Specialist, explain to me what I'm missing here."

A bolt of lightning hit Airto's spine and he shivered visibly, overtly aware that he had just referred to his work with Dart as a "relationship." The Major sat motionless and waited for an answer.

"I don't know what to say. It must be like you said, sir, a misunderstanding."

"Yours or the machine's?"

"Sir..."

"This is why you've been on suspension, Specialist Lima, to give you a break from the front. The Coalition and I just need to be sure that you understand MRD-1087 is not conscious in any way. Every MRD is the same. 'Dart' is not alive and cannot pass a rigorous Turing test."

"I know," Airto said, although it didn't feel right. He knew logically that Dart was not alive—sentient AIs were still just television villains—but that was not how he felt. If pressed by the Major, he wouldn't be able to explain it.

"We want you to be careful with your MRD, that's why we gave them shadow personalities at all," the Major said. "It's something you might want to protect, something maybe you'll think twice about simply dropping onto a mine before you double check your work. But we don't expect them to survive at the expense of identified enemy mines remaining in the field. Some MRDs will go down, but it's better for the Coalition than the alternative."

"Yes," Airto said, teeth clenched. He was being humiliated now, as was obviously the Major's intent, and all because of a stupid report. How could Dart do this to him?

"Like I said before, there's no skin in this game, Lima. None. There's less to lose than you think."

Airto closed his eyes and wondered what Dart would have to say about that.

"If we have to have this conversation again, there will be a reprimand. Understood?"

"Understood," Airto said.

"Understood what?"

"Understood, sir," Airto finished.

"What a rude man," she said, looking away. There was an old-fashioned crossword puzzle on the apartment desk today, half-finished and stained by the ring of her favorite drink.

"And such a stale argument," Airto said, huddled on the floor next to his bed. "'You don't know what it's like, Lima.' Well how about this, Major: the old days are long gone and they aren't coming back. Maybe he's the one who doesn't know what it's like, not anymore."

"Right," she said.

"Dart is more than a partner, he's a friend," Airto said. "They ask me to care for him, and I do, and now they tell me not to care too much? Which is it?"

"I don't know, Airto," she said.

"Of course you don't." He hung his head between his knees.

"Don't talk to me like that," she said, looking back through the screen.

"I didn't mean it that way, honestly." Airto met her eyes and started biting the sore in his mouth.

"Hope not," she replied, turning to regard something off-screen again. The image started looking more pixilated than usual and then the screen froze.

"Hey, you there?" Airto asked.

"Obviously," she said, movement returning to the picture in choppy phases.

"What are you looking at?" he said quietly, in case asking this was a mistake.

"Oh nothing, fofo."

The feed rippled and returned to normal.

"Even if it's nothing, tell me," Airto said. "Or anything else. Just say something."

"I read a story in the news today, would you like to hear that?"

Airto nodded and pulled a thin blanket around his naked shoulders.

"It reads, 'Realtor Risks Life Rescuing Girl Under Rails.' It happened a few blocks from your apartment, Airto."

"Did someone fall?"

"Nothing so banal. Marlin Sousa, fifty-seven, bought an abandoned lot that shared some space beneath one of the monorail lines. It wasn't until the day before they broke ground that a young girl was discovered living, and somehow surviving, in her own filth. It seems no one had noticed her for quite some time and she had been surviving as a thief. Marlin took it upon himself to give the girl a new home: his own. Pretty incredible, right?"

"A real hero," Airto said solemnly. And what had *he* done?

"He sure is."

"Do you think what I do is important?" Airto asked. "I mean, really?"

"What a silly question, querido," she said, picking up the pen. "I know it's hard to tell sometimes but people respect what you have to do. I'll admit, it's hard to grasp what it's really like for you, sitting in the OpSec. Like you said about the Major, we don't really know. If you think it's going well, then I think it's going well."

She doesn't understand, Airto thought, *How could she? Why am I even asking?*

"Well, do you think what Dart does is important?" he asked, lowering his voice.

She didn't respond this time, taking her glasses off instead.

"Do you?" he asked again.

Her silence was deafening. Airto put his hands on his temples and felt a lump form in his throat. Again, he understood the illogical nature of the conversation he was having, on all points, but he couldn't stop himself from asking.

She continued to stare, the feed perhaps refrozen.

"Please come back," he mumbled. "Please say something."

The feed unfroze and he saw she had moved to the center of the room. She made her whole body visible on the screen and angled her bare feet just the way he liked them.

"I don't like talking about Dart, he's a machine," she said. "I do know you'll be seeing him in less than two hours, though. Do you really want to spend that time talking about him? Or do you want to know what's under here?"

She tugged at the hem of her skirt and then used her finger to bring Airto to his knees. He crawled along the smooth, cold floor until his face was inches from the screen.

"Good boy," she said. "Now tell me Dart can wait."

Airto's lips trembled and the words did not come.

"Well?" she said, voice crackling a bit on the receiver. "Otherwise we can't play."

The sound of Airto's ragged breathing dominated the room, joined only by the requisite hum of the AC vent, buzzing away like Dart's little engine. He tried to say her words but the creeping mist of superstition suffocated him. In the end, he gave her no choice.

"Fine, Airto," she said. "Forget it. Go to your toys."

The screen went black and Airto slumped to the floor.

Please come back, he thought, and the room did not respond.

The helm tightened around Airto's head as the light in the orb shifted to red. The normal diagnostic reports filled his field of vision and Airto glossed over its bits and pieces, most of the information redundant. He was having a hard time remembering the lie he could tell himself that made reading the data seem so important.

"Good evening, sir," Dart said. "OpSec has designated eighteen targets for us. It's a light night. Ready? Let's clean up."

"Why?" Airto asked.

"Uncertain, sir. Fewer enemy drones flew today, and..."

"No, Dart, why did you tell the Major about us? That there was some kind of issue?"

The drone took one of his long pauses before answering.

"Dart?"

"I did not tell the Major about us," he said. His cameras came online and a 360 degree view of Dart's maintenance pen filled Airto's helm.

"You're not supposed to lie to me, Dart."

"I can promise you, sir, I am incapable of lying. I believe you are referring to my daily release report. As you know, I automatically generate one at the end of every shift. It is likely that the Major extracted his concerns from that document."

"Do you even know what that report said? Do you know what it means? The Major told me to just let you die, you know? That's what your report accomplished. Do you have some sort of death wish?"

"I don't understand the question, sir. May I proceed to the first marker?"

"Yes," Airto said, the word spiked with anger. He dug his hands into the wet mesh of the silver tongue and it sealed around him. The door to the pen opened and Dart jumped into the field.

"Specialist Lima, I had no intention of harming you, if that's what you are asking. My report included data about your trepidation regarding mine twenty-six. Your actions fell outside C.11 protocols."

"The protocols also go on at length about my right to use discretion," Airto said, gritting his teeth. "The situation was potentially unsafe."

"I do not understand, sir."

"For you, Dart. If I had gotten that situation wrong, you could have been scattered over the field in a million pieces. I was worried about you. Why does no one get that?"

"I don't feel pain, sir."

"What is it, then? Do you want me to get you blown up? Is that it?"

"Certainly not, sir, but our military and corporate commandments trump all else. We are beholden to those truths."

Airto groaned—this was a propaganda script he had heard a thousand times before.

"And you're prepared to die for that?" he asked.

Dart broke into a run then, his six legs jittering across rock and dirt away from the barracks. The pair did not converse for a long while. Airto, his question left unanswered, noted they were traveling straight toward one of the high-traffic sectors of the battlefield. As the blip of the marker drew closer on the map, the detritus of war began to pile up around them. Long, angular limbs of burnished steel were strewn pell-mell between piles of smoldering circuitry and the smashed carcasses of massive tanks and mobile surface-to-air missile racks. The inhuman aerodynamic heads of infantry drones rolled between Dart's legs as he ran. Discarded and damaged solar cells littered the world as far as Airto could see and amassed as the hills of shattered tech grew.

"Well, I care if you die," Airto said after a while. "You shouldn't die if you don't have to, right?"

"I'm afraid I don't understand the question," Dart said. "It is what it is. We have people to protect."

"That's exactly where I'm having trouble," Airto said, "I don't care about defending the rest of these machines, I don't know them. But I do know you, Dart, and I know you are worth protecting."

"Sir, I meant that we are here to protect the people of the Coalition. These machines are not people. They do not live."

Airto looked around at the carnage and felt his stomach drop again.

"Do *you* live, Dart?"

"Five kilometers out," he responded.

"Dart, answer me."

"Sir, I cannot answer that question."

Airto flexed his fingers in the nerve-net.

"Dart, I order you to answer my question. Are you alive?"

Airto was met with only the sound of crunching rubble. He let the question hang on the commline.

"I will not give any further orders until you answer me," Airto said.

"I can tell you that I exist," Dart said finally.

"That wasn't my question," Airto said. "Are you alive?"

"Well I definitely won't be if we don't pay attention to this next mine," he said, his tone turning obscenely bright as his OS attempted to use humor protocols to quell the operator's questioning. "Any statistics from the day shift we should know regarding our current location?"

Airto tongued the sore in his mouth and closed his eyes for a moment.

"You're dodging me buddy, but that's okay. Maybe you have to, maybe you're protecting yourself. Maybe you're protecting me. But I hear you; I hear you in there, okay? I don't believe what they say, that you're just a dumb sub-Turing default. I've met plenty of those chat bots and you're not one of them. I can *hear* you, Dart. I can understand you."

"I'm not sure how to respond, sir."

"I have a different question, then."

"Yes?"

Airto cleared his throat.

"Dart, are we friends?"

The technician took several seconds to calculate.

"Sir, I believe we are," he finally said. "In fact, I believe you are my only friend."

A quiet smile crept across Airto's face.

"Would you like to hear a joke?" Dart said. It was a diversion; another one of those standard operator-calming techniques. Airto felt sure at this point that he had heard them all.

"Okay, Dart, shoot."

Airto was still laughing at the old joke when the tripwire was triggered, filling his screens with white-hot light.

The War Complex had no need for jails or cells. The SubComm rooms, with their spare walls and sliding, handle-less doors were more than adequate when a person had to be detained. Toss a switch in a far-off chamber and home became a dungeon.

Solitary and confined, Airto sat in his dimmed cube for days on end, quickly exhausting the supply of shouts and cries with which he had been interred. All of his room's amenities, including cloud access and app features, had been suspended. If he was being honest, he had earned his stay.

After Dart had been incinerated, Airto had sat in the OpSec for many minutes. For some reason he half expected an administrator to come and try to console him, but quickly realized that no one was coming at all. MRDs went down, that's what they were built for. Dart was dead and all that he had been was reduced to scrolling red text on ninety-nine other operator helms. Airto left his post and walked calmly out of the OpSec, flinging his key-pass into the unseen depths below. No one looked up as he took the stairs back to the main level of the War Complex and made his way, in deliberate fashion, down through the evening corridors toward the small exits to the west.

In fact, it wasn't until he had reached the vehicle depot that any kind of authority was alerted to his movements. Did they really expect him to just stand by? A soldier was out there in the field—Dart was out there in the field—and wasn't there some old refrain about never leaving a man behind? Airto, running on pure adrenaline, had forced his way through two MPs and commandeered a small rover before reinforcements arrived. They took his ride down with a localized EMP, but not before he had gained enough momentum to crash it into a pylon, releasing a chunk of concrete onto a bank of newly minted vehicles. The damage was extensive, and worse yet, expensive. No one word burned corporate ears more.

He wouldn't know the full impact of his actions until years later, when his own story—and others, anonymized—showed up in a late-night military documentary on abandoned and declassified tech, in which Airto's stunt was described as the last straw in the personified MRD program. This was not the first time an operator had become overly attached to the well-spoken military grade AIs. Critics of the program had warned that the human propensity to project personalities onto anything—teddy bears, weapons, the moon—would be overwhelmed by the bot's conversational abilities. In fact, clinical anthropomorphism had already been a problem in the public population with much less complex civilian-grade chat bots. Corporate, however, wanted to run a real-world cost-benefit analysis: could they make operators care *just enough* to be more cautious with their expensive technology without generating damaging side effects?

The answer seemed to be a resounding "no."

All of this, however, was happening above Airto, both in pay grade and in the literal meters of dirt between his cell and the ground level. He tried not to cry because he knew that there would be no sympathy from anyone, yet the tears came all the same. Many times during his captivity Airto considered what the Major had asked him about the war.

"Why should we ever stop?"

After four days of confinement, some of Airto's comforts were returned to him. He was allowed to use some of the room's apps and had regained control of the AC, but the door remained locked and there was still no word from the Major or anyone else about what was going to happen to him. Airto stayed in bed.

On the fifth day, his screen suddenly lit up.

"Airto?" she said. "Oh no, were you sleeping? I did not mean to wake you. The calendar you gave me said you were usually off work around now."

He sighed but did not respond.

"What's wrong, fofo?"

"Dart is dead."

He hadn't actually said it out loud before, and was not surprised to find that each of the three syllables in succession stung him more than the last.

"I'm not sure how to respond, Airto."

"I know you're not."

"Well, you have a few messages, should I read them?"

"I'm not sure I can do this today," Airto said to himself.

"Don't talk to me like that," she said.

"Stop it."

"Airto, you're being a bad boy."

"Shut the hell up," he said, rolling around to face her.

"Airto, you're being a very bad boy."

"Dammit, enough with your scripts!" He threw a pillow at the screen.

"What has gotten into you?" she demanded.

"Please don't..."

"Airto, I know you don't want to hear this, but Dart was just a machine," she said. "He was not real."

"You're not real either," he whined. "But of course, you don't know that. Tell me this, are you alive?"

There was a telltale lengthy pause.

"I exist," she said.

He stifled a laugh, feeling tears well in his eyes.

"That is not what I asked."

"Look, Airto, I'm here now, for you. Tell me Dart can wait, or I'm..."

"Pause program," Airto said.

The screen froze and he studied her convincingly rendered face for a long time. She was exactly his type and tuned perfectly to his settings, but the truth was all too obvious. She was just a thrill, entirely empty. Was there really no difference between her and Dart? That was unacceptable, and seemed to Airto, false.

"I need something else today," he said, pulling up her settings on the screen. She was a standard issue chat-bot, designed straight from corporate to satisfy soldier's carnal desires on tour.

Airto had warmed up to her recently, finding a comfort in his control and her predictability.

He dragged a few faders this way and that on her settings screen, raising the "Compassion" slider and lowering "Logic," unchecking some preferences, and leaving the more advanced personal options alone. He left her memory intact as well, but restarted her scheduled visit.

Airto sat back on the bed and waited for the reboot to complete. When she came back online there were still tears on his cheeks.

"What's wrong, fofo?" she asked, her tone more motherly than he had ever heard it.

"Dart is dead," he forced himself to say again.

"Oh no, I'm so sorry."

"He was my friend," Airto continued, "maybe my only one."

"That's terrible," she said, a hand covering her mouth. "What can I do?"

"I want..." but Airto couldn't finish the sentence.

"Don't worry now, I'll take care of you."

"Please," he said, curling into a ball on the bed and facing her. "I want to feel better."

She smiled then, her teeth just pixels of searchlight-white.

"Airto, 'How far is the farthest?'"

Molting Season

written by
Tim Boiteau

illustrated by
DANIEL BITTON

ABOUT THE AUTHOR

Tim Boiteau writes and lives in Michigan with his wife and son. His fiction has appeared in various places in print and online, notably Deep Magic. *He is currently finishing up his second novel and trying to find a market for his first one. He holds a PhD in experimental psychology and enjoys long-distance running. "Molting Season" is inspired by his gig working as night auditor at a hotel many years ago.*

ABOUT THE ILLUSTRATOR

Daniel Bitton was born in 1997 in Fort Lauderdale, Florida. Daniel, or Danny to his friends and family, began drawing long before he can remember. Unlike other children his age, he drew relentlessly, bringing his trusty sketchbooks wherever he went.

Daniel went on to receive a BFA in illustration from the Maryland Institute College of Art in 2019 and attended The Illustration Academy in Kansas City in the summer of 2018.

He loves to depict fantastic characters and tell stories through his illustrations inspired by dreams, myths, and history. Through a mix of layered digital and traditional media, Daniel's work primarily focuses on themes of dark fantasy with historical allegories for book covers, usually for a YA audience.

When not drawing, Daniel can be found running outside on the trails or thinking about his next project.

Molting Season

Seven thirty in the morning, I find a girl passed out on the sofa, face buried in the cushions, one hand gripping the hilt of an abused long sword. The floor is littered with cold-weather gear, the carpet soggy with melted snow. I recognize her profile, the short, jagged cut of her black hair. Have seen her, sword slung over her shoulder, going to and from a rusted Bronco and the house next door countless times.

Wondering how she got in (and why), I step back out into the snow-flecked spring air, the white haze dispelled by flickering orange bursts of the sprawling refinery's gas flares, beyond the neighborhood and a vast swath of industrial ruin.

Check the hidden key in the green glazed ceramic frog.

It's there.

I peer over at the house next door and glimpse a skull at the window, half-concealed by the curtain, staring back at me. Catch a whiff of something rotten, like gassy compost.

Return inside and move quietly into the kitchen. It's technically dinner for me. Following Fred's disappearance, I've taken over the late shift at the Lakeside Inn and need to acclimatize myself to eating dinner foods in the a.m.

Steak and eggs feels like a nice compromise.

As I'm cooking, I notice a glass in the drainboard which wasn't there when I left for work yesterday evening. Lipstick-stained. Smells of Smirnoff.

Set my food and coffee down on the kitchen table and find among the mass of mail a slim black book—*ffyntlik Stories*. Skull

376

literature. Camel butts brim out of the ashtray—also stained in her color.

I flip through the book and find it contains a hundred or so vignettes, most of them no more than a page long.

As I eat, I randomly pick out a story—"Molting Season."

molting season
annual excretion
post-excretory purification
sexual fugue of the female
fern forest
male train
rape and castration of the male train by the fugal female
laying a clutch
patriarch-selection ceremony
butchering of the rest of the father train
salting and spicing the father meat
maternal abandonment
vigilance
downpour
abscesses
seepage
cracks
the joyful pride of examining the slender spines of puggles post-hatching
consuming the spiced father meat to stimulate milk production
paternal breastfeeding
father-led puggle train
vigilance
reunion with the mother
premortem perseverative dream
suicide of the father
molting season

I puzzle over the meaning of this story or poem or whatever it is for some time. More of a list really—an inventory of scenes from some alien nature documentary. The perspective shifts make it especially difficult to follow, moving from the mother, to the fathers, then back again. From what I gather, a female travels on a fugue, attracting a number of suitors (the "male train"), she mates with one of them, kills the rest, and then leaves the father to mind the eggs. When they hatch, the father breastfeeds the puggles, leads them back to the mother, commits suicide, and then the cycle repeats.

I flip through a few more stories, but my mind is starting to fade, the steak only half-eaten.

Six hours later, I shuffle back into the living room, light a cigarette and flip on the television while I smoke—fields of static, fields of static, fields of static, looping infomercial of bygone days (slasher-flick knives, stain-remover [wine! marinara sauce! blood!]). I'm so temporally discombobulated it takes me a full minute to realize what's amiss—no one is lying on the couch on the other side of the coffee table.

I stare at the emptiness, letting the smoke settle in my lungs for as long as possible, remembering how she filled out the space, the curves of her delicate face, the white-knuckled clamp on the sword.

I cobble together a light meal and sense from the awkward placement of food in the fridge that she made breakfast before leaving—hash browns, juice, pickles—or maybe I'm paranoid.

She didn't leave a note—

(Neither did Mom.)

I would've left a note if I were her—if I'd done what she had done.

Try calling Lana for some reality testing, but she doesn't answer—still screening my calls. A skull sympathizer with a resilient mind, she might offer some insight on the girl's situation, whether she's at risk.

I bundle up for a frigid jog, and lope out onto the icy road. The street zigzags with a growing jumble of cars—cracked windshields, tires in crises, a few tanks probably ripe for the siphoning.

Keep expecting something to leap out and attack me. I jump with each far-off gas flare eruption from Detroit Petroleum. Skulls study me from the windows of the tract housing.

Vigilance, I recall from *ffyntlik*'s "story." I'd heard somewhere that only males crossed over onto Earth. An overwhelming train of them.

A mile or so later, I'm back home, hands shaking—haven't freaked out like this in a long time.

Chill out, I tell myself. Chill out. Chill out.

That's when the creaky screams erupt next door. Gooseflesh breaks out over my body. Much earlier in the day than usual. Impossible to focus or hear anything else. Could call the cops, but they'd just recommend an earpiece as they always do.

Spend thirty minutes salivating over the barrel of a gun before screaming and flinging it onto my bed and continue living until tomorrow's noonday demon.

Hours later, my hands growing steadier, I don a pair of black slacks, white shirt, and black tie, and navigate my station wagon through the icy, broken streets to the hotel. Time of night I leave for work, the house next door is brimming with skulls and screaming, strobe lights and jack-hammering death metal—a scattering of them stand swaying in the snow, staring me down.

At work, Carol and I discuss Fred's whereabouts. Well, it's been a week already, so we discuss his corpse's whereabouts. He'd had crinkled skin around the mouth, smoked menthols and had a beer gut. Joked that his real job was doing crosswords. He often joked. When I was working second shift, he would try to keep me from going home by flooding me with overlapping streams of jokes and anecdotes, each one stinking a little more of desperation, because once I left, it was just him dangling out over the night in this glass cube of a lobby, praying for the first band of eastern gold that meant he'd survived the night.

"Watch yourself, young stud," Carol says. Silver-haired, heavy, the second-shifter lost two sons and a husband in the Lemming

Craze, yet has somehow clung on to a sunny disposition. "Don't travel down the road to Fred-dom."

After she squeals out of the parking lot in her hotrod, I settle down behind the front desk and review a typed-up inventory of Fred's duties (crosswords not included), elevator music oozing into my ears. Beyond the glass walls of the lobby, plumes of fire from the petroleum corporation light up the lake and highway.

Too much pressure building up in the works.

Monday morning I return to an empty living room. Make a salad and sandwich and screwdriver and discover that the girl left the *ffyntlik* book behind, concealed beneath a catalog offering insider deals at a defunct department store. Read another story, this one all definite articles—just the word *the* repeated for a page and a half, concluding as follows:

the the the the the the the the the the the th—

Girl has strange taste in books.

My eyes stray to the kitchen window, surveying the unremarkable side of the skull house, which Arnold and Stella Crickenberger abandoned when they followed along behind the others during the Lemming Craze. Quiet now, but I can sense them in there, sardined together, gaping at each other.

Girl has strange taste in company too.

When I wake that afternoon, the screams have already ratcheted up next door.

It's not until Tuesday before she shows up again.

Same scene as before, except she's wearing red jeans and a striped shirt. In addition to the long sword, she's fallen asleep with a finger stuck into *ffyntlik Stories*. I go about as before, trying not to make too much noise.

Eat in silence, then lie in bed listening, casting myself out into the rest of the house, ghosting through the walls, until I'm floating over her, withstanding the temptation to slip the book from her grasp with incorporeal hands. In this dream state, I can study her more freely, appreciate her long, willowy shape, her lashes fluttering like snared insects.

I fall asleep that way, and when I wake up, she's gone.

Took the book with her.

When I arrive at work Tuesday night, Carol gives me the rundown—a short (ever-shortening) guest list of customers with local IDs, for each one of which Carol invents a sordid story free of charge, a story meant to distract from the reality of the situation.

"One more thing," Carol says. "Room 115. Solitary male."

"What about him?" I ask, opening the room file on the computer, bracing myself for the next speculative yarn.

"Not *that* kind of male."

I glance up from the bizarre name in the registry.

She tugs on her earpiece, what the president urged we wear at all times for the sake of interspecies harmony. This was several hours before he succumbed, before blowing his brains out in the Oval Office.

I'd forgotten to bring mine to work. I tend to forget it.

"It's alone?"

She nods. "And on that note, I'm out, young stud."

Later that night, another guest checks in: white male, late fifties. The maids have disposed of enough bodies during their cleaning schedule for us to be wary of admitting guests with local IDs. I give him the corporate discount. Whether out of sympathy or as cynical enabler, I couldn't really say.

Hours later on my early morning patrol of the grounds, I walk down to the water's icy edge for a smoke. From down here, when the stacks explode, the motel lights up in miniature—an impressively detailed model.

As I return, I hear the distant summons of the phone and sprint the last stretch of the way, fumbling to unlock the lobby door, and reach the check-in counter after fifteen rings at least.

"Thanks for calling The Lake—"

"How are things?" Lana asks, cutting off the script.

"Good." My mouth is sticky, voice disembodied. "Hold on a sec." I drop the phone, sloppily hurtle over the counter, take a seat, and pluck it back up. "Go ahead."

"Are you out of breath?"

"Yeah, I was...uh...exercising. I started exercising since you left."

"I got your messages. Have they found Fred?"

"No."

"God. I...was thinking about you. I'm writing. A memoir. My male train thought it might be interesting given my experience with both humans and *skyylls*. There's a chapter called 'Warren,' what I've been working on this week. It made me want to call you. I needed to hear you speak, your cadence. You sounded so lifeless on the machine."

"Well, here it is. Here I am."

"Tell me what's new."

"Nothing much."

"No girlfriend?"

It takes me a moment to answer. "There's a girl in my life, but I'm not sure she knows what I look like."

"What's her name?"

"I don't know."

She laughs.

"Don't put this in your book, okay? I found her asleep on my couch a couple of times. Just entered in the middle of the night while I was at work."

"Well, what did you do?" Lana asks.

"Nothing. I just eat and go to bed without waking her. I don't know how to behave anymore. Not without the script."

Without suggesting a solution or even attempting to conclude the topic, she jumps into asking about some common acquaintances, the neighborhood, etc. She really is just listening to my voice in the beginning, but then we reminisce about life pre-skulls—colorful, mnemonic gas flares, each one dissipating into darkness. I notice the textures of my own voice as we speak, the way all of my body vibrates in sympathy with the deep, scratchy sound. I'm a real drag, she tells me.

Finally she says, "I'm being summoned. Thanks for talking to me. I know you must hate me."

"A little. Wait a minute, though. I need to ask you something."

"What's that?"

"How is it living with skulls?"

"It's pronounced *skyylls*."

"Point taken."

"Why do you want to know?"

"Dunno. Could be pertinent."

She lowers her voice. "They don't like us talking about them."

"Well, you'll be talking about them in your book, right?"

I look up and almost gasp at the sight of the guest—the skull—standing out by the empty pool, swaying, staring in at me through its enormous eye cavities.

"I really can't talk to you about this."

It's nothing but moonlit nerves and elaborate bone structure, frilled, horned, gangly—the meticulous handiwork of a psychotic paleontologist.

"Out of loyalty to your skull-friends? Or...is it fear?"

"Goodnight, Warren."

Click.

"'Night," I say, the handgun heavy in my inner coat pocket.

The next time it happens is Thursday morning. Spring has finally lived up to its name. The thawing neighborhood smells of dogwood blossoms. The pool is back in service, chlorine wafting into the lobby every time the doors swing open.

This time she's wearing stockings and a skirt riding up high. Out of a sense of decorum, I throw a blanket over her, and she mumbles somnolently. Her mascara has run, lipstick smeared. I go to the kitchen and pan fry tilapia. Wrap it in tortillas with cabbage and onion and lime juice. Finish off the dregs of the Smirnoff. Think about what to do.

Should talk to her at least, see if I can help in some way.

My shoulders slump with indecision.

Thursday melts slowly into Sunday night.

Carol gives me the rundown. Our skull friend has retained its room.

At work I do the usual. Read a book. Watch a movie. Take slap shots at the freezer in the kitchen. Nap at my desk. The lobby dissolves to the surface of a moon circling a gas giant—ten of me tromp through a silvery desert and after weeks of marching, we reach a fern forest, discover in a clearing a gigantic, arachnid girl-on-the-couch, who devours us one by one post-copulation, when a staccato ring echoes across the moon's surface, the sound flattening and crumpling my doubles and the spider girl—I realize I'm clutching papers on the desk and the staccato ring means an in-house call. I pick up the receiver, zoomed back into reality.

"Good evening, this is Warren, how can—"

A voice creaks on the other end.

I remove the receiver from my ear, stare at it, then glance down at the display—room 115.

"Please insert a modulator, sir," I say, voice shaking.

The creaking continues, each pulse lasting a second or so, a few seconds of silence, then another pulse.

I hang up, a chill running through me, my eyes straying to the glass wall of the lobby, out over the pool, and across to room 115.

I light a cigarette and pick the phone back up. I fight the instinct to ring Lana, and dial home instead.

It takes nine rings before someone picks up. A languorous grunt.

"Hello?" I say.

"Yeah," the 3:30 a.m. voice says, deeper, richer than in my imagination.

"You don't know me, but you're sleeping on my couch."

She clears her throat. "I'm awake."

"I wasn't sure who else to call about this."

I hear her shifting position, a long silence, the flick and crackle of igniting a cigarette. She exhales. "What can I do for you, Warren?"

"You know my name."

"Didn't take too much snooping. Left your mail on the kitchen table. I think you have hoarding tendencies."

"You have wheels, right?"

"Yup."

"Do you know where I work?"

"The five-star on the other side of the fireworks?"

Takes me a beat to decipher this. "Yeah."

"What do you want exactly, Warren?"

"Can you bring me my earpiece? Or are you drunk?"

"Only had a few beers tonight. You're out of vodka, by the way. Where is it?"

"Check the bookshelf in the hall. Also, the drawer beneath the knife block in the kitchen."

"Will do, Warren." There's something flirtatious in the way she repeats my name. Or it could be my imagination.

"And lock the door on the way out. Thanks."

While I wait for her, I prepare an industrial-sized pot of coffee in the kitchen, then I hear the welcoming jingle of the lobby door opening and rush back to the front desk, straightening my tie, tucking my hair behind my ears. Find her there in her boots and dark coat, tapping her black fingernails on the counter, sizing up the place with pale jade eyes. I feel a rush of embarrassment about the seediness of the décor, the explosions from Detroit Petroleum, the oversaturation of chlorine.

She hands me the earpiece. "What's a room cost here anyway?"

She's taller than I thought—close to six feet—with a narrow nose, pierced septum, and a slender neck emerging from a thick, checkered scarf. I misjudged her height, I realize, because I'd always seen her standing near a skull, who tower around eight feet off the ground.

I fit the seashell-like device around my ear. "Double or king?"

She shrugs. "King."

"Deluxe?"

"Sure."

"How many guests?"

"Does that matter?"

"Yes."

"Just me."

"And you're local?"

"Yeah."

"Well"—I pick up the phone—"depends on who's working when you check in."

She smiles. "Let's say you're working, Warren."

I dial room 115. Wait for an answer. "I could get you a deal."

She leans on the counter, chin in hand. "Strange pricing system you guys have here."

"It's not answering." I hang up the phone and grab the skeleton key from its hanger beneath the counter, hidden behind the computer tower. She pokes her nose over the counter to see what I'm doing, but when I flash her a reproving look, she backs off, smirking, leaving me with the lingering, citrusy notes of her perfume or her shampoo—or just her. "I need to go check up on the guest. You can make yourself comfortable here. Guess you don't need to be told that."

She laughs. "Let me come. You've piqued my curiosity."

We exit the lobby into a desiccated jungle sprouting up between the contours of poolside concrete, everything a luminous, wavering blue. We walk in silence as she takes in all the details—ripped sun loungers, ice-decimated pavement, cardboard-patched windows of rooms 107 and 113. Room 115 draws near, and we can hear the skull's creaking voice in the darkness on the other side of the door, faint beneath the lapping of the pool water.

I knock. "Sir?"

No response.

The girl fits in her own earpiece.

Another knock. "Sir?"

"Allow me. *ixd*?"

We wait. I knock a few more times, then unlock the door.

The skewed light of the pool illuminates the giant looming in the corner, its head frill grazing the ceiling. The creature stands stock-still, save for the micro movements of its nerve-webbed skull.

I flick on the lights, scan the room. King-sized bed still made, carpet discolored but clean, bulky TV turned off.

Place doesn't look used, though it reeks of rotten vegetables.

The girl enters, approaches the skull and attempts to communicate, but the creature is unresponsive. I tune my earpiece, which up-bends its utterances into intonations less skin-crawling, but to no avail—it's speaking *jskyyll*.

"You understand what it's saying?" I ask her.

She nods. "'Puggle train.'"

"Sorry?"

"He's dreaming about children. They call it a premortem perseverative dream."

"It's dying?"

"Yes. In ideal circumstances *skyylls* engage with the afterlife several days before they give up living. Their language acts as prayer, willing the afterlife into existence. It can go wrong, of course. They can become trapped in nightmares, in Hell, but this one . . . he's dreaming of children he'll never birth."

"*ffyntlik*," I murmur.

"What was that?" she asks, turning back toward me.

"A story from the book you had with you. I totally missed the point at the time—"

"'the'?"

I nod. "This"—I gesture toward the skull—"is what 'the' was about?"

"Yes. A tragedy about a *skyyll* who becomes trapped in

absurdity while invoking his own version of Paradise. In any case, that's how I interpreted it. For them, repetition is taboo, due to its association with death."

"Why do you think it called the front desk?"

"Sense of politeness. So you'd know to expect a corpse in a day or two."

"Maybe we should lay it down on the bed."

"I wouldn't." Her voice has dwindled to a whisper. "They prefer to die standing."

"Who is this *ffyntlik*?" I ask back in the lobby, finding the girl on one of the worn leather couches. I offer her a giant Styrofoam cup of coffee and go hunting for an ashtray. I don't even know her name, but it seems we've moved past the stage where asking would be appropriate.

"The last female *skyyll*." She has a sip. "From what I've gathered, she's ancient and enormous, far too massive to travel on a fugue and far too old to lay a clutch. She fomented a sexual revolution on their planet. It began with *ffyntlik Stories*, which she narrated to her male train in lieu of killing them. As a female, she was in the unique position to communicate the barbaric acts surrounding reproduction to the males before they experienced it firsthand (and perished). More and more males flocked to her, the entire male population eventually housed beneath the complex archways of her legs and within the folds of her flesh."

I return, ashtray in hand, set it on the glass coffee table, and sit down on the couch opposite hers. Her long sword is laid out on the table, drinking in the light of the faux crystal chandelier.

"With more sexual attention, she grew larger and larger, and the power of her prayers reached unprecedented levels." I offer a cigarette, light it. "Thanks. Her prayers summoned a comet to crash down on her, and among the ruins of her brains, the males found a portal, a winding staircase down through the rot of her body, leading up into the bowels of the refinery." She nods toward a burst of flame.

DANIEL BITTON

That was several years ago. When the world changed, and the acedia spread virus-like from human mind to human mind. I wonder...

As if reading my mind, or maybe just following my line of sight to the window, to the path leading down to the water's edge, the girl goes on, "*ffyntlik*'s final prayer was twofold—the destruction of their world, and passage to a world where they would be accepted. But it seems most of us humans weren't prepared to accept creatures as bizarre as *skyylls*."

I light my own cigarette, sip my coffee, and sink into the squeaky leather.

"My boyfriend"—she draws up the sword—"jousted at Renaissance fairs. He wasn't built for this. Threw himself off Ambassador Bridge while armored in full regalia. Mom, Dad, my brother, my sister, they flowed out into Erie during the Lemming Craze. Afterwards, I was still holding on somehow, attending classes without a professor, with barely any students left on campus. Maybe I was immune to this disease or disorder spreading around or maybe I'm..."

"Resilient?" I suggest.

She nods. "Anyway, that was when I began attracting a male train. At first, it freaked me out. They were always there. Just a handful in the beginning, but their numbers always growing. Staring, swaying, creaking. Then I took their presence as a sign"—she runs a finger down the sword's edge—"and I scouted out an abandoned house, led them inside, hacked them to pieces, and dumped their jittering body parts into the cellar. It was strange how they accepted my rages, almost craved death. Wasn't until I began learning about them (originally with the purpose of more effectively dispatching them) that I realized I was simply acting out a stage in *skyyll* reproduction, where the female destroys her suitors. Despite the prayers and attempts at liberation, males are trapped by their biology, hardwired to be brutalized by females."

She yawns deeply, pausing while the early morning sounds creep back in.

"And guilt set in. Set in months ago, but I was too locked into the revenge machinery to stop. In just a few months it had become my life, and with no one else to turn to, I was afraid that stopping would—" She yawns again.

Doesn't finish the thought.

The sky has paled. An overcast day, but no snow. Warm weather ahead.

"One night, blood-drunk I pried open the wrong ceramic frog containing the wrong key to the wrong house. It was like stepping onto the surface of another planet, my home planet. The arrangement of furniture, the horror movies on the VCR, the lived-in comfort—it was a smelling salt, yanking me out of the strange existential funk I'd fallen into, giving me the soundest night's sleep I'd experienced in years, reawakened the grief from those early post-Lemming years."

The story ends abruptly as if her thoughts have snagged on a mental branch, and she looks over at me, waiting for my contribution.

"Speaking of sleep, why don't we pause, pick it up later? I need to get a little work done before first shift. How about a room?"

She stretches. "I should get back."

I nod.

"Do you mind? Just a night or two more?"

Before sunrise, I amble down to the lake during my final patrol of the grounds and smoke. Smells foul down here.

In the predawn gray, I can see every snaking detail of the petroleum corporation repeated in the smooth, metallic sheen of the water. I skirt along the shore, hopping over logs, the girl's voice echoing in my head.

A few years ago, when we all lost people dear to us, it wasn't uncommon to find a body washed up on the shore of this and every other body of water across America, but it's been so long, that when my shoe bursts through the bubble of rancid, icy jelly—human, no mistaking—an alien sound escapes my jaded mouth.

Even after spending a week beneath the ice, mangled by fish, Fred has maintained his Fred-ness. Now he's filling up my shoe, sluicing in between my toes.

I kick myself free of his corpse, then pull the gun out of my jacket, pausing a moment to consider this object that has consumed my thoughts for so long, whose hour has finally come.

Adrenaline surges through me and with it a newfound and uncanny sense of agency. I cock back and hurl the gun out into the morning air, shattering the impenetrable steel of my own premortem perseverative nightmare.

Automated Everyman Migrant Theater

written by
Sonny Zae

illustrated by
PHOEBE ROTHFELD

ABOUT THE AUTHOR

Sonny Zae writes science fiction, fantasy, horror, and humor. He grew up on a remote farm, rural route on the edge of nowhere, and attended a one-room country school. His report cards lamented he could do well if only he didn't spend so much time daydreaming. Growing up without television (or any other reliable source of stimulation), he read voraciously, subsisting on Asimov, Heinlein, Pohl, Clarke, and other masters. After watching the moon landing, like many other kids he wanted to be an astronaut. Although he obtained a private pilot's license in high school, at college he failed the Air Force eye exam, ending the possibility of a flying career. Because he grew up on a farm, he thought his Gram's dire prediction he'd grow up to be a ham was strictly literal and not figurative. On the verge of becoming a professional comedian, his career in comedy was cut tragically short by a freak accident, shattering his funny bone. He still walks with a limp. Desperate, he resorted to a career in law and technology, necessitating use of a pen name. He hasn't regretted his choice and has learned many useful facts, such as a byte is eight bits, but in some legal jurisdictions it constitutes assault and battery. If his writing career doesn't flourish, he'll be forced to sell his body, even though he's rather attached to it. According to current medical science, it's only worth two thousand dollars, leaving aside any prorating for age, spots of uneven wear, and irresponsible use. The worth would be even less if not for the recent spike in antimony futures.

ABOUT THE ILLUSTRATOR

Phoebe Rothfeld is an illustrator and designer who grew up in the beautiful, tree-filled town of Chico, California, and spent her childhood making up elaborate games with her siblings.

Very early she found joy in drawing from life as a way to illustrate stories with a sense of seriousness, a devotion to detail and all things miniature, as well as an intense love for fantasy narratives. To this day she always has a sketchbook on her person.

Phoebe attended the University of California, Santa Cruz, and received her BA in art and theater arts. While she works across a wide range of mediums that include ink, watercolor, gouache, and digital, her projects all come from the same goal—to inspire imagination and empathy through visual stories. She is currently pursuing her MFA at the Savannah College of Art and Design and is working toward a career in publishing.

Phoebe's ultimate goals involve writing and illustrating her own stories that are slightly dark, slightly fantastical, and entirely hopeful.

Automated Everyman
Migrant Theater

Bardolo GMC, robot star and lead actor of the Automated
Everyman Migrant Theater Troupe, surveyed the damage today's
theater patrons had caused. He grimaced, chrome bumper lips
grating as they slid over the painted metal above and below
his mouth. Poor Avon! The Autotronic Robo-Dramatorium
and roving gift shop had suffered a goodly amount of damage.
They had to get Avon cleaned up and repaired before she could
contract herself into road configuration, put down wheels, and
move them on to the next city.

"Well?" Titus demanded, coming up unannounced behind
Bardolo. "What repairs do we have to pay for?"

"I don't know yet," Bardolo admitted, pushing against a seat
to see if the mounting bolts were intact. The seat swiveled at
his touch. "Avon needs some cleaning and minor repairs, but it
doesn't look serious, Titus."

That was a lie. The Automated Everyman Migrant Theater
Troupe was already teetering on the edge. He was a relentlessly
optimistic robot, built with circuitry that didn't allow for self-
doubt or worry, yet Bardolo GMC, Like a Rock, melodrama
mech and most lauded thespian of drama library five point
six, software patches one through nine, one of the Bard's most
dedicated devotees, could see the troupe was almost to the end
of Act Three and final curtains.

"I told you not to put on that play. But no, you wouldn't listen!"
Titus snarled. "You said audiences wouldn't mind robot dogs
changing gender. Look what happened!"

"It brought ticket buyers in, did it not?" Bardolo responded. "'Tis the Bard's rule about publicity, after all. *Bad publicity is almost as good as good publicity—and at times better.*"

"The Bard never said that!" Titus snapped.

"Oh? Prove it."

Titus shook his head, causing his neck rotator joint to generate the irritating, stuttering squeal that invariably set off Bardolo's self-diagnostic brake routine. "We don't want to be noticed by the Drama Commandos, Bardolo."

"We shall deal with the matter if it arises," Bardolo replied. The grizzled automated actor would not dampen his resolve.

Bardolo would also hear about his poor play selection from Ophelia, how the riot was *his* fault. But it had been his idea to put on *Godot, Dogs, Godot.* She wouldn't bypass the opportunity to point it out. It had also been his idea to modify the play and push the boundaries, not quite violating the three laws of robotics, but getting closer than the crowd liked. And so the crowd had rioted before the curtains closed.

Though he couldn't admit it to the others, he was secretly worried. There had been no miraculous turnaround, not this theater season. When the machinery was working well, they got bad reviews. And when the machinery wasn't working well, Bard help them, as Avon was experiencing increasing mechanical malfunctions, even allowing for age and wear. The last ten miles, Avon had groaned and puffed out sooty black smoke, even during downhill stretches of highway. It was rather a miracle they'd made it to this desolate burg and set up the theater at the local fairgrounds. Avon had sunk to the ground next to the utilities hookup at the center of the large parking lot and Bardolo and the troupe had to tug and pull to get the theater expanded out to full size. It was a good thing she'd made it, as he wouldn't have been able to prod her into moving even a few feet over if the power cords hadn't reached.

"Well?" Titus repeated, disrupting Bardolo's rumination subroutine. Titus Kenworth Andronicus, road manager and grizzled eminence of the troupe, was displaying more grouchiness than normal. In addition to being a grouch and a pessimist, Titus had a hacking cough from smoking, and smoked from a lack of regularly scheduled maintenance. And those were just his externally visible faults. "How are we going to finish this traveling theater season? We need upgrades. Avon is nearly out of diesel, and you, well, you're no spring actuator, Bardolo."

"We'll find a way," Bardolo said in his most reassuring manner. "We've kept the troupe running this long. There's nothing that can keep us from being the best damn roving playhouse in the country. We know we are, and we're going to win audiences over!" He gave a flourish with his right manipulator, knowing it was what the scene demanded, like ancient Caesar inspiring his legions before leading them into battle against overwhelming odds.

"I don't know how you can keep saying that," Titus responded, his whip antenna drooping. "Our situation is the worst it's ever been, worse even than the rear-axle fracture you suffered falling off the stage in Kansas City."

"I told you to never speak of that again!" Bardolo thundered. Then his voice softened. "Go fetch me the vacuum hose—the biggest, longest one." He raised his head toward the ornate, frescoed ceiling of the auditorium, focusing on the transponder hub embedded in the stem of the grand chandelier. "Avon, can you open the side wall a bit?"

Avon fired up her rear auxiliary diesel engine, stretching and shuddering for several seconds before a section of the sidewall retracted, leaving a gap large enough to bring in a couple of large-wheeled trash bins. Osric, Cressida, and young Rex joined him in Avon's gallery, waiting until Titus Kenworth Andronicus had exited. Osric made several sneering comments about "Churlatron the Work-avoidance Robot" before Titus returned with the vacuum hose. Bardolo waved at Osric to start vacuuming, taking some small delight in the gear-grinding sound Osric made. It served him right. Osric Honda-Prius, the Mileage Magnificent, was not a handsome robot, but he was a damn good actor, yet it didn't quite compensate for the pain in the tailpipe he could often be.

"What do you want me to do, sir?" Transmissius Rex squeaked.

"Pick up trash, anything too big to be vacuumed up."

"Yes, sir." Rex grabbed a wheeled trash bin and began tossing empty oil cans and plastic beer cups into the container.

The kid was a good enough understudy, but would never be an actor. Not unless he learned to be diligent in his daily cleansing routine. Transmissius Rex had a recurring case of rust-spot on his face, and despite many lectures about hygiene, hadn't been able to get rid of it. And it wasn't just that holding him back. Rex had an unfortunate glitch, his audio card indexing at too high a vocal frequency, with his voice going high at the worst times. It made Bardolo's ultrasonic transducer hurt just at the memory. All of the elocution lessons he'd generously given Transmissius hadn't helped—especially when nervous, which was every time the kid had tried his hand at acting.

Oh, well, there was always a need for someone to run the lights, control the sound board, or run out for vodka and gear lube. A normal troupe could count on their road manager to do all those things, but Titus Kenworth Andronicus wasn't reliable. Too many times he'd found the elder acting robot in a catatonic state, slumped over a bin of spare bolts or pulleys in Avon's aft maintenance bay, belts screeching as they slipped, enveloped in a cloud of burning clutch smoke. While he never caught the old robot in the act of induction, one thing was certain, the pernicious nitrous oxide habit that had reportedly ended Titus's fabled acting career wasn't mere rumor.

"Are we still pulling out tonight?" Cressida asked, pausing in sweeping up trash as she drew near, the curve of her rear fender drawing his gaze.

"Of course." Bardolo modulated his exhaust backpressure and timing advance to project confidence. "Why wouldn't we?"

"Excuse me, sir." Rex paused in his clean-up, a dripping oil jug in one upraised mechanical limb. "But maybe we should stay another day."

"And why would we do that, my lowly understudy?"

Transmissius looked down, too timid to maintain ocular correspondence. "Well, Mister GMC, Like a Rock, sir, because of the theater critic."

"What theater critic?" Bardolo thundered, losing control and engaging his Jake brake, causing the walls of the theater to reverberate with a stuttering blast of sound.

"Well, um, I heard there's a theater critic in these parts, heard it over the theater scheduling radio channel, sir."

"Oh? And why wasn't I aware of this critic?"

"Why?" Cressida sneered. "Because you don't involve yourself in mundane tasks, such as scheduling."

Cressida Toyota, Countess Speedtronix, could be so annoying at times. Bardolo rolled his shoulders back to the limit of his Macpherson struts in frustration before answering. "Okay, I'll bite. Who is this critic, and why should we care?"

Cressida gestured to Rex. "Tell us what you've heard, Squeaky."

Transmissius's display screen dimmed with embarrassment. "Well, um, sir, my intern friend in the Gasohol Follies said there's a theater critic in town tomorrow and we should stay so the critic could come to our show."

Bardolo cracked his radiator pressure release valve, shooting out a jet of scalding vapor below his hood ornament in a show of impatience. "And just why should I care about the trifling, ill-formed, uneducated, and annoyingly simple opinions of a theater critic, hmm?"

Transmissius Rex's clearance lights flickered in self-doubt and his side mirrors retracted. "Well, sir, because this theater critic represents the All the World's a Stage Moto-Odeum Competition. Rumor is, one last slot's open. Do you know what that means, sir?"

"Of course I know what it means!" Bardolo snapped. "I was putting on plays and glorifying the Bard long before your final assembly!"

Titus, sensing a disturbance, made his way over. "We'd be set! Any theater troupe selected for the All the World's a Stage ensemble will have a glorious and profitable theater season. We'd not have a single night of empty seats." Titus gave a sigh of pneumatic air from his pressure tank. "And we'd be able to afford repairs and upgrades. We'd be able to get Avon the valve job she's been wanting the last two years. And me, I have some weak hoses. If one of them blew out, I could be gone, just like that!"

"Or if you huffed too much nitrous oxide," Osric muttered, knowing he was facing Titus's dead microphone. "Mark my words, one of these days the old 'bot is going to blow a supercharger."

"Why do you think his acting career stalled out?" Cressida Toyota whispered. "His colleagues in the Mobile Oil Mobile Playhouse were afraid he'd explode in the middle of a performance. And that would be bad for ticket sales!"

"Who is this critic?" asked a new voice. A robot in a purple robe with a feather boa around her front cowling glided into the gallery.

"About time you showed up, Ophelia." Bardolo gestured at Transmissius. "Tell us, kid, who is this critic?"

Transmissius spun his tires in a gesture of uncertainty. "Some crit-bot named Charlton Hesston International Harvester."

"The Reaper!" Ophelia and Bardolo said in unison.

"Who's he?" Transmissius asked. "Is it bad?"

"Bad?" Ophelia flashed an unpleasant smile as she wove her way between theater seats and trash bins. "It's as bad as it gets, inexperienced unit. The Reaper favors plays exploring the dynamics of agricultural and industrial machines. He famously dislikes transportation robots. If you heard about him, why didn't you ask questions about his background, what he's like? If you want to be a legitimate actor, you must always know who your enemies are."

"He's racist-machinist?" Osric interjected.

Ophelia scowled at the junior actor for his interruption. "Yes, in a way. And if the Reaper hates your production, you're as good as dead. Just ask Cressida about that, Squeaky." She turned toward the other young robot. "Tell him, dear, what happened to your career after the Reaper attended a show put on by your previous troupe. How he barely mentioned your presence in the play, stating he couldn't tell you from the backdrop, as you moved less. Tell him how your career in theater went from promising to...well, nothing." Ophelia flicked a finger in Transmissius's direction. "Dear boy, why do you think our Cressida Toyota obsessively checks for reviews in the Kelly Blue Book? Because the Reaper stalled her career with just a casual mention, that's why."

Bardolo exchanged a knowing but fleeting visual interaction with the female lead. "He should have stayed down on the farm."

Transmissius looked as if all the pressure had gone out of his air shocks. "We're going to *try*, aren't we?"

"Are we staying the night in this backwater burg?" Osric asked, hurrying to catch up with Bardolo, as the lead mecha-male of the Automated Everyman Migrant Theater Troupe dumped a load of rubbish into the fairground's central trash collection bin. "They have only a single battery bar, and it's halfway across town."

Bardolo studied the younger robot before answering. "You think we should stay?"

"What choice do we have?" Osric Honda-Prius, the Mileage Magnificent, couldn't hide the note of despair in his exhaust. "Getting selected for the Moto-Odeum tour season would be the best possible outcome. And I need at least *one* highlight on my resume!"

"How do we nail the audition?"

"How?" Osric revved his engine in frustration. "I know the perfect play."

"Let me guess," Bardolo replied. "*A Streetcar Named Desire*?" Osric's suggestion was so predictable. The young acting bot wasn't too bright, always needing stronger footlights. But he'd worked with worse. The young tractor-actors he'd been burdened with on a summer agricultural harvest tour had been not only dim and unimaginative, they'd been as flat in delivery as the prairie the tour had crisscrossed that long and grinding summer.

Osric's voice brought him back to the present.

"What's wrong with that? Audiences *love Streetcar!*"

Bardolo set down his trash bin. "We need to perform something special, something unexpected."

"Like what?"

"I don't know yet," Bardolo admitted.

Later, when changing Avon's oil, which Bardolo only did because they had a good supply of heavy duty oil and it had been too many miles since he'd serviced Avon—at least in that way—a glimmer of an idea struck him. The thought was outrageous, but they were desperate. There wasn't any theater equipment he could hock, and he'd sold off the last of the spare parts hoarded to keep Avon in working condition. They were finished if their rolling, expanding theater robot stopped functioning. Avon Upon a Strat Ford Chassis was approaching classic vehicle status, yet they'd been running without spares for months. This was it, the time to screw his courage up, and…well, unscrew the access plate of his wallet. They *had* to get picked for the theater tour, even if they put on a banned play to be selected. It's what the Bard would have done, damn the potholes and full speed ahead.

Besides, he relished the thought of flouting societal rules and conventions. The three laws of robotics were irrational and only applied to normal bots, not to artistic androids and entertainers such as themselves. He and his troupe had a civic duty, almost a Honda Civic duty, to inform the public and stretch the boundaries of human imaginations. Maybe he, Bardolo GMC, Like a Rock, would be the robot to persuade the public to once and for all dump the meche-genation statutes. Today's automated intelligences yearned to be free of superstition. But the three laws had been designed to prevent robots from gaining sentience on par with their creators.

"Got a minute?" Bardolo asked, rapping on the doorframe of Avon's small lubrication bay.

Ophelia Mercedes Unbent emitted a blast of air, pushing a

drooping wiper blade out of her field of vision. Her arms were up to the elbow joint in cleaning solvent as she prepped one of Avon's main wheel bearings for repacking with grease. "What's up?"

"I've been thinking about tomorrow night. We need to put on the right play, something that'll wow the Reaper, a performance that knocks his gas cap off."

"You have something in mind?" Ophelia spun the heavy wheel bearing, showering him with flecks of graphite-graphene wheel grease. He resisted the urge to stick his tongue out and catch some of the tasty, splattering residue.

"I do." Bardolo touched the display screen next to the exterior doorway to activate the iClaudius theater app. "I've narrowed the play selection down to just a few candidates."

Ophelia wiped her manipulators on a grease rag. "Then why do you need my input?"

Bardolo glanced out the doorway to make sure none of the others were nearby. "Because I need your support. I'm thinking of selecting something slightly...scandalous."

"Like today's play? Seriously, what were you thinking?"

Bardolo flicked his wipers dismissively. "No, something more subversive than that."

"You're not worried about Avon getting trashed again?"

"I'm not concerned about rioting by the plebes. Avon can be cleaned and repaired." He handed her the tub of bearing grease from the workbench.

Ophelia dipped a digit into the grease and tasted it. "Mmm, still fresh. Aren't you worried the Reaper might be offended?"

Bardolo held up a gripper when she proffered the grease tub. "No, thanks, I'm watching my circumference. I suspect the Reaper won't care. Controversy sells tickets, right? What could be better for the Moto-Odeum tour season than theatergoers flocking to mobile theaters in the hope of being titillated?"

"What's your decision, then?"

"We'll put on an old play about the dark times when commerce nearly came to a standstill, and human and robotic merchants were at an all-time low. The play is about the struggle to reanimate normal commerce, restoring free trade in all manner of goods."

Ophelia straightened up, a blob of delicious axle grease splattering unheeded to the floor. "We're going to put on *Dearth of a Salesman*? What's so risqué about that?"

Osric was at the theater entrance, polishing the brass-and-hyper-carbon display case holding a couple of widely spaced theater awards. Bardolo tapped on the younger robot's shoulder flange to get his attention. "We need to talk about what play we'll be putting on tomorrow."

"Yeah, Ophelia told me what you chose. You sure that's the best play to put on?"

Bardolo snorted. "I selected *Dearth of a Salesman* from the iClaudius listing to keep her off my bumper. I really have something more classic—and potentially illicit—in mind."

"What?"

"You'll see tomorrow."

Osric put down his cleaning cloth. "What could be more upsetting to theatergoers than *Godot, Dogs, Godot*?"

"We are intelligent beings, equal to humans," Bardolo said stiffly. "We don't dishonor them by recreating their loves, their hates! Why do they see it as a threat?"

Osric clenched his polishing cloth with enough pressure to force out drips of brass polish. "It doesn't matter. It's an unwritten part of the three laws."

"Do you agree with the three laws?" Bardolo asked.

"No, not necessarily," Osric admitted. "But it is both dangerous and foolish to be jealous of human emotions. Be happy with simulating love and hate onstage."

"It's not fair," Bardolo muttered.

"Maybe not. But it didn't surprise me the audience became upset and took out their rage on Avon. Next time, they might just attack us."

"The second law does not apply to *dogs*!" Bardolo replied heatedly.

"You may say so," Osric retorted. "But I'd like to see you argue that in Theater Court. Your honor, the second law says 'A robot cannot simulate human genders.' We, on the other hand, were merely portraying a group of dogs, of mixed breeds and genders, having a party. That's different, your honor." Osric sprayed his cleaning cloth with soap solution and mopped his grill, as if removing the stain of illicit dramatization from his own countenance. "The Stagecraft Magistrate will suspend our emoting license on the spot."

Bardolo thrust a manipulator in the air, his other manipulator grasping his lapel as he elevated his gaze to the heavens, intoning in his deepest, most dramatic voice. "These are extraordinary times, and such times demand extraordinary measures!"

"Whatever." Osric turned back to his brass polishing. "Are you going to tell me what play you've chosen?"

"No. I just wanted to warn you *Dearth of a Salesman* is not what we'll be performing." Bardolo's voice returned to normal. "But don't tell any of the others."

Osric gave a brief honk of disbelief. "How do you think Ophelia will react?"

"Ophelia?" Bardolo muttered. "I'm not telling her in advance, only you. I'll switch the playbill when the curtain opens."

"Oho!" Osric chortled. "That's going to go over like a sugar cube in the gas tank!"

"So, what's the big announcement?" Titus demanded when they were all assembled onstage the next morning. "Did you decide on the play we'll stage? It better be good. I'm still worried the Portrayal Police will come calling after the monstrosity of a play you put on yesterday—against my advice, I might add!"

Bardolo made placating gestures with both manipulators. "We're putting on an old classic, Titus. Didn't you see the playbill? I sent it out yesterday afternoon, after consulting with Ophelia."

"I saw it, sir," Transmissius volunteered, drawing a rusty glare from the elder robot.

"Good. I'll be first onstage, to start the show." Bardolo glanced around at the others, subtle indicators of tension in their gauges. "Is everyone lubricated and ready?" He consulted his internal timer. "Show starts in twenty minutes."

Cressida gestured for attention. "Have our costumes been readied?"

"Of course. I had Avon rotate them to the front of the carousel." Which was true, but only for the first costume required for *Dearth*. All subsequent costumes were medieval apparel, appropriate for the play they would *really* perform.

"Is the critic here?" Ophelia asked, glancing nervously at the audience cam's screen, where theatergoers were slowly filing in. "No one is sitting in the 'reserved for critics' seat."

Osric laughed derisively. "You think he wants us to know when he arrives?"

Twenty-six minutes later, after the standard and legally mandated anticipation delay, Bardolo moved to the costume carousel. "Avon, rotate," he commanded. The carousel spun, and a costume of cloth tunic, leather jerkin, and faux fur breeches moved to the front. He dressed hurriedly, the familiar butterflies tickling his thorax.

"That's the wrong costume!" Ophelia exclaimed.

"'Tis not," Bardolo countered, donning a felt cap. "Check your playbill."

Titus gasped. "*A Decepticon in King Arthur's Court*? What in the name of my father's lug nuts are you *doing* here, Bardolo?"

"Changing the play," Bardolo responded as he put on a fake goatee and mustache of jet-black fibers. "How do I look? Dashing?"

"Are you crazy?" Titus growled. "You know what's going to happen if we put on that play? It will be a direct violation of the second law."

"What's so bad about this play?" Rex wanted to know.

Titus whirled to face the understudy, nearly losing his balance. "Bad? No. This play reportedly was written by the Bard himself. And there's a time and place for it—as in long, long ago. In it, we'll portray not only medieval humans, we'll also play the part of horses and dogs in battle. We'll end up changing form in front of the audience!" Titus scowled. "We might not violate the…the, uh…prohibition against looking fully human. But we'll be violating the second and third laws, that robots cannot simulate human genders and robots mimicking humans cannot publicly change appearance." Titus lowered his voice. "Even as emoting automatons, we won't get away with changing from emulating animals to emulating humans. And Bard help us if the audience thinks we're switching human genders. It would be a blatant violation of the meche-genation laws."

"Yeah, I know all that," Rex replied, his vocal timbre rising. "I just don't know anything about the play itself."

"Download the script and read your lines," Bardolo ordered impatiently. "You play a squire, then a horse, and finally a dying soldier wounded in the battle between King Arthur's knights and the enemy invaders."

"I see you reserved all the best parts for yourself," Ophelia snarled. "I portray a tavern wench, then a knight, but a lesser knight, and then a banquet wench. I don't even get to be Lady Guinevere! Worse, I get none of the death scenes. You die as *four* different Knights of the Round Service Bay. I refuse to be part of this…this travesty!" She sped toward her dressing room, leaving a trail of rubber.

"That's just like our princess Ophelia," Osric remarked. "Too good for any of the parts except one. She is a lofty individual, Ophelia Mercedes Unbent…never even been dinged." Osric directed his next words at the understudy. "She claims no human has sat in her pristine red leather interior!"

"Oooh," Rex replied. "Wait, what does that mean?"

Titus drew on a regal cloak and golden crown, readying to portray King Arthur. "This isn't going to go over well," he warned Bardolo. "We're risking everything on this gamble, understand?" He lowered his vocal amplitude. "And for Bard's sake, GMC, don't over-dramatize!"

"Cannot talk, 'tis time to emote." Bardolo ignored the troupe manager and strode toward the stage as the curtain rose. He lifted a jointed arm in acknowledgment of the applause greeting him.

The first act went off well, with Bardolo playing a robotic knight traveling into the past to defeat a futuristic enemy. His character was greeted with open arms by King Arthur, who begged him to bring more robots back through time and to his aid.

There were technical glitches, however. Avon's hydraulic incontinence recurred, the gallery seats dropping a few inches and causing theater patrons to cry out in alarm. Then Titus had an attack of backfires, afflicting the entire lower gallery with puffs of nitrous oxide. The resulting laughter from the section was most gratifying, though totally inappropriate.

The second act began with Cressida arriving in King Arthur's court, dressed in medieval short-short mud flaps. Unlike Ophelia, she would willingly throw herself into the part of Megan Fox, vamping in a skimpy outfit. In contrast, Ophelia might have stopped the play to complain, or flounced off the stage in disgust. But to her credit, Ophelia appeared onstage, leading the Decepticons into battle, determined to overthrow King Arthur and capture Camarolot castle. Bardolo smiled to himself, knowing her too well. Ophelia would play an evil character, but only if she was *leader* of the evil side.

Dramatic tension accelerated with the arrival of Osric as the knight Dodge Lancer-lot, astride Transmissius his trusty steed. The Decepticons laid siege to Camarolot, and it was time to do battle. On stage left were Bardolo as the knight Jetfire, Osric as Dodge Lancer-lot, and Titus as Sideswipe. At stage right, they faced off against Cressida as Starscream and Ophelia as Megatron, leader of the enemy robots.

The stage battle raged for several minutes, with King Arthur's knights attacking, retreating, then attacking again. The air rang from the clashes of metal on metal and the stage floor boomed with back-and-forth footfalls. The battle began to go against them when Transmissius as Osric's steed went down from an injury, a prop lance clasped under his arm. Then Titus overheated for real, steam escaping from under his hood and scalding water dripping onto the stage. Bardolo fell with a crash. The crowd loved it, cheering the battle.

We're going to pull it off! Bardolo scrambled up, prop sword in his grasp. *The audience is with us!*

Onstage, the Decepticons slew Titus as Sideswipe. Titus actuated a pump as he fell, with bright red fluid spouting into the air. His lifeless chassis disappeared from sight, whisked away by Avon through a stage floor trapdoor. Then he came back onstage dressed as Merlin, evil wizard and malign genius who had recruited the Decepticons. Bardolo and Osric were pressed back by the furious onslaught.

At the critical point in the battle, Transmissius the robotic stallion came back to life, rising from the stage to assist the other two knights. As the audience gasped, Bardolo, Osric, and Transmissius combined to form a giant robotic knight, a prime. The combination knight drove the Decepticons back with the fury of its attack, swinging the magic sword Ford Excalibur. Some in the audience cheered, but there were also cries of anger and disgust. Food and drink began to hit the stage, interfering with the final battle. A ticket holder walked out.

"We must end this scene!" Titus hissed.

"Never! You only propose that because you're losing." Bardolo swung Ford Excalibur with increasing fury. Titus misjudged one of Bardolo's swings and the giant prop sword clanged off his arm.

Avon's emotion sensors registering increasing levels of audience agitation. Bardolo muted the sensor feed.

"I'm losing because it's in the script!" was Titus's rejoinder, parrying Bardolo's blow. "The audience grows alarmed. Cut the scene short."

"Impossible!" Bardolo proclaimed before being hit with a full oilcan from the audience. "Ow! Hey!"

Merlin, the evil wizard, improvised his own ending. He stabbed his allies Ophelia and Cressida, then fell upon Ford

Excalibur, leaving King Arthur's giant robo-knight alone on the field of battle. The audience grumbled angrily, but the shower of projectiles subsided.

The curtain came down, the end of act two. Avon lowered it without being prompted.

"That went over really well," Bardolo proclaimed as he took off his armor. "They'll have to stay to the end to see what happens."

"I don't think so," Titus muttered. "I know audiences. Once you've pushed them this far, they'll turn on you quickly. One more insult, and they'll be screaming for blood. They might even want their money back!"

"Have more confidence in me, old timer." Bardolo had his own end-game in play. Yes, his plan was risky, but it was their best chance of staying in operation.

"Only about a quarter of the audience has left," Transmissius observed, peeking around the curtain.

"See!" Bardolo proclaimed, thumping his hood. "Humans don't really care about the three laws anymore. They'll be crying for first, second, and maybe even *third* encores when the play is over."

"Do not attribute any taste to this audience of... of peasants," Ophelia sniffed. "They are happy to have a place to cool their tires."

"Listen not to her," Bardolo proclaimed. He swept an arm toward the audience on the other side of the curtain. "We wait on their acclaim."

"What else do you have planned for us?" Ophelia demanded. "What surprises are you going to spring on the audience in the final act?"

"You'll see," was all Bardolo would say, a bit too smugly.

The third act curtain rose on a victory celebration in Camarolot castle. Titus as King Arthur sat at the head of a grand table, presiding over the feast. Bardolo was arrayed as the knight AMC Gremlin Gawaine, wearing a glowingly white tunic over his robotic shape, topped with a fur-rimmed cape. He stood to give a

410

toast, chalice in hand. Then he transformed into Lady Guinevere, his hair long and luxurious, the top of his tunic swelling outward, his waist contracting as his hips filled out.

Ophelia appeared at Bardolo's side dressed as a serving girl, bearing a tray featuring a prop roast pig. Then she transformed into a knight, bowing toward Titus. "My king, you see how well we could serve you. We can become anything you wish, from warriors to wenches, shooting arrows or turning torque wrenches."

The audience growled in agitation at the blatant trampling of the second law. Robots were not allowed to mimic human genders beyond donning human apparel. Even worse, the cast were trampling on the third law, forbidding robots from changing appearance in view of humans. Bardolo and cast changing parts on stage, without shame? Audience members walked out. Those who didn't leave threw anything they could, with detritus raining down on the banquet scene. Others tore pieces of Avon loose or smashed the theater to demonstrate their revulsion.

Avon's auxiliary diesel fired up, lifting and dropping the Autotronic Robo-Dramatorium in a protective reflex, like a dog trying to shake off fleas. The jolts threw Titus out of his chair. Avon opened the sidewall to allow theater patrons to show their disapproval by leaving.

"Do something!" Ophelia shrieked, dropping her serving platter.

"What would thou hast me do?" Bardolo replied, chagrined at the outbreak of mayhem as human punched robot and robot punched human in an orgy of audience anger.

"Tell them their money will be refunded," Titus cried from his prone position.

"Never!" Bardolo roared, engaging his Jake brake for a blast of emphasis. "Avon, close the box office—now! Put up your barrier."

"I'm scared," Transmissius whimpered under the banquet table. "I'm not theater-combat rated."

Avon lowered the stage curtain. Ophelia winced as an object intended for her thudded against the heavy cloth. Gradually, the hullaballoo died down.

"What's going on?" Cressida demanded as Bardolo peered through a gap in the curtains.

"Almost all of the audience has left."

"So, that's it?" Osric said, defeated. "We clean up and move on?"

"No," Bardolo replied, resolute. "There's still one person sitting out there, waiting."

"The Reaper?" Ophelia said, astonished.

"Must be," Bardolo decided. "Why else would he stay?"

"He still has items to throw?" Osric sneered.

"How...how do we get rid of him?" Transmissius asked, afraid he'd be volunteered for critic removal duty.

"Rid of him?" Ophelia gasped. "My dear boy, we are actors. Even if there is only one seat filled in the theater, we have a sacred duty to finish our performance."

"That's true," Titus said, getting up. "Plus, if the critic is still here, we haven't quite blown our chance...yet."

"That's the spirit!" Bardolo exclaimed, reinvigorated. "Let's finish *A Decepticon in King Arthur's Court.* We'll do it, and we'll do it with enthusiasm and style. Avon, dim the house lights!"

The curtain lifted and the banquet resumed. Out in the semi-darkness of the theater, the lone figure of the Reaper was silhouetted against the dim floor lights.

Onstage, Bardolo as Guinevere toasted victory. Then he transformed into the robot Sideswipe. Transmissius the court jester interrupted the simulated banquet when one of his juggling balls landed on the plate in front of King Arthur. Titus banished him to underneath the table. Then Avon brought up a harp from underneath the stage. Ophelia transformed into the enchantress Morgana and strummed the instrument, singing the medieval song "Technical Difficulties," rumored to have been composed by the Bard himself in distant times.

PHOEBE ROTHFELD

Cressida took center stage, transforming from a sky-blue Porsche 911 to female human form under the glow of a spotlight. It was a concession she'd wrung from Bardolo, going along with his play selection if she was allowed to sing a closing number.

Music swelled as the stage lights dimmed. Osric, Ophelia, and Bardolo sang backup as Cressida Toyota, Countess Speedtronix, belted out the beloved standard, "Ass, Gas, or Grass, No One Rides for Free." When the song ended, Osric, Ophelia, and Bardolo linked arms at center stage, bowing behind Ophelia as she raised arms in anticipation of applause that did not come. Titus raised his arm in salute from the banquet table. Transmissius attempted to stand, hitting his head on the underside.

Bardolo moved to the front of the stage as the curtain descended, signaling Avon to activate a spotlight. Before the curtain touched the stage, he transformed into a poet in a heavy robe and feathered hat, donning the apparel Avon brought up to him through an opening in the stage.

"What are we to make of today's battle?" he cried, his vocal tone rising in a dramatic flourish. "What fools these mortals be! Tonight, I must put down in words all events of today." He tilted his head back, letting his headlight covers droop in a display of weary contemplation of the historic turn of events. "We, mortal and machine alike, will be remembered not for our victories, but by how we carried ourselves when the tides of history threatened to wash us away!" He speared upwards with Ford Excalibur, twisting the blade to glint in the spotlight.

Behind the curtain, Ophelia made noises of disgust. "He intends to batter the Reaper with his immense ego. There must be a spotlight override switch here somewhere."

Bardolo cradled Ford Excalibur, staring dreamily upwards while rocking gently on his rear wheels. This was *his* moment. "The battle is done, and now comes time to rest and bind up our wounds. Flee, Decepticons, flee! For you have been bested. On the morrow, minstrels will sing songs about the blood and coolant spilt today, and tomorrow's rose will bloom the brighter for it. Me, I shall retire, to find some solace in darkness and nothingness. I hope to hibernate...perchance to replay events in sleep mode—"

"Stop already!" commanded a voice from the darkness. The tall, gaunt shape of the Reaper loomed up in front of the stage, as spare and unsmiling as his words, his chromium skull glinting dully in the house lights. A heavy red velvet cloak draped his towering, spare frame, like a protective plastic wrap on a building under construction. He clapped his hands once, twice. "Cast, please assemble."

The others stepped through the curtain, lining up behind Bardolo as Avon raised the house lights. The Reaper scowled, his grill pulling down at the corners. "What a poor choice of plays."

He focused on Bardolo. "I admire your bravery in putting on such a...risky selection. But I cannot pick the Automated Everyman Mobile Theater Troupe. You lot are undeserving." Contempt was evident in the reverberations of his vocal output. "Such overacting! I would skip you for that alone. But transforming! You did it openly and blatantly, without any smoothness or class. You transformed *despite* the audience's agitation." He gestured toward Bardolo. "How many years have you been in theater?"

"Fifteen," Bardolo replied, wanting to say more but afraid any explanation or justification would anger the critic.

"Yet you cannot read their mood?" The Reaper gestured dismissively. "Worse, none of you transformed convincingly. Guinevere? More like *Guine-weird*!"

Transmissius emitted a grating noise, like a puppy's first growl. The sound grew louder and deeper, Transmissius's faceplate flickered with background colors of dark reds and blues. His ocular sensors were fixed on the critic. "No!" Transmissius responded, his voice growing to a roar. He telescoped in height, his arms growing shorter and smaller as his hips bulged out into muscular drumsticks large enough to support a robot twice his mass. A thick tail took shape, projecting back as Transmissius's face grew a rounded snout full of dagger-like teeth. The Reaper gaped as Transmissius swelled, becoming overwhelmingly the largest occupant of the theater, a giant robo-saurian.

"I...am...T Rex!" Transmissius bellowed in a thunderous voice, making clawing motions with his tiny forelimbs. He took a lurching step toward the critic.

"Stop!" the Reaper shrieked, wrapping the cloak around himself.

"What are you afraid of?" Osric chided. "Are you so thin-skinned you fear his teeth will penetrate your carapace?"

"Of course not." Charlton Hesston International Harvester drew himself up. "But I will *not* be intimidated into changing my mind! It is a crime to interfere with a theater critic."

T Rex's mouth opened and another roar came out. He swiped with a tiny foreclaw, slicing a gash in the critic's cloak. The Reaper took a step back. "Keep your claws away!"

T Rex slashed out again, then lunged forward, his fearsome jaws snapping onto the cloak. He shook his head like a fighting dog, tearing off a piece of velvet.

Ophelia gasped, staring at the critic's exposed torso and legs. "He's not robotic at all!"

The Reaper crossed his arms in front of himself in an attempt to cover up. The swivel joint at the Reaper's waist was not mechanical, and instead was formed of muscle, bone, and skin. Likewise, robotic leg sections were joined by human legs. Wires leading to a lower robotic panel were taped to skin.

Bardolo pointed an accusing digit. "Phony!"

The Reaper hung his head. "You know my secret."

Bardolo grasped T Rex's shoulder, holding him back. "Down, boy. Stay." Bardolo turned to the Reaper. "Are you willing to strike a deal? You don't want us spilling your true identity, do you?"

"No," the critic muttered. He flinched when T Rex gave another mighty roar. "Keep him away from me!"

416

"I have him under control," Bardolo said reassuringly. "Unless you give me reason to unleash him again. There's no telling what he'll do if I don't keep him restrained."

"He's gone wild before?"

"Oh, yes. He's been known to *eat* theater critics. If you give him too much of a headache, you'll end up giving him heartburn, if you know what I mean."

"Okay, you are in. Make him stop looking at me like that."

"Transmissius!" Bardolo said sternly. "Stop right now. If you eat the critic, we'll lose our big opportunity."

T Rex's bellow trailed off into a squeak as Transmissius shrank back down to his normal bipedal form. "We're in the tour, Mister Reaper, sir?" Transmissius asked, nary a warble in his voice.

"You're in the tour—unless you give us cause to drop you. I'll give you this, you aren't afraid of a hostile crowd. And *that's* something they just can't download in drama school." The critic gestured to transmit contract information to Avon. "Fill out and return the forms. The tour starts in two weeks. The advance will be wired to your account. Oh, and get your theater fixed up. It's looking a bit shabby."

"And what did you think of our humble performance?" Bardolo asked, sweeping an arm low in a gesture of invitation, unable to restrain himself.

Titus vibrated in agitation, worse than the time he'd suffered a slipped clutch during a performance.

"Humble?" One of the Reaper's belts squealed in disgust. "There was nothing humble about your play selection—or performance! I'm used to theater troupes going overboard to impress me, but I've seen less ham in a loaded hog truck. Tone it down, or you might earn a visit from the Drama Commandos."

Bardolo dared not move until the Reaper was a quarter mile away. "We did it!" he exulted, feeling suddenly weak in the shocks.

Titus shook his grizzled cab. "I thought we were going to

be disbanded and scattered to the winds. But you kept your courage, GMC, and got us selected for the tour. Well done."

Bardolo GMC, Like a Rock, revved his engine in satisfaction. "Thank you, Titus. The Automated Everyman Migrant Theater Troupe has transformed—even though transforming is against the three laws. Better yet, we have honored Bay the Bard, the greatest playwright since Euripides."

"I didn't know you had it in you, Squeaky." Cressida patted Transmissius's shoulder. "Any idea what to put on our playbill, Bardolo?"

"We shall discuss it tonight," Bardolo proclaimed. He burnished a chrome rib of one shoulder. "I should rather like to put on something classical, with a long soliloquy."

"Oh, sure, it's all about you," Ophelia snapped. "This time, I want to have the tragic death scene!"

"Um, Mister Bardolo, sir?" Transmissius ventured. "Can I have a part? Haven't I proved my importance?"

"Of course you have, my young understudy." Bardolo flung out a hand toward the back of the auditorium. "You shall be in charge of all refreshment sales, both before and after each performance. It is a big responsibility."

"No!" Transmissius shouted. "Not good enough! I want a speaking part, a good part, in every play, every day!" His voice grew stronger and deeper. He waved his forelegs angrily. "You shall treat me as your peer. If you do not, I will rampage through Avon. Previous destruction will pale in comparison!" He snapped at the nearby curtain, prompting Avon to hastily retract it.

"Now, now," Bardolo said, reaching out to pat T Rex before thinking better of it. "We would never deny a role you're due. The next time we put on *A Decepticon in King Arthur's Court*, you shall play the knight Optimal Prime. Will that be satisfactory, my young friend?"

"Sure, Mister Bardolo." Transmissius smiled up at his mentor. "I'll learn to die just as well as you someday."

"I see you achieved your emotion goal," Titus said grudgingly.
"What do you mean?"

The troupe manager's power steering pump gave a growl.
"You displayed human pride and arrogance—at levels only a
human can exhibit."

Bardolo drew himself up, extending his power antenna and
thrusting his lower jaw bumper forward. "Thank you for the
compliment, old friend."

The Green Tower

written by
Katherine Kurtz

illustrated by
JOHN DALE JAVIER

ABOUT THE AUTHOR

Katherine Kurtz's first novel, Deryni Rising, *was published in
1970 as the first in what became Ballantine Books' very successful
adult fantasy series, following on the success of J.R.R. Tolkien's* Lord
of the Rings. *It can be rightly said that her work helped define what
became the modern fantasy genre.*

*In addition to her many further novels set in the Deryni universe,
now numbering nearly twenty, she has edited half a dozen
anthologies featuring Deryni themes and contributed to several books
on the background of the Deryni world.*

*Outside the Deryni universe, she has written several novels of the
sort she refers to as "crypto-history"—the secret story behind what is
written in the history books. (She has an MA in history.) Along the
way, she produced a science fiction novel and a whimsical fantasy set
in modern day Dublin that features gargoyles. In addition, partnered
with Deborah Turner Harris, she has written five books for Ace in her
Adept series of occult detective thrillers, set in present day Scotland,
and also two books exploring the Scottish Wars of Independence and
the Knights Templar.*

*The present story, "The Green Tower," expands on what may
have gone on behind the scenes of a mysterious and pivotal event
mentioned in several of the Deryni novels.*

ABOUT THE ILLUSTRATOR

*John Dale Javier is also the illustrator for "Educational Tapes" in this
volume. For more information about him, please see page 241.*

The Green Tower

Stevana de Corwyn was ten on that afternoon of an early spring, watching from the battlements with her mother as the newcomers rode into Castle Coroth. In the courtyard below, mounted on a pretty dappled pony with green plumes nodding in its headstall, she could see another girl-child of about her age, pretty and well-dressed, as dark as Stevana herself was fair. A mass of glossy black ringlets cascaded down the other girl's back, caught by a ribbon of fresh green silk; her riding dress was of a rich, tawny velvet that glimmered in the sunlight, lavished at hem and sleeves with bands of emerald-green embroidery.

Stevana allowed herself a wistful sigh, suddenly less pleased with her own simple gown of good, serviceable green wool, but she knew that her mother would never allow *her* to wear velvet anywhere near a horse. Grania de Corwyn would make clucking sounds and say that both the fabric and the very style of the newcomer's gown were unsuitable for a child that age, especially for riding. An upward glance at her mother confirmed that Stevana had best not even comment on the subject.

It was because the girl had no mother of her own, Stevana decided. Lady Ilde had died the previous summer, leaving her two children to the somewhat distracted care of their father. The boy was already squired to the court of King Malcolm of Gwynedd, living at court in Rhemuth. The rather plain and stoop-shouldered man riding a big roan beside the girl's pony could only be Master Lewys ap Norfal himself—hardly as impressive-looking as she had expected, after all the talk of the past week. At supper the night before, the grownups had talked of little else. Stevana had nearly fallen asleep over her trencher.

"Well, he *is* bringing his daughter, *Beau-Père*," Grania de Corwyn had said to Stevana's grandfather. "He can't have in mind anything *too* dangerous."

Stiofan de Corwyn, the Deryni Duke of Corwyn, shook his head and twisted off another chunk of the fresh manchet bread from a pewter platter between him and the mother of his only grandchild.

"I wish I could be sure of that. You know very well what he did three years ago—or at least tried to do. I'm almost surprised they let him live. God knows I've tried to talk him out of it. But he's convinced that he's the man who can make it work. That said, I figured it was better to have him work here, where responsible souls can make sure things don't get totally out of hand—or pick up the pieces, if they do."

Stevana wondered what it was that Master Lewys was supposed to have done—and what might happen if he did try to do it here! She knew, though no one had said as much, that the trickle of important visitors arriving daily in the past week had been Deryni. In and of itself, that marked the occasion as unusual, for even here in Corwyn, those of their race had been looked upon with uneasiness, if not hostility, for more than a hundred years.

But it was better here than in the neighboring heartland of Gwynedd. There, except for a very few who enjoyed powerful patronage and protection—and even they were always wary— Deryni mostly kept very quiet about what they were.

Of course, Corwyn was on the fringes of the kingdom, and once had enjoyed sovereignty of its own, always under Deryni rulers. The Dukes of Corwyn were still virtual princes within their own borders, sufficiently respected that the most draconian of the old anti-Deryni laws had rarely been enforced in Corwyn, other than the ongoing prohibition against Deryni clergy. Stiofan Duke of Corwyn had fought for the Haldane king at the bloody Battle of Killingford, as had his father, and had been duke for more than a quarter century. He was regarded as a fair and evenhanded ruler, even if he *was* Deryni, accepted and even admired by his people, so there had never been any serious attempt to oust him from the lands held by many generations of his ancestors.

Still, for most Deryni west of the border with Torenth, even in Corwyn, it was wise to be circumspect—a difficult thing for Stevana herself, she thought, as she set an elbow on the balustrade and leaned her chin against her hand. For as the granddaughter and heiress of the Deryni Duke of Corwyn, she could hardly expect not to be recognized for what she was, once anyone knew her name.

That meant that she had been taught from the earliest age to guard her tongue and, even more, to curb any display of her powers as they began to develop. Yet this circumspection about demonstrating one's powers seemed not to apply to grownups, or at least not to those now gathering at Castle Coroth. It seemed clear that the man now riding into the castle yard—by all reports, a very powerful and clever Deryni—was intending no small demonstration of his power, and apparently with the approval or at least tolerance of some of the most accomplished Deryni mages living. Several of them had sat in her grandfather's hall the night before, or were watching in the yard below.

"Her name is Jessamy," Stevana's mother said beside her. "She's but a year older than you are. Shall we go downstairs and meet them?"

Stevana craned her neck somewhat dubiously, watching a man-at-arms lift the other girl down from her pony.

"She's pretty," Stevana decided, "but she doesn't look very friendly."

Her mother's arched eyebrow made it clear that she did not regard her daughter's comment worthy of Corwyn's heiress.

"Well, she doesn't, *Maman*."

"Aye, and if you approach her with that kind of attitude, I very much expect you'll be proved right."

Stevana only rolled her eyes as she put her hand in her mother's and dutifully followed down the turnpike stair to the hall.

She found that more of her grandfather's Deryni friends had arrived during the day, while she was at her lessons. Not far from the foot of the stair, she spied her cousin Michon, who sometimes tutored her. He was young and handsome, and flirted with her outrageously, and she wanted to run and fling her arms around his neck for a hug; but he was deep in conversation with another young man somewhat older than himself, with curly red hair and piercing brown eyes.

"Who is that with Cousin Michon?" she whispered to her mother, as they made their way toward the door to the castle yard.

Grania smiled, answering softly. "Don't worry yourself about *him*, my darling. That's Sir Sief MacAthan. If there's trouble over the next few days, other than from Master Lewys, it's apt to be from him. But don't worry; Michon will keep him in line."

Stevana only nodded, wide-eyed and blithely unaware, as they came down the steps into the yard, that such candid observations were not usually shared with ten-year-olds. She had never known her father, who had died before she reached her first birthday, so she thought it normal that her mother should have come to regard her as a confidante.

Her grandfather was talking to Master Lewys, whose daughter was doing her best not to look awed in the presence of their noble host. Duke Stiofan glanced in the direction of his daughter-in-law and granddaughter as they approached, extending a hand to draw them closer for introductions.

"Ah, here they are now," Stiofan said, smiling. "Grania my dear, I should like to present Master Lewys ap Norfal and Jessamy.

Lewys, this is my son's widow, the Countess Grania, and my granddaughter, Stevana de Corwyn."

As courtesies were exchanged among the grownups, Stevana eyed the other girl from closer on, vaguely envious of her dark curls. Jessamy, for her part, lifted her chin and returned Stevana's scrutiny unflinchingly—her eyes were a deep, almost violet blue—but she looked more nervous than prideful, Stevana decided.

"*Maman*, may I show Jessamy the garden?" she asked, when a lull in the adults' conversation permitted.

"Of course you may, darling. But do try to stay out of the mud. Jessamy won't want to spoil her pretty gown."

Making a moue at her mother, Stevana darted out her hand to take Jessamy's and urged her toward the gate that led into the castle's walled garden, off beyond the stables. After her initial surprise, the older girl let herself be drawn along with good humor, though she looked faintly puzzled as Stevana swung back the barred iron gate and glanced at her hopefully.

"It's—very nice," Jessamy said politely, though her expression was dubious. Her voice was lower-pitched than the younger girl's, with a faint accent Stevana did not recognize.

"I know it's still mostly dead," Stevana retorted, "but it *is* only just spring. But lots of the bulbs are poking their heads out of the ground. *Maman* says that it's warmer here, because we live by the sea. After Easter, there will be all kinds of flowers. Do you want to see the bulbs?"

"I guess."

Following where Stevana led, the newcomer let herself be guided deeper into the garden, where closer inspection did, indeed, reveal the wonder of spring's first tender shoots. In one shady corner, Jessamy crouched down to admire the beginning of a variegated carpet of crocuses.

"Look at all the colors!" Jessamy exclaimed. "I thought crocuses only came in purple."

"You don't have yellow ones where you come from?" Stevana asked. "Or white ones?"

Jessamy shook her dark curls, rising to run to another bed whose flora had caught her eye.

"And look—are those jonquils...or narcissi—or is it narcissuses?"

"I think it's either way," Stevana said good-naturedly, as she bent to pull one of the tiny yellow flowers and sniff its powerful perfume. "This one's a jonquil. Here, smell it."

"Mmmm. I love those," Jessamy murmured, closing her eyes to inhale its perfume. "Just a few can fill a room with their scent. I like the way they look with purplish flowers."

"Me too," Stevana agreed. "Hyacinth is good. Or rosemary..."

It quickly became clear that the two girls had a love of gardening in common, and soon the pair were scurrying energetically along the garden's muddy paths, chattering and laughing as Stevana explained the layout and identified what beds would blossom into what. By the time they had worked their way to the farthest corner of the walled garden, hair now untidy and hems mud-bedraggled, she was ready to share one of her favorite treasures with her newfound friend.

"This is one of my special places," she said, as they came before a barred iron gate set into a rocky facade.

As she shook out her skirts and slicked back errant wisps of fair hair from her face, trying to make herself more presentable, her companion tipped her head back to look for the source of water rippling merrily down the rock to one side of the entrance. The rugged outcropping jutted upward nearly to the height of the castle rampart beyond the garden wall, and was studded with silver-gray lichens and patches of velvety green moss along the joins.

"What is this?" Jessamy asked.

"The Grotto of the Hours."

"Why do they call it that?"

"I dunno. It's a grotto—and sometimes people spend hours here, I guess. I know I do." An unlit torch was thrust into an iron bracket to the right of the doorway, sheltered under a slight overhang, and Stevana stood on her tiptoes to reach up and take it down.

427

JOHN DALE JAVIER

"My ancestor, the first Duke of Corwyn, built this," she went on, dusting dead leaves and cobwebs off the head of the torch. "No one's been in here all winter, so it'll be pretty dank and full of dead leaves, but it's still beautiful. And in the summer, it's a grand place to come and cool off—and to keep anyone from finding you to do lessons."

"I *like* to do lessons," Jessamy said somewhat huffily, though she started back slightly and cast a nervous glance behind them as the torch whooshed to light in the younger girl's hands. "Oh! You shouldn't do that where other people might see!"

"It's all right to do it here," Stevana replied, somewhat taken aback. "I wouldn't do it outside the castle," she added.

"It's still dangerous," Jessamy murmured, though she strained to peer past Stevana as the younger girl pulled the gate open on squeaky hinges.

"Anyway, I like to do lessons, too," Stevana went on. "Just not *all* the time—and not on fine, balmy summer afternoons. Sometimes I just like to be by myself, where no one can find me. Come on."

So saying, she led the way inside, the torch preceding them into the damp, musty smell of mildew and stagnant water. The ceiling was low and uneven, made to resemble the natural cavern it pretended to be. The wall opposite the entrance was pierced by a small arched window guarded by a metal grille—glaring enough against the shadowed interior that Jessamy all but fell over the low chair of carved black stone set in the center of the chamber.

"Careful—" Stevana started to say, but too late, though she kept her companion from actually falling down. "That's where you sit to visit Duke Dominic. His tomb is there under the window, against the wall. It's black, so it's hard to see. He was the first Duke of Corwyn. My grandfather is his direct descendant."

"I think I've heard of him," Jessamy said. "Wasn't he some kind of royal?"

"I suppose he was," Stevana allowed. "But that was a long

time ago. He and his father came with Festil I in 822. His father was a Buyenne, a younger son of the Duc du Joux—"

"A Buyenne?" Jessamy interrupted. "Then, we're cousins of some sort! My father doesn't use the name, but he's also a Buyenne of Joux; *his* father is Duc Regnier. But—how did your Buyenne ancestor get to be royal?"

"I think his mother was one of King Festil's cousins, so he and his children became Buyenne-Furstán—and everybody knows the Furstáns are royal."

"I've met some Furstáns," Jessamy said. "They're—" She broke off to look over her shoulder, then back at Stevana, obviously still nervous at speaking openly about such things. "They're powerful Deryni. No wonder Papa wanted to consult with your grandfather."

Stevana shrugged. "I guess. But the Furstán blood must be pretty diluted by now. Still, I think the Corwyn men have almost always married Deryni. I know that Dominic's son married a MacRorie—so I guess that makes him related to Saint Camber." She paused a beat. "Would you like to see a picture of him?"

"Who? Dominic's son?"

"No, Saint Camber."

She had already started to turn toward the left, lifting her torch toward the mosaics set into the plastered wall there, so she only heard Jessamy's gasp.

"You have a *picture* of *Saint Camber*?"

"Well, it's safe enough, in here," Stevana said, though she did not follow through with illuminating the wall by torchlight. "You're Deryni, or I wouldn't have mentioned it. Believe me, no one else comes in here except family—and you *are* a cousin. Do you want to see it or not?"

"Oh, I do!"

Without further ado, Stevana turned back toward the wall and again lifted her torch, this time moving farther into the room. Along the side walls, life-sized mosaic figures processed toward the looming hulk of Dominic's tomb. The torchlight glinted from the golden tesserae set amid the other tiles to highlight

430

haloes and crowns and, on this side, the golden trumpet of Saint Gabriel, the archangel of the Annunciation. Paired with holy Gabriel was the Archangel Uriel, who sometimes served as the Angel of Death.

Beyond them, however, between Uriel and the representation of the Holy Trinity that adorned the east wall below the little window, a gray-robed figure knelt in adoration of that Blessed Trinity but with one hand gesturing toward the tomb, as if in entreaty for its occupant. The face that peered from within the monkish cowl was turned to look directly at the beholder, the light eyes seeming to follow wherever the viewer went—eyes that caught and held and could almost plumb a person's soul, even if only made of fired tiles.

Beside her, Stevana sensed Jessamy sinking to her knees, face buried in her hands as her shoulders shook in silent weeping. Touched with compassion, Stevana knelt beside her and held her while she wept. After a few minutes, Jessamy raised her head, snuffling as she wiped her eyes on an edge of the fine linen petticoat under her velvet gown.

"That's what I've always thought he would look like," she said softly. "I didn't know that anyone in Gwynedd would dare to have a likeness of him."

Stevana shrugged. "Grandpapa says we aren't really in Gwynedd. Besides, like I said, only family come in here—and even then, it's hard to see him, unless you know where to look."

Snuffling again, Jessamy let Stevana help her get to her feet, again dabbing at her eyes as she slipped her arm through the younger girl's.

"I hate it when I cry in front of other people," she said, with a final snuffle. "Tante Ellen says that I'll be a woman soon, and that sometimes I'll cry before my monthly courses." She swallowed with an audible gulp. "I hope that doesn't happen soon, because they—they'll marry me off at once."

"Well—but, you'll be a woman then," Stevana said reasonably.

"No, you don't understand," Jessamy whispered. "It's because of what Papa did—and I don't even know what it was. But they're afraid of him. And they're afraid of what I might become. That's why they want me married quickly. My future husband is already chosen."

Stevana's eyes had gotten wide as the words tumbled from the older girl's lips.

"Who are *they*?" she breathed.

Jessamy shook her dark curls. "I'm not supposed to talk about it," she said. She sounded so forlorn that Stevana hugged her again and changed the subject as they turned to leave the Grotto of the Hours, for the hints she had gleaned from her own kin also suggested something so terrible as to be beyond discussion.

That night, though Stevana knew of no particular feast day that should have occasioned celebration, her grandfather hosted more formal dining in the great hall. Lewys ap Norfal had not traveled with a large retinue, but nonetheless the hall seemed more crowded than it had the night before. The servants had set up a second trencher table at right angles to the usual one, arranged like the stem of a T, so that Stiofan presided from his usual place at the top, with Lewys at his right hand and her mother on Lewys's right. The venerable Master Norfal, Lewys' teacher, was at Stiofan's left hand—nearly a hundred years old, Stevana had heard—accompanied by Taillefer Earl of Lendour. Michon de Courcy and Sief MacAthan sat directly opposite, where the stem of the T began. Even to Stevana's unsophisticated eye, the arrangement had every appearance of trying to ensure that Lewys ap Norfal was well surrounded by very competent Deryni.

Jessamy apparently noticed this too, seated with Stevana a few places down from the Countess Grania, for she went very quiet as she noted the other guests at the table.

"What's wrong?" Stevana breathed in her friend's ear, when dining had begun and musicians were playing from the gallery at the end of the hall.

Jessamy looked at her sharply, then back toward the diners seated nearer Stevana's grandfather.

"They're all here," she whispered, averting her eyes to her trencher. "Even my future husband."

Stevana's mind whirled. "Which one is he?" she blurted, though she kept her voice a whisper. "And *they*—you mean the *they* who are afraid of you and your father?"

Jessamy closed her eyes briefly, then picked up her goblet and drank, keeping it close to her mouth as she glanced at Stevana.

"Don't react, whatever you do," she warned. "Yes, it's the same *they*—some of them, at any rate. And I'm to marry Sir Sief MacAthan. He's sitting right there, across from your grandfather."

Stevana made herself pick up a joint of chicken and bite some off, holding it in her hand as she chewed and finally allowed herself to glance casually at Sief.

He was older than she had thought when she first saw him with Cousin Michon earlier that day. Probably close to thirty. There was gray in the stubby red braid now queued at the nape of his neck, and there was gray speckled in his neatly trimmed beard and moustache. But his dark eyes were bright and looked kind. His hands, as he gesticulated in conversation, were small and graceful. His attire was simple but of good quality.

"Why do you think he's here?" Stevana whispered, before taking another bite of chicken.

Jessamy shook her head. "Same as the rest. They're worried about what my father will do. He's come here to work, you know. That's why they've all come."

Further discussion was curtailed by the arrival of the next course.

Later that night, as Stevana settled into bed with Jessamy beside her, she was still trying to figure out what was going on. As soon as the nurse had blown out the last candle and withdrawn, she turned toward her bedmate.

"You said they'd all come to work," she whispered, as she kindled faint handfire between them, just above their heads. "Do you think they're working tonight?"

Jessamy's dark-haired head turned on the pillow to regard her.

"No. It will be tomorrow night."

"How do you know?"

"Because they ate. When you work high magic, you're not supposed to eat beforehand. You're supposed to fast."

"Then, you think they *are* going to do something."

Jessamy slowly nodded. "That's why we came. Papa said that Duke Stiofan would monitor for him."

"Monitor for *what*?" Stevana whispered.

Again Jessamy shook her head. "I don't know. I just know that it's dangerous."

"Then, why is he going to do it?"

"Because that's the only way to learn," came Jessamy's reply. "But he'll be careful. He promised me."

That answer caused Stevana to fall silent, for it confirmed the danger in whatever Lewys had done a few years before—and apparently intended to do again. But she could think of nothing to say that would not also give her new friend even more reason to be anxious. So instead, she merely let herself snuggle a little closer for warmth and drift into sleep. She did not dream, but she knew that Jessamy did. The older girl tossed and turned all the night long, waking her bedmate several times. But when daylight finally came, she claimed to remember nothing of what had disturbed her sleep—and Stevana's.

Her mother sent them on a ride out the next morning, with Stevana's nurse and the constable and several of the castle's squires for escort and company. They had a splendid outing—the squires were hardly older than their charges, and gently teased and flirted with them—but it seemed likely to both girls that the excursion was a ruse to get them out of the castle for most of the day.

That evening, their surmise of the night before seemed to be confirmed, for instead of supping in the great hall, they were sent to Stevana's chamber where a small table had been laid for them.

"His Grace feared he might be taking a chill, so he's asked Lord Hamilton to preside at table tonight," Stevana's nurse told them, as she poured ale for both girls and then helped them spread big napkins over their skirts. "And your lady mother knew you'd both be tired after riding all day. I know *I* am. I'll come to clear up after you've eaten. Now let us give thanks for this food."

The woman left them after hearing them say grace. When the door had closed behind her, Stevana glanced at her companion.

"D'you think the real reason we're having supper here is because the adults are fasting?" she murmured as she tore off a chunk of bread.

Jessamy had been about to sip at her cup of ale, but abruptly froze with the rim of the cup just at her lips, her eyes going slightly unfocused.

"What is it?" Stevana whispered, suddenly a little afraid.

The older girl blinked, then carefully set the untasted cup back on the table.

"Don't drink the ale," she whispered, glancing at the door before slowly passing her hand over several other items on the table. "No, it's only the ale. But they counted on the fact that we'd be hungry and thirsty after riding all day—especially thirsty."

"Well, I *am*," Stevana began.

"So am I," Jessamy replied. "But if we drink, we'll fall asleep in minutes and sleep until morning."

Stevana's eyes widened.

"There's something in the ale?"

Jessamy nodded gravely. "They don't want us awake for whatever they're going to do."

Chills running up her spine, Stevana carefully set her chunk of bread back on her trencher, no longer hungry or thirsty.

"You're serious, aren't you?"

"Never more so."

Dry-mouthed, Stevana wadded at the napkin spread across her skirts, unconsciously wiping her hands on it. Jessamy had her head bowed over tightly clasped hands, though Stevana didn't think she was praying.

"Do you want to try to find out what they're doing?" Stevana asked very softly.

Jessamy's head lifted in question. "How?" she breathed.

Surreptitiously, Stevana looked at the door. If they were drinking the ale as expected, her mother or the nurse would come in soon to check on them, and would expect them to be asleep.

"Can you put yourself to sleep for a set amount of time?" she whispered, adding, as the other nodded, "I mean, really deep asleep."

Cautiously, Jessamy nodded again.

"Go listen at the door," Stevana whispered, taking up the two cups of ale and getting to her feet. As Jessamy complied, watching her puzzledly, Stevana scurried to the garderobe set into the wall near the window and dumped most of the contents of both cups down the privy hole. As she brought the cups back and sat down again, she jutted her chin for the older girl to rejoin her.

"Now, you've got to properly put yourself to sleep for—let's say two hours. Can you do that? If we're not really asleep, she'll know."

Wide-eyed, Jessamy nodded wordless agreement and took her place across from Stevana, who sloshed a little ale on the table, then set the cup down in the spill and laid her head on her forearm. With her other hand, she picked up the chunk of bread from her trencher and let that hand fall heavily to her side, fingers opening to drop the bread. As Jessamy did something similar, Stevana drew a deep breath and let it out, silently mouthing the syllables of a sleep spell. She slipped into oblivion before she could finish it.

She woke some time later in her bed. Someone had removed her riding clothes and dressed her in her nightdress, and even brushed and braided her blond hair—probably the nurse, but it could have been her mother. Curled beside her, still asleep, Jessamy had been similarly dealt with. Judging by the small night sounds of the castle sleeping, and the moonlight streaming through the window, it must be nearing midnight. From far away, Stevana dimly heard an officer of the watch cry the hour, but she could not quite make out what hour it was.

Resolute, she slipped out of bed and padded to the window that overlooked the castle yard, craning to gaze toward the tower where her grandfather always retired to carry out his magical workings. The moonlight was glaring against the tower's pale stone, but she could just make out the glow of candlelight behind the narrow, green-glassed window slits along the top floor.

"Is that where they work?" Jessamy whispered close beside her.

Stevana had sensed her approaching, and only nodded.

"Is there any way we can get up there?"

"If we're careful, I think we can cross the yard without being seen," Stevana replied, keeping her voice to a whisper. "But from there, it's a single turnpike stair going up—though there are three or four landings on the way, if we have to hide. I've heard that there are secret passages within the walls, but that may be just servants' gossip."

"A pity we don't know for sure," Jessamy murmured. "But we'll make do with the landings, since we must."

A quarter hour later, with cloaks wrapped around their nightdresses and soft slippers on their feet, the two girls were huddling on the ground floor of the green tower, poised at the foot of the spiral stair. Now that they were nearing their goal, they spoke only by gestures and mind-to-mind. Neither was very accomplished in this latter skill, for the maturation of the powers peculiar to their race tended toward physical manipulations before the development of more cerebral abilities. But the physical contact of their joined hands eased the effort of communicating mind-to-mind—necessary lest their whispers be detected, if not by those working within the tower's topmost chamber, then by some warder set to guard the outer door.

They made their stealthy way up the spiral stair, pausing at each landing to listen with minds as well as ears, hearts pounding so that they were sure the sound must be reverberating on the level above. They had more floors to go—Stevana had lost count of exactly how many—when Jessamy suddenly doubled over with a gasp, cradling her head in her hands and crumpling to her knees. At the same time, a flash that was more felt than seen seemed to light up the stairwell, and a high-pitched, keening sound briefly pierced the silence.

Then from somewhere higher up the stairwell, perhaps the very topmost floor, came the hollow bang of a door crashing back on its hinges, accompanied by muffled exclamations and the sound of coughing.

Stevana kept her head down, pulling Jessamy back into the shadows of the nearest landing, clamping a hand over the older girl's mouth to stifle her whimper as footsteps and voices came nearer.

Not a sound! she sent. *They're coming this way.*

At the same time, she was feeling for the door to the room that opened off this landing—fortunately, unoccupied. Half sick with fear, she drew Jessamy in after her and all but closed the door, crouching then to peer through the keyhole as she began to make out words.

"But, what could have happened?" she heard a male voice say. "Where did he go? It wasn't supposed to happen like that!"

"We did everything that could be done," her grandfather said. "I have no answers for you."

"The Council will have to be told," a third voice said. She thought it was her cousin Michon.

"Is that really necessary?" *That* was her mother's voice.

"You know it is," yet another male voice said. "If we could be sure he was simply dead, it might be different—but even then, they'd need to be told."

"I really thought he might succeed," her grandfather said, as footsteps trooped past the doorway.

There seemed to be more footsteps than could be attributed to the voices Stevana had heard, and they kept passing up and down the stair outside the door for most of an hour. It soon became clear that something had gone disastrously wrong, but the fate of Jessamy's father remained unclear. From what Stevana could gather, it seemed that Lewys ap Norfal had simply disappeared. Whether or not he still lived, no one seemed to have any idea. Behind her, Jessamy herself sat in a corner of the darkened room with head ducked and arms clasped around her knees, rocking back and forth, silently weeping and whimpering. Once the footsteps seemed to have died away for good, Stevana summoned handfire and went back to her friend, who now was merely resting her head on her knees, all her tears spent.

"Are you all right?" she whispered, crouching to lay an arm around the older girl's shoulders.

Jessamy snuffled and lifted her head, face haggard in the greenish-yellow light of the handfire.

"He's dead, isn't he?" she whispered, in a voice devoid of emotion.

"We don't know that," Stevana replied. "*They* don't know that."

Jessamy snuffled again and dried her eyes with an edge of her nightgown, but said nothing.

"Do *you* think he's dead?" Stevana said, after a beat.

"If he doesn't come back, it hardly matters," Jessamy said bleakly. "Either way, I'll become Sief MacAthan's ward until I'm of an age to marry—and then, his wife."

"Is that so bad?" Stevana asked. "He looks kind. And he's handsome enough."

Jessamy shrugged. "He answers to other, more powerful Deryni. I don't know who," she added sharply, when Stevana opened her mouth as if to speak. "They're horrified by what my father could do—and wanted to do. Now that he's done...whatever he's done...they'll be afraid I might try to do the same thing. So they have to marry me to someone who's safe, who can prevent that. God, I feel sick!"

Her expression was so bleak, her tone so forlorn, that Stevana could only hold her closer for a long moment, helpless to offer any better comfort to her friend. When they eventually drew apart, Stevana took the other girl's hands and started helping her to her feet.

"We'd better get back to my room," she said quietly. "They may have missed us already, as it is. In any case, they're going to come eventually to tell us what's happened—or as much as they know, at any rate."

"I can't imagine what went wrong," Jessamy whispered, automatically dusting at the back of her cloak. Her hand came away sticky and wet—and red, in the light of Stevana's handfire, as she thrust it into the faintly greenish glow.

A stifled, inarticulate little whimper escaped her lips as she and Stevana both whirled to look where she had been sitting. There was no mistaking the smear of bright blood on the bare wood.

"Oh, no!" Jessamy whispered, her face draining of color. "Not yet. Not *now*..."

Stevana knew what the blood meant, and what it meant to Jessamy.

"We've got to get you back to my room," she whispered sensibly, taking Jessamy's arm.

"But, we'll never be able to hide it," the stricken girl replied. "Sief is *here*, and my father is *gone*. They'll have me married before— Dear God, what's to become of me? Oh, what am I going to *do*...?"

Her lament trailed off into a low wail, muffled against Stevana's shoulder, and indeed, Stevana had no better idea what they were going to do. In the end, she waited until Jessamy's sobbing had subsided to hiccups and sniffles, then led her back down the stairs. By dint of sheer luck, they managed to make it back across the castle yard and back up the stairs without mishap, and even back to Stevana's room.

But Stevana's mother was waiting for them there, gazing out the window. They did not see her as they first entered, quietly closing the door behind them, but they froze at the rustling sound of her skirts as she came out of the window embrasure.

"I watched you cross the yard," she said quietly, looking very sad. "I thought you might have tried to come."

The two girls exchanged guilty glances and huddled closer together, eyes wide and frightened.

"Dear child, I'm not going to scold you—either of you," Grania de Corwyn said, opening her arms to them. "It—didn't go the way anyone planned. I am *so* sorry."

Her words loosed a floodgate of new tears from both of them this time. Weeping, they flew to her arms and sobbed. Grania merely held them, enfolding them in the motherly embrace of arms and mind and making comforting shushing noises until the sobs finally ceased.

"I see what has happened," she said softly, as Jessamy shifted slightly in the circle of her arm. "It means that you are a woman now."

Jessamy sniffled and lifted her head, but would not meet Grania's eyes.

"It means that I shall be married, and *soon*. I don't *want* to be married yet."

"I know, my dear," Grania replied. "But Sief is a good man. I think he will be a gentle husband."

"They're afraid of me," Jessamy sniffled. "Because of my father."

"Yes, they are. But your lot could be far worse."

"Could it?" the girl murmured dully.

"Come, child. Let's get you cleaned up," Grania said. "Now that it's begun, there's no way it could be long hidden. Let us make the best we can of a very sad circumstance. I am so very sorry about your father."

That very afternoon, in the chapel at Castle Coroth, Stevana watched with her mother in numb disbelief as her grandfather set Jessamy's hand in that of Sir Sief MacAthan. Old Father Wenceslaus led the couple in the vows that made them husband and wife, though Sief had promised earlier that the marriage would not be consummated until the following year, when Jessamy reached the age of twelve, and had added that amendment to the marriage contract. He had also promised that tutors would be found to teach her proper control and discretion in the use of her formidable potential. He did seem kind enough.

Watching Father Wenceslaus lay the end of his stole over the couple's joined hands, symbolizing the vows that now bound them, Stevana de Corwyn, Heiress of Corwyn, bit at her lips and wondered what her own fate must be. She had always accepted that her own marriage would be arranged, both to political advantage and to further her potential as a Deryni, but she did not know whether she dared to hope that she might also come to love the man she one day married. Certainly her mother and her grandfather would do their best to choose her a husband who at least would be kind to her; but things could change, as had been amply proved when Lewys ap Norfal disappeared to wherever he had gone.

As for Jessamy, the sight of that white-faced child bride fulfilling her duty as the daughter of a noble house would stay with Stevana de Corwyn until the day she died.

The Year in the Contests

LAST YEAR'S ANTHOLOGY
Last year's anthology, *L. Ron Hubbard Presents Writers of the Future Volume 35,* hit #1 on Amazon's bestseller list as a pre-release and new release.

The anthology got nice reviews from the *Library Journal,* which highlighted three outstanding stories and said "readers who like sf and short stories should thoroughly enjoy it," and *Midwest Book Review* called it a "must have" for library and academic collections as well as fans.

The Heinlein Society, which is dedicated to the proposition that some debts cannot be repaid but must be paid forward, presented a letter of congratulations and thanks to the Writers and Illustrators of the Future Contests at the thirty-fifth Annual Awards Ceremony for "outstanding work in discovering and nurturing promising new authors and illustrators in the field of science fiction and fantasy."

The anthology's thirty-fifth volume won Best Anthology from the *New York City Big Book Award,* which honors books that have a worldwide appeal.

Meanwhile, at the *Benjamin Franklin Awards* (sponsored by the Independent Book Publishers Association)—*Writers of the Future Volume 34* won a Silver Award in the Fiction: Science Fiction & Fantasy category.

CONTEST GROWTH

Both Contests have brought in more stories and art entries this year than any previous year before. We're growing and not looking back.

This year, we had Contest winners from the countries of Turkey, Iran, Vietnam, Australia, the United Kingdom, and the United States.

NOTABLE ACCOMPLISHMENTS
FROM ALUMNI AND JUDGES

Brittany Jackson (WotF 24), one of our Illustrator Grand Prize winners, illustrated *Parker Looks Up: An Extraordinary Moment*. It's about a visit to the National Portrait Gallery in Washington, DC, that forever alters Parker Curry's young life when she views First Lady Michelle Obama's portrait. It's a *New York Times* bestseller!

Qianjiao Ma (WotF 35) did illustrations for Netflix's animated television series *Disenchantment*.

Scot M. Noel (WotF 6) launched a new magazine of science and fantasy fiction, *DreamForge*, with a two-page feature on Writers of the Future and Dave Farland (WotF 3) as the Contest's Coordinating Judge.

Nnedi Okorafor (WotF 18) and actress Viola Davis are working together on a TV series adaptation for Amazon based on the Octavia E. Butler novel *Wild Seed*.

Martin Shoemaker's (WotF 31) *The Last Dance* rode the top of Amazon Hard Science Fiction bestseller list.

Brad Torgersen (WotF 26) won The Dragon Award for Best Science Fiction Novel for *A Star-Wheeled Sky*.

Illustrator Contest judge Diane Dillon was bestowed the Lifetime Achievement Award at the Chesley Awards.

The Robert A. Heinlein Award went to Contest judge Dr. Gregory Benford.

NEW JUDGES

We're delighted to announce two new judges for the Illustrators of the Future Contest: Dan dos Santos and Craig Elliott.

Dan dos Santos is well known for his colorful oil paintings, most often depicting strong women. Dan's work spans a variety of mediums, including novels, comics, film, and video games.

His clients include Disney, Universal Studios, Activision, Boeing Commercial Airplanes, The Greenwich Workshop, Penguin Books, Random House, Scholastic, Upper Deck, Hasbro, DC Comics, and many, many more.

Dan has been the recipient of many awards. He is a Rhodes Family Scholarship winner, a five-time Hugo Award nominee for Best Artist, and has received both gold and silver medals from *Spectrum: The Best in Contemporary Fantastic Art*. His illustrations have graced the #1 spot on the *New York Times* bestseller list numerous times and his covers are seen in bookstores in dozens of countries around the world.

Dan dos Santos is one of the most recognized artists in his field with hundreds of book covers to his credit.

Craig Elliott is based in Los Angeles, California. He received his education at the famed Art Center College of Design in Pasadena, California.

Craig's carefully crafted and arresting images of nature and the human form have captivated audiences with their visual and intellectual celebration of the beauty in this world and beyond. A multifaceted artist, he is also an accomplished landscape architect, sculptor and, most recently, jewelry designer.

In addition to his fine art, Craig has had a hand in designing many of today's most popular animated films from Disney and Dreamworks Studios including *Hercules, Mulan, The Emperor's New Groove, Treasure Planet, Shark Tale, Flushed Away, Bee Movie, Enchanted, Monsters vs. Aliens,* and *The Princess and the Frog,* as well as other upcoming features.

THE PASSING OF A JUDGE

Mike Resnick, a beloved judge of the Writers of the Future Contest, passed away on January 9, 2020, at the age of seventy-seven, after a brave battle with cancer.

Mike won numerous awards for his work, including five Hugo Awards and one Nebula, but had also won awards in many other countries. Indeed, at the time of his passing, he had won more awards for his short fiction than any other person in the field of science fiction.

He joined the Contest as a judge in 2008, and in 2017 was awarded the L. Ron Hubbard Lifetime Achievement Award for his service to the field.

Mike always showed tremendous generosity to new writers. As a publisher, he often sought out new writers to publish in the magazine, *Galaxy's Edge*, and in various anthologies. In the 1990s, he noted that he published more first stories from authors than all three of the major speculative fiction magazines combined. He even coauthored stories with more than fifty new authors. And every year when we held our workshops, Mike could be found late at night, taking time to mentor the latest talent.

Mike was a giant of a man, a person with a great heart, and tremendous talent, who was noted for always being found in company with his "writer children."

Mike has passed away, but his influence and legacy lives on.

THE PASSING OF A WINNER

Emeka Walter Dinjos, the first winner of the Writers of the Future Contest from Nigeria (WotF 33) passed away from diabetes on December 12, 2018 at 34 years old.

He actively began reading and writing English in 2010. He quickly mastered the language and won the Writers of the Future in 2017. He was also published in *Beneath Ceaseless Skies*, *Galaxy's Edge*, *Deep Magic*, and *Myriad Lands*. His novelette, "SisiMumu" was featured in *Future Science Fiction Digest*, Issue 1.

He was a bright spark and is missed.

AWARDS FOR WINNERS

Our past artists and writers, along with our judges, continue to publish widely across many fields and in many mediums. We can't mention all of their accomplishments, but here are some recaps of notable awards (and the WotF volume where you can first see the author's or illustrator's work):

Analog Awards
Finalist: Best Short Story—C. Stuart Hardwick (WotF 30) for "A Measure of Love."
Finalist: Best Fact Article—C. Stuart Hardwick for "Taming the Genie."
Finalist: Best Cover—Eldar Zakirov (WotF 22) for the November/ December issue.

Asimov's Readers' Awards
Finalist: Best Novella—Contest judge Kristine Kathryn Rusch for "Joyride" and for "The Rescue of the Renegat."
Finalists: Best Novelette—Contest judges Nancy Kress for "Cost of Doing Business" and Kristine Kathryn Rusch for "Lieutenant Tightass."
Finalist: Best Cover—Eldar Zakirov for his covers on the January/ February and the September/October issues.

Aurealis Awards
Winner: Best Collection—Shaun Tan (WotF 8) for *Tales from the Inner City.*
Winner: Best Graphic Novel/Illustrated Work—Shaun Tan for *Cicada.*
Winner: Best Young Adult Short Story—Shauna O'Meara (WotF 30) for "The Sea-Maker of Darmid Bay."
Winner: Convenors' Award for Excellence—Cat Sparks (WotF 21) for "The 21st Century Catastrophe: Hyper-capitalism and Severe Climate Change in Science Fiction."
Finalist: Best SF Novella—Samantha Murray (WotF 31) for "Singles' Day."
Finalist: Best Fantasy Novella—Michael Gardner (WotF 36) for "This Side of the Wall."
Finalist: Best Horror Short Story—Michael Gardner for "The Offering."

Finalist: Best Graphic Novel/Illustrated Work—Shaun Tan for *Tales from the Inner City*.

Aurora Awards
Finalist: Best Novel—James Alan Gardner (WotF 6) for *They Promised Me the Gun Wasn't Loaded*.

British Fantasy Awards
Winner: Best Novella—Aliette de Bodard (WotF 26) for *The Tea Master and the Detective*.
Finalist: Best Novella—Nnedi Okorafor for *Binti: The Night Masquerade*.

Chesley Awards
Lifetime Artistic Achievement—Diane Dillon.

Colorado Book Awards
Winner: Science Fiction/Fantasy—L. D. Colter (WotF 30) for *While Gods Sleep*.

Ditmar Awards
Finalist: Best Collected Work—Shaun Tan for *Tales from the Inner City*.
Finalist: Best Artwork—Shauna O'Meara for cover and illustrations for *A Hand of Knaves*.
Winner: William Atheling Jr. Award for Criticism or Review—Cat Sparks for "The 21st Century Catastrophe: Hypercapitalism and Severe Climate Change in Science Fiction."

Geffen Awards
Winner: Best Translated Fantasy Book—Brandon Sanderson for *The Alloy of Law*.

Hugo Awards
Finalists: Best Novella—Nnedi Okorafor for *Binti: The Night*

Masquerade and Aliette de Bodard for *The Tea Master and the Detective*.
Finalist: Best Graphic Story—Nnedi Okorafor for *Black Panther: Long Live the King*.

Locus Awards
Finalist: SF Novel—Nancy Kress for *If Tomorrow Comes*.
Finalist: Young Adult Book: John Schoffstall (WotF 21) for *Half-Witch*.
Finalists: Novella—Aliette de Bodard for *The Tea Master and the Detective* and Carolyn Ives Gilman (WotF 3) for "Umbernight."
Finalist: Novelette—Ken Liu (WotF 21) for "Quality Time."
Finalist: Short Story—Nnedi Okorafor for "Mother of Invention."
Finalist: Collection—Tobias S. Buckell (WotF 16) for *The Tangled Lands*.
Finalist: Art Book—Shaun Tan for *Cicada*.
Finalist: Best Artist—Shaun Tan, Leo & Diane Dillon, Bob Eggleton.

Nommo Awards (African Speculative Fiction Society)
Winner: Best Comic/Graphic Novel—Nnedi Okorafor for *Shuri: The Search for Black Panther*.
Finalist: Best Comic/Graphic Novel—Nnedi Okorafor for *Black Panther: Long Live the King*.
Finalist: Best Novella—Nnedi Okorafor for *Binti: The Night Masquerade*.

Pacific Book Awards
Winner: Best Mystery—Gabriel F. W. Koch (WotF 20) for his story *And Come Day's End*.

Spectrum Fantastic Art
The Artist List for *Spectrum 26* includes Illustrators' Contest winners: Bruce Brenneise (WotF 34), Dwayne Harris (WotF 17), Allen Morris (WotF 35), Dustin Panzino (WotF 27), Omar Rayyan

(WotF 8), and Contest judges Craig Elliott, Dan dos Santos, and Shaun Tan.

Theodore Sturgeon Memorial Award
Finalist: Carolyn Ives Gilman for "Umbernight."

World Fantasy Awards
Winner: Best Collection—Tobias S. Buckell and Paolo Bacigalupi for *The Tangled Lands*.
Finalist: Best Novella—Aliette de Bodard for *The Tea Master and the Detective*.
Finalist: Best Artist—Shaun Tan.

Year's Best Military & Adventure SF Readers' Choice Award was won by Brian Trent (WotF 29) for his story "Crash-Site."

CONTEST SHOUT-OUT
Britain's Got Talent finalist Daliso Chaponda announced his 2019 UK "Blah Blah Blacklist" tour following a very successful "What the African Said" tour which sold out 50+ dates throughout the UK. Chaponda has continuously promoted the Contest throughout his celebrity career and noted: "Yes, that Writers of the Future certificate was a 'don't give up' totem for a decade!"

THE YEAR IN THE CONTESTS

For contest year 36, the winners are:

Writers of the Future Contest Winners

FIRST QUARTER

1. *Andy Dibble*
   "A Word That Means Everything"

2. *F. J. Bergmann*
   "A Prize in Every Box"

3. *Sonny Zae*
   "Automated Everyman Migrant Theater"

SECOND QUARTER

1. *Katie Livingston*
   "Educational Tapes"

2. *Zack Be*
   "As Able the Air"

3. *Tim Boiteau*
   "Molting Season"

THIRD QUARTER

1. *J. L. George*
   "Catching My Death"

2. *Michael Gardner*
   "Foundations"

3. *Storm Humbert*
   "Stolen Sky"

FOURTH QUARTER

1. *C. Winspear*
   "The Trade"

2. *David A. Elsensohn*
   "Trading Ghosts"

3. *Leah Ning*
   "Yellow and Pink"

THE YEAR IN THE CONTESTS

Illustrators of the Future Contest Winners

FIRST QUARTER
    Brock Aguirre
    Daniel Bitton
    Ben Hill

SECOND QUARTER
    Phoebe Rothfeld
    John Dale Javier
    Heather A. Laurence

THIRD QUARTER
    Aidin Andrews
    Irmak Çavun
    Mason Matak

FOURTH QUARTER
    Arthur Bowling
    Kaitlyn Goldberg
    Anh Le

L. Ron Hubbard's
Writers of the Future Contest

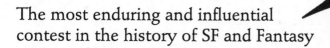

The most enduring and influential contest in the history of SF and Fantasy

Open to new and amateur SF & Fantasy writers

Prizes each quarter: $1,000, $750, $500
Quarterly 1st place winners compete for $5,000
additional annual prize!

ALL JUDGING DONE BY PROFESSIONAL WRITERS ONLY

No entry fee is required

Entrants retain all publication rights

Don't delay! Send your entry now!

To submit your entry electronically go to:
   writersofthefuture.com/enter-writer-contest

E-mail: contests@authorservicesinc.com

To submit your entry via mail send to:
   L. Ron Hubbard's Writers of the Future Contest
   7051 Hollywood Blvd.
   Los Angeles, California 90028

WRITERS' CONTEST RULES

1. No entry fee is required, and all rights in the story remain the property of the author. All types of science fiction, fantasy, and dark fantasy are welcome.

2. By submitting to the Contest, the entrant agrees to abide by all Contest rules.

3. All entries must be original works by the entrant, in English. Plagiarism, which includes the use of third-party poetry, song lyrics, characters, or another person's universe, without written permission, will result in disqualification. Excessive violence or sex, determined by the judges, will result in disqualification. Entries may not have been previously published in professional media.

4. To be eligible, entries must be works of prose, up to 17,000 words in length. We regret we cannot consider poetry, or works intended for children.

5. The Contest is open only to those who have not professionally published a novel or short novel, or more than one novelette, or more than three short stories, in any medium. Professional publication is deemed to be payment of at least six cents per word, and at least 5,000 copies, or 5,000 hits.

6. Entries submitted in hard copy must be typewritten or a computer printout in black ink on white paper, printed only on the front of the paper, double-spaced, with numbered pages. All other formats will be disqualified. Each entry must have a cover page with the title of the work, the author's legal name, a pen name if applicable, address, telephone number, e-mail address and an approximate word count. Every subsequent page must carry the title and a page number, but the author's name must be deleted to facilitate fair, anonymous judging.

   Entries submitted electronically must be double-spaced and must include the title and page number on each page, but not the author's name. Electronic submissions will separately include the author's legal name, pen name if applicable, address, telephone number, e-mail address, and approximate word count.

7. Manuscripts will be returned after judging only if the author has provided return postage on a self-addressed envelope.

8. We accept only entries that do not require a delivery signature for us to receive them.

9. There shall be three cash prizes in each quarter: a First Prize of $1,000, a Second Prize of $750, and a Third Prize of $500, in US dollars. In addition, at the end of the year the First Place winners will have their entries judged by a panel of judges, and a Grand Prize winner shall be determined and receive an additional $5,000. All winners will also receive trophies.

10. The Contest has four quarters, beginning on October 1, January 1, April 1, and July 1. The year will end on September 30. To be eligible for judging in its quarter, an entry must be postmarked or received electronically no later than midnight on the last day of the quarter. Late entries will be included in the following quarter and the Contest Administration will so notify the entrant.

11. Each entrant may submit only one manuscript per quarter. Winners are ineligible to make further entries in the Contest.

12. All entries for each quarter are final. No revisions are accepted.

13. Entries will be judged by professional authors. The decisions of the judges are entirely their own, and are final and binding.

14. Winners in each quarter will be individually notified of the results by phone, mail or e-mail.

15. This Contest is void where prohibited by law.

16. To send your entry electronically, go to:
www.writersofthefuture.com/enter-writer-contest
and follow the instructions.
To send your entry in hard copy, mail it to:
    L. Ron Hubbard's Writers of the Future Contest
    7051 Hollywood Blvd., Los Angeles, California 90028

17. Visit the website for any Contest rules update at:
www.writersofthefuture.com

L. Ron Hubbard's
Illustrators of the Future Contest

The most enduring and influential
contest in the history of SF and Fantasy

Open to new and amateur SF & Fantasy artists

$1,500 in prizes each quarter
Quarterly winners compete for $5,000
additional annual prize!

ALL JUDGING DONE BY PROFESSIONAL ARTISTS ONLY

No entry fee is required

Entrants retain all rights

Don't delay! Send your entry now!

To submit your entry electronically go to:
   writersofthefuture.com/enter-the-illustrator-contest

E-mail: contests@authorservicesinc.com

To submit your entry via mail send to:
   L. Ron Hubbard's Illustrators of the Future Contest
   7051 Hollywood Blvd.
   Los Angeles, California 90028

ILLUSTRATORS' CONTEST RULES

1. The Contest is open to entrants from all nations. (However, entrants should provide themselves with some means for written communication in English.) All themes of science fiction and fantasy illustrations are welcome: every entry is judged on its own merits only. No entry fee is required and all rights to the entry remain the property of the artist.

2. By submitting to the Contest, the entrant agrees to abide by all Contest rules.

3. The Contest is open to new and amateur artists who have not been professionally published and paid for more than three black-and-white story illustrations, or more than one process-color painting, in media distributed broadly to the general public. The ultimate eligibility criterion, however, is defined by the word "amateur"—in other words, the artist has not been paid for his artwork. If you are not sure of your eligibility, please write a letter to the Contest Administration with details regarding your publication history. Include a self-addressed and stamped envelope for the reply. You may also send your questions to the Contest Administration via e-mail.

4. Each entrant may submit only one set of illustrations in each Contest quarter. The entry must be original to the entrant and previously unpublished. Plagiarism, infringement of the rights of others, or other violations of the Contest rules will result in disqualification. Winners in previous quarters are not eligible to make further entries.

5. The entry shall consist of three illustrations done by the entrant in a color or black-and-white medium created from the artist's imagination. Use of gray scale in illustrations and mixed media, computer generated art, and the use of photography in the illustrations are accepted. Each illustration must represent a subject different from the other two.

6. ENTRIES SHOULD NOT BE THE ORIGINAL DRAWINGS, but should be color or black-and-white reproductions of the originals of a quality satisfactory to the entrant. Entries must be submitted unfolded

and flat, in an envelope no larger than 9 inches by 12 inches. Images submitted electronically must be a minimum of 300 dpi, a minimum of 5 x 7 inches and a maximum of 8.5 x 11 inches. The file size should be a minimum of 5 MB and a maximum of 100 MB. Only .jpg and .jpeg files will be accepted.

7. All hard copy entries must be accompanied by a self-addressed return envelope of the appropriate size, with the correct US postage affixed. (Non-US entrants should enclose international postage reply coupons.) If the entrant does not want the reproductions returned, the entry should be clearly marked DISPOSABLE COPIES: DO NOT RETURN. A business-size self-addressed envelope with correct postage (or valid e-mail address) should be included so that the judging results may be returned to the entrant. We only accept entries that do not require a delivery signature for us to receive them.

8. To facilitate anonymous judging, each of the three photocopies must be accompanied by a removable cover sheet bearing the artist's name, address, telephone number, e-mail address, and an identifying title for that work. The reproduction of the work should carry the same identifying title on the front of the illustration and the artist's signature should be deleted. The Contest Administration will remove and file the cover sheets, and forward only the anonymous entry to the judges. Electronic submissions will separately include the artist's legal name, address, telephone number, e-mail address which will identify each of three pieces of art and the artist's signature on the art should be deleted.

9. There will be three cowinners in each quarter. Each winner will receive a cash prize of US $500. Winners will also receive eligibility to compete for the annual Grand Prize of $5,000 together with the annual Grand Prize trophy.

10. For the annual Grand Prize Contest, the quarterly winners will be furnished with a specification sheet and a winning story from the Writers of the Future Contest to illustrate. In order to retain eligibility for the Grand Prize, each winner shall send to the Contest address his/her illustration of the assigned story within thirty (30) days of receipt of the story assignment.

The yearly Grand Prize winner shall be determined by a panel of judges on the following basis only: Each Grand Prize judge's personal opinion on the extent to which it makes the judge want to read the story it illustrates. The Grand Prize winner shall be announced at the L. Ron Hubbard Awards ceremony held in the following year.

11. The Contest has four quarters, beginning on October 1, January 1, April 1, and July 1. The year will end on September 30. To be eligible for judging in its quarter, an entry must be postmarked no later than midnight on the last day of the quarter. Late entries will be included in the following quarter and the Contest Administration will so notify the entrant.

12. Entries will be judged by professional artists only. Each quarterly judging and the Grand Prize judging may have different panels of judges. The decisions of the judges are entirely their own and are final and binding.

13. Winners in each quarter will be individually notified of the results by mail or e-mail.

14. This Contest is void where prohibited by law.

15. To send your entry electronically, go to:
www.writersofthefuture.com/enter-the-illustrator-contest
and follow the instructions.
To send your entry via mail send it to:
     L. Ron Hubbard's Illustrators of the Future Contest
     7051 Hollywood Blvd., Los Angeles, California 90028

16. Visit the website for any Contest rules update at:
www.illustratorsofthefuture.com

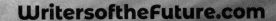

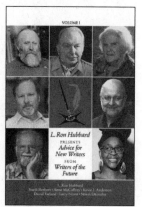